GET TO YOUR BOAT. SOMETHING IS WRONG HERE . . .

On the edge of the deep-sea cavern they call the Abyss, a salvage diver ignores the inner voices warning him of danger. Here, where the warm Caribbean waters turn dark and cold, he has found a new prize. A sunken German sub—an iron coffin buried in a tomb of sand.

He digs furiously, driven to unearth it, to explore it, to discover its mysteries. Until something in the eerie silence of the deep freezes his heart in ghastly horror . . .

It is the haunting, hollow hammer of something inside. The frantic, ceaseless sound of something pounding, raging . . . *dying* to get out.

THE NIGHT BOAT

HARBOUR SQUARE
LIBRARY

Books by Robert R. McCammon

Baal
Bethany's Sin
Blue World
Boy's Life
Mine
Mystery Walk
The Night Boat
Stinger
Swan Song
They Thirst
Usher's Passing
The Wolf's Hour

Published by POCKET BOOKS

ROBERT R. McCAMMON

THE NIGHT BOAT

POCKET BOOKS

New York   London   Toronto   Sydney   Tokyo   Singapore

*For my mother, who helped me
find that special island*

POCKET BOOKS, a division of Simon & Schuster Inc.
1230 Avenue of the Americas, New York, NY 10020

Copyright © 1980 by Robert R. McCammon
Cover art copyright © 1988 Rowena Morrill

All rights reserved, including the right to reproduce
this book or portions thereof in any form whatsoever.
For information address Pocket Books, 1230 Avenue
of the Americas, New York, NY 10020

ISBN: 0-671-73281-1

First Pocket Books printing October 1988

10 9 8 7 6

POCKET and colophon are registered trademarks of
Simon & Schuster Inc.

Printed in the U.S.A.

Author's Note

It may be interesting to note that U-boats were referred to by both captains and crews as "Iron Coffins." Rightly so; 736 German submarine crews still lie with their boats on the ocean floor.

R.R.M.

God how the dead men
  Grin by the wall,
Watching the fun
  Of the Victory Ball.

—Alfred Noyes,
A Victory Dance

Evil . . . has infinite forms.

—Blaise Pascal,
Pensees

Prologue

CLOUDS SWEPT ACROSS the yellow oval of the moon, one moment obscuring it, the next opening chasms so that its ocher light could stream down upon the plain of black ocean beneath. The moon hung motionless, while around it the clouds roiled. It was as if they possessed a life of their own, whirling upon themselves, breaking into pieces and attaching themselves, leechlike, onto others. They were first the maws of fantastic monsters, then men's faces with mouths open and screaming, then bare, bleached skulls shattered slowly into fragments by the Caribbean winds.

There were two lights panning across the surface of the sea—one high, over a dark mass of land, flashing intermittently, and the other floating low, just above the stern of a rusty-hulled American freighter hauling eight thousand tons of raw sulfur.

And one hundred yards beyond the freighter's wake was something else.

Quietly and smoothly a dark cylinder of iron rose up from the depths on a slender tower. The metal had been painted black to avoid reflection, the viewing lens sheathed in concrete—a single freezing eye.

The periscope turned, the only noise betraying its presence a soft *hisssss* of foam rushing around the tower; it sighted the island beacon, paused a few seconds, and turned several degrees to study the specter of the merchant vessel. Moonlight glittered off railings, off porthole rims, off the glass in an upper-deck wheelhouse.

Easy prey.

The periscope descended. A gurgle of water and gone.

Then, with a noise like the death threat of a striking serpent, the first G7A concussion torpedo, loaded with eight hundred pounds of explosive, left its forward tube. Powered by compressed air, it left a thin trail of silvery bubbles on its course toward the freighter's stern. It moved with a fluid grace, a smaller replica of the huge machine that had borne it across six thousand miles of ocean. Gradually it rose to within ten feet of the surface and hurtled onward toward its rendezvous.

When the torpedo slammed into the freighter's screws, it ripped open a gash below the waterline with an explosion that lit the sea with fire and fury. There was a long scream of iron as ton after ton of sea broke open the freighter's stern plates. Then there came a second explosion, hotter and redder than the first, sending up a gout of heavy black smoke through which burning men leaped over the shattered deck railing for the sea. Flame spread along the lower deck, greedily chewing its way toward the wheelhouse. A third explosion; a spray of metal and timbers tossed into the sky. Shuddering, the freighter veered toward the beacon light less than a mile away. The captain did not fully realize what had happened. He was perhaps thinking that they had struck something underwater: a reefhead, a sunken wreck. He did not know the screws were mangled and useless or that the fires were already out of control; he did not know the great shafts of the diesel engines had been thrown forward by the blast, grinding men to bloody pulps before them.

When the second torpedo hit, just to starboard of the first strike, the explosion collapsed the stern section of the lower deck. Supports shattered and fell away, and men struggling blindly through smoke and flame were crushed beneath tons of iron. The entire superstructure trembled and began to cave in.

Bulkheads moaned, split, burst as the sea gnawed its way through; iron crumpled like waxed paper; men clawed at each other as they sank, drowning. Some, above decks, were quickly burned into stiffened crisps. The dying ship, filled with the hideous racket of screams and moans, of shattering timber and glass, lurched sharply to starboard and began to sink rapidly at the stern.

A red emergency flare was fired from the remains of the burning wheelhouse; it exploded in the sky with a sharp crack and floated lazily back down toward the sea. Black smoke churned over the freighter, becoming thicker and thicker, filling the air with the stench of scorched iron and burned flesh, until finally it turned the moon ebon.

The surface of the sea began to part beyond the freighter's fiery shape. A rush of swirling white foam marked the ascent of the hunter. Its periscope tower broke the surface, then the rectangular shape of the conning tower appeared, and finally its superstructure, which gleamed as the sea ran off it in red-reflecting streams. The U-boat began to move nearer its victim, its bow slicing cleanly through a carnage of bodies and timber, crates, pieces of railing, ship's furniture. Here a man holding a bleeding comrade and calling out for help, here another in a blackened life jacket, raising up the bloody stumps that had been his arms. A sheen of oil had spread across the sea from the freighter's ruptured tanks, and it too was afire. Flames reflected off the iron hull of the U-boat, burned in the eyes of the men who watched from the conning tower's bridge, glowed in the submarine commander's wolflike eyes.

"*Ja.* A good hit," he said over the noises of the explosions. It had been ten minutes since the second torpedo left its tube. The freighter was doomed. "Die," he said very softly to the floating blanket of debris and the mass of the sinking ship. "Die."

The black smoke, carrying the scent of death with it, drifted around the U-boat in heavy swirls. Through it the commander could hear a final, long shriek as the freighter headed for the bottom. This was deep water, a thousand feet or more, a trench surrounded by steeply sloping coral reef and sand walls. He cocked his head, listening to a loud gurgling and bubbling of water, the hissing of steam, the half-crazed outcries of drowning men. This was a symphony to him, the almost overpowering music of destruction. He narrowed his eyes and moved his gaze to an object floating off the port bow. It was a life preserver. "All slow," he said, speaking into the voice tube that relayed his orders to the control room. The ring would bear the freighter's name and possibly the registry number; he was fastidious about keeping his leather-bound war diary accurate. "Schiller," he said to the lean blond man who stood nearest him. "You and Drexil get that ring for me."

The two crewmen clambered down the conning-tower ladder to the deck and began to move forward, careful of their footing on the slippery, algae-slimed wood.

The U-boat's bow pushed through a mass of blazing wreckage. Somewhere a man was calling out for God, over and over again; the voice died away abruptly, as if the man's throat had filled with water. Hanging on to the port-deck railing, the oily, littered sea washing around their ankles, the two sailors waited, watching the preserver carried toward them by the waves. Three more of the choppy swells and it would be close enough to grasp by hand. The commander watched, hands folded before him, as Drexil, with Schiller holding his legs, reached over to get it.

And then there was a high, piercing noise that made the commander whirl around. His eyes widened. The noise, coming from the midst of the black smoke, rose until it became a metallic shriek. From the open tower hatch the exec's black-bearded face emerged, his mouth a silent O. At once the commander understood. A battle-station siren. A subchaser, coming up fast on their stern. He roared into the voice tube, "CRASH DIVE! CRASH DIVE!" even as the U-boat's alarm bells shrilled below. Then a second shrieking siren: a second subchaser joining the first. Both of them roaring full-speed, bearing down on the U-boat. The exec dropped through the hatchway, and the commander peered anxiously out across the bulwark. His sailors had the preserver and were

5

frantically making their way through the deepening black troughs.

A bright circular light hit the sea just across the U-boat's bow, and now the sea vibrated with the noise of the subchasers' engines. With a muffled thud a geyser of water rose up to starboard of the conning tower, followed by an explosion that almost tore through the eardrums. The sea heaved around them.

The commander looked into the spotlight, his eyes aching from its brightness, his teeth clenched. Schiller and Drexil would not make the bridge in time. Without a second glance, he threw himself into the yawning hatch and sealed the lid shut over his head.

Like a huge reptilian beast, the great gleaming U-boat slid without hesitation into the depths. The two sailors, floundering in rising water, felt iron and wood drop away beneath their feet. They clutched at a railing, screaming out, focused in the eye of the light.

"THE RING!" Schiller shouted to his mate. "HOLD ON TO IT!"

But then a churn of white water tore it from Drexil's grasp, and it skittered away into the flames. Schiller opened his mouth to cry out, seeing the conning tower sink away, passing him like a descending monster's fin, but salt water streamed into his throat and he almost choked. He kicked forward, trying to grasp hold of the periscope tower, but as he did his leg slammed against something, and he felt himself being pulled down. He jerked at the leg, jerked again; it was useless. Something had caught his ankle and was pulling him after the boat. The sea blinded him, closing over his head. *Get free!* he heard himself shriek. *Get free!* The currents enveloped him, carrying him down. He cried out, air bursting from between his teeth, and wrenched at the leg. It came free at last, but there was a sharp cracking noise and pain almost overcame him. He fought his way to the surface. *Stroke!* the mind commanded the failing body. *Stroke!*

Schiller found himself amidst a maelstrom of noise and foaming sea. The sky was filled with the smell of cordite and the spinning red and green comets of flares. Shells were dropping all around him, hammering at his brain, and through the nightmare he grasped on to an empty crate and wrapped both arms around it.

When Schiller cleared his eyes he saw Drexil's head bobbing only a few yards away. He cried out, "DREXIL! HOLD ON!" and began swimming, his leg a useless appendage. In another moment he realized he was weak and growing weaker, that he could not tread water, and land was too distant. There was something stringy, like dark clumps of jellyfish, in the waves. Gouts of blood. Intestines. Brains. Bodies torn to pieces. The offal of war. He reached Drexil and it was only when he took the man's shoulder that he realized this man had black hair, and Drexil's had been red.

The corpse, floating in a tattered life jacket, had no face.

White teeth grinned from a pulp of tissues and membranes and nerve fibers. Schiller shouted hysterically and pulled his hands back as if they had been contaminated. He began swimming into the green-glowing ocean, the fires still burning around him, but he was swimming without direction. Ahead was a solid plain of flame, and in the midst of the flame he could see the blackened, shriveled corpses, whirling around and around as if they were spinning above a gigantic whirlpool. He could feel the power of the water over the freighter wrenching at him. He tried to move away from it, but the sea had him and was pulling him down, and he couldn't swim anymore. He wondered where Drexil was and if there were a true peace in death. He lowered his head and opened his mouth to fill his lungs before he went down.

Hands grasped him. Pulled him up from the surface. Threw him down into the bottom of a boat. Men standing over him, peering down.

Schiller blinked, could not make out their faces, could not move his body.

"A live one," someone said, in English.

One

SOMETHING LAY AHEAD, dark against the thick blue-green swells.

David Moore reached back and cut the sputtering motor. The sharp, hot sun lay across his bare back and shoulders like a bright tropical jacket. The battered fisherman's skiff slowed, rolled lazily across the next swell, and Moore turned the tiller so whatever was in the water would come up on his starboard side. Squinting from the glare of sun off sea, he reached over the gunwale and brought the object up.

It was another piece of timber—God only knew where it had drifted or been torn from. It was a new piece, though, not yet gnarled and aged by the salt water, and he placed it in the bottom of the boat to examine it. On one side there were the remnants of red-painted letters against a white background. An S and an A. Salty? Sally? Samantha? It was evidently a shard of a boat's transom, perhaps one of the Coquina boats, perhaps one that had drifted from a long way

9

off. He knew the names of most of the island's fishing fleet: *Jolly Mack, Kinkee, Blue Lady, Lucy J. Leen, Gallant,* a dozen others. This boat had probably been destroyed in some distant harbor or maybe it was one of the unfortunates caught in the teeth of the tropical storm that had screamed across the island three days previously. Some fisherman might have lost his life clinging to this boat, Moore thought, staring at the plank. He didn't want to think about that. It brought up too many bad memories.

He started the motor again and swung the tiller so that the skiff's prow was aimed at a point directly into the opening of Kiss Bottom Reef some forty yards ahead. The sea was still fairly rough, "somewhat jumpin'" as the Caribbean fishermen said, and as he neared the reef passage the swells struck hard against the hull. There was debris all around: more splintered timbers, driftwood that might be worth salvaging, tree branches, roof tiles, even a rusted tin placard that read COLA, BEER, WINE. He had seen it ripped off the front of the Landfall Tavern from his hotel terrace. The sign had spun high across the island roofs and had been tossed in a wild, rain-swept spiral into the sea. As Moore passed through the channel he could see the ragged edges of the reef, stubbled with brown and green coral growths, just grazing the surface. A lot of boats had been torn open by those treacherous devil's-horns, and had had to be dragged off to be patched up at the island's boatyard or to die in deeper water. Outside the reef were two "clangers," brightly painted orange buoys that banged and rattled as they were jostled together by the rough currents.

Moore steered between them, following the path of blue-green water before him, and then he headed toward the deeper, almost purple sea in the distance. It was still shallow just off Kiss Bottom—thirty to thirty-five feet—but the sand and coral bottom quickly shelved off into what was respectfully and fearfully known as the Abyss.

Moore turned in his seat and glanced back at the island he'd just steered from to get a correct bearing. The dark, tire-lined piers, the fishermen's cluster of tinderbox shanties, the village of Coquina with its houses and shops of stucco brilliantly painted in wild reds, oranges, pale pinks, blues, browns, light greens. In the white sunlight the colors were dazzling. He let his eyes move up the island, where High Street left Coquina village and wound its way, on a path of ruts and gravel, to a small dark-blue structure with a white gabled roof and white wrought-iron terraces overlooking the harbor. The Indigo Inn was his hotel; he'd made the purchase three years before from an elderly man who was moving back to the States. In the last few days Moore and Markus, his handyman, had been busy replacing broken windows, shattered porch railing slats, and shutters that had been ripped away by the high winds. They did a patchwork job replacing things that had been broken before and would surely be broken again. In the islands, decay was the only certainty.

He turned out from land and steered toward the deeps, searching the water around him. Most of the debris had been washed ashore in the previous few days and whatever was still usable had been gathered up by the islanders. The storm had been a particularly fierce one even for September, one of the most furious of months during the autumn hurricane season. It had blown in from the east, almost unheralded except for the ominously yellow sky. Smashing first into the Coquina harbor, sending boats flying against the piers, the storm had torn a few of the fishermen's dwellings to pieces, then screamed into the interior jungle, uprooting palms and shrubs, and miraculously veered around the shanty village of Caribville on the island's northern point before finally heading out to sea again. The few radios that were the island's sole method of communication had been knocked out by electrical interference. It was a wonder there had been so few serious injuries: only a few broken bones and lacerations, which had been tended by Dr. Maxwell at the clinic.

The sea darkened under his boat. The squat stone tower of the Carib Point beacon lay over his shoulder, a sighting point still used on stormy, wild nights to aid merchant freighters out in the channel. Since it lay near the Carib settlement, it had been allowed to fall into a state of near-ruin. Moore corrected his course a few degrees. In another few moments he was in the right spot; the beacon was just over his left shoulder and the tin-roofed structures of the boatyard drydock shelters over his right. He cut the motor, went to the bow, and heaved a lightweight grapple anchor over the side, allowing the rope to coil out from a hand-winch reel. When the line stopped, he knew that he'd been correct; he was in about fifty feet of water, at the very rim of the Abyss, where the bottom suddenly dropped off into infinity.

Moore moved back to get his diving gear and tank in the stern. He sat down, almost comforted by the skiff's slow rocking, and took off his khaki slacks and thongs. He wore dark-blue bathing briefs underneath, and he pulled a thin cotton T-shirt over his shoulders to guard against strap-burn. When he'd turned on his tank's air supply, he hoisted the tank to his shoulders and strapped it on securely. Then he looked out across the Abyss.

In the distance he could see the faint shapes of far-off land masses: Chocolate Hole, Sandy Cay, Starfish Cay. They were much smaller than Coquina— mainly long spits of hot, palm-edged beaches—and of the three nearest, only Chocolate Hole was really a village. It was a tiny settlement of only fifty or so people who made their living selling green sea-turtles to the bulky industry boats that dealt in local island products. Here, out in the open, the breeze was strong and warm on Moore's face. He let his eyes wander the plain of purple water above the great depths.

Only a few fishermen sailed here; they generally stayed nearer Coquina or fished for albacore and jacks in the shallow waters to the south. The Abyss was a haunted place, so the old islanders—the superstitious ones—said. A score of them had sworn they'd seen or heard things out here. There were those who'd been vehement: a great blazing ghost freighter, burning with a spectral emerald fire, in the midst of the Abyss, water hissing all around her, the moans of her doomed crew carrying out into dawn's twilight. Though Moore was a man who made up his own mind about such things, he was sometimes inclined to believe it wasn't just bad rum or Red Stripe beer talking. Not from the looks some of those men had in their eyes.

But now, in the clear afternoon sunlight, with the entire sky a huge unbroken canopy of hot blue, he could not believe in ghosts. At least, not sailing the surface.

When Moore looked into a mirror, he saw first his

father's eyes, as blue as the Caribbean depths themselves, crackling with intelligence and caution. He had let his beard grow when he reached the islands from Europe, and by the time he'd stepped off a tramp steamer onto Coquina's shore he was a hard-muscled, tanned, and lean figure with black hair that curled around his collar, and a dark beard and mustache. He would be thirty-four in November, but he was light-years away from the life he'd led in Baltimore, his birthplace. No one in Baltimore—no one who remained in the life he'd left behind—could have recognized him, except perhaps by his eyes. He was a different man entirely, no longer the one who'd been a rising young executive in his father's bank; who'd lived in a modest if expensive home in a fashionable Baltimore suburb with his wife, Beth, and eight-year-old son, Brian; who'd fought for a membership at the Amsterdam Hills Country Club; who'd owned a beautiful, teak-decked sailing sloop, custom-built by a Canadian firm, that he and Beth had christened—with champagne and all—*Destiny's Child*. In those days he had worn "the uniform," dark-blue or gray suits with regimental-striped ties, to quiet business luncheons and discussions in oak-paneled drawing rooms where he had struggled to stifle his yawning and restless unease.

He slipped into his black swim fins, strapped a sheathed knife around the calf of his right leg, then secured a weight-belt to his waist. Putting on a pair of gauntlet gloves, Moore rinsed out his mask with seawater, spat into it to prevent it from fogging, and then rinsed it out again. He eased the mask down over his face, put the regulator mouthpiece between his teeth, sucked and exhaled to make certain it was clear, then flipped himself backward over the gunwale in an easy, practiced motion.

Below, in the great room with light-blue walls streaming with sunlight, he waited for his bubbles to clear, watching the rise and fall of the hull above him. When he had adjusted to his underwater world, Moore swam toward the bow, found the taut anchor line and began to follow it hand-over-hand into the depths, his breath appearing before him in crystal globes that ascended to the surface. He went slowly, clearing his ears by squeezing his nostrils shut and blowing every few seconds. In another moment he sighted the bottom, ridges of sand and high walls of tangled coral, and he let go, kicking smoothly away, when he came to the end of the anchor line. Following the bottom, he swam toward the curtain of blue before him, his legs doing all the work, his arms held loosely at his sides. Familiar sights told him he was in the right place: the bulbous mass of brown brain coral that had amazed him the first time he'd seen it; magnificent forest of staghorn coral, now filled with the dart and shimmer of dwarf herring; an angelfish, strikingly blue and yellow, moving gracefully past him.

Through thick clumps of algae that stirred with the currents below, Moore saw a brigade of crabs on the march, freezing solid when they sensed his movement. The reefs were alive; fish flew like birds through the coral openings or whisked themselves into holes to await his passing. The reef dwellers were too accustomed to the predators to take any chances. A shadow covered him, and he looked up. Thirty feet above an eagle ray swam, the wings rippling like beautiful muscle. It vanished into the blue gloom.

Moore had been angling down as the bottom dropped away, and now he faced a wall of gnarled dark coral. He swam through a maze of sea fans, then rose above the wall and stopped abruptly.

Beneath him stretched the Abyss: dark, forboding. The sea turned from blue to black in those depths, like the huge mouth of something waiting to devour him. Though he'd been prepared, the sight of it sent an electric chill through him. Abruptly the vision of the ghost ship, lit by moonlight, glowing green and iridescent, came to him. He brushed it away. If ghosts did exist, Moore thought, they probably *were* down in that awesome hole. He glanced up at the silvery surface, then thought of the brass ship's compass he'd found last year and began to descend.

There *was* a freighter down there somewhere, Moore knew; probably so deep his lungs would explode before he could ever reach it. It had gone down sometime in a battle during World War II—that was all he could glean from the stories that floated about the island. Details were sketchy, and no one here really liked to talk about the war. He had gone diving in this area the year before, after another fierce storm, and had discovered a ledge littered with pieces of metal, railings, even the bow portion of a shattered lifeboat. On that dive Moore had found an old ship's compass, the glass missing but the brass still shining. He had taken the compass back to the inn, but when he'd returned to the Abyss a few days afterward the sand had settled back like a flat white carpet, and nothing remained. Another storm had hit soon after, but he hadn't had the chance to dive again, so he'd had to wait for the following season in hopes of finding something else he might be able to salvage.

He continued downward. *Where's that ledge?* he wondered suddenly, trying to pierce the deep-blue mist. *It's dropped away entirely.* But then it materialized and he reached it, swimming along a high ridge of rock-dappled sand. There was something metal a few feet ahead: a rusted can. He picked it up. It was still sealed, though badly dented. He let it fall, swam on. In the midst of clumps of coral, probably ripped from the reef at the Abyss rim, there were shards of timber and more cans which gleamed brightly. He held one up and saw himself reflected in the scoured metal. It had been buried. Food supplies for that freighter's crew? he wondered. Maybe. What would be inside? Peaches? Vegetables? He wondered if out of curiosity he should open one to see what was included in a 1942 merchant seaman's diet.

The Abyss stretched down beneath him like the empty socket of a huge eye; there was a series of ledges, all sand choked with rock at various depths, one beneath the other until they faded from sight. One of them, a massive Mt. Everest of sand, caught his eye. It had a definite shape, but he couldn't determine what it reminded him of. Moore descended, intrigued by the mound; he hadn't noticed it before, but then his attention had been on an upper ledge, not the lower ones. He was perhaps ten feet above it when he realized something was protruding from the mass of sand and rock; his heart began to beat more rapidly.

Moore hovered over it, fanning the sand back with quick motions of his fins. The top of a cylinder of some kind protruded vertically. He felt it gingerly. Iron. Unmarked by marine growth, the object, like the cans, had been completely covered over by sand. There was glass in it, very heavily scarred. *What in*

God's name? he wondered. He reached down and pulled at it, only half-expecting it to come free; it wouldn't budge. Moore began to dig the sand away from the object, then wrenched again at it. *No use, David old cock,* he told himself. This—whatever—is stuck tight. He checked his wristwatch. Time to head for the surface. But this cylinder: the scars of sand abrasion glinting, the glass inset. Fascinating as hell. It could be something worthwhile, he thought. Or perhaps . . . he gazed down at the sand stirred by his every movement.

Or perhaps something was buried beneath it.

Moore unstrapped his knife from its sheath and dug rocks away from the cylinder's base. He uncovered more iron, gleaming and pitted, an inch at a time. Digging in wrist deep, he pulled the sand away in handfuls. He pried the rocks loose with his blade and let them roll off into that deep hole below him. Another glance at the watch. Time to go! But he was functioning like a machine now, digging and lifting, slowly uncovering what appeared to be a thick, gleaming iron support for that cylinder. There were no growths; it had been buried here for a long time. His knife scraped across flat rock and he shifted his digging to another section.

And then he froze. Forgot to exhale, then exhaled, the bubbles rattling toward the surface over a hundred and fifty feet above.

He had heard something, muffled and far away, like iron being hammered underwater.

Moore waited, his heart pounding, but the noise didn't come again. What was it? He looked around and then realized something very odd: he hadn't seen any fish at this depth. Very odd, in waters teaming with snapper, grouper, jacks, albacore. Moore glanced up, looking for the reassuring distant glow of the sun. There were remnants of jagged rock hanging over him, as if what had once been a ledge just above had given way. He tried to quiet the inner voices. *Get to your boat,* they whispered. *Something is wrong here.*

Where were the damned fish?

He continued digging, lifting out coral clumps.

The sand completely obscured his vision, like the roil of white clouds; it had to be extremely deep here, he thought. A mountain of sand and below him the valley of darkness. He plunged in his hands, the fingers closing around a rock, and pulled it out from the mound. When he did, sand cascaded in sheets off the sides of the mountain and on into the Abyss.

Then Moore saw something exposed a few feet away from the strange cylinder and the iron tower. He pulled at the new object. It was a large barrel of some kind, also made of scarred, dented metal. He freed it and it began to slide down the sand slope, and as he clung to it he saw the detonation cap of the device, and the chill of fear raised hair on the back of his neck.

It was an unexploded depth charge.

Moore wrenched his hands back as if they'd been burned. His tank clanged sharply against coral debris, and he fought his way up the mountain away from it, his fins churning water. He could see himself turned inside out by the thing's blast, his body reduced to a mass of bloody shreds. Then the predators would come, and there would be nothing left. He half-sank into the sand, fought himself free in a blinding mist, looking back over his shoulder to see the forgotten charge pitch off the ledge. Then it began to fall into the depths, spinning end over end. Moore reached the summit; the charge had vanished into the dark mists and he stared fearfully after it, praying that if it did explode it would go off hundreds of feet below, where the shock might not kill him. Otherwise . . .

And then there was a burst of white light far below. The shock came roaring out of the depths, an undersea whirlwind that reached inside him, through the flesh, gripping the bones and twisting.

He gritted his teeth against the pain and roaring noise that almost shattered his eardrums; a fissure split open in the sand, releasing a pulsating globe of air that tore past him and rocketed up toward the surface. The blast echoed all around, the water crazily shifting in all directions, trying to rip him to pieces. The sand parted, cracked open in a dozen seams. It slid under him; an avalanche of it covered Moore and he fell backward, toppling toward the wild Abyss, his tank slamming against coral. Great bubbles of air were roaring all around him, some of them ripping their way free of the sand. Something struck him like the blow of a fist; his mask was torn from his face and the water blinded him. When he felt for a grip, frantically, his hands closed around a solid object. He held on, the currents twisting at him, the noise a throbbing pain at his temples. And then a realization came to him that almost caused him to shout out in terror: he was rising.

There was a shudder beneath him, and through the blue-green distortion he saw a dark, massive shape towering above him. His lungs were filling; he was rising too quickly. He let go his grip and kicked out with his fins against a hard surface that slid past him. He was thrown away from the thing, twisted and turned and mauled by the fierce currents, lost in the explosion of sand and sea. When he could see again he was looking toward the surface into the sun.

Or where the sun had been.

For now it was obscured by the huge shape; the thing was rising to the surface, trailing sand; its shadow covered him, and he felt lost in its darkness. He watched it, eyes stinging. The shape broke through the surface in a roil of foam, and through the ringing in his ears he heard the thunder of sea surging against iron. It hung there, rocking slowly from side to side.

Get up! Moore screamed to himself. *No, no. Control. Control.* He swam furiously out of the thing's ominous shadow and began to stroke very slowly for the top. He had been thrown almost to the rim of the Abyss, and he concentrated on following the slope of the shelving bottom. He found his anchor line, pulled the anchor free and began to climb. He stopped for decompression at ten feet, watching the hull of his skiff being battered by the waves. When his head finally broke water, he spat out his mouthpiece and hung on to the skiff's gunwale, staring at what lay not more than thirty yards from him.

"Dear God," he whispered.

Its hull was over two hundred feet long; red sunlight had settled into splices in the iron flesh, like the bleeding wounds of a giant saurian. Water foamed around a sharp, evil-looking prow. Remnants of an iron railing hung twisted over the side, partly submerged; there were long dents and gashes in the superstructure and in the bulwark of a conning tower. Moore could hear the sea hissing against its sides.

A submarine.

One of the old World War II types, with a flat deck

and a hungry-for-battle look about it. It seemed to be a monstrous predator reawakened, eager for prey.

Moore hung from the skiff's gunwale, unable to think what he should do. And as he watched, he saw the bow of the thing begin to turn. The currents had it now, shoving against its mass. Alive again, the submarine began to move slowly and inexorably toward the island of Coquina.

Two

WHEN MASON HOLCOMBE picked up his next card he knew Lady Luck with her shining golden hair and dress of crackling folding money was standing at his right shoulder. He tried to keep the look of the barracuda out of his eyes, but it was damned hard to do. He had a pair of queens and triple jacks; he raised his eyes very carefully . . . *oh, mon,* he told himself, *do keep that look innocent!* . . . to Percy "Pudge" Layne, who sat across from him at the up-ended, rusted fuel drum they used as a card table. Percy, a rotund black with a high forehead and close-set oval eyes, regarded him in silence.

"Come on, mon!" said Mason carefully, trying to affect an off-handed aggravation. "How many cards?"

"Three." He tossed the three down, took another three off the top of a dog-eared pack that had been used in boatyard games for as long as both men could remember.

"Okay, what you puttin' up?" Mason said, ready to get on with it.

Percy shook his head, his face wrinkled up and worried. He gazed out across Mason's broad shoulder at the plain of the sea beyond, then dropped his eyes back to his hand. Without a word he reached beside him to a pack of cigarettes that had been broken in half. He put four halves before him.

"Fine." Mason put out his four cigarette halves, raked out three more. "And three."

Percy shrugged, met the raise.

"What you got, my fine friend?" Mason asked, ready to leap.

"Not so good, I doan think," said the other man. He laid down his cards in a fan shape. "You can beat that, I know." Before him on the drum were two aces, two wild deuces, and a six.

Mason sat, numb from the neck up. He dropped his cards down. Percy laughed out loud and took the cigarette halves to add to a growing heap. "Came up lucky as all hell on that draw," he said quietly.

"I ain't playing no more with these old cards!" Mason said. "You can just damned see through the back of 'em! Jesus Christ!"

"Oh shaddup," Percy said, "and lay down your ante."

The afternoon breeze off the sea was cool and fresh. It was a welcome relief to get out here when the sun was high, away from the heat of the wharfs and the stench of fuel oil, grease, and battery acids. They could hear the banging of a hammer against timber and the drawing of a handsaw repeated over and over again—someone still working in the boatyard. Probably J.R., or the foreman, Lenny, burning themselves up in that sun to finish replacing the *Ginger*'s broken hull planks. The old man who operated her, Harless, or "Hairless," as the boatyard men called him, was a good friend of the yard's owner, Kevin Langstree, and so that accounted for the rush that had been put into the repair work.

The Langstree boatyard had seen better days. It was a jumble of wharf pilings, huts, piles of timber and empty oil drums, crates and boxes strewn everywhere, heavy ropes coiled like thick brown pythons, and a morass of bald tires stacked up to protect the hulls of boats. It had been affluent once, bustling with traffic from the island harbor, an anchorage for both British and American freighters. Now it was kept up primarily to service the island's fishing fleet and to do repair work if necessary on the yachts that cruised through here during the tourist season. The work force had been cut to a third of what it had been during the early part of World War II, when the boatyard was paid handsomely for repairs made on the huge Allied warships that had fought the Germans in the Caribbean. In those days, as the aging Langstree liked to tell everyone, the boatyard had worked fifty men on two shifts; the work was plentiful and hard but the men knew what they were doing. They were all tough, muscular islanders with a common-sense, natural knowledge of both the small fishing trawlers and the larger, more complex steel-hulled craft. They had learned the art of fast patching, of making use of available materials until what had seemed hopeless was again ready for the sea. They could take down and put back together ocean-going diesels blindfolded, restore the snapped rudders and broken hulls of sailing sloops, rebuild skiff motors by spit and wire.

But no more. Many of those men had moved away from Coquina in search of better-paying jobs after the war had ended; some of them had died in action, for a boatyard servicing warships in a combat zone was a prime target for the enemy. Now most of the yard was abandoned. Of two tin-roofed wooden structures used as drydocks only one was in use, and that only occasionally when a larger boat needed a patch job or some such serious work. The other, allowed to fall to pieces in the salt air, had been constructed by the British navy for the purpose of storing damaged warships until they could either be patched or until the heavy naval tugs could arrive for them; it was filled with supplies and equipment left over when the warships were no longer needed to patrol the Caribbean. Although the jobs had dried up, the boatyard had always maintained a proud reputation and was the only thing that kept Coquina on the map. Most of the workmen made ends meet for their families by moonlighting either as fishermen or farmers.

"Deal," Percy said over the noise of the hammer. He glanced across; the bulkheadlike doorway to the nearest drydock had been opened and he could see J.R.'s head as the man worked in the concrete-reinforced pit. Beside the shelter were the bleaching bones of an abandoned ketch, its splintered hull as white as the grass-thatched sand around it. A few dozen yards away, beneath a block-and-tackle assembly, were the wharfs, where a couple of fishing boats were moored. A sign on long stilts at the far end of the wharfs, facing the sea, read in weather-beaten red paint: LANGSTREE BOATYARD.

Percy was not really concentrating as the cards were placed face-down before him. He was looking out at the sea. He had watched the little skiff with the white man in it move on through the bommies of Kiss

Bottom, and while he and Mason played he gazed curiously out at the Abyss, where the skiff, only a white dot against the blueness of sea and sky, floated at anchor. He wondered what the white man was doing there. In the middle of the sea, beneath that searing orb of sun! Moore had to be crazy as hell. Even he, Percy, with his black flesh thickened by years of outdoor work, avoided the early afternoon heat, preferring instead to play poker beneath the shading palm fronds or drink beer and swap old stories with the other men up at the Landfall.

He picked up his hand. Four and six of clubs, heart's king, ten of hearts, and ace of diamonds. What to discard, what to build on? He suddenly felt like a fool sitting here. He had nets to mend for the next morning's fishing. Without them he'd have to depend on trawling lines, and he didn't want to. The fish were getting too smart to grab just any old bait these days, and the huge nets on the industry boats that worked these waters on an erratic basis frightened away the fish that weren't scooped up. Damn it, he thought angrily, it's gettin' tough for a man to feed his own mouth, much less a wife's and two children's.

"What you want, mon?" Mason asked him.

And when the other man looked up, intending to ask for three cards, his gaze froze.

The sea was boiling like a hot cauldron out in the Abyss, just beyond where Moore's skiff lay. Percy could see the great turbulence of it. Something was wrong. Bad wrong. He dropped his cards, rose up from the battery crates he'd been perched upon. He pointed. "What the hell's that?"

Mason twisted around, narrowed his eyes. "Jesus," he said, quietly.

The men could see foam crashing over the skiff; it was jerked down the side of a wave, then bobbed back into view again. And as they watched, spellbound, they saw a massive shape burst from the sea in a white geyser of water. They thought at first it was a whale emerging from the depths but then the sun glinted sharply off what appeared to be a hard surface; the thing rocked back and forth as the ocean continued to churn around it.

"Damn!" Mason said, leaping up from his seat. He put a hand across his forehead to shield his eyes from the reflection and stared.

"J.R.!" Percy shouted, cupping his hands around his mouth. The hammering ceased and a man appeared at the shelter entrance. "GET OUT HERE QUICK!"

On the Abyss rim, Moore clung to the skiff gunwale. He was trying to sort out what had happened, dazed because it had happened so quickly. One moment he had been digging on the great mountain of sand, the next he had been gripping that depth charge, the next scrabbling wildly away as the charge hurtled into the depths. He wasn't bleeding anywhere, but his flesh felt raw and bruised and his head ached fiercely. And then, as he stared at the hulk that had begun its eerie movement with the currents, he realized what he'd been trying to dig out: the uppermost portion of a periscope. He'd been digging above the mass of the submarine; it had been buried beneath the tons of rock and sand, and the explosion had ripped it free.

Moore unfastened his straps and heaved his tank over into the boat's bottom. Then he painfully pulled himself over, his muscles tight and unyielding, and quickly cranked up the anchor with the hand winch.

He laid the anchor in the bow, started up his motor, and swung the skiff around to follow in the thing's wake.

He drew up alongside it off the starboard beam, keeping well away in case it suddenly turned or heeled over for the bottom. It was riding low, the waves sliding across the bow and crashing with a hollow *boom* against the conning tower. A mass of black cables and wires, secured to the forward deck, writhed like angry snakes. The paint was almost completely scoured away to reveal the dark, sea-weathered iron, but here and there remained patches of rust-colored primer and even the original dingy gray. Moore could almost have sworn the old relic was operating under its own power, so straight was its direction, but of course the thing was long deserted—there was no noise of racketing diesels, only the relentless pounding of the sea. He turned the tiller a few degrees, moved in for a closer look. From the distance of only a few yards he could see the rivets in the conning-tower plates, and the sight was oddly disturbing. The plates looked like scales on a huge, prehistoric reptile. A cable as thick as Moore's arm hung down across the tower bulwark, slapping iron. He recalled a picture he'd seen in an encyclopedia as a child: a black-finned monster rearing high above storm-tossed waves to snap its jagged teeth through the neck of a pterodactyl.

He was entranced by the thing, lost in its aura of power and ancient menace. In another few moments he heard the noise of the sea rushing around the Kiss Bottom reefheads; there were figures standing on the fishing wharfs and beach, others watching from the boatyard. The submarine began to turn, almost imperceptibly, for the opening in the reef, drawn by the influx of water there. Moore turned his skiff to avoid scraping across a gnarled, green-slimed bommie, then found himself in the midst of jagged reefheads. Someone shouted something from the fishing wharfs, but Moore couldn't hear. The hulk looked like it might pass unscathed through the reef into Coquina's tranquil harbor, but then he heard a loud grinding of iron across coral. Sea foamed at the bow, and the forward deck began to rise. The currents were driving the hulk across the reef; bits of coral shattered and collapsed under the thing's weight. The submarine shuddered, grinding forward, the bow rising out of the sea like a knife's black blade. And then, abruptly, the grinding noise stopped. The submarine was wedged on Kiss Bottom, its bow out of the water but its stern deck still awash. Moore could clearly see the closed vents of the two forward torpedo tubes on the starboard side, and a chill touched the flesh at the back of his neck.

There was more shouting from shore, but Moore wasn't paying attention. Gulls swooped down from the blue; they circled, screaming, above the hulk, then sailed away on their currents of air as if disdaining contact with the thing. Moore drew nearer; the submarine loomed above him, angled crazily, now motionless. As the breeze swept across it he caught the stench of age, of a slow decay; it smelled to him like the carcass of a pilot whale that had beached itself in a directionless search for the sea. Moore's skiff moved into the submarine's shadow, and it towered over him. He cut his motor, tied a line onto the collapsed deck railing, and with a smooth, powerful movement, pulled himself up the railing to the submarine's deck.

Part of the forward deck had caved in; he could see where the deck plankings had given way. There was still a lot of sand left aboard; it slithered with quiet hissing sounds around Moore's feet and lay in clumps among the twistings of cables. Just forward of the conning tower there was a deck gun, still firm on its mount and apparently in good shape but for the wet sand that dripped from its muzzle. Moore moved toward the bow, walking gingerly on the slippery planking. He reached the deck gun and hung on to it. Forward of the gun was the square outline of a deck hatch which appeared to be secured. Ahead of him the bow's sharp spear challenged the sky; railings were twisted and broken, iron scarred and gouged. He left the gun and worked his way forward as if climbing a steep hill. When he glanced back he saw the gun's bore, black and deadly looking.

He had taken only another step when the planking gave way beneath him. As he slid through the hole he reached out, grasping a cable; it held and he pulled himself back up on deck, his heart hammering. Through the splintered opening Moore saw a gleaming, massive metal tube. He knew very little about submarines, but he figured that the tube, protected by the iron and timber of the superstructure, was actually where the guts of the boat lay. The pressure hull, he remembered it was called, was resistant to the great depths at which these boats had moved. Along the iron sides of the superstructure, the shell that protected the intestines, were dozens of ducts that allowed the water to stream in, cushioning the pressure hull. The engines, the control room, the crew's quarters, all the other compartments and stations necessary to the submarine's operation were inside that tube. It looked smaller than he would have imagined. How many men would have manned this thing? Twenty-five? Thirty? Fifty? It seemed impossible that they could have found space to move.

Now there was only the noise of the sea swirling across the submerged aft deck, a series of whispers and groans.

A dead relic, Moore thought, staring at the mass of the conning tower. He saw above it the periscope he'd been trying to dig out. There was a second shaft that looked like another periscope, but this was battered and slightly bent to one side. As the sun baked down, the smell of decay rose all around him. *When did this thing go down?* he wondered, *and what boat was it?* There were no identifying symbols or numbers; if there had ever been any, the sand had scraped them off. He felt like a fly crawling along the maw of a crocodile that had come up to sun itself on the rocks. Why, he wondered, did he sense something living about this boat now so long dead?

Moore heard the distant pounding of engines. At first the sound chilled him until he looked toward the harbor and saw one of the beat-up old fishing trawlers approaching with men at the gunwales. A cluster of islanders had gathered on the wharfs, and children were running up and down the beach as if at some kind of festive celebration. He waved a hand at the trawler and a man at the bow waved back.

The trawler, its engines rumbling, pulled up alongside; two brawny islanders leaped over onto the submarine's deck. Lines were thrown and secured; an anchor chain rattled down and a gangplank was tied into place between the trawler and the hulk. Most of the men seemed reluctant to come aboard but one, a broad-shouldered black wearing a dark-blue cotton shirt and khaki trousers, crossed the gangplank and came over to Moore, avoiding the holes that gaped in the planks.

The man was not quite as tall as Moore but stockier, with iron-gray hair and a firm, chiseled face. He looked into the white man's eyes and then gazed the length of the thing, as if unsure of what he was seeing.

"It came up from the Abyss," Moore said, still shaken.

"Christ Jesus!" The black shook his head, peering down with deep-set, wary eyes through the broken planking at the pressure hull. "Tell me what happened."

"I was salvaging, looking for stuff off that freighter down there. This was buried beneath a mound of sand and coral; there was an explosion . . ."

"An explosion?" He looked up, sharply.

"An old depth charge. The shock blew it free, and this thing corked for the surface. God only knows how long it's been under there."

"You're okay?"

Moore nodded. "Got a hell of a headache and my ears are ringing like Sunday at the Vatican, but mostly the bastard just scared hell out of me."

"I've told you before about diving in the Abyss, David," said the man in a West Indian accent polished with a British veneer. Steven Kip had been Coquina's constable of police for some seven years. He stabbed a finger at Moore. "I've warned you about all that junk lying underwater, all that war crap. It could've been your bones at a thousand fathoms. So you found one damned brass compass. So what? Now this! You're a fool to go diving alone in there!"

Moore said nothing, because he knew the constable was right. The currents were dangerous, the risks great for a group of divers and astronomical for one alone. *What was it,* he thought grimly, not looking at the other man. *His death wish? Damn it to hell!*

"She's an old one," Kip said quietly, staring at the deck gun. "Sand's kept her as clean as a new tooth." There was a sudden sharp clatter. One of the islanders was pulling at a cable that snaked off into the water at the stern. "Hey! Let that be!" The islander looked up, dropped the cable, and backed away from it. "How deep?" Kip asked Moore.

"Hundred and fifty. Pretty close to the surface for one of these."

Kip shook his head. "Didn't want to stay down, did it? There's supposed to be a main hatch up on the tower. Did you check it?"

"No," Moore said.

"Then let's get at it." Kip turned from him and made his way past two more islanders who had come aboard.

"Watch your step," Moore called to his friend. "Deck's weak in places."

They stepped over the tangle of cables, reached a ladder, and climbed up to the tower bridge.

The bridge was ankle-deep in gray sand and seawater, littered with pieces of planking and clumps of coral. Droplets splattered onto them from the periscope shafts above, ricocheting off the iron bulwark. Kip bent down into the water and parted sand with his hands until at last he uncovered the slab of a hatch. "Sealed tight," he said, wiping his forehead with a dripping hand. "If we want to get in we'll have to burn through, and I'm not so certain we want to do that."

"Why not?"

"Still anxious to do some salvaging today, are you?" Kip fixed him with a cynical stare. "You might be doing your salvaging in Heaven if this thing's carrying live torpedoes." He stood up, looking toward the stern. "There should be a crack somewhere in this boat's guts. Otherwise what was it doing in the Abyss?"

"It seems to be stable enough now," Moore said. "No indication that it's sinking."

Kip grunted. "I can understand a dead boat going down. I *can't* understand a dead one coming back up. This beats all I've ever seen. One thing's for sure, though. Kiss Bottom's got a hold on it, and the hulk's not going anywhere soon." He looked closely at Moore as he leaned back against the bulwark and ran a hand over his face. "You want to see Dr. Maxwell, David?"

"No, I'm okay. I guess I'm still a little shaky. I knew the storm would have uncovered a lot down there, but I never figured on anything like this."

The constable was silent for a moment, gazing along the wide decks. "World War II crate, I'd say. No markings. Could be British, American, Italian, German . . . who knows? They all prowled these waters during the war. Now that it's up we're going to have to do something with it. I can't leave it out here, but for the life of me I'm stumped as to . . ."

There was another sharp noise of something striking iron. Kip peered over the bulwark, expecting to see one of the islanders again trying to gather up that heavy-duty cable.

But the men were all standing together at the bow. They had been talking quietly, and now they stared up at the constable, their faces frozen, their lips drawn into tight lines. The others on the trawler stood where they were, watching and listening.

And all around a deep, hollow booming—something striking iron with a rising, feverish intensity.

One of the islanders cried out in fear; they all backed away from the tower, moving toward the gangplank and the safety of the trawler.

Moore felt a chill streaking up his spine. "What the hell . . . ?"

"Get off it!" a bearded man on the trawler called out.

"It's the sea!" Kip said loudly, so they could all hear. "What's wrong with you men? The sea's coming up and banging around underneath the hull, for God's sake!" But now their eyes were wide and terrified; they were chattering among themselves, and even as they did the noise grew louder and sharper, more frenzied, out of pace with the sea's rhythm.

Then nothing. And the silence was ten times as bad.

"It's about to come apart," Kip said quietly. "Let's get off this thing." He swung himself easily over the bulwark and descended the ladder to the deck, then stepped back for Moore to come down. Kip paused a few seconds, looking over the side where the currents churned about under the hull, while Moore cast off the lines of his skiff. One of the men secured it so the boat would drag along with the trawler.

"Let's get out of here," Kip said.

They took the trawler's gangplank back aboard, freed the lines, and pulled them back. With a throb of its engines the trawler veered away from the submarine, swinging around for the clear entrance through the reef. Moore turned to look back at the thing. Its bow jabbed the sky, the maw of a beast. It unnerved him to think he'd been underwater with something like that, clinging to it, his unprotected network of flesh, nerves, muscle, and bone so close to an armor-plated creature of cables, gears, rivets, iron beams.

He was unable to turn his eyes away. *Where have you come from? And why are you here?*

No one spoke aboard the trawler. The sun beat down on the men, and the safety of harbor lay just ahead.

The eerie hammering noises still echoed within Moore's head. Had it been the sea, as Kip had said? He'd heard the same thing underwater, as he worked around that exposed periscope. But it had seemed to him then that the noise had come from inside the thing, as if something were striking metal over and over again, with a terrible strength.

Something trying to get out.

Three

THERE WAS LAZY WATER within the harbor; Kiss Bottom held back the swell and surge of the waves. Moore stood on the deck of the fishing trawler watching his own reflection break into halves, thirds, fourths by the boat's bow-break. The wharfs were coming up, and young boys stood ready there to catch and secure the thick fore and aft deck lines. Beneath the tangle of wharf pilings, where the steady surf washed in on a beach, crabs rustled through thorns and grass. The remains of a fishing skiff were half-buried there, and now no one remembered to whom it had belonged. Other small boats were beached along the semicircle of the harbor; nets were drying over timber racks, and a solitary fisherman sat beneath a cluster of palms, watching the trawler as it neared.

The larger trawlers were moored in their places, their tire-browed sides rubbing aged timbers. A sheen of oil floated across the water, tinting it in a kaleidoscope of thick colors; a dead ghostfish hung in the midst of it, the oil coloring it. In another moment the trawler's bow had ground it under.

"I've been in these islands for all my life, David," said Kip, coming up beside him and speaking over the din of the diesels' hoarse voices. "But I've never seen anything like that happen before. Like I say, it's a holy wonder you weren't killed." He scowled inwardly when he realized Moore wasn't listening.

Kip had been born into a poor fishing family on Hatcher Key, a small island perhaps a hundred miles to the east of Coquina, so named because of its turtle hatchery. Often he dreamed of being a youth there again, running with his friends across mountains of gleaming ivory sand, and beyond the shore into the surf with its unbroken patterns of white. Then his father had broken his arm and shoulder running the family's boat aground on an uncharted sunken steamer. The bones had never knitted correctly and his father had had to give up fishing, so the family had gathered up their belongings and moved to the Kingston slums, a mass of twisted clapboard and streets of shifting sand. Survival there had meant making miniature straw figures for the tourists, or in Kip's case, acting as a guide for a few pence. His aunt and uncle lived just outside Kingston, on the fringe of the woods. They had frightened Kip—their beliefs and practices had seemed peculiar—unnatural—and altered their everyday personalities in some inexplicable way. Kip had hated his visits with those people.

His mother had barely known how to read, but she insisted on teaching him. *If you can read,* she said, *you can think. And in this world a man got to think to survive.* While the woman had read to Kip, his father had sat apart from them in the tiny room, watching the lantern flicker and listening to the roll and call of the sea.

Kip had gone to the United States, to Florida, to seek his own living and there he had run into trouble. The grinning, tallow-faced white men either tried to beat him or steal whatever money he made sweeping floors in a Miami poolhall. They weren't all like that, of course, but he thought then he'd seen enough badness there to last a lifetime. By day he absorbed everything he saw or heard, and by night, in an upstairs room with holes in the plaster, he read all the books he could beg or borrow. One of them impressed him greatly: a novel about the bobbies of London, called *The Long Arm of the Law.* And so he worked his way across the Atlantic on a tramp steamer that docked in Liverpool, finding work as a deckhand on a harbor tug. He had had trouble at first, as the object of scorn and derision of the white old-timers. He had gradually won their respect, if not their friendship, simply because he could work like any three of them put together. Kip had gotten into a program in law enforcement and, returning to the islands in the sixties with his education and his eyes full of the world, he had landed a post as an officer in the Bahamas. On Grand Bahama he'd met his wife-to-be and fathered his first child, a boy named Andrew. Then he was offered the position of constable on Coquina. He had accepted because of the responsibility involved and the sense of doing something worthwhile.

He and Myra had stayed on Coquina because they'd found life good here, peaceful and secure. Mindy had been born just after they'd arrived, and five years later, Andrew, then seventeen, had gone to the United States on a factory boat to find his own path in the world. Kip saw the cycle repeating again and though he'd miss his son, he knew there was no use in trying to hold back what must be. Which was, he knew, the way of the world.

The trawler cut its engines and coasted toward the wharf. The boys caught the deck lines and made them secure around the stumps of pilings. Moore took Kip by the arm. "Look who's coming," he said.

"His excellency," Kip said, watching the black man in a dark suit and white shirt approaching them.

Moore climbed over the side of the boat and stepped onto the wharf; nearby two old men were cutting the heads off snappers to use as bait the following morning. Their knives gleamed with blood. As they worked they kept looking up at the thing that hung crazily across the reef.

"What's that?" another black with a gold front tooth asked Moore; he squinted to look out to the reef. "Big fish someone landed."

"That's right," Moore replied. "A hell of a big fish."

"Moore!" called the man in the dark suit, making his way past piles of crates, drying nets, and barrels of fish offal covered with motionless flies.

Kip had stepped onto the wharf behind the white man to watch the mayor's approach. Reynard never failed—he was always there as soon as something happened that might make him look bad.

"Where did that come from?" Reynard asked as he reached Moore, looking over Kip's shoulder at the hulk. He was neatly dressed in a clean suit, but the tight knot in his dark-blue tie was stretched badly, and the collar and cuffs of his shirt were frayed. When he squinted the lines around his nose and beneath his sparse field of white hair folded into deep trenches that gave his face the appearance of an aged oil painting about to crack. "My God!" he said, not looking at either the white man or the constable. "Do you know what that is?"

"It corked from about a hundred and fifty feet in the Abyss," Moore told him. "And, yes, I know what it is."

"Is it open?" The mayor turned to look at Kip.

"No."

"It's wedged in there, is it? Thank God it didn't come into the harbor or we'd have hell to pay, gentlemen. It looks from here to be almost intact . . ."

"It is," agreed Moore. "All two hundred feet of it."

The mayor made a face, as if he had swallowed something bitter. "What's going to be done with it, constable?"

"Right now I don't know. It's safe here for the time being. As long as it doesn't slip off the reef, it's not going anywhere."

"Isn't there some way to sink it again?" Reynard said, glancing nervously from one man to the other.

"Unseal the hatches or torch a hole in it under the hull," Kip said. "But I'm not so sure that's our decision. There are salvage laws to consider; the thing may belong to Moore."

Moore looked at him. He hadn't thought of that before, but now he realized it was entirely possible. He had found the thing and, in a sense, excavated it from its vault on the Abyss ledge. It wasn't something he would ordinarily have tried to claim as a salvage; few submarines were worth much except as historical relics. But, still, one in such good shape, and on the surface . . . it was something worth thinking about.

"And," Kip continued, "that's an old boat. No identification markings, but I'd say quite a few naval historians and museums would be interested. So I wouldn't be in such a hurry to put it back under again. David, if you like I'll fill out a witness form for you. I doubt if there's anything aboard that's not crumbling, but at least you might get a nice bronze plaque in a maritime museum . . ."

"I want it off my reef," the mayor said brusquely. "I don't like it being so close to the harbor. What if something exploded?"

"I say we don't do anything until we think over the possibilities," the constable said firmly. "I don't know a lot about submarines and nothing about explosives, but moving it could be worse than letting it stay as it is."

Reynard took a handkerchief from a back pocket and dabbed at his glistening cheeks and forehead. "I wish to God that thing had never come up! It should be rotting like a thousand other sunken ships out there, not hanging on Kiss Bottom like a black leech! God knows I've never seen anything like it before!"

"Do you have any idea what boat it might have been?" Moore asked him.

"I didn't come here until after the war," the mayor said defensively. "I'm not certain what lies in the Abyss, probably all manner of trash. But that thing . . . I don't know."

"The fishermen may be able to tell us something," Kip said. "In the meantime, David, let's get started on the salvage claim. We'll go from there."

As the constable and Moore started down the wharf Reynard called after them, "Just remember, both of you. The boat is as much your responsibility as mine. I hold you both accountable."

"Understood," Kip said.

The two men left the wharf, moving through the crowd that had streamed down from the village to gawk. They climbed into the constable's old rust-eaten jeep, which was parked beneath a group of high palms. Kip started the engine and drove along Front Street, through the tangle of fisherman's clapboard dwellings to the intersection of High Street, which would carry them directly to the heart of the village. They passed a cluster of bars, a few small stores, and drove on toward the Square, where the constable maintained his office.

A thin, hard-eyed black in dungarees watched the constable's jeep as it passed along High Street. Then he turned his attention back to the harbor and the object he'd seen driven upon the reef by the currents. *Dam' my eyes if that ain't it,* he said to himself. He lifted the burning stub of a hand-rolled cigarette to his lips and when he did the fingers trembled. *That got to be it, got to be. But thass so long ago . . . thirty-five, forty year . . . and now this bastard come up from the Abyss. It ain't right. Ain't no sense to be made from it. But I see it and by God I know thass it.* He flicked the cigarette stub to the ground and stepped on it, then began walking quickly down High Street, past the bars, past the men who sat on porch stoops watching him, past the few easy ladies hanging around trying to coax money. Ordinarily he would have been inclined, especially when he saw that slender high yellow who'd come in from Old Man's Cay a few days before, stopping to make money enough to get to Trinidad. But there was no time now.

He walked around to Front Street, past islanders who milled around the wharfs gaping and talking about the boat; he saw the looks in the eyes of a few of the older fishermen, and he saw they knew and did not wish to know just as he did not. He left the wharfs behind, moving by the fishermen's shanties, kicking at a black dog that came at him fiercely from underneath a house with the paint peeling off. Beyond the village, where the green jungle grew up wild and thick and the birds screeched from perches high in gnarled red bottlebrush trees, and where Front Street turned into a rutted sand path. He continued on, deeper into jungle, hearing the sharp, plaintive cries of the birds. When he came around a thicket of thornbushes he saw the church just ahead.

It was a small squat white structure with a high, pointed steeple. Front Street ended here. Beyond the church was a cemetery bordered by an ill-kempt picket fence and a chicken coop off to one side. The jungle was creeping in, grasping wood-plank grave markers with long green and brown vine fingers. Painted across the sides and front of the church itself were drawings: faces, numbers in circles, and names: *Erzuli, Zoka, Legba*. The paint, black and red, had streamed down in thick rivulets, staining the ground. There were two shuttered windows, both closed.

The black man approached the church door, took hold of the unornamented metal knocker, and rapped sharply on the wood.

Silence.

He put his ear to the door, then rapped again.

"It Thomas Lacey, rev'rend!" he said after another moment.

There was a long pause, the silence unbroken but for the birds and the breeze sweeping through foliage. Then the noise of a bolt sliding back. The door was pulled open. A face—gray goatee, eyes saucer-shaped behind thick wire-rimmed glasses, prominent cheekbones, and jutting chin—appeared in the opening. The eyes moved, slowly, taking the other man in, and then the reverend said in a thick French accent, "Enter."

Thomas stepped into a bare-floored room with a few long wooden pews. There was an altar at the center and a podium off to one side. He could smell sawdust, dampness, and age within the church, the odor of incense which was almost overpowered by the reek of tobacco. When the reverend shut the door the room was dark save for the light that squeezed through broken places in the window shutters, casting dim shadows about the walls. The reverend slid the bolt home and turned to face the other man. "What is it you wish?"

"It what come up out of the sea," Thomas said in a voice that was almost a whisper, the whispering echoing around the walls, moving like smoke in a box. "It what been thrown up on Kiss Bottom."

The reverend's eyes, dark marbles floating in yellowed whites, narrowed a fraction. His tall, almost frail body bent anxiously toward Lacey. "What are you saying? I don't have time for you."

"The white mon, Moore, he go divin' into the deep water today," Thomas said, trying to speak slowly. "It was him brought it up; it was him raised it. You say it

46

was gone. But right now that thing, that thing be across the reef. . . ."

"Ma foi!" The reverend was motionless, most of his face in shadow, only the lips moving.

"The boat!" Thomas said, a droplet of spittle catching in the corner of his mouth. "It come up from the deep water. . . ."

"No," the reverend said, very softly.

"I seen it with my own eyes. I seen it there!"

"No." The voice was still soft, but a commanding note had crept into it, and Thomas Lacey stood looking at him fearfully.

When Thomas found his voice he said, "It be under the water a long time. It tore up, twisted, but thass the one."

The reverend stared into the other man's eyes, examining them, as if he didn't want to believe what Thomas was saying. *"C'est possible?"* he asked quietly, without expecting an answer. His shoulders sagged forward perceptibly, the sharp blades protruding. *"Non, non."* A bird screamed outside, in the tangle of a protective perch. "The white man?" the reverend asked.

"Thass right."

"Leave me alone. Please. I want you to go away and leave me alone."

Thomas stood where he was, blinking, worried that he had somehow hurt the old man. He wiped his hand across his mouth.

"Please," the reverend said, turning away.

Thomas backed toward the door, unbolted it; the reverend was walking down the aisle between the pews, moving toward a doorway on the far side of the podium. He disappeared into the shadows as if consumed by them. Thomas stood there a moment, then he opened the door, squinting from the harsh glare. He left the church quickly, without looking back.

In his meager, cramped living quarters the reverend lit a candle and watched the flame grow to a tall white point. He reached into a dresser drawer and brought out a locked black box, setting it on top of the dresser. He took a small key from a pocket and unlocked the box. He looked through the contents—a white rabbit's foot, a vial of dark-colored liquid, grains of something dark in a paper packet, silver-painted candles, a pair of glasses with tinted lenses. Finally he found what he sought. *Oui.* There.

A silver case.

He withdrew it and opened it; inside there was a glass eye—blue—on a coiled silver chain. He put everything away again but the eye, and this he fastened carefully about his neck so that it lay across his chest outside his shirt.

He stepped forward, cupped a hand about the flame, and blew it out.

Standing in the thick darkness, he asked in French, very softly, as if speaking to someone standing just beside him, "What do you see? What do you see?"

Four

MOORE WAS CHOKING for air, tumbling head-over-heels down into a maelstrom of water. Around him loomed the huge gray-green walls of the sea; he was captive in a liquid mansion, falling through the thousand rooms, falling from attic to cellar, from light into darkness.

You've left them alone, his voice shrieked at him. *You've left them alone and they're afraid and they don't know what to do . . .*

The water had him, closing in, pounding pressure squeezing his lungs.

They're afraid . . . they're afraid . . .

He braced his shoulders against the sea, straining, fighting it; he kicked upward, encumbered by something yellow and bulky on his body. The foul-weather slicker. He kicked again, clawing at the sea, fighting upward against it, the air ebbing from his body with each second. *Don't leave them, you musn't, no, no, no. Reach them, please oh God give me strength, let me, let me please this time . . .*

When he reached the surface he was able to drag in only a small bit of air before the water crashed down over him, driving him under again. He fought free, staring about wildly in the darkness. There was a scream of wind and water, as though they were crazed beasts fighting madly. And caught between them, their boat creating a foaming wave, heeling sharply to port, the water pouring in sheets across the deck. He could see them reaching out for him, but the ocean separated them and the wind was drawing them away. He called out for them but the roaring shriek of the storm took his words and ripped them to pieces, spinning them out into space. He reached out his hand but then the wave came, a mountainous jagged thing of glistening stone, and he watched it, horrified as it crashed down over them, splintering through wood, driving them down in a spray that exploded with the shards of what had been a teak deck. He could only see them an instant more, frozen in the stucco of foam and black walls, and when he heard his name cried out he wanted the sea to sweep down his throat and take him too, but that was when the spinning section of transom came up under him, forcing him to dig in his nails and cling to it. It lifted him from height to height and on and on; before him he could read the red letters, the name that seared his brain as if each letter were a point of flame: *Destiny's Child.*

Please . . . don't leave them alone . . . they're afraid . . . please . . . please . . .

". . . please," he said, opening his eyes and feeling the pinprick beads of cold sweat on his eyebrows. A soft night breeze wafted in through the open terrace doors. Palm fronds clattered gently just outside, and he could see their shadows, like fingers, in the pale ivory moonlight that painted one wall of his bedroom. Somewhere far away, past the village, a dog was barking. A cockatoo cried in the jungle, a sad and mournful sound of the night. Moore put his face into his hands, waiting. *God,* he breathed. *God.* Some nights they were worse than others; some nights they were so real he couldn't shake them, and they laid back yet another layer of raw flesh. This one he'd had before, though they were all variations of the same thing. He hadn't been taking the sleeping pills Dr. Maxwell had given him for some time, because he always convinced himself he could sleep soundly without them. Now he wondered if there were enough in the little amber bottle to get him through the rest of the week. He lay there for a few more moments, and when he wiped his face he realized his eyes were moist. When he started to get out of bed the girl beside him reached out and caught his arm. "What is it?" she asked, coming fully awake.

"It's nothing," he told her. "Go back to sleep."

She stared at him, her dark eyes darker against the tint of her flesh. Her hair was cut short—like they were wearing it in Kingston and easy to manage, she had said when he complimented her. She drew her knees up, lifted her purse from where she'd put it on the floor, rummaged for a cigarette, found one, and lit it. He sat beside her on the edge of the bed, and she traced a line down the center of his back with a fingernail. Her name was Claire, she was from Old Man's Cay, and a few more as generous as this one and she could pay a freighter for passage to Trinidad. "Come on," she said. "I'm not sleepy anymore."

He said nothing, listening to the roll of the ocean. After a while she stabbed her cigarette out in an ashtray beside the bed and stood up, her lean, firm body and carnelian-tipped breasts catching moonlight. She took the clothes she'd folded over a chair and began to dress. Moore sat where he was. "I'd better go," she said. "I don't like sleeping in a strange bed."

"Neither do I," he said quietly.

"My sister's going to get me a job on Trinidad," she said, trying to lighten his mood with some casual conversation. "She's a dental receptionist." She narrowed her eyes at his back, struck by his defenseless, unmoving posture. He had a strong body, he was young and had seemed okay when they'd met at the Landfall Tavern that afternoon, but now he was so detached and distant. "Wasn't everything as you wanted it?" she asked him finally.

"Yes." He wiped the moisture from his face, stood up. "It was fine." He got a striped terry-cloth robe out of his closet and put it on. When he turned back he saw the sea shimmering, patches of silver and black, through the terrace doors. The moon hung in the center of pendulous, free-form clouds. From its position in the sky Moore estimated that it was a little past three. His gaze moved, as if drawn, to the dark line that lay just outside the sheen of the harbor. He could see the flashes of white breaking around the reef's exposed bommies; then he saw that other thing, that long black shape lying across the reef. It seemed still wedged tight in the same position it had been in when he'd looked last. He was afraid the surf would eventually beat the hulk free, but it was still angled toward the sky, the sea foaming in silver and green swirls of luminescence along its hull.

The hulk, dappled with moonlight and cloud-shadow like an eerie camouflage, sent a slow crawl up his spine. How the hell did it come to be buried beneath the sand? he wondered. And, more importantly, whose boat was it? British? American? German? He focused his eyes, aware of the rustling of the girl's skirt across the room. A U-boat? One of Hitler's wolf-boats prowling the deep currents, here in the placid Caribbean? It looked like a dark coffin recently exhumed. He shook off the image quickly; but he couldn't shake a strange idea he'd had all day, something that had made him want to get to the Landfall Tavern, down a few comforting shots of rum, and seek some companionship for the night ahead.

It was almost as if he'd felt compelled to try to dig that thing out underwater; he had known he was approaching his diving limits and he shouldn't have been that deep. He had this feeling he'd been lured there, enticed by that periscope jutting from the sand. He wasn't responsible for finding the submarine; rather, it had somehow found him and pressed him into service.

Claire was buttoning her blouse, still watching him, tired but half-hopeful he would warm to her again, offer her a bit more money. He was an attractive man and he had made love to her in a gentle but demanding way that had nearly succeeded in exciting her.

Suddenly he turned from the window. "I'll make you something to eat before you go," he told her.

She closed the last button. "I can't eat in the middle of the night," she said, laughing.

He shut the terrace doors and waited until they were out in the corridor before he switched on the lights. They descended a stairway, and when they got to the front room Moore turned on a pair of lamps, which surrounded them with a warm, smoky glow. Claire squinted a fraction through sleep-swollen eyes and smoothed her skirt down over her hips because she knew it was wrinkled. "I don't look too good in the light," she apologized.

Moore gazed at her; she was a pretty girl, very young, hardly out of her teens, but already the lines were showing. Very few women were able to keep their looks after a few years under the searing Caribbean sun, and she would be no exception. But he smiled at her, knowing she was fishing for a compliment. "I think you're very attractive. Sexy. How about a cup of coffee?"

She gave a half-nod and sat down in one of the wicker chairs. She put her purse, made a bit heavier by his money, on the long table made of a solid piece of driftwood, sanded and oiled. Across the bare wood floor there was a rug of woven seagrass; there were book-lined shelves, most of them old paperbacks, a small fireplace with a stone mantel. A group of primitive paintings, done in wild and vivid splashes of color by some island artist, decorated one wall.

Moore went back through a connecting doorway down another corridor to a kitchen; he made two cups of the strong, rather sweet, island brew and brought one of them to her. He crossed the room and took a decanter from a shelf to pour a stiff shot of dark rum into his cup. He sipped at the fortified coffee, feeling it light up his insides and chase the bad dreams away. As he turned back to her he caught a glimpse of the harbor stretched out below the hotel through one of the many square windows that lined the room. Moonlight glistened on the submarine, giving it shadowy teeth.

"Too early for that," Claire said, indicating his cup. "You drank a good bit down in the tavern."

He shrugged offhandedly and sat down in a chair across from her, unable to concentrate on anything but his dream and the events of the previous day. He had filled out some forms at the constable's office and Kip had witnessed them. He was uncertain about procedure on a military vessel but, he'd said, at least they were getting something down on paper. Then, there were two ways to go: contacting the Coast Guard to have the boat towed off and possibly sunk in deeper water, or sending out feelers over the radio-telephone to the two nearest large islands. Jamaica was approximately two hundred miles to the northwest and Haiti one hundred to the north. Kip had a cousin working for the police in Kingston, who could probably fill them in on the procedures so everything would be aboveboard and legal. If anyone wanted a look at the boat the word would get out. Moore had decided to wait on informing the Coast Guard and see what developed. Kip had agreed, for as long as he could placate Mayor Reynard. Then he cautioned Moore against any more diving in that damned Abyss—at least until the mess was cleared up. "Where'd that thing come from?" Claire asked him.

He looked up at her, finally registering what she'd said. "What thing?"

"I saw you lookin' at it, upstairs, and then out the window. The boat."

"Underwater," he said. "Other than that I don't know."

The girl was right: It was too early for rum. *You're older and wiser and this only compounds the sickness.* Or so the doctors had said. *Time doesn't heal,* Moore thought suddenly, *it only makes you forget the name of your illness.* And what was it called? There was a medical term for it that Moore didn't remember. The layman's label was much simpler: "survivor's syndrome."

Claire looked up, putting the empty cup aside, went to the window, and gazed down. "It's a big one. The men are already talking about it in the taverns."

"Are they? What do they say?"

"Funny things, things I don't understand so good. It's made some of them afraid, and there's a lot of whisperin' goin' on."

"Are you afraid of it?" he asked.

She paused, then smiled awkwardly, but the smile was quickly gone. "I've never seen nothin' like it before. But . . . I don't know. Mebbe. A closed-up thing like that, as huge as it is, like something from a bad night. I get chills thinking about it." She watched him, seeing his gaze go through her as if she were invisible. She picked up her purse. "I should go."

"Let me get dressed and I'll walk you down," he told her as he got to his feet, but she shook her head.

"No need. I be all right. You ever want to see me again I'll be down by the tavern somewhere, but I figure to be leaving here soon." As he approached her she reached out and touched his hand. It was as cold and hard as stone. She smiled again, showing teeth sharpened by chewing sugar cane, and then she was gone out the door and along High Street. She headed for the dark village below, keeping her eyes away from the thing lying across the reef. For a long while Moore stood in the doorway and watched her walk away, knowing she'd be okay but wishing all the while he'd gone with her just so that he could be with someone.

And then he couldn't see her anymore and he closed the door.

He felt weary suddenly, and after a while he turned off the lights and climbed the stairs in darkness.

On Kiss Bottom, surf surged in around the hulk, hammering at iron, foaming in and then back, again and again. A dog howled in the village, and another began barking, brokenly, in answer.

There was a manta ray sailing across the moon.

The aged black fisherman could clearly see its lines, the ridges along its extended wings, the long, sweeping tail trailing after it. It was a big one, he thought, plenty big enough bait for hungry snappers. As he watched, the wide cloud changed, curled in upon itself, became the silver image of a flying fish reaching for a height its ocean brothers could only dream of. Then the wings melted and it became a man's face with an open mouth. He could see the wide eyes, the cheekbones, the point of a chin. But there was fear in that face, and as he continued to observe the cloud, the look of the thing frightened him. The mouth opened wider, wider, in the outcry of one who has seen a terrible vision but does not yet know what he has seen. He felt the breeze knife through his bones. The mouth, opened as wide as possible, suddenly split from the face and became a separate cloud; now it was no longer a face but something grotesque and unrecognizable, turning in on itself like a maddened beast.

Abruptly the fisherman turned his gaze away.

There was a sharp bark, then a subdued growling.

"Hey!" said the old man. "Hey! You leave them be!"

The old man's terrier mutt, perched on top of the

fishing skiff's wet-well, had been watching the bone-white squid as they darted and dived, their tentacles tangling together. "You put your nose in there, Coconut," said the fisherman, "and one 'o them boys bite it off sure as I tells you!"

The mutt scampered away from the wet-well and to the stern, where his master sat with one hand on the tiller of a small trolling motor. "I ought to throw you to the merrimaids," the old man said, feigning disgust.

There were less than two hours until first light, and the fat squid that usually rose around Kiss Bottom at this time of the morning were nowhere in sight. He had caught what he could, mesmerizing the fish with the beam of a flashlight and then scooping them out, twisting and coiled, with a net. He could tell time by the rise of the squids, and in twenty years of foraging them from the reef that clock had never been off. Where were they this morning? He sat back in the stern, seeing the huge angled shape just ahead, hearing the soft thunder of the sea around it.

It was that bastard scaring the squid away. Damned thing prob'ly rustin' into the sea, and the squids taste the rust and go back down for the sweeter depths. He had seen the thing wedged onto the reef, and he'd marveled at its size. He'd never seen a boat like that before, all tight and sealed shut. How did the captain breathe, or any of the crew? Damn, but it was a mystery! His wife hadn't wanted him to go out this morning, but in all of twenty years only the storms had kept him from squidding. No damned rusting shell was going to scare him off, he'd told her. "And besides," he'd said, "the thing is dead." "No, no," she'd told him, "you don't know nothin' about it. I was here then. You don't know 'cause you came after it was over and done."

Superstitions. They was all the time eatin' at a woman, tryin' to get at a man too. Not that he didn't listen hard to the winds and the tides, or believe in the power of Rev. Boniface. But some things—old things his father and grandfather had sworn by a long time ago—he refused to put his faith in.

The water hissed along the thing's spine as he neared it. *Damn thing got a nest of snakes in it,* he thought. He looked toward the towering bow, ran his gaze past the rise of the conning tower. The boat was battered pretty bad, but no algae growths marked the iron. That was plenty peculiar. As he watched, a swell rolled across the stern leaving a trail of dull green phosphorescence and brown seaweed. It was an underwater boat, his wife had told him. Something bad and unnatural about it, she'd said. How could it stay under and then come back up again? He shook his head. It was a mystery, one that was beyond him. Coconut barked sharply again, stirring him from his thoughts.

Strands of weed, as long and brown as a woman's hair, rolled across the reef. His skiff was jostled by swells, and he put a hand on each gunwale to steady himself. He realized he was getting a little too close to the bommies, and he'd had a skiff peeled open before, so he turned his tiller to get away. Across the reef the seaweed swirled, a dance of the morning tides, and the phosphorescence gleamed like liquid emeralds.

And then, as if from a distance, came a low grinding noise.

The old man's flesh crawled; beside him the dog jumped, yipped.

Silence. The sea, the breezes whining around broken railings.

Coconut began to bark again. "Hush! Hush, I said!" The old man reached down for his flashlight and snapped it on, pointing it into the water at the submarine's hull.

A rush of foam kept him from seeing anything; he moved the light toward the stern, his mouth suddenly gone dry. Then the grinding noise returned, full force, and from the foam came a clump of coral and weed that looked like a decapitated head. Water rolled in, hammering, pulling. At first he didn't understand, but as he followed the beam of the light the realization came clear to him, and it clawed at his heart. The boat had moved, just slightly, but it *had* moved. It was sliding backward, grinding over the reef. The currents were freeing it.

"Great God!" he cried out; the hulk shuddered, and he almost dropped his light. The grinding quieted, almost vanished, then picked up again: a hideous scream of iron ripping coral. "Hey!" the old man shouted toward the sleeping village. *They had to hear it. They had to, the sleepin' fools!* "HEY! HEY!" But now the grinding was too loud, it filled his brain and ears and mouth so he could neither shout out nor hear his own words. When the skiff rose over the next swell he tripped over the dog; as he grabbed for the starboard gunwale the flashlight fell from his fingers and into the sea. In blackness, he reached for the tiller.

But before he could grasp it, he was riveted in place. His eyes, accustomed to the darkness now, saw the shadowy thing begin to slide off the reef with a low, ominous groaning and a hissing of foam. *Something unnatural,* his wife had said. Water roiled across the boat's deck as it settled down; it gurgled through vents and sloshed across the deck debris. Something was hammering, hammering, hammering. . . .

It's sinkin'! he thought, glad to see it go. He twisted the tiller around, his breath harsh and forced, and made for the reef entrance. The dog was whimpering at his feet, but even when he shoved him with a foot, Coconut wouldn't stop crying. He could see the swirls of water at the entrance, and the two buoys were clanging simultaneously, like church bells, again and again and again. He was only a few yards from the passage when he turned in his seat to watch the hulk go under.

But there was something black behind him, something huge, bearing down on him, cutting the sea to ribbons on either side. It twisted his guts in utter terror and forced his mouth open in a soundless scream. He let go the tiller, held up his hands to try to ward it off. The skiff, out of control, turned broadside in its path.

The looming bows drove across the fisherman's craft, splitting it, grinding it down; timbers exploded into the sky, then whirled in circles and fell back. Iron roared, tearing through reef bommies. The buoys clanged madly, the sea almost smothering them. With a long, piercing shriek the hulk passed through the entrance, struck sand bottom with a hollow, reverberating *boom* and finally lay still, the water still churning all along it. The submarine lay just inside the harbor, stuck on a narrow sandbar. Behind it, spreading like an oil slick, was a mass of timbers. In the midst of it was a crushed thing that had been a human body.

Lights began to come on in the village, one yellow dot at a time, and a dog howled as if trying to scare the moon away.

Five

In the pearly morning light three men waded through the surf, pushing aside shards of timber, and lifted out what was left of a corpse. An old woman in a tattered green gown screamed on shore as she watched.

"Careful, careful," Kip told the other two quietly. "Come on back. Watch your step, now." The body felt like something made of straw in their arms, a sack of broken bones hardly recognizable as something that once walked, breathed, lived. The gases hadn't had time to build yet. One arm was thrown out, a frail lance defending against attack. Teeth glistened in the remnant of a face. Kip averted his eyes, controlling himself with all the willpower he could muster. *Christ, what a terrible way to die!* he thought. One of his helpers in the grim chore shook his head back and forth; the other simply stared straight ahead at the group of people who had congregated on the beach. The old woman could not stop shrieking, and the rest of the women couldn't quiet her. Staggering out of the surf, the men came up the beach; the onlookers backed away, faces drawn. The men laid the corpse on a canvas tarpaulin and Kip closed the folds over it.

"You bastard . . ." Kip breathed at the submarine. He found himself mesmerized by the thing. Painted in vivid reds and black shadow by the rising disc of the sun, the massive hulk was now motionless. The currents must have lifted it off Kiss Bottom, and then . . . and then what? How did it crush the old man? The hulk could have turned before the man got his skiff away, but how in God's name did it clear the passage so perfectly? Now it was within the reef, sitting right inside Coquina's harbor. He walked forward a few feet, the surf swirling around his shoes and sucking the sand from beneath them. It must have happened very fast, he reasoned, and the old fisherman had panicked, losing control of his skiff. How many tons did that boat weigh? Seven, eight hundred? Something bumped his foot and he looked down; a gray, spongy mass had washed up. He realized what it was when he saw the eye: the severed head of the old man's terrier mutt.

He stepped back and the head was dragged away by the surf.

The woman had stopped her shrieking now; her eyes were fixed on the canvas-enclosed form, and one of the others was soothing her.

"Take her home," Kip told the women. "And one of you get Dr. Maxwell for her."

They pulled at her but she resisted, shaking her head violently. Her gaze didn't move from the tarpaulin, as if she expected her husband to throw it aside like a sheet and get up, whole and alive again. "Go on," Kip said softly. "There's nothing you can do."

She looked at him and blinked; heavy tears

streamed copiously along the deep trenches of her face. "I tell him," she said suddenly, in a weary voice. "I tell him. *Masango!*"

One of the women gently grasped her arm.

"Masango!" she said again, her eyes flickering from Kip to the submarine. Then she allowed them to lead her, like a sleepwalker, back to her house further along the harbor. Kip watched them leave, wondering what she was talking about. *An evil spell?*

A battered green pickup truck drove toward him along Front Street; it slowed, pulled off into the sand. Moore climbed out and came quickly across the beach to where the constable stood. "Who was it?" Moore asked, and Kip saw that there were deep hollows under his friend's eyes, as if he'd only slept for a couple of hours.

"Kephas, a fisherman," the constable said. "I don't think you knew him."

Moore gazed down at the tarpaulin; when he looked up, his eyes fixed on the submarine. "How did this happen?" he asked, a strange note in his voice.

"The currents must have worked the boat free; it went right over his skiff. He's not a pretty sight." He glanced over at the group of islanders. "All of you get on, now. I need a couple of men to carry the body, but the rest of you go on home."

"My God," Moore muttered as the people dispersed. "I saw from my terrace that the thing had gotten into the harbor, and I knew something bad had happened when I saw the commotion on the beach, but I didn't know . . ."

"We gon' take him to the rev'rend?" one of the men asked, coming forward.

Kip started to agree, but then shook his head. He

was staring out past the black's shoulder. "No need," he said finally.

Moore and the others turned to look. Standing in the shadows that stretched across the sand was a tall, gaunt figure in black, leaning on a thin ebony cane. The man blended with the darkness except for the circles of light that caught in the lenses of his glasses. He stood where he was for a moment more, then approached, his cane probing the ground in front of him. Moore saw something glittering around the man's neck: It was a glass eye on a long chain. Boniface did not look at any of them, but instead he bent down and drew aside the canvas. He crossed himself, closed the folds, moved past Moore and the constable, and faced the submarine as if confronting an ancient enemy. Moore saw his eyes blaze and then narrow into slits.

"I see it has come through the passage," he said. He took a long breath and sighed deeply. His breath came in a tortured gasp, as if he couldn't get enough air into his lungs.

"It crushed Kephas . . ." Kip began.

"Oui. One of the women came for me." Boniface regarded the two blacks. "You men, take his corpse to the church and leave it there."

Without hesitation they lifted up the canvas, holding it between them, and made their way toward Front Street.

"Where did you find this thing, Moore?" Boniface asked, not looking at the man but at the boat.

"On a ledge in the Abyss, about a hundred and fifty feet down, maybe a little more."

"And what's to be done with it?"

"For the time being," Kip said, "it's going to have to stay where it is."

Boniface whirled around to face the constable. "You must not . . ." the reverend said; the orb hanging around his neck glinting in the sun. His eyes had a power which Kip had rarely seen before. "You must not allow it to stay in this harbor. You must take it back over the Abyss, cut a hole in its hull and let it sink. Do you understand what I'm saying?"

"No," Kip responded, "I don't."

"One man is dead," the reverend said quietly. "Isn't that enough?"

"Just a minute," Moore interrupted. "It was an accident."

"Certainly," Boniface said, with a hint of sarcasm in his voice. "Do as I say," he ordered Kip. "Get it out of the harbor. Where that thing goes there is much to fear."

"That's voodoo talk!" Kip said disdainfully. "That's an old, dead machine out there. I think it's right you're concerned, but . . ."

"Concerned?" A thin smile slithered, lizardlike, across the man's lips. "Concerned, *oui.*" He lifted up the eye so both men could see it; sunlight flashed, reflecting an arc of light. "This is my sight, my *aché*. I have seen terrible things, and I ask you to do as I say."

"I don't believe in your visions, Boniface," Kip said. "Or your voodoo."

"I don't ask you to believe!" The reverend's voice was sharp, and his words had meaning behind them he evidently could not divulge. "I ask you to be warned. Everything the gods have created on this earth has a power . . . including that machine."

"No gods created it," Moore said. "Men did."

Boniface nodded gravely. "And are men not guided by their gods, be it the god of peace or the god of war?" He stared into Moore's face for a moment and saw something there that disturbed him. Then he turned to the constable. "All manner of things have their life forces, for good or for evil, and I am very familiar with the forces that rule that boat."

The man was openly talking voodoo now. "You speak of it as if you really thought it was alive. . . ." Kip said impatiently.

"Because I know!" Boniface hissed. "I remember . . ." He caught himself, looked away into the harbor.

"Remember what?" Kip asked.

"The fire," Boniface said very quietly.

Kip had heard hushed mention of it since he'd been on Coquina. It had happened during the war—a great blaze that had consumed most of the island's dwellings, sweeping out across the jungle and killing a score of people. He'd tried to learn more, for the sake of curiosity, from Langstree at the boatyards and some of the other old-timers, but it was a subject no one wished to discuss freely. "What about the fire?"

The sun was slowly filling in the shadows of the reverend's face, settling into the lines. They were like wrinkles in an ancient piece of parchment. He was silent for a long long while, and when he spoke it was with a genuine effort.

"It began with a screaming in the sky, as if all the heavens were wailing, as if the night sky had gone mad. At first it sounded distant . . . very distant . . . then louder and louder, cloaking the senses in noise

68

and heat. There was an explosion in the boatyard, and another and another; glass burst from windows and people were thrown to the ground by the blow of an invisible fist. I remember; *oui,* I remember too well. Something exploded among the fishermen's houses and the flames began there. The wind whipped in, tossed sparks into the sky, scattered them through the jungle. The strongest of us helped whomever we could to get away from the village, and we escaped to the sea in the few boats that were still moored to the broken wharfs." He paused, his eyes bitter; his tongue darted out and licked his dry lower lip.

"We could see the blossomings of the fires all along the beach and stretching toward the jungle. The British had a few freighters and a patrol boat moored in the burning boatyard, and they were trying to get them out to the open sea; there was much shouting and screaming, and their patrol boat crew was firing at something beyond our boats. At that time there were shore batteries—the big, ugly guns in their concrete bunkers—near the yard and built higher up on Coquina; their yellow tracks streaked across our heads into the distance."

He looked from Kip to Moore. "It was such a long time ago, you see, and the cruelty of it is that I recall every detail so clearly, so terrible and perfect. We were all in the mire of a nightmare, jammed together in skiffs and sailing sloops. There were many hysterical and wild, others trying to keep order as we watched our island burn. *Mon Dieu,* there can be no worse torture than that! Coquina was a mass of fire. There was no fleeing, for those of us who had taken to the sea could still hear our brothers and sisters screaming on shore. The heat touched our faces; we saw the bodies contorted in pain, racing into the surf where they only felt a worse pain as the salt hit their raw burns. The wailing, the terrible wailing . . . the night was full of it. I can never forget it as long as I live.

"And through the thick curtain of whirling smoke a noise reached us, more terrible even than that of human agony: It was a heavy pounding that made the ocean tremble. The timbers of the boats shuddered under us. We thought we would be capsized, and perish. We waited, and then out of the smoke came a thing that could drive a man mad, haunt his sleep until he despaired of ever finding rest again. One of the men aboard my skiff had a pistol and in his rage he fired at the thing, but there was no stopping nor slowing it. The sea thundered around it. Its great rolling bow-wave came under us, throwing our boat over; we clung to its upturned hull like rats. The monstrous thing, all black and gleaming like a huge, hungry predator, passed just before us.

"And that was when I saw the man. He stood high up on a platform of some sort. He stared at us for a moment and then he disappeared. The boat—for I had realized it was such—passed on and then suddenly dropped away like a stone into the sea. The waves rushed across it, and we sat stunned in the midst of the sea. Still we could hear the terrible screams of the dying from Coquina. We always had the fear that the monster might return."

Boniface raised his cane and pointed it like a rapier. "And *that* was the thing I saw. The thing of iron and evil; it came from the night and returned into the night."

"A sea-to-land shelling," Moore said after a moment. "Then it was a German submarine after the island boatyards." The thing looked wicked enough, like some sort of vengeful iron demon; Moore could understand why the islanders had feared it.

"To us it was a thing from Hell, crewed by faceless, inhuman creatures of another world. We wanted no part in that white man's war and yet it was forced upon us. We were not to be spared. The boat came again, and brought death until it was itself destroyed."

"How?" Kip asked him, intrigued. "What destroyed it?"

"That I don't know. But many nights I stood on this beach, perhaps in this exact spot, and watched the fires burning out at sea, the strange green and crimson comets streaking the black. And each morning the debris washed in, parts of ships and men. Frozen bodies with twisted, terror-struck faces; sometimes only a tide of blood or of arms and legs." He drew in his breath. "That . . . is the Night Boat, risen from its tomb at the bottom of the sea."

The men were silent. Kip could hear the buoys clanging out past the reef, and their sharp metallic sound grated on his nerves. The sea washed strands of clinging weed across the U-boat's deck, and made a *rhuthummmm* noise along the iron. "There's nothing for anyone to fear anymore," Kip said. "It's a dead hunk of metal now."

Boniface turned slowly to face the constable. "Not dead. Only waiting. And I beg you as I have never begged any man on this earth. Return it to the Abyss."

"For God's sake!" Kip said, irritated by the man's persistence and more than a bit uneasy beneath his

71

powerful gaze. "You've preached spirits and voodoo for so long you're seeing jumbies in a junkyard relic!"

The reverend said nothing for a long while, looking from one man to the other, probing their belief and fear. *"Dieu vous garde,"* he said softly. "I have a body to attend to." He turned from them and, picking his way with the tip of the cane, he moved away up the beach. He stopped once more on higher ground to stare back at the submarine, and then he disappeared among the clapboard houses fringing Front Street.

Kip saw that Moore looked concerned. "Don't listen to him," he said. "Superstition's become his second nature. But damn it all, I don't see how that bastard cleared the reef and got through into my harbor!"

The trawlers were preparing to move out for the fishing grounds from the commercial wharfs across the beach. Diesels rumbled; men shouted back and forth from boat to boat, and lines were cast off. There would barely be room for them to swing past the obstruction of the submarine and out to sea. The sun was rising now, a hot yellow orb in a sky that promised to be a clear azure blue. A few moments before, the hulk had indeed looked dark and spectral, with the weeds entwining its deck and railings. Now, in the clearer light, it simply appeared to be a battered, aged wreck.

"Can you give me a lift back up to my office?" Kip asked, and when Moore nodded they began walking toward the pickup truck. "A hell of a mess," Kip muttered. "The whole island probably knows about this by now, and if I judge Boniface correctly he'll use it as an opportunity to strengthen his hold on these people. I've got to do something about that boat, David. I can't let it rot here, but for the life of me I don't . . ." He stopped suddenly, his eye caught by the sun glinting brightly off the tin roof of the abandoned naval shelter off in the distance. *No, that would be one hell of a huge risk.* Then he asked himself: *more risk than leaving it unattended on the sandbar?*

The constable's office, a small stucco building painted a light green, was on the village square. There was an oval park of palmettos in the center of the street, and the weather-etched granite statue of a black man hefting a harpoon that had been erected by the British as a peace concession to the Carib Indian tribe. It honored one of the Carib chieftains—a man named Cheyne—who in the 1600s had led a rag-tag army against a band of pirates who were trying to seize Coquina as a fortress. The Caribs had been here at least a hundred years before the first British settlers had arrived; they lived off the sea and the land, keeping to themselves unless feeling threatened, and then their wrath could be awesome. It was clear that the Caribs were to be left alone, judging from the number of British settlers who were laid in their graves in those early years. Now they were mostly quiet, and Moore didn't know much about their current way of life. Across the Square were brightly painted buildings: Everybody's Grocers and Cafe, Langstree's marine supply store, an open-air market where the inland farmers displayed their goods on Saturdays, and the Coquina Hardware Store. Dirt-track streets cut back through the jungle to more houses. Beyond those, the foliage grew thick and wild.

Coquina was fifteen miles around, housing a population of a little more than seven hundred. In centuries past it had served as a battleground between the British and the French; the island, along with a dozen other small spits of sand in the area, had been possessed first, in the early 1500s, by the Spanish, who had left it pretty much alone, then a hundred years later by the British, who'd fought the Caribs to make a go of sugar and tobacco plantations. The French had attacked when the plantations had proven profitable. And so on in a spiral of naval and diplomatic warfare, until finally the British seized it as a permanent possession. Some of the old plantation great houses still stood in the deep jungle although now they were cracked mounds of rubble through which the vines and growth had reclaimed their own territory. When Moore wandered these old plantation houses through the long corridors and empty, ghostly rooms, he thought sometimes he could feel how it must have been: the land barons gazing out over their sloping fields to the seas beyond, the schooners with billowing sails slipping across the ocean to take on new cargoes for mother England. Coquina had been a good and inexpensive investment for the British, until the Caribs had rebelled and killed most of the plantation owners.

The island was so named because it was shaped like a coquina's shell; also because the beaches were filled with the little clamlike sand-diggers. They were thrown up by the surge of the surf and then would rapidly scurry down again into the safety of the wet sand, their paths marked only by bursting bubbles of air.

And now, over two hundred years since the French and British had battled here, Coquina was home to

David Moore. Perhaps it would not be home forever, but for now it was good enough.

God, how the years have passed, he thought as he drove into the Square. Rapidly flashing by in swirls of color, of experience, of memories he kept close to his chest like a deck of cards. In the space of seven years, everything had changed and the changes had led him here. His mind sheered away from the old vision: riotous gray waves, soaring whitecaps, a storm that had swept up without warning, thunderclouds torn from the sky above the Atlantic into Chesapeake Bay. The ragged images tortured him, filled him with a sense of dull, throbbing rage and left him with the knowledge that at any given instant, the security and hope of a man's life could fall away like rotten flooring.

"You okay?" Kip asked, gently touching Moore's arm. "You just passed my office. Slow down."

Moore shook himself from the memories. "Sure. Guess I wasn't thinking."

He turned the pickup around and parked in front of Kip's office.

"You had your breakfast?" Kip asked.

"Not yet."

"Come on in and I'll throw something on tne griddle." He opened the door and Moore followed him inside. Kip's office was piled high with varied and assorted things—there was scarcely room to turn around. There was a desk and a reading lamp, a few chairs, a bookshelf with legal volumes; behind the desk a locked gun cabinet, faced with glass, holding two rifles. On a wall hung framed certificates of merit from Kingston, and there was also a crayon drawing of a scene in Coquina harbor—the trading vessels with masts like telephone poles and all of them colored a different hue—done by Kip's five-year-old daughter, Mindy. Gunmetal-gray filing cabinets stood against the opposite wall next to a storage closet; another door with an inset of glass at eye-level led back to two cells.

Kip drew open the blinds; sunlight flooded in. He slid a couple of the windows open so the sea-breezes could enter, and then he went to the far side of the room. There was a small sink with a shelf above it holding a few plates and cups as well as a hot plate, which Kip plugged into a wall socket, and a portable icebox. He rummaged in the icebox, found a couple of eggs, and knifed strips from a slab of bacon.

Moore settled himself into a chair before the constable's desk and ran a hand across his face. He sighed wearily.

"What's wrong with you?" Kip asked him. "You not getting enough sleep?" He threw the bacon into a skillet he had placed on the hot plate. He smiled. "I understand your problem, my friend. You had too much company last night."

"How'd you hear about that?"

"I'm supposed to know everything that goes on around here." Kip picked up two of the cups, saw that they were clean but rinsed them anyway. He filled a teakettle and waited for the bacon to crisp. "You ought to stop living out of damned cans like you do, David. It's no trouble for Myra to set an extra place."

"She'd strangle you if she heard you say that."

"Possibly." The bacon was curling; the scent of it wafted about the office. One of Kip's duties as constable was to keep whatever prisoners he had confined in good health, which meant feeding them three times a day, and on his budget he couldn't afford to send out for food. "I made a call to my cousin Cyril in Kingston yesterday evening," he said after a pause.

"And . . . ?"

"He couldn't offer any suggestions; he thought I was joking at first, and I had a bad time convincing him. In any event, Cyril's promised to pass the information along to the *Daily Gleaner.*" Kip forked the bacon out of the skillet and onto the plates; he cracked the eggs and let them fry.

"It bothers me." Moore said quietly.

"What does?"

"The submarine. What made it go down? And what about the crew?"

Kip looked over his shoulder as he lifted out the fried eggs. "What *about* the crew?"

"I wonder . . . what kind of men they were, and how did they come to be so far away from home. . . ."

"Well, there were a lot of U-boats patroling the Caribbean in the early part of the war," Kip reminded him. "You needn't be concerned about the crew. Most likely they're old men relaxing in slippers by their hearths, puffing their pipes, sipping their steins of beer, and swapping war stories. Here. Take this while I do the tea."

Moore took the plate. "But the hatches are sealed. How could they have gotten out?"

Kip shrugged. "All those old crates had to have an emergency hatch of some kind. I don't know; I'm certainly not an expert. Are you going to stare at that egg or eat it?"

Moore probed it with his fork. "I'm not sure; I think I might be safer just staring."

The kettle whistled. Kip poured water over a teabag in each cup and offered one to Moore, then he sat down behind his desk and began to eat. "I'm more concerned with the present," he said, in a graver tone. "I'll be going by to see the Kephas woman, and I'm not quite sure what to say to her. Damn it! The chances of an accident like that happening to her husband are one in a million." His jaw clenched. "Boniface worries me. Oh, he's pretty much harmless, but a lot of people on Coquina pay him heed. I don't want him stirring up trouble over the submarine. You've heard those drums going out in the jungle as many times as I have; God only knows what he's up to during those ceremonies. And of course there's no legal action I could take, if I wanted to—which I don't. I don't care what gods the islanders pray to, I just don't want undue and irrational fears taking over." He picked at his egg and then shoved his plate away. "I wish to God Boniface had stayed in Haiti where he belonged."

"Why didn't he?"

Kip drank down the rest of his tea. "Local trouble." He began to roll a cigarette for himself, using an island-grown tobacco. "A feud between him and another voodoo priest—a *houngan*—over territorial rights, I suppose. From what I gather there was a lot of bad stuff going on; Boniface's home was burned down and his family chased off into the jungle. Not long after that the other *houngan* was found in the Port-au-Prince bay, weighted down by a gutfull of nails. The police got on the track but nothing was ever proven; you know how those things go. But this *houngan* was supposed to have had some powerful friends, and they went hunting Boniface's head. One way or another he got out of Haiti and wandered around the Caribbean for a while. He settled here just before the war. Some day I'd like to find out just how many skeletons I can pull from his closet. Which brings us to that damned hulk. I'd love to donate it to Langstree to be hammered into scrap, but some museum curator would probably slit my throat. Now, with the thing in my harbor . . . something's got to be done." He lit the cigarette and stood up, taking the two plates over to the sink.

Moore got up and went to the door. "I've got things of my own to do. Shutters and drainpipes still need some patching."

Kip walked out to the truck with him, and they exchanged a few more comments about the ferocity of the storm that had just passed. Kip could only think of one thing: he dreaded the way the Kephas woman would stare at him when he said, I'm sorry, there's nothing I could have done, it was an unavoidable accident. Unavoidable?

Moore swung up into the truck and started the engine, waving back at his friend. He drove along the street toward the Indigo Inn. After he was out of sight, Kip turned toward the flat blue-green expanse of the harbor, watching the thing that grew across the sandbar like a cancer.

He drew on his cigarette, exhaled smoke. A trawler was moving out through the passage, with a gang of men on its starboard deck making sure they cleared the submarine's bulk. Far out at sea, an industry freighter was swinging in to take on a load of fish, coconuts, or tobacco.

It would take three trawlers to break it off the bar and guide it, he decided. Langstree would scream like hell, but that was something Kip had encountered before. He closed and locked the office door and in another moment was in his jeep, driving out of the Square toward the harbor below.

Six

A SWIRL OF dark smoke from straining diesel engines
stained the blue of the afternoon sky. The men on the
trawlers' decks called back and forth to each other as
they yanked at thick hawsers and cables, securing
them around heavy-duty cleats and bollards. Lines
drew tight, coming up out of the sea with a popping
sound, sending droplets of water flying. Someone
called out, "Pull! Break her ass, there!"

Timbers creaked; the noise of diesels mounted,
their vibrations pounding decks and churning the guts
of the blacks who worked there. Sweat rolled off their
backs beneath the hot sun. "Give 'er more," the
captain of the *Hellie* shouted out, the stub of a
Brazilian cigar clenched firmly in his teeth. "Come
on, mon!" Water boiled at the stern. The captain
looked across to the other trawler, the *Lucy J. Leen,*
stretched tight on its spiderweb of hawsers. The
Lucy's diesels were smoking, and it looked as if her
captain was going to have to drop his main lines.

The *Hellie*'s master squinted and exhaled a large cloud of blue smoke. Christ A'mighty! That big bitch had her nose stuck tight in sand; she wasn't going to move, no matter how much power they squeezed into the engines. One of the starboard lines was fraying fast; he saw it and pointed, "Hey! You men watch your fuckin' heads when that baby comes flyin' back, you hear me?"

Another trawler, a rickety old boat with a smaller draft, had secured lines onto the hulk's bow, pulling its nose out of the sand while the other bigger boats hauled at its length. The thing was heavy—heavier than she looked. The *Hellie*'s master didn't want his diesels wrecked, and he was almost ready to tell his first mate to shut them down. But he'd told Steve Kip he'd do his best, and by God that's what he was going to do. "We're heatin'!" someone cried out, and the captain yelled back, "Let 'er heat!"

The props were foaming wild water at the sterns of the trawlers; now sand was coming up, too. That was a lot of power working in there. Shit! The captain grunted and chewed the butt. Fuckin' thing won't move!

But suddenly there was a sliding sound and the *Hellie* lurched forward. "Ease up!" the captain called out sharply. "Drop her down a few notches!" The diesels immediately began to rumble more quietly, and a man in the stern on the trawler securing the bow lines waved his arms.

"Okay," the captain called out toward the squat wheelhouse. "Full ahead."

"Full ahead!" The order went back, by way of two or three crewmen.

The *Hellie* began to move back, as did the *Lucy J*.

Leen, still smoking badly, and the sliding noise inten-
sified. Then, abruptly, it ceased. The submarine's bow
began to swing free, and the beat-up trawler tightened
its hawsers to keep control over the thing. Holding the
U-boat secured within their circle, the trawler armada
moved at a crawl past the wharfs where the crew of a
Bahaman freighter watched from their aft deck. The
swells rolled in toward the fishing wharfs, bobbing the
small boats up and down against their tire-brows and
bumpers, spreading out beneath the pilings, and
smashing into the beach in a mass of oil-streaked
foam.

The trawlers moved along the semicircle of the
harbor, past the village toward the boatyard beyond.
Past a couple of old, submerged wrecks with masts
and funnels protruding from blue water, past another
large trawler at anchor, past the boatyard wharfs they
moved. The *Hellie's* captain looked along the port
deck and could see the aluminum drydock shelters.
The largest one, the one used as a temporary shelter
for patrol boats during the war, was right on the lip of
the sea. It had been built on a concrete bedding with a
large door that could be raised or lowered and a dam
and pumping system that could allow flooding; now
the captain could see the open shelter doorway. It was
set amid a jumble of unused, rotting piers the navy
had built and then abandoned. It was going to be
damned tricky getting such a length in there, damned
tricky.

He watched the angle of the swells as they flowed
around Kiss Bottom's bommies. The sea was running
a bit rough this afternoon, and that was going to cause
more problems. The *Hellie's* master had been a first
mate on a British ocean-going salvage tug, and that

was the primary reason Kip had asked him to oversee the operation. He'd towed for the British navy in the latter years of the war and had brought in many dead or dying ships to the Navy facilities here in this very harbor. He twisted around to check the lines. Number four fraying badly, number two as well. *Goddamn it!* he snarled to himself. No good rope in the islands these days! The *Lucy J. Leen* was cutting back somewhat due to her overtaxed diesels; someone was going to catch hell about letting those engines get in such a shit-awful shape.

Dark-green water roiled inside the abandoned naval shelter. He could see the workmen waiting with their sturdy hawsers to secure the hulk. The trawlers passed the shelter; the smaller craft with the bow lines turned in front of the submarine and made for the open doorway. Diesels shrilled, but in another moment the hulk responded and started moving bow-first toward the shelter. Simultaneously the larger boats cut their engines; now it was up to the small boat to line up the submarine with the shelter and take it in. Moving steadily and slowly, the bow trawler maneuvered into position, heading its own nose into the darkness of the shelter. The other boats swung around, using their combined power to haul the U-boat forward. At the last moment the small boat dropped its lines and swung sharply to starboard; the U-boat was cutting a bow-wake, moving too fast, so the trawlers cut back on their engines to slow it.

The U-boat moved into the shelter, and though its speed had been reduced, it still sent water crashing into the concrete sides of the shelter basin. Its bow crunched against concrete even as men leaped aboard her and caught lines to tie the boat to iron cleats. The trawlers dropped their lines then and swung off, and for a moment the heavy swells thrown up by the action of the boats sent foam and spray flying inside the drydock basin. The dock workers fought to lash the hulk down, but as the swells subsided the water smoothed out and the boat held firm between tightly pulled fore and aft hawsers.

Kip stood and looked at the thing. *God, what a machine!* He took a last puff on his cigarette and tossed it into the brackish water; the butt hissed and went up underneath the hull. He was standing on a wide concrete platform level with the hull which ran around the entire shelter. Ladders leading off the platform that would normally have gone down to a dry pit were almost submerged. Behind Kip was an abandoned work area now jammed with old crates and forgotten machinery, a carpentry area where a stack of timber lay, an electrician's cubicle now cluttered with pieces of iron and thick coils of all-purpose wiring. The concrete flooring was coated with a film of aged oil. The entire shelter smelled of sweat, diesel fuel, and oil, and compounding the odors was the fetid smell of the hulk itself. It was decaying, Kip thought, right in front of his eyes.

"She's in tight," said a tall, barrel-chested black with a gold tooth gleaming in his mouth. "Sure hope you know what you're doin'."

"I do, Lenny," Kip said.

"Mr. Langstree, he be back from his trip to Steele Cay tomorrow or the next day, and when he find out what he got in here . . . well, I don' think he goin' to like it too much, you know?" Lenny Cochran was Langstree's foreman. He had agreed to go along with this because Kip was the constable and a man he respected, but he was still worried his boss was going to come down hard on him.

"He's never had need to use this basin," Kip reminded him, sensing the man's unease. "It's just full of junk the British navy left behind—just a damned storage warehouse. If he jumps, you tell him I ordered you and the rest of the men, and send the old goat over to see me."

Lenny smiled. "Shouldn't talk 'bout Mr. Langstree that way."

There was a rattle of chains and the sound of a winch in operation; the far bulkhead slid down into the water, just missing the stern and submerged propellers of the submarine by a few feet. The only light in the shelter streamed through a series of large, rust-edged holes in the roof almost thirty feet above them. Water gurgled noisily around the U-boat's hull vents; its conning-tower and periscope shafts loomed high. Shadows played across the shelter's opposite wall as several of the men moved about, examining the boat at a respectful distance.

"She ain't in such bad shape," Lenny said softly. He looked down the boat's length and whistled. "Mon, she must've been hell in her day, you know?"

"I'm sure of it." The deck was fully out of water now, and the sea streamed in rivulets through the mass of debris, making strange whispering noises that echoed within the shelter. Kip looked past the tower bridge toward the stern, then something caught his eye and he jerked his head back. *Jesus!* he thought, stunned. *What was that!*

He was almost certain he'd seen someone standing there, hands on the iron coaming, a dark, lean figure of a man staring down at them. He saw now it was an interplay of shadows and light, locking together like pieces of a jigsaw puzzle, through one of the roof holes. Christ, that had given him a shock! *Jumbies,* he told himself sarcastically, and then chided himself. *Don't go thinking voodoo, Kip; there are no such things as haunts.*

"What's the matter, Kip?" Lenny asked him a second time—Kip had not seemed to hear before.

"Nothing." He blinked his eyes and looked back to the bridge again. A shadow, that was all.

And then he was certain someone was staring at him.

Kip turned his head. In the corner, near the wreckage of timber that had once been a naval carpentry shop, a red dot glowed. As Kip watched, the dot flared and a stream of smoke rolled out, like a ghostly essence, through a splotch of light. A black man smoking a thin cigar, wearing faded jeans and a sweat-stained T-shirt, emerged from the shadows. He had no expression on his hard face; there was a cold, rather cunning set to the line of his lips, but he moved with an animal-like grace.

"That the boat killed old man Kephas?" the man said to Kip. His eyes didn't seem to register the men's presence; they focused somewhere on the submarine. His name was Turk; he had only recently arrived on the island, and Kip had already had trouble with him, throwing him in the cell two Saturdays before for brawling. Langstree had bailed him out; the young man was supposed to be an expert hand at a torch, and Langstree was paying him top wages for a welder. But Kip had seen a lot of these island drifters pass through, and he knew Turk was a rootless, undisciplined type of man.

"What happened to Kephas was an accident," Kip said.

The young man had a tough face, thick eyebrows, a black goatee. "I saw the body this mornin'. Bad way to die." He exhaled smoke through flared nostrils. "Why you put that thing in here, to hide it?"

"Go on about your business, 'mon," Lenny cautioned him.

Turk ignored him. "I hear some things 'bout that fucker. I hear it's a Nazi sub."

Kip nodded.

"How 'bout that, huh? Goddam bitch jus' corked off the bottom, ain't that so? I never heard of that happenin' before. What's inside her?"

"A few tons of corroded iron, twisted bulkheads, maybe a couple of live torpedoes." Kip said. *And what else?* he wondered suddenly. *What had Moore mentioned about the sealed hatches?*

"Why don't you open it up and have a see?" Turk raised an eyebrow.

"Too dangerous. And I'm not that curious."

Turk nodded, smiling thinly. He turned and stared at the boat for a moment, then took the cigar stub out of his mouth and flicked it. It hit iron, falling in a shower of sparks into the placid water. "Off the Caymans couple or three years ago," he said, "somebody found a German gunboat sunk in about a hundred feet. They used an underwater torch to get through a few collapsed bulkheads, and they burned into a vault. You know what that fucker yielded?" He looked from one man to the other. "Gold bars. Made those fellas rich. Fuckin' rich."

"Gold bars?" Lenny asked.

"That's bullshit." Kip interrupted quickly. "And if

you think this beat-up crate's carrying gold bars you're out of your mind."

Turk shrugged. "Maybe not gold. But maybe somethin' else. Those goddamn Nazis carried all manner of stuff with 'em. You never know 'til you look."

"The only thing in there is a lot of old machinery," Kip told him.

"Maybe so, maybe not." Turk smiled again, his eyes still blank.

Kip recognized that hungry look. "Now you hear me. If you're thinking about doing a bit of free-lance torching, forget it. Like I say, you spark some explosives and you'll be picking gold bars off the streets of Heaven."

The other man held up his hands defensively. "I'm talkin', that's all." He smiled again and walked past the constable toward the battered frame door set into one wall. He opened the door, admitting a shaft of blinding sunlight, and was gone.

"He got no respect for elders," Lenny said. "He's trouble, but he damn good at what he does."

"So I hear." Kip gazed at the U-boat for a few more seconds, feeling a chill creep up his back. He could hear the sounds of it settling; creaking timbers, water sloshing around, the groan of a deep metal bulkhead—eerie, distant voices. "Lenny," he said, "keep the workmen away from here, will you? I don't want anybody fooling around with this thing, and what I said about explosives maybe being on board is true."

"Okay," Lenny agreed, nodding. "I do what you say." He raised his voice and called to the rest of the men, "She down now, let's get on with our business!

J.R., you and Murphy got a hull-scrapin' to finish up! Percy, you done paintin'? Come on, let's get back!"

Kip clapped the man on the shoulder and made his way out. But even in the fierce sun, his eyes aching from the glare, he saw the image of a dark form standing on that conning tower, as silent and motionless as Death itself. *Keep it up,* he told himself, starting the jeep's engine. *You'll be seeing jumbies in your soup.* He drove out of the boatyard, heading for the fishermen's shanties. Like it or not, he had to pay a call on the Kephas woman. There was work to be done, and a sorry task it was indeed.

But before his jeep had made a hundred yards more he felt that chill again, like a premonition. He had a wall inside him, cutting him in half, blocking off a dark place where he feared to look.

That boat had been built to destroy; it had been baptized in blood and fury, and God only knew how many ships and good men had gone down in the wake of its torpedoes and guns. Boniface's words haunted him: *Take it out of the harbor. Sink it. Sink it. Sink it.*

"How, by God?" he said aloud.

Abruptly the bright colors of Coquina village came up around him, and his mind had just begun to wonder how he could soothe the Kephas woman when he felt the first slow scrape of jagged nails across the wall inside his soul.

Seven

HE PAUSED IN the darkness, took from a back pocket a flask and uncapped it, tilted it to his lips, and let the good strong Blackjack rum flow down. Then he wiped his mouth on his sleeve, returned the flask to the pocket, and continued walking the road.

The darkness was absolute, the midnight breezes thick. They clung around him. No lights burning in the village. Everyone asleep. No, no—there was a light burning up at the Indigo Inn. A single square of light in an upstairs window. He didn't know the white man, but he'd seen him around the village before. It was the white man found the submarine.

The jungle grew wild just beyond the road; cicadas were singing like sawblades in the trees, and every now and then a bird skreeled. It was just enough noise to unnerve him. Out at sea there was only the blackness; he could hear the surf on the coral and he knew the beach was near, but he couldn't see it.

He'd gone back to the naval shelter three more

times that day to look at the U-boat, to think about what might be waiting for him inside. The gold bars found in Cayman waters had flamed his greed. Of course, he didn't know if the stories were true or not—he'd heard them from a rum-rag in a bar—but if it was true! It was. It *had* to be true. He quickened his pace. The boatyard was around the next curve in the road, and he had hard work to do.

Something about that vessel had eaten into Turk; there was a strangeness to it, he had a weird feeling about it. He'd spent all day thinking about it, wondering what treasures it could be hiding. Maybe that damned policeman knew more than he was saying, too. Why else would he have wanted to put it away inside that shelter? Why not just let it rot in the harbor? No, somethin' was real strange. The policeman was hidin' somethin'. And nobody had ever hid any secrets from Turk Pierce.

The whitewashed wooden gates to the boatyard entrance were straight ahead. It would be easy to either slip under them or climb over. Hell, who was going to know? He had almost reached them when a shadow detached itself from the other jungle shadows and stepped out into the road.

Turk stopped, frozen, his mouth half-open.

In the darkness the apparition was huge, a hulking form with wide bare shoulders, its chest covered by the thinnest cotton shirt. He took a step back before he realized it was real—it was a man. He was bald-headed, his flesh a tawny color instead of pure ebony; he had a white beard and mustache, cropped close to his shadow-covered face, and Turk caught the sudden gleam of a small gold ring hanging from one earlobe. The man was carrying a crate of some kind, and Turk could see the muscles defined on his forearms. The figure stood perfectly still, watching.

"Hey, you scared the fuck out of me," Turk said easily, trying to control his voice. Christ! He didn't want any trouble, especially not with a bastard as big as this. "Who are you?"

The man said nothing.

Turk stepped forward, trying to see the face, but the figure had vanished, swallowed up by the foliage. A knot had caught in Turk's throat; he thought he'd seen one side of the face, and it had been a hideous mass of scars. He stood still for a long time, then took his flashlight from his belt and shined it into the jungle, cautiously. Nothing there. If the man was still around, he was moving silently. Turk shivered, fighting off a cold wave of nameless fears. What was that thing, a damn jumbie walking the road maybe hunting a soul? Something lookin' for a little child to suck the blood out of?

He kept the light on, moving it from side to side before him. When he reached the gates, he saw there was enough room for him to slide beneath them on his belly. Crossing the yard, moving through discarded piles of machinery, empty oil barrels, around beached boat hulks, he saw the naval shelter. He paused for a moment, standing against a mountain of cable, and switched off his light. He'd heard a noise, like the sound of someone walking along wharf planking. A goddamn night watchman? There was the noise again, and then Turk realized it was just the breeze, slapping the weathered boatyard sign against its support posts. He could hear the sound of the clangers in the far distance, and the bass rumble of breaking waves. Turk snapped his light on again, still uneasy from his encounter with that figure on the road, and approached the shelter. Cochran hadn't put a chain or padlock on the door, thank God; it was closed, a few crates blocking it. A handpainted sign read: *Keep out. Cochran.*

Turk pulled the crates away, scowling when he found they'd been filled with heavy odds-and-ends—bolts and broken tools. He opened the door, shined the light around inside, then entered. It smelled like a burial vault and the stench was almost overpowering, but he swallowed and tried to keep his mind off it. Light reflected off the water and rippled across the walls, undulating beneath the thing's hull. Strange shadows moved away from the beam of light, like phantoms scurrying for the safety of darkness. He worked the light over the conning tower, up to the tops of the shafts, and then back along the superstructure. *You ain't so much hell now, are you?* he asked the thing. Something clattered sharply behind him, and Turk sucked in his breath; he flashed the light into a corner, his heart hammering. It was only a rat, panicked by the unfamiliar light, squeezing among a clutter of oil cans and rag scraps.

There was a gangplank between the concrete walkway and the U-boat's deck, and Turk crossed it, careful of his footing. He had already climbed to the bridge and examined the main hatch there during the day; water and sand more than an inch deep still swirled over it. There was another hatch on the aft deck, covered with the tendrils of cables, and he couldn't work them away alone. But on the fore deck, near the gun's snout, there was a third hatch, the seam line marking a large rectangular opening. It was covered over by a broken planked lid.

Turk bent down, his eyes following the circle of the light, and lifted the hatch cover to examine the iron again. *How thick would this bitch be?* he wondered. He banged a hand against the iron and knew it was going to be a hell of a job. He sat back on his haunches and swung the light toward the spear-point of the bow far ahead. *Hell of a big mothafucker,* he thought. His impulse to burn through was stronger than ever, though he was oddly unnerved by the sheer size of the boat. There was probably no gold inside, but what about souvenirs? he wondered. The dealers in Kingston and Port-au-Prince could move anything. And there was a collector for everything under the sun. He might be able to get a good price for some of the equipment inside, maybe find himself the skeleton of a pistol or intact instrument gauges. And what about bodies? *Maybe they in here, may they ain't. Come on, come on; you got a job to do.*

Something made a noise on the other side of the shelter; Turk swung his light around, swearing softly. The rattle of a can. The flashlight beam shone through thick clumps of brown weed that hung down from the tower bulwark, and he could smell the sea in them. Another rat, Turk told himself. The shelter was filled with the things, big bloated wharf rats that ate the dockside roaches. He'd best get on with it.

Hidden back in the carpentry shop, covered by an oily tarpaulin, was a cylinder truck—an apparatus like a pushcart—with a cylinder of acetylene gas and a larger cylinder filled with oxygen. From the two cylinders there were hoses that connected to the welding-torch unit, providing a flammable mix of the gas, in this case, for the cutting process. Turk had wheeled the unit over to the shelter just before quitting time and had hidden it in the carpentry shop. He was taking a chance, if Cochran had decided to take a check of the supply shed, but the worker in charge of the equipment was a lazy bastard, Turk thought. Which had worked out fine for him.

Now he wheeled the truck over the gangplank onto the deck, carefully because it was fairly heavy and the planks groaned beneath its weight. He got the truck positioned as he wanted it before putting on the welder's mask he'd left hanging on the truck frame. Turning on the valves to release the gas and oxygen flow, he used his striker to spark the torch tip and it sprang into life, a soft orange glow in the darkness. He adjusted the mix until he was ready, then bent down and began to work, his hand moving in a smooth semicircular motion.

Over the soft *hissssss* of the burning gas he heard the great boat moan, like a sluggish and heavy creature awakening from sleep.

In the small bedroom of a brown-painted stucco house across the island, Steven Kip jerked suddenly and his eyes opened.

He lay very still, listening to the repetitive voice of the surf, wondered what it was that had awakened him. Beside him his wife, Myra, was sleeping peacefully, one slender arm thrown out across his chest, her body pressed against his side. He turned his head and kissed her very softly on the cheek, and she rustled the sheet and smiled. They had been through a lot together, and though the years had made Kip tougher and more cynical, they had been gentle with her. There were laugh lines around her eyes and mouth, but they were lines of good living. He kissed her again. He was a light sleeper, so anything could have awakened him: a wave breaking, the clatter of a coconut palm, the shrill of a nightbird. He waited for a few moments. Still nothing. All familiar sounds he had heard a thousand times before. He lay his head back on the pillow beside hers, and closed his eyes.

Then he heard it again.

A muffled stacatto of drums, echoing from somewhere distant.

He sat up, drew the covers aside, and rose from the bed. Myra stirred and lifted her head. "It's nothing, baby," he whispered. "Go back to sleep. I'm going to have to go out."

"Where are you going?" she asked, rubbing her eyes. "What time is it?"

"After three. Lie back now, and sleep. I won't be long." Already he was getting into his trousers, then buttoning his shirt. Myra pulled the sheet up around her, and Kip crossed the room to peer out through a window that faced the harbor. It was pitch black out there except for the stars, tiny clusters of light in the sky like the wheelhouse lanterns of a thousand spectral ships against a black ocean.

Then, again, echoing through the jungle, the sharp rattle of the drums; Kip's skin tightened at the back of his neck. Damn it to hell! he thought, pulling on his shoes and leaving the house as quietly as possible.

He drove the jeep to Front Street, turned along the dark shanty village on the harbor rim and toward the jungle, the wind sharp in his face. He watched the windows for lights and searched the streets for moving figures, but no one was stirring. Who else was listening to those drums? How many lay in the dark, eyes open, trying to read the message that was swept across the island with the early breezes? Kip knew what it had to be: Boniface conducting a ritual over the boat. Damn the man! Kip cursed silently, still watching for lights. *I'm the law here, the only law, above and beyond Boniface's voodoo gods.*

Along Front Street where the jungle bent down low in strange shadowy shapes, he saw several men standing in the road. When his headlights touched them they twisted away before he had a chance to recognize any of them. They leaped into the surrounding underbrush and were gone in a few seconds. When Kip came to the church, he found it darkened and deserted. He stopped the jeep and sat there for a few moments, listening. When the next brief flurry of drums came, still somewhat distant, Kip caught their direction. He took a flashlight from a storage box on the rear floorboard, clicked it on, and climbed down from the jeep.

There was a narrow path leading past the chicken coop and Kip walked along it as silently as he could, the thorns catching at his shirt. The jungle was densely black on all sides and quiet but for the persistent, steady drone of insects. In a few more minutes he could hear fragments of voices, the sudden crying out of what sounded like several women at once, the forceful voice of a man, all punctuated by sudden bursts of the rapid drums. He went on, following the path even when he was forced to crawl beneath a thick cluster of wiry brush. The voices became progressively louder, more frantic, and at last he caught a glimmer of light ahead. The drums pounded a steady rhythm, three or four patterns intertwining, louder and louder, each beat accompanied by a scream or a shout as if the drums themselves

were crying out in either pain or ecstasy. The noise
grew until the drumming was inside Kip's head, a
wild and unconfined frenzy of sound. And through the
drum voices there was the voice of a man, rising from
a whisper to a shout: "Serpent, serpent-o, Damballah-
wedo papa, you are a serpent. Serpent, serpent-o, I
WILL CALL THE SERPENT! Serpent, serpent-o,
Damballah-wedo papa, you are a serpent . . ."

The jungle was suddenly cut away to make a clearing; Kip quickly turned off his light and stayed hidden
in darkness. Blazing torches formed a wide circle
around a small three-sided, straw-roofed hut. Directly
in front of the hut, surrounded by black and red
painted stones, was a fire that licked up toward the
jungle ceiling high overhead. A strange geometric
figure had been traced in flour in front of the fire, and
placed at points on the figure were various objects:
bottles, a white-painted steel pot, a dead white roost-
er, and something wrapped in newspapers. The drummers sat behind the fire, and thirty-five or forty people
made a ring around them—some lying on their bellies
in the soft dirt, some twirling madly in circles, still
others sitting on the ground, staring with open, glazed
eyes into the depths of the flames. The drumming was
furious now, and Kip saw beads of sweat fly off the
half-nude forms that circled the fire. One of the
dancers lifted a bottle of rum and let the liquor pour
down into his mouth, then he doused the rest of it
over his face and head before spinning away again.
Empty bottles lay scattered about. Sweat streamed
from faces and over torsos, and Kip caught the
powerful smell of strong, sweet incense in the air. One
of the dancers whirled in and threw a handful of
powder into the flames; there was a burst of white and

the fire leaped up wildly for a few seconds, illuminating the entire clearing with red light. A man in a black suit leaped in the air and crouched down at the base of the flames, shaking a rattle over his head. It was Boniface, the fires glinting off his glasses. Sweat dripped off his chin as he shook the rattle and cried out, "Damballah-wedo papa, here, Damballah-wedo papa, here . . ."

A woman in a white headdress fell down beside him, her chest heaving with exertion, her head revolving in circles and her eyes glistening with either rum or ganja. She lay on her belly, snaking along as if she were trying to crawl into the flames. It was the Kephas woman, the same woman Kip had seen that very afternoon sitting in a dark corner of her house muttering something he had failed to understand.

Boniface shook the rattle, now in time with the drum beating, and reached into the white pot with his free hand to withdraw a thick snake that instantly coiled about his forearm. At the sight of the snake there was a chorus of screams and shouts. He held it up, crying out, "Damballah-wedo papa, you are a Serpent. Serpent, serpent-o, I WILL CALL THE SERPENT!"

Kip's heart was hammering, his head about to crack from the noise. The drummers stepped up their rhythms, the muscles standing out on their arms, droplets of sweat flying in all directions. Kip could barely hear himself think; the screaming and the drums were bothering him, reaching a part of his past he had closed tight, to a place of fearful memories and grinning faces hanging from straw walls. Boniface turned and draped the writhing snake around the woman's shoulders like a rippling coat, and she cried aloud and stroked its body. The reverend put aside his gourd rattle, lifted the object wrapped in papers over his head and began to spin in front of the fire, shouting out in French. The old woman let the snake slide from arm to arm. She played with it, teasing it with a *tetettetette* noise. Boniface lifted a bottle of clear liquid, poured it into his mouth and held it there while he unwrapped the object. In the light of the fire Kip saw it was a crude wax image of the submarine; Boniface tossed the paper into the flames and sprayed the image with the liquid from his mouth, and as the others shouted and urged him on he held his hands out to the fire, his eyes wild and his teeth bared in a grimace. In another moment the heat began to melt the wax, and Boniface began to knead the image until wax dripped down his hands and arms. When nothing was left but a misshapen blob, he cast it into the fire and stepped back. The others screamed louder and danced like possessed souls. Boniface spat into the fire.

The old woman stared into the face of the snake, then lifted her chin and let it explore her lips with its questing tongue. She met the tongue with her own; they seemed like nightmarish lovers. When she opened her mouth to let the reptile probe within, Kip could take no more and stepped out into the light.

One of the drummers saw him first; the man gaped and faltered in his rhythm. The others noticed at once; heads turned, and someone shrieked as if in pain. A few of the dancers leaped up from the edge of the fire and ran for the jungle. The Kephas woman looked at Kip in horror, the snake slithering from her arms into the grass, and then she too ran away, her skirts billowing behind her. The rest of them were gone almost at once, the jungle closing behind them, the darkness swallowing them up.

And in the silence, still echoing with the beat of the drums and the shouting, Boniface stood framed against the fire, staring across the clearing at the constable. "You fool," he said, trying to catch his breath. "It wasn't yet complete!"

Kip said nothing, but walked to the edge of the fire. He examined the assortment of bottles. One of them looked as if it were half-filled with blood.

"IT WASN'T YET COMPLETE!" Boniface shouted, his hands curled into fists at his sides.

There was another pot filled with water; Kip picked it up and poured it over the blaze. The timbers hissed and smoke twisted toward the sky. "I've let you carry out your ceremonies," he said quietly. "I haven't raised a finger to interfere. But, by God"—he turned to face the other man—"I'll not have you making something out of that boat and the old man's death."

"You young ass!" Boniface said, wiping beads of sweat away from his eyes. "You don't understand, you could never begin to understand! You fool!"

"I asked for your help." He kicked at the embers and dropped the pot to one side. "Is this how you're helping me?"

"OUI!" Boniface said, the anger white-hot in his eyes. He held Kip's gaze a few seconds longer, then looked back into the remains of the fire. His shoulders were stooped, as if he had been drained of all strength. "You can't see, can you?" he asked, in a tired whisper.

"What was the Kephas woman doing here?"

"It . . . was necessary."

"God, what a shambles," Kip said, looking around the clearing.

"All necessary."

"I don't want any trouble, Boniface. I thought I made that clear. . . ."

Boniface glared at him sharply, his eyes narrowing. "You and the white man are to blame. Both of you brought that thing into the boatyards. Now you are to blame!"

"For what!"

"For what may take place if I'm not allowed to take a hand against it!"

Kip looked down into the glowing remains of the fire and saw the clump of wax there, blackened by the heat and ashes. He kicked it out into the grass and looked across at the reverend. "What kind of madness is this?"

"I expected better from you," Boniface said bitterly. "I expected you to be able to see. The white man, no, but you, Kip . . . you could open your mind if you wished, you could feel it. . . ."

"What are you saying, old man?" the constable asked him harshly.

"I know about you; you think you can hide it but you're mistaken!"

Kip took a step forward. "What are you saying?"

Boniface stood his ground; was about to explain but then thought better of it. He bent down and began to gather up the bottles that stood along the lines of the geometric figure. He put them down into the white pot that had contained the snake, and they rattled together.

"What do you know about me?" Kip asked very quietly.

The reverend began to smear the geometric lines with his foot. "I know," he said without looking up, "who you could have been." His head came up, and he stared fiercely into the constable's eyes. A strange, almost tangible power riveted the other man where he stood. He could not have moved even if he'd wished.

"Listen to me well," Boniface told him. "If you refuse to take the boat to deep water, you must do these things: Lock that shelter securely. Let no man go near it. Let no man touch his hand against that iron. And for all our sakes do not try to break the hatches open. Do you understand what I say?"

Kip wanted to say no, that Boniface was a raving fool, that the man didn't know what he was talking about, but when he spoke he heard himself say, "Yes."

And in the next instant the reverend was gone, melting away into the darkness beyond the circles of torchlight. Kip had not seen him turn to go, nor did he hear the man making his way through the underbrush; he had simply vanished.

Gradually the night sounds returned, filling in the spaces left when the drums and the shouting had stopped. Insects called to each other across the jungle, and the cries of the nocturnal birds sounded like the voices of old men. Kip covered the embers with dirt until he had completely extinguished the fire, then clicked his light back on and retraced his path to the jeep. There was a yellow glimmer of a light behind a window shutter at the church and a shadow moving about within.

He climbed behind the wheel and started the engine. He was actually eager to get away from this part of the island; it was Boniface's kingdom, a place of shadows, jumbies and duppies, faceless things that walked the night seeking souls. He drove back toward the harbor, along Front Street and through the village.

Still no lights, no sounds. And before he realized it, he had passed the road leading toward his house and was driving to the boatyard as if drawn there by something beyond his control. There was a sheen of sweat on his temples and he hastily wiped it away. He couldn't shake the image of Boniface, standing before him, touched with amber light that glittered in his thick glasses. *I know,* the man had said, *who you could have been.*

And then Kip's foot came down hard on the brakes.

The jeep started to spin in the sand, but Kip let the wheel turn and then corrected its direction; the jeep straightened, whipping grit up behind it, and then stopped abruptly as the engine rattled and died. Kip sat and looked straight ahead for a long time.

The boatyard gates were shattered, the weathered timbers broken and lying splintered on the ground. The timbers that still remained in the gate sagged forward, like bones in a broken rib cage, their edges raw and jagged.

An ax, Kip thought. *Some bastard has taken an ax to Langstree's gates.*

He picked up his light, climbed out of the jeep, and went through into the yard. Nothing else seemed to be wrecked, though in the disarray it was difficult for him to tell. He swept his light in an arc. Nothing moved. There was no noise but for the sea and the slow creaking of a boat moored to the wharf. This would be the right time for someone to break in, with Langstree away. Why the hell didn't the man hire a watchman? *That cheap old bastard!* he thought angrily, knowing it was his own responsibility if someone had made off with something valuable.

As he moved deeper into the yard, he tried to keep

his mind off the U-boat ahead in the naval shelter. The image of the rotting thing was a searing flame in his mind. He moved past a great heaping tangle of ropes and cables and walked faster, heading directly for the shelter.

He saw immediately that the door was open; he stopped in his tracks, shining the light about, and then slipped through into the stench of decay. He moved his light slowly along the hulk, not knowing what to expect, not even knowing what he was looking for. And when the beam picked out the form of the cylinder truck on the forward deck he swore and let his breath out in a hiss.

As he crossed the gangplank he shined the light down onto the deck, and then he saw the gaping, smooth-edged void where the hatch had been burned out. The hatch itself, the bottom of it encrusted with some kind of yellow fungus, lay several feet away on the deck. Kip thrust the light down toward the hole, aware that his heartbeat had picked up, that there was something . . . something . . . something . . .

Aware that blood was splattered around the yawning opening.

At once Kip sucked in his breath, stunned. He bent down and touched a hand to the thick globs of blood. He wiped it off on his trouser leg. The blood was so dark it was almost black, and he realized he was standing in it. Puddles had collected around the hatch opening like oil seepage. And now he smelled it as well, like a thick, coppery taste in his mouth. There was a larger lump of something beside him, and it was only when Kip had bent to examine it that he realized it was a piece of black flesh.

The U-boat moaned softly, and a timber creaked,

the echoes filling the inside of the shelter. He turned, played the light up the conning-tower bulwark and toward the stern. A sharp, piercing fear was inside him, jabbing at his guts, and he fought to keep hold of his sanity. He backed away from the hatch, keeping his light on it, until he'd reached the gangplank.

The flashlight beam played across the murky green water: A Coke can floated against the hull, and beside it a beer can. The water, pulled in through the sea bulkhead, was dotted with cigarette butts, and his light touched the staring eye of a white, bloated fish. Something else was there as well, floating just under the gangplank at Kip's feet.

A welder's mask.

Kip got to his knees, reaching down with one hand to pull it from the water. And as he did and the mask came free, the body underneath it rose to the surface. The eyes were wide and terror-stricken, the open mouth was filled with water. Beneath the battered face the throat had been torn open. Bare bone glittered in a red, pulpy mass that had been a larynx and jugular vein. Half the face was peeled back, the teeth broken off or ripped from the mouth. The arms floated stiffly at the corpse's sides, and already tiny fish were darting in to taste the blood at the mangled throat.

Kip cried out involuntarily and pulled his hand back, the welder's mask dangling from his fingers. The body began to turn in a circle, bumping against the side of the basin. Kip felt the place closing about him, felt the darkness reaching, and beyond the darkness things that grinned and clawed at him with filthy bloodstained fingers. He backed away from the U-boat, his legs like lead, and then half-walked, half-ran into the fresh air outside, drawing breath after breath to try to clear away the sight of that dead, gray-fleshed face.

"My God," he muttered brokenly, supporting himself against the shelter wall. "My God my God my God . . ."

For he had recognized the expression on Turk's dead, puffed face. It was a glimpse into an unnamable horror.

Eight

DR. THEODORE MAXWELL, a heavyset black in his mid-fifties, let the blood-spattered sheet drop down over the ruin of a face. He wore a smock smeared with human fluids over his clothes. Rays of morning sunlight streamed in dusky patterns through the drawn blinds of the Coquina clinic examination room. He shook his head, pushed his eyeglasses off the bridge of his nose, and let them rest on top of his balding head. He had seen bad things before: men whose noses had been cut off by rusted razors in barroom brawls, automobile accident victims, the mangled remains of a young child caught in the screw of a trawler. He was familiar with the ugly wounds of life, and familiar as well with the sight of death. But in his experience most people died in their sleep, with an expression of peace and almost of relief. This one was different. This young man who lay before him had seen Hell before he died.

Maxwell reached for a clipboard and began to jot notes for later reference.

"What's your opinion?" Kip asked wearily, his eyes hollow from lack of sleep.

Dr. Maxwell looked up quickly, then went back to his clipboard. He finished writing, then said in a soft, quiet tone of voice that belied the tension he felt, "Perhaps the most brutal beating I've ever seen. All manner of things were used: fists, fingers, some kind of blunt instruments. Maybe a wrench, and there's indication a hammer was used on his skull."

Kip frowned, staring at the outline of the corpse.

"Any next of kin?" Dr. Maxwell asked.

"No. I don't even know where he was from. He was an island drifter."

The doctor put his clipboard aside, steeled himself, and lifted the sheet again. The muscles of the face had frozen in that hideous grimace, and Maxwell shuddered as he gazed into those staring eyes again. He took a small penlight from his breast pocket and leaned over the throat. Yes. Those marks were unmistakable.

"What is it?" Kip asked.

Maxwell snapped off the light, returned it to his pocket; he placed the sheet back down. "This man is missing a great quantity of blood," he said, turning toward the constable. "But I believe he was dead before he received that throat wound."

"Then one of the blows to the head killed him?"

"I'm not sure. I want to go into the chest cavity and look at the heart. The frozen facial muscles, the coloration, the teeth locked through the tongue—all those may indicate instantaneous heart arrest. Perhaps brought on by a sudden and severe shock."

Kip blinked, letting the words sink in. "A shock? Fright, is that what you're saying?"

"That I don't know. I've heard of it happening before, but I've never seen it."

Kip shook his head in disbelief. "Christ Almighty!" he said softly. "What could scare a man enough to kill him?" He looked into the doctor's eyes for an answer, but the other man had turned away. Kip crossed the room to a desk with a metal tray which contained items the young man had had in his pockets. A few coins, a small penknife, a rusted key, cigarette papers, and a bit of ganja. And also something the doctor had pried from the corpse's rigid fingers. It was a few inches of filthy cloth, matted with yellow streaks of fungus. Kip picked it up and held it under the desk lamp to examine it for the third time. At one time the cloth had either been brown or green, but now it was a sickly, faded color somewhere in between. *What was it?* he wondered. Something Turk had grabbed at during his horrifying ordeal?

The constable gathered up the items and buttoned them in the back pocket of his trousers. Coins, a key, enough ganja for a few wild highs; it was one hell of a legacy to leave behind. What a terrible way for any man to die.

"Kip," the doctor said quietly, looking from the covered corpse back to the other man. "What types of wild animals would you say were out in the jungle?"

At first he thought he'd misunderstood Maxwell. Then Kip answered. "Not many. Maybe a few small boar, and if you're not counting snakes, that's it." He narrowed his eyes, seeing the puzzled expression on the doctor's face. "Why?"

Maxwell folded his arms before him and leaned back against the examination table, keeping his gaze steady. "There are teeth marks on this man's throat and on the right cheekbone. Some of them have broken bone, as if . . . something was trying to get at the bone marrow. All I can think of at this point is some kind of animal."

What kind of animal would do that? Kip shook his head, ran the back of his hand across his face. No, he knew of no vicious animals in that jungle, though there were probably several places so choked with growth that anything might be hiding in there. He had seen a couple of the boar on occasion, but they were too small to be of any consequence.

"An animal big enough to take on a man?" Kip asked. "Impossible, not on Coquina. But . . . teeth marks? You're sure it's not the mark of some kind of tool or something?"

"Yes."

Kip took a step toward the corpse and then checked himself, realizing he couldn't bring himself to look at it again. Teeth marks? No, it didn't make sense! "Do this for me, please," he said. "I want you to keep that opinion to yourself. Do whatever you have to, an autopsy or whatever, but I don't want anyone to know about the marks. At least not until I can figure out what the hell's going on."

"All right," Maxwell said, "I understand." He made a move to wheel the table out of the examination room, and as the doctor turned the table around, Kip felt that scrape of nails inside again, and this time a chunk of mortar fell away. He watched the doctor push the table through a pair of doors into a hallway and then into another room. Kip had to get out; his mind was numbed and his senses on edge.

Leaving the clinic, he walked in the hot sunlight

toward the Square, his brain filled with questions he couldn't begin to answer. What if there *were* something out in the jungle that could attack and kill a man by ripping his throat into bloody rags and gnawing on the bone? But then why hadn't some of the inland farmers seen it? They'd been out there for years, and if an animal like that prowled the jungle at least one person should have seen it. But no, no; Turk had been struck by blunt instruments as well as fists; Maxwell had said so himself. What had probably happened was that someone . . . or more than one? . . . had killed the man, leaving the body for the big wharf rats that had eaten through the dead flesh. That made sense, but then how did Turk's body wind up in the water?

Kip was stunned by the brutality of the crime. A murder on Coquina was practically unthinkable. There were always barroom fights, of course, and often those got pretty damned ugly, but murder? Who among the islanders would be capable of such a thing? At once he thought of the Carib Indian men. They were a rough, fierce breed, and whenever they came down to the village, which was fortunately rare, Kip had to wield a billyclub to break up the trouble. The Caribs were hot-blooded people who—island rumor said—had practiced cannibalism on their enemies less than a hundred years before. Was it possible Turk had run into one, or a group of them, who had come down from their settlement to see the submarine? It was all speculation, of course, but maybe worth a drive over to Caribville to ask some questions.

No, he decided. It was rats. The rats had crept out and torn into the corpse's flesh, and that accounted for the teeth marks.

Kip saw David Moore's truck parked over by the hardware supply in the Square. There was a stack of timber in the truck bed, and as Kip approached, Moore came out through the doorway, carrying another load of wood in his arms. He laid the timber down, wiped sweat off his face, and started to go back inside when he saw the constable and raised a hand in greeting.

"Business so good you're building an addition?" Kip asked him.

"Not hardly. I'm setting this aside in case we have another blow during the season. The old roof might not take much more this year."

Kip nodded. There were three elderly men on a porch in front of the hardware store, two smoking pipes and the third just sitting with a straw hat pulled low over his face. They had been talking quietly until the constable had walked over; now they listened, eyes moving from Kip to Moore. Kip greeted them politely and then said to Moore, "Anything I can help you with?"

"That should do it, except for paying my bill. If you really want to help you can talk Yarling into extending my credit."

Kip tried to smile but found it difficult because he couldn't shake the image of Turk's dead face; the eyes of the old men were on him and he felt uneasy. "Sorry. No favoritism."

"That's what I was afraid of." Moore dug for his wallet and then turned to go back into the hardware supply.

"Constable," said one of the three on the porch, a lanky man with snowy hair and teeth clamped around the bit of a pipe. "What happen' to that boy las' night?" He leaned forward in his chair, and Moore stopped where he was.

"Never you mind about that," Kip told him.

"Is it true what they say?" one of the others asked. "About his neck bein' broke and all the blood gone out his veins?"

"Whoever told you that has got one hell of an imagination. I'd have to go far to think up a better one." Kip kept his voice light and easy, but he was fooling no one; the old men's eyes were sharp and direct. Moore was watching him, his mouth half-open in astonishment.

"Dan Miles saw the body," the man in the straw hat said. "He say somethin' got hold o' that throat an' . . ."

"Dan Miles drinks too much, too," Kip said, more sharply than he'd intended. "If listening to lies was a crime I'd throw all of you in jail."

"They say somethin' come out the jungle," the man continued. "Mebbe be somethin' nobody got the right to see. I seen a jumbie back in there when I was a boy. Him a mean thin', a tall white thin' moved so fast you could hardly see. Moved with the wind, and the wind around him go wheeooooo . . . wheeooooo, like that. I'd seen that face and I ain't never forgot. Ugly thin', with bright red eyes and teeth hangin' out the mouth. I run and I run and I run 'cause I wasn't s'posed to be out there at night, you know? But I seen that face and I ain't never forgot."

Kip leaned a hand against a porch slat, keeping his movements casual. "No such things as jumbies."

"I seen the ghost of the Ritter woman long time

115

back," the first man who'd spoken added, his eyes wider and brighter. "Damn me if I didn't see her over on the fishin' wharf where her man's boat used to lie. She wave her arms at me, and I seen the stars shinin' through her, and she say 'Follow me. Follow me.' And then when I step back, she walk right on off the wharf into the sea and she gone." He looked at the other two men, and they nodded appreciatively.

"Kip," Moore said, "what happened last night?"

"You'd best go pay your bill," the constable told him. "Yarling's been known to get mean."

"Young buck name o' Turk got hisself killed," the one in the straw hat told Moore, sharing the secret. "It happen' over in the yard where that dam' boat be. Thass a bad thin', constable. Unlucky as all hell. That dead boat draw the jumbies out from the jungle, and they all flock around in there when everybody sleepin' and they have a hell of a party, all them dead thin's together. And they laugh and scream and roll them eyes up and they look for the livin' man 'cause they jealous, and they hate the livin' man and want his soul. And thass what happen' to that young Turk."

The other old men had settled back in their chairs, saying nothing, pipe smoke swirling about their heads.

"What happened last night?" Moore asked again.

Kip said, "Come over to my office when you're finished here. We've got things to talk about." He glanced again at the men on the porch and then turned away, crossing the Square toward his office. Kip went inside, drew the blinds, and brought the dead man's belongings out of his back pocket, laying them together on the blotter on his desk. He sat down, rolling himself a cigarette, and then snapped on his desk lamp. Picking up each item in turn, he examined them under the light; when he came to the rotten cloth he felt a dull throbbing start somewhere inside him, at the pit of his stomach. He traced a finger along the ridges of yellow fungus. *This is important,* he told himself, *but I don't know why. This is important and I can't yet understand it.* And deep within him, in the hidden recesses, he felt the brick wall tremble, as if something were pushing against it from the dark side.

There was a knock on the door. "It's open, David," Kip said.

Moore came in looking puzzled by the secrecy and intrigued by what the old men had been saying. He stepped toward Kip's desk, seeing the items there on the blotter. "What's going on?" he asked quietly, noting the strained, tired look in his friend's eyes.

"The submarine was torched open early this morning," Kip said. "A welder for Langstree did it, a crazy fool by the name of Turk."

"Did he say why?"

Kip gazed at Moore through a blue haze of cigarette smoke and shook his head. "No. Someone beat him to death over at the boatyard. I know what he was looking for, though, because just yesterday afternoon he was rambling on about gold bars and a wrecked German ship. I tell you, David, someone did a hell of a job on him, and when they were finished the rats took the rest. It's possible he got into the hulk, found something, and whoever killed him took it away from him." He waved at the items on the blotter. "This was all we found in his pockets, and this scrap of filthy cloth was gripped in his hand. Could be he ripped at something before he went down."

Moore was speechless. A murder on Coquina was unbelievable; there had never been a murder while he'd been operating the Indigo Inn. Hell, he'd come to this island because he'd believed it was set apart from all the bitter cruelties of men. Now he realized his fantasy was just that—a ridiculous dream. "How'd he get into the boat?" he asked after another moment.

"Torched through a hatch on the forward deck, just in front of the main gun." Kip put the items into a plastic bag; he sealed it and put the bag away in a lower drawer. "He was a drifter; maybe he had enemies, and one of them caught up with him. I don't know." He pulled on the cigarette, then crushed it out in his ashtray. "Anyway, dead men tell no tales, as they say." He pushed his chair back and went over to the storage cabinet, unlocking and opening it. From its recesses Kip withdrew a flashlight and a bull's-eye lantern; he tossed the flashlight to Moore. "I'm going to have a look inside the U-boat. Want to come along?"

"Yes," Moore said, taking a deep breath. "I'd like to see what's in there."

"All right, then. We'll be taking a chance if there're live explosives in it, but if a cutting torch didn't blow anything to hell I figure it's pretty safe." He glanced over toward the gun cabinet, but he quickly dismissed the idea. What was there to arm himself against? The rats? He was certain the shelter was filled with them, but they certainly weren't man-killers. *For God's sake,* he told himself, *settle down.* He clicked the lantern on and off a couple of times to check the battery and then motioned toward Moore. "Let's see what the old relic's carrying," he said, and stepped toward the doorway.

"God only knows," Moore said.

Yes, Kip told himself, as they stepped out into the harsh white glare of the sun's eye and Kip climbed into the driver's seat of the jeep.

God and perhaps one other.

Nine

MOORE COULD FEEL the tension radiating from Kip as they passed through the boatyard gates' broken slats and drove across the yard. Kip was chewing nervously on a match he'd taken from his breast pocket. When they came around a lumber pile Moore saw the other man's eyes narrow a fraction. There was the shelter and the delapidated wharfs just ahead. As Kip pulled the jeep to a halt alongside the shelter Moore himself began to feel uneasy; he stared at the weathered wall, knowing that behind it was the thing that had lured him down to the depths. It had broken free by his hand. Violence had followed it, marring forever the naïve, pure pattern of life on Coquina. Moore thought that the thing's purpose—giving death—had somehow, horribly, been revitalized. And *he* had brought it here.

Kip climbed out, waving a hand to a few of the men working some distance away on a storm-beaten trawler at the wharf's end.

Turk's frozen, horrified face burned at the back of his brain. He could see every detail, and for the first time in a very long while he realized that a strange and vague fear crawled inside him. *What was it?* he asked himself. *There's nothing to fear. It's irrational, stupid, childish.* But something bothered him, something terrible, something he did not want to think about. When he realized Moore was standing beside him, he clicked on his lantern and pushed against the door.

It swung open hesitantly, on rusted, whining hinges. A foul darkness lay beyond the doorway, as if they stood on the rim of day and were about to cast themselves on the mercy of the night beyond. *The Night Boat,* Boniface had called it, Kip thought suddenly. A creature of the night, a thing that used the darkness as a defense. They stepped through into the shelter, Moore following the constable, their lights leading the way. A wall of overpowering stench hit them.

"Jesus," Kip said. "This bastard's rotting from the inside out." He motioned with the light into the sheen of water beneath the gangplank. "That's where I found the man. You'll see the dried blood up around the hatch opening."

Moore scanned the length of the U-boat. It lay entirely in the darkness except for the stream of murky light that flowed down from the roof holes. The water around the hull was oily and thick, a deep emerald green in which a few bloated fish had met their death. Their carcasses, white bellies up, bumped against the iron, and each slow movement scattered flies that were exploring the decaying flesh. A chill ran up Moore's back; he could imagine the terrible rumble of the boat's diesels. *God,* he thought, *what a machine that must have been, gliding through the deep canyons like some kind of sea predator.*

"Just a minute," Kip said quietly, moving his light past Moore. He focused the beam on a pile of timbers that lay on the forward deck near the hatch. A coil of cable sat against the conning tower, on the port-side deck. He didn't recall seeing either the cable or the timbers earlier that morning, but then, he couldn't remember anything very clearly except the dead man's face breaking water. He moved his light over the cable, then back to the wood. The timbers looked as though they'd been stacked there, haphazardly. Kip probed with the light back in the far shadows, where the carpentry section had been. The timber had been over there the last time he'd seen it. Or had it been? He couldn't remember. As his light brushed the mound of crates and rags red eyes glittered and they heard the sound of high, panicked squealing.

"What's wrong?" Moore asked him.

Kip shook his head. "Nothing." He stepped into the darkness, away from the warm sunlight, and Moore followed him across the gangplank onto the U-boat's deck. Moore stepped into something, and drawing back with his flashlight he saw a little heap under the looming bulk of the tower. There were small shattered bones, grisly whiskered heads, curled black tails. A mound of offal, of mangled things that had been fat wharf rats. Glassy gelatinous eyes caught the light and Moore quickly looked away, stepping over them. A cat must somehow have gotten in and out of the shelter.

Clots of blood marked the area where the young man had been killed at the yawning circular hole. Kip played his light across them; the splatters looked like brown paint flung wildly from a brush. Beneath them the plankings creaked softly, and the rustling of the rats filled the shelter with echoes.

And then the two men aimed their lights down into the hole.

A ladder descended into the boat, but there seemed no room to move around in there. Moore bent lower and shined his light in at varying angles. Pipes, bare bulkheads, thick bundles of cables, all illuminated briefly and then reclaimed by the dark. Beneath the opening he could see rusted floor platings and a sheen of water perhaps three inches deep. He saw his reflection there, a shadow without form or face.

Kip, his teeth clenched around the match, his breath coming in short gasps, lowered himself carefully through the opening, his feet groping below for the rungs. He stepped onto the floor plates, splashing water, and waited for Moore to join him.

They stood in a narrow, cramped chamber filled with pipes, flywheels, and complex machinery. Kip swung his light around and motioned. There were four sealed torpedo tubes at the bow, with hatches the size of upended kettle drums. Two torpedoes seemed to rise up from the floor plates on iron tracks; thick clumps of dried black grease, veined with a greenish fungus, clotted the tracks, but the torpedoes themselves seemed almost clean. Moore ran a hand along one of them.

"Careful," Kip cautioned, the sound of his voice an eerie noise that rang from one bulkhead to the next. He moved his light again, illuminating the thin, fungus-coated mattresses which had been hung on chains so they could be folded back when not in use. A narrow path led between the bunks into the black guts of the U-boat. Beneath the bottom bunks were more torpedoes, secured in place with metal clamps. Kip shined his light on the bulkheads; there were photographs, badly faded and hardly recognizable, still in place among the mattresses. A young dark-haired woman stood in the midst of an amusement park, smiling; a middle-aged man and woman embraced on a bench with a fountain in the background; there was a postcardlike photo of a huge house surrounded by woods; a pretty blond woman stood on skis, against a backdrop of snow-covered mountains, and waved to a lost love.

The lights revealed crates stowed in every possible nook and cranny. A bucket had overturned, spilling out something that resembled thick, whitish globs. Everything was covered with the sickly hues of decay; a shoe, caught in the miniature swells made by the men's movements, bumped against one of the stored torpedoes. Moore lowered his flashlight and saw what was left of a shirt, coiled like an octopus in a shadowy corner. Moore thought: *And what happened to whoever wore that?*

Kip sloshed through the water, bent down and picked at the shirt. It fell into pieces in his hand, covering his fingers with a yellowish residue. He held a scrap of it before the light as if mesmerized by it, and then abruptly let it drop back into the water. The shirt fragments floated out of sight beneath a bunk. Kip wiped his hand on a trouser leg.

A passageway stretched ahead of them. The air seemed putrid and thick here; Kip found it difficult to draw a full breath. There had probably been no air at all in here until that hatch was torched through, and not enough had circulated yet. Over the graveyard stench there was another odor: cloying, sickly sweet, harsh on the lungs. Some kind of noxious gas? Something that had been collecting inside here for forty-odd years? Kip waited until Moore's light caught up with his and then he crouched forward, ducking under pipes, and started into the corridor. The darkness seemed to gnaw away at the lights, and up ahead small shadows scurried for safety. The men couldn't walk side-by-side because the corridor wasn't wide enough. It was like crawling down the throat of a huge beast into the sodden entanglement of tissues and organs and bone. "Jesus," Moore said softly, hearing his voice jump back at him, "it's hard to breathe in here. It's a claustrophobic's nightmare."

There was a large central pipe above them that wound its way through the boat like a rusted spine. Kip shined his light through one of the openings off to the side, toward a cramped storage space filled with crates, two more bare mattresses, and a table bolted to the floor plates. A row of white shirts hung from the ceiling, and more lay in water. He moved on, his shoes stirring swirls of rust and filth from the plates.

The crewmen had gone about their duties here, all part of the efficient mechanism, like cogs in a terrible weapon. But how they managed to keep their sanity in this place day after day, week after week was beyond comprehension. The smell of humanity, of sweat, of cigarette smoke and urine mingled with the stenches of diesel oil and fuel must have been all but overpowering. Even now Moore felt trapped, as if the bulkheads and ceiling were gradually closing in on him, and he was walking downhill instead of straight ahead. What had started as an irritation had become a raw burning at the back of his throat, and when he drew in a guarded half-breath his lungs were seared. He heard Kip cough violently once, then again.

Moore leaned inside the next opening, probing with the flashlight as Kip moved on ahead. On a metal table there was a radio console; a set of headphones dangled from wires, and a chair had been overturned. The shadows were deep and thick, clinging to the corners like solid cobwebs; they resisted the thin spear of light. Rising off the rotted debris in the water was that terrible crypt smell, dry and sweet. Moore drew back, inhaling sharply. He was about to rejoin Kip when he thought he heard something move.

He froze, listening.

There was only the sound of Kip moving ahead, sloshing water. The echoes were merging, doubling and tripling, vibrating full force off the bulkheads. Moore flashed his light into that radio room again. A pulpy mass bumped against the back of the chair, and it took him another moment to realize it was more torn rat carcasses, entrails floating behind. Rats down here? What had they done, gotten down into the boat after the hatch had been opened, lured by the smells of fetid food? But they were all mangled, ripped to pieces like the ones piled on the deck. He shuddered. How had that occurred? What in God's name had done that?

Moore backed away from the cabin, feeling the ooze of the water at his feet; he shined the light back in the direction they'd come. The sound he'd heard had been the noise of something moving back down the passageway; he knew he hadn't imagined it. He kept his light steady for a few more seconds, and then he began to move toward his friend.

Kip was examining the filth that floated around

him: articles of tattered clothing—shirts, underwear, shoes—empty crates. There was part of a magazine, showing a picture of a girl coyly hiking a skirt up over a thigh. There was a date on it: November 1941. Racy stuff for that time, Kip thought. He was about to move on when a feeling of dizziness swept over him; he thrust a hand out against iron to keep himself from falling face-forward. Black spots swirled before his eyes and his lungs seemed filled with fire.

Moore caught his shoulder. "Are you all right?"

"Just a minute," Kip said thickly, trying to catch his breath. "There's bad air in here, David." He shook his head, waiting for the spots to clear. "Okay. I'm better now."

"Can you go on?"

Kip nodded, looking ahead. Beyond the narrow beams of light the darkness was clinging and ominous, like something hideous and alive. On either side, fungus and rust had scrawled strange multicolored patterns. The boat was a fester of decay. Moore felt filthy and contaminated; his throat was burning but he made an effort to suppress the urge to cough. Oddly, he feared making more noise than was necessary. The lack of oxygen and the fumes were beginning to take their toll.

Kip was sweating profusely, the droplets running down his arms and beading up on his face. He wiped his forehead with the back of his hand, wondering what it was that frightened him so much about being inside here. It was only a machine . . . a machine of war, yes . . . but now only a dilapidated relic of days past. It was not the closeness of the place, or the darkness, or the sense of being buried alive. No. It was something else, a sixth sense he had and had possessed all his life, that was now trying to whisper to him, to reach into his soul and shake it.

Kip's light moved past more openings on each side and came to rest on the outline of a sealed iron hatch farther down the passage.

His legs began moving, sluggishly, and carried him to that hatch as if he were drawn to it. It was not closed after all, but cracked open an inch or so. An empty crate lay in his path and he pushed it aside. Before him was the grisly, crushed body of a large rat. Flesh still clung to the head and front half of the thing, but its hind quarters and stomach had been ripped away, leaving bare bone, as if something had been gnawing greedily at the carcass.

Get out, he heard a whispering voice say; his skin crawled, writhing on his spine and arms. *Get out while you can.*

Moore stepped to one side of the passage and drew back the remnants of a green curtain; it fell away, across his arm. There was a bunk, a small writing table with a mold-smeared blotter, a few metal lockers. There was a paperweight, amid a clutter of old books and papers on the table, and Moore held it up to the light.

It was a heavy glass cube, and a scorpion was frozen at its center. The gold letters etched across it, some of them chipped away by time, spelled out: WIL E M KO RIN, SEPTEMB R 1941. And directly beneath, a portion of a swastika. "Kip," he said quietly. "Look at this."

Kip turned from the hatch and came over, shining the light around the small cubicle. He examined the paperweight for a moment and then handed it back to the other man. "I'd say this must have been the commander's quarters," he said, his voice sounding hollow. "You'd best keep that. It's probably all you'll get to salvage off this goddamned crate." Moore slid it beneath his shirt. It was like the touch of ice against his flesh.

Kip focused his attention on the hatch again. He slid his fingers into the crack and pulled at it; steel grated across steel, but the hatch came open more easily than he expected. Wiping the sweat from his eyebrows, he aimed the light inside.

"David . . ." Kip said, hoarsely, not moving from where he was. He didn't think Moore had heard, so he called again, more loudly this time.

"What is it?" Moore stood next to him and peered through, following his beam as it crept across the flooring.

They were staring into the control room, the U-boat's heart. At the ceiling hung a mass of pipes, flywheels, and tubing. There were banks of controls, rows of gauges and dials. The glass caught Kip's light and glinted back. In the center of the room stood a chart table, surrounded by machinery and more gauges, their needles frozen in place. Equipment took up almost every inch. It was suspended from the ceiling in clusters, jammed into the corners: multiple rows of toggle switches, levers, flywheels, blank-faced dials.

And something else.

The corpses.

Some of them were still at their stations, obedient to a long-dead commander, but now they wore the rags of uniforms; they were the ghost crew of a dead boat.

And they had been mummified.

One whose face was half-covered by a white veil of

129

fungus had crossed his brown, shriveled arms on a table before him; a grinning, eyeless mask stared into their lights from the aft shadows; bone showed in a misshapen skull. Here were empty brown eye sockets, here one with the nose rotted away and the facial features collapsed around a cavernous hole. On the flooring, washed by less than an inch of water, a corpse stared directly at them, its mouth a straining O, broken teeth showing. More littered the rear of the control room, lying singly or in groups, some with facial features still distinct, others coated with yellow and gray fungus, which had covered them like a thick and creeping leprosy. The lack of oxygen had helped to preserve the bodies, had mummified them and left their flesh brown and crusty-looking. Skin was stretched tight over bones and tendons, and the dark eye sockets were deep, fathomless pits in front of solidified brain matter. In one corner a corpse held up both stiffened arms before its face, as if trying to hide from the lights.

Kip released his breath from between clenched teeth. Moore could feel the tension holding his own body upright. Kip's stomach was churning from the reek of decay. He coughed, the pain throbbing in his tissues. What was it? Gas, vapors oozing from the guts of the U-boat, from the aft section where the diesel engines lay? It was an airless crypt, an iron coffin that had taken these men to their deaths. There was an opening at the far end of the death-chamber; the men aimed their lights into it but they could see nothing except a murky curtain of black.

"Must be other bodies back through here," Kip heard himself say, realizing they were the first words to be spoken in this terrible place for nearly half a century. "Could be they were trapped in the aft section when this bastard headed down, and none of them could get out."

Moore shivered involuntarily, moving his light from corner to corner. The drawn, hideous faces stared back, as if watching them. The darkness seemed to be closing around him. The cone of light was a weapon of protection he held before him. The beam glinted across a bronze plaque mounted on a bulkhead: KIEL—1941. As he stared at it the lettering faded out of focus, and every breath he took seemed to draw the stench of decay deeper within him. He wiped his face, his skin cold and clammy. He could barely move his hand from his face, as if suddenly paralyzed.

"Let's get the hell out of here," Kip said, but the words were distant, muffled sounds. Kip coughed violently into his hand, and had to support himself again in the frame of the hatch.

And then something in the aft section, beyond the range of their lights, clattered. The sharp sound of iron against iron riveted the men, raising the hair on their necks, causing their hearts to pound with the fear of the unknown.

"Jesus," Moore whispered. "Jesus, what was . . ."

"Back away," Kip said, slurring his words. "Back away from . . ."

And then the hammering, the frenzied clattering of hellish noise, exploded through the aft opening and pounded at the two men before they could get away, the echoes building, sweeping wildly past them, filling the boat with more echoes, and more, a thousand others a hundred thousand others and no escape from it no way to get out get out get out get out. . . .

"GET OUT!" Kip shouted, his voice lost. He couldn't see; the black motes had obscured his vision, and he could no longer make out his light. Moore reached for him, slowly, too slowly, grasping the man's elbow and trying to pull him away from the hatch opening. The entire boat seemed to vibrate, and Moore heard something like the shrieks of the damned roaring in the passageway just above his head. He twisted around, staring into the control room, gritting his teeth in terror.

Things stirred within, uncoiling themselves like reptiles rising from the water. A wave of cold, pure hatred hit the men like an icy blast. Moore could see the inhuman forms reaching out with black-taloned fingers, ruined faces gaping, black eyeholes now red and hungry. Moore pulled Kip back, shouting out but not knowing if he actually had because he couldn't hear himself. He threw his full weight against the hatch, forcing it closed, and as he did he saw the greedy mouths open and the teeth glitter. Kip had turned and was staggering back down the passage, flailing at the unseen with his light. Moore started after him, tripping over a crate and falling to his knees in the water, losing his flashlight. He struggled up, dripping, trying to hold back the panic about to burst out of him. He fought on, locked in the nightmare, his feet thickened in the cement hold of the water. God what was it God what was it MY GOD WHAT WAS IT! He opened his mouth to cry out but all that emerged was a dry, dusty rattle, like the voice of something long buried. GET OUT GET OUT GET OUT GET OUT GET OUT. . . .

Kip, almost blind with terror, tripped, slamming his head against a pipe. He struck out with his arm,

132

cracking the bull's-eye lantern against metal. It flickered to a dim yellow.

And in the shadows that lay beyond him, between the two men and the way out, something was rising up, a skeletal thing with a half-consumed rat clutched in one clawlike hand. Kip tried to warn Moore, but he was struck dumb and frozen with fear. The thing's other hand came up quickly, and an object flew at Kip's face from the blackness, turning end over end, whistling as it passed his head. The hammer slammed into a bulkhead and bounced off even as Kip steeled himself and threw his lantern at the walking corpse. There was a sharp crash of shattering glass and then the darkness claimed all.

Moore reached Kip and they stayed together, moving as rapidly as they could toward the bow section, still dazed and staggering. The light was growing stronger, the noises of hatred and madness falling behind. The open deck hatch was ahead, and the ladder. Moore grasped it and hurtled up into the rush of clean, pure air. He fell across the deck, the strength drained from him, and crawled toward the railing like a madman. Behind him Kip, his face a tight, drawn mask, rocketed up and slid the heavy hatch lid back over the hole to seal it. He threw himself across it, breathing raggedly, shivering and unable to stop. He thought he must be losing his mind. "No," he protested in a raw, pained voice. "NO!"

Moore reached the port railing and leaned over, vomiting into the water. "What was that?" he said, wiping his face. Then he demanded in a choked whisper, "WHAT WAS THAT?"

Kip listened. No sounds, no movement. He couldn't stop shaking; his body was out of control.

"They're dead. . . ." he spat out finally. "They're DEAD!"

And then the echo, coming up around them, engulfing them with a word that seemed strange and terrible.

And untrue.

Ten

THE SQUARE-SHOULDERED black fisherman dealt cards to the four other poker players arranged around a central table in the Landfall Tavern. Evening was rapidly falling and the trawler crews had long since finished their labors. The place was now a maelstrom of noise and movement; on the other side of the plank-floored room a jukebox blared a raw, insistent reggae, and several of the men were trying unsuccessfully to get the bar girls to dance with them. It was Friday night, a time for drinking and wildness, tall tales, and an occasional fight to blow off steam, and with Saturday a market day the crews wouldn't be working until Monday. Cigarette smoke swirled above the men's heads, drawn by the lazily turning ceiling fans; glasses clinked against bottles, and there was a din of loud laughter and talking. On the rough plank walls tin signs advertising Red Stripe and Jaguar beers and Bacardi rums almost vibrated from the noise level.

The card dealer settled back in his chair and calmly

surveyed his hand. Then he looked from face to face, trying to read the other men's hands from their expressions. They had been playing for over an hour and he had won most of their money; he was feeling loose now, all good and warm inside. He had been drinking hard on purpose, hitting the rum bottle time after time, because he wanted to forget the stories he'd heard about that young buck Turk. He had played cards with the man here in this bar, on another Friday night, and thinking about the way Turk had died unsettled him. There was no sense to it, no reason for it at all. Now Turk was cold and dead, lying on a slab over at the clinic. The dealer reached over for his bottle and swigged again. *Damn. Could have been anybody lyin' over there,* he thought. *Damn, it was a bad thing!* He raised the rum bottle and took another slug; suddenly he didn't feel quite so warm after all.

"Hell of a thing," James Davis said from across the table, throwing down a card. "I hear they find the boy with his head almos' cut off. God A'mighty, I'da hated to been the one who find him. God A'mighty."

Smithson shook his head. "No, mon. It was his back broke clean in two. Somebody got him in one hell of a hug."

"His head was split open," Youngblood told them over his cards. "I hear that from one of the doctor's nurses. He go messin' round that fuckin' boat and he find bad trouble. Me, I wouldn't go near that t'ing."

"What you know?" the dealer, a bulky man named Curtis, asked sharply. "Put down your money."

"It's trouble, thass what I know," Youngblood continued, throwing a few coins into the pot. "Been trouble since the white man brung it up. Me, I say take the thing out and get rid of the sonofabitch!"

Percy leaned over the table, looking from one face to the next. "They say his eyes was starin', like he seen Death comin' for him," he whispered. "The talk's all over the yard. He seen Death reach out for him, and take him by the throat and . . ."

"Stop that talk!" Curtis said.

"Oh yah," said the other man. "If you doan believe a man can see his Death comin' then you crazy. That boy did and he die right there on the spot. I hope to God I never see it comin'. I hope it sneak up on me and take me from behind so I go quick."

"*You* crazy, mon!" Davis told him.

"How many cards?" Curtis asked the men, trying to get off the subject.

Youngblood said, "Few years ago I crewed on a freighter out of Jamaica, big industry boat. We runs through a squall an hour out, slowin' us down, and we cuts to the west a few points to keep away from Jacob's Teeth. We travelin' at night, and ever'thin' dark as hell and that wind blow bitter through our riggin'. Oh, that wind be bitter, mon, cut you to the bone. And the helmsman lose the way, him lost after thirty damn years at sea and a storm buildin' at our asses! Wireless go out, nothin' but crackle, then even the goddamn crackle gone. We goes on and on, zigzaggin' for marks, seein' nothing, no lights nor land, and all of a sudden we comes out in a place where the wind and the sea go flat. And by God there come up a moanin', hard to hear at first but then louder and nearer, things bein' said in different tongues, and wild screamin' and laughin' and carryin' on . . ."

"Shit!" Curtis said fiercely.

". . . and then we sees we not alone. On all sides goddamn boats. Steamers, freighters, sloops with full riggin' catchin' a breeze that wasn't there. All of 'em green and glowin', like St. Elmo's fire cracklin' up their lines and along them timbers. Oh, mon, I tells you I ain't never seen a thing like that before, and I ain't seen it since. Them boats criss-crossin' in front of us, then passin' alongside. And we sees men in the lines and workin' the goddamn decks! They was just outlines of men, y'know, with hardly any faces, but you knew they was men . . . or they was men mebbe a long time ago. You see, we had come out in that place where the dead world and the livin' one meet. Me, I hid my face and started to shake like mad. And them ghost crews all callin' for help, y'know, because they stuck on that place forever, right there on the rim between the two worlds. Mebbe they not ready to pass on, or they tryin' to find the way back to harbor, but all the time their boats layin' down deep and just the specters ridin' the caps. God knows, that place be Hell itself, all the shriekin' and moanin' so pitiful. The helmsman spin us about and we tracks into the storm. In a while he sight the buoys at the tip of the shoals, and we goes back the way we come, and by God no man ever kissed ground so happy like we did in Kingston."

The men were silent for a few moments, pretending to be absorbed by their cards. Curtis reached over for his bottle, swigged, and then peered into Youngblood's haunted eyes. "I doan believe a word o' that shit! I never seen nothin' like that!"

"Best pray you don't, mon," Davis said quietly. "Three cards."

A hefty black woman in a red dress passed by their table, glancing down to see if anything was needed. She cast her eyes around the bar, from the tables illuminated by harsh ceiling lights to those in the shadows at the rear. Damn Frankie King was getting drunker, louder and louder, and soon she was going to have to have Moe throw the bastard out. Two men had cornered a bar girl named Rennie, trying to work up something for later, but the girl looked bored and disinterested. *Serves 'em right, the horny fuckers,* she thought, with a grim smile. And then that other table back there, the two men sitting together, talking quietly.

She had seen many things in this world, but nothing like the expressions on the faces of Steven Kip and the white man when they'd come in and taken that back table. She had served them drinks—beer for the constable, dark rum for the white man—and wanted to talk but they seemed to have no use for her. There was something in Kip's eyes that made her go about her business, cleaning glasses behind the bar, watching for inevitable trouble. Now she approached them, moving her bulk through a group of drinkers, and looked down at their table. "Get you men something else?" she asked.

"No," Kip said, without once glancing up, and the white man shook his head.

She paused a few more seconds, then shrugged her shoulders and turned. Frankie King was roaring drunk; he had a fighting look in his eyes.

Kip watched her walk away and then coughed into his cupped hands; the cough tore at the linings of his lungs. He gazed into the sputum in his hands and wiped it off on a napkin. "Hallucinations," he said quietly. "There were all manner of damned gases inside the thing."

"No. I'm not going to pass it off so easily." Moore

139

looked intently into the constable's eyes. "How could we see the same thing? Even if we were affected by some kind of fumes, how the hell would we see the same thing?"

Kip paused, taking a sip from his Red Stripe. When he put the bottle down he asked, "And just what was it we saw, David? Shadows, a boatful of debris . . ."

"Come on, damn it!" Moore said, his eyes blazing. "By God, I know what I saw! I'm not going crazy!"

"I didn't say you were."

"I didn't mean it like that." Moore shook his head, ran a hand over his face. "I was never superstitious; I never believed in any of the stories about jumbies and all that, but this shakes me, Kip. Something was moving inside the U-boat, and I felt . . . I felt . . ."

"What?"

"I felt hatred," Moore said, "I felt the presence of hatred and evil inside there. Maybe my lungs were clogged with gases; maybe my eyes were failing me and I was half-mad with fear, but those things hated us, Kip. And they wanted to rip us to pieces."

"I didn't see anything but old corpses inside the boat," Kip said brusquely. "If you think there was anything else, you're mistaken. Nothing but shadows, tricking the eyes. An echo that sounded like something banging iron. No telling what the gases did to our senses—amplified noises and made shadows into, well, into whatever you think you saw."

"Then where the hell is your lantern?" Moore asked him pointedly.

"I couldn't see where I was going; the damned walls were closing in on me, and I suppose I dropped it."

"You suppose?" Moore asked incredulously, a wave

of anger and emotions rising within him. "YOU SUPPOSE?"

"Keep your voice down!" Kip cautioned.

"Goddamn it, don't play me for a fool! I was standing beside you! I couldn't say for certain what it was, but . . ."

Kip suddenly reached over and grasped his friend's sleeve, his gaze hardening. "Okay," he said in a low, controlled voice. "Now you listen to me. These people are a superstitious, fearful breed, David. Tell them a story like this, let it leak out so the island gossips get it, and they'll be carrying damned guns in the streets and locking themselves behind their doors."

"Maybe they should," Moore insisted, unwilling to give any ground. "There's something terrible about what's inside it, Kip. You know that as well as I do."

Kip looked at him uneasily for a moment. He lay some money beside his empty bottle and stood up. "I'm going home and get some sleep. I hope you'll do the same." He paused, then clapped the white man's shoulder gently. "There's been too much trouble over the boat. On Monday morning I'm going to have it towed out to deep water and have the hull cut open. You've got your Nazi trinket, and I've got a murder to solve. I think that's enough."

"I hope to God you can get rid of it that easily," Moore said in a hollow tone.

Kip turned away and vanished in the crowd as he moved toward the doorway, leaving Moore sitting alone.

As the constable wound his way through the clustered tables he passed the group of poker players, and one of them was leaning over, talking eagerly, eyes widened and voice lowered. Kip strained to hear, seeing the taut expressions on the faces of the others. ". . . it that goddamn boat bringin' badness here," the man was saying. "Me, I afraid to even go down there and see it. I doan want nothin' to . . ." He looked up suddenly into Kip's face, as did the other men. Kip paused, gazing around the table.

The man who'd been speaking glanced across to the dealer. "Two fuckin' cards," he said.

Kip made his way out of the whirling circles of smoke and noise into the coolness of night. And as he walked along the street to his jeep he caught the fetid odor of rot, a stench hanging in the air, blown across the island in the grip of the evening's breeze. He knew what it was: the decay from the thing in the shelter oozing through the cracks and holes like a disease to infect all of Coquina.

He reached the jeep, slid behind the wheel, and paused before starting the engine. He could lie to David Moore; he could lie to all of them, perhaps, as part of his responsibility as peacekeeper of Coquina. But he could never lie to himself. There was something terrible, something unspeakable in its evil, down in the guts of that U-boat.

The wafting coils of rot came down around him, tightening at his throat. He started the engine, put it in gear, and drove through the darkness toward home.

Eleven

WHEN HE WAS a young boy running free and wild on the waterfront streets of St. Thomas, Cockrell Goodloe had seen a woman stabbed to death.

It had been very fast, a blur of motion and color as a man in a red shirt darted from an alley, catching a lithe young black woman in a brown-striped dress around the throat. She had dropped a sack of groceries at her feet, and Goodloe had seen the sharp glitter of a blade as the knife drove down into her midsection once, then again. "You bad!" the man had shouted mindlessly. "You dirty bad!" The young woman had opened her mouth to scream. At first nothing came out but a terrible choking sound, and then the shriek came, a sound that raised the flesh all over him, that caught at his throat and made him clap his hands over his ears. The man had cast her aside, dropping the knife, and had turned to run. A few older men shouted and chased after him; on the blood-pooled earth the woman shrieked, on and on, a cry of desperation and horror. And then she was silent, and that was when someone bent down beside her.

And now, forty years later, in the middle of a dreamless sleep, he heard that shriek again.

At once he had pulled himself out of bed, his nerves tingling and heart pounding as they had done that day a long time ago. He was still groggy from sleep, and he stood in the center of his room, bare feet on harsh timbers, groping for the lantern at the bedside.

"What that?" his wife asked, rising up in bed, a shadow in the darkness. "What that sound?"

"Jus' wait now," he said. Matches. Where them goddamn matches? He found them, lit the lantern wick. The flame grew, warming the sparsely furnished room. He put on a threadbare shirt over his shorts and, taking the lantern, he crossed the floor to the single open window. He drew aside a tattered curtain and peered out into the night. His wife came up beside him and clutched at his shoulder.

There was another loud, pained shriek. Sounded like a woman, stabbed and screaming. But no, that couldn't be it. Goodloe's farm was two miles to the north of Coquina village, and the next nearest place was another mile on. The shriek continued for a few more seconds, ending in a high, wild grunt. Then came the rooting of the hogs in their pen behind the storage shed.

"Somethin' at the hogs!" Goodloe said. He turned from the window, moving quickly past his wife, through a tiny kitchen to the back door. "Don't you go out there!" the woman cried out in a frantic burst of words. "Don't you go . . . !" But he was already through the door, grasping a hoe he had propped against a wall. He followed the lantern's track toward the hog pen. Now more of the hogs were squealing, that terrible, almost-human sound of fear and pain, and Goodloe's skin crawled.

"Don't go!" his wife called out, running after him, her gown flying.

He hefted the hoe like a weapon as he neared the storage shed; it had been torn open, and one door sagged off its hinges. *What the hell?* he wondered, his mind racing. And then he had rounded the shed and stood near the fenced-in pen where he kept his live-stock.

The reddish-brown beasts, fattened for Saturday market, churned madly within the pen, jostling each other in a frenzy, rooting frantically and emitting squeals of terror. Goodloe couldn't see for the dust they were kicking up, and he lifted his lantern over his head.

In the dim shafts of light that pierced the haze of dust he saw that two of the largest hogs were down. Black blood glistened around their bulks, and he could see the gleam of bone through their wounds. The other hogs were startled at the light; their eyes were wild and red, and they jammed into each other to get away from the reek of death. But there was another noise, a sound above the squeals.

It was the sound of flesh being ripped by the handfuls.

And another noise, an unrestrained sucking, made Goodloe back away a few paces from the pen. He bumped into his wife, who grasped at him and trembled, her eyes widening because she had seen.

There were other figures in the pen, forms that huddled around the hogs' carcasses and feverishly tore the flesh, then bent over to suck from the flowing rivers of liquid. The beams reflected off the backs of the hogs, piercing the shadows and briefly illuminating things that appeared human and inhuman at the same time. When the light grazed them they looked up into the beams, and Goodloe caught his breath in terror. There were three of them, huddled over the flesh and pools of blood, and the light catching in their eyes burned like the raging centers of hell.

"Oh God Jesus," Goodloe whispered hoarsely.

And then the things drew themselves away from the light, throwing up skeletal arms before their faces. Beside him the woman screamed, and then the forms got to their feet, half-hidden by the dust. Goodloe dropped his lantern down and when he did the things melted into the darkness, moving like aged men plagued by some terrible bone-rotting disease.

Goodloe and his wife stood where they were for a few moments more, the woman crying and the man murmuring "Be quiet. Be quiet," over and over again. In the distance they heard the brittle noise of the things crashing through jungle growth, and it wasn't until long after that noise had faded that the man moved unsteadily toward the animals.

"Get back to the house," he told his wife. She shook her head, and he yelled, "GO ON!"

She stepped away, looking fearfully beyond him toward the veil of the jungle, and then ran back to the farmhouse.

Goodloe moved around to the opposite side of the pen to the place where the fence had been torn open. Stepping over shattered timbers, he knelt over the carcasses and examined the wounds. The throats had been ripped wide open, veins torn and bone gnawed. Large pieces of flesh and hair lay scattered at his feet.

The other hogs, still unsettled and fearful, stayed crowded together in a far corner, seemingly mesmerized by the lantern. Goodloe stood up, stepped through cooling puddles and gazed off into the underbrush. The things had attacked and killed like animals, but in the dim light they had appeared to be men. They'd looked old and . . . yes . . . diseased. Sort of like lepers: pieces of their faces missing, a two-fingered hand thrust out, a head covered with what looked like yellowish sores. He trembled, staring off into the darkness.

And when he left the pen he began walking quickly for his house, knowing that whatever they had been . . . men, animals, or some nightmarish breed of both . . . they might be back, and there was a rifle under the bed he had to load.

Twelve

THE SHIP'S BELL mounted in front of Everybody's Grocers tolled six times. As the morning light strengthened across the island, the Square was filled with people in all manner of clothing and a wild rainbow of bright hues. There was much talking and laughing, and a couple of the island's musicians had set up their steel drums on the grocery's porch, intertwining their delicately sweet rhythms and motioning occasionally to an upturned hat used to catch coins.

There were tables of goods for Saturday market—bananas, coconuts, papaya, corn, tobacco, a myriad of vegetables—and beneath the shade of a thatched-roof shed there were large ice-filled buckets containing snapper, amberjack, squid, and grouper. Bundles of sugarcane were arranged in stacks, and children paid for them by the stick. There were cardboard boxes filled with chickens, and hogs grunting and pulling at the rope collars attaching them to poles in the ground. An aged man in a straw hat sat in a patch of shade, moving back and forth in a rocking chair, telling ghost stories to wide-eyed children who crowded around to hear. There was much probing and handling of goods, and voices were raised in the babble of haggling for the best price and determining whether corn grown to the east or to the north was the sweetest.

David Moore, carrying snapper fillets wrapped in newspaper under one arm and a sack of vegetables under the other, moved gingerly through the crowd, in the midst of its furious blare of voices, music, and colors. There was a man selling drinks from a cooler, and Moore paused to buy a lime soda before being swept up again in the crush of people. He saw people he recognized on every side, but no one spoke to him, and those who caught his gaze quickly looked away, whispering and motioning. He knew he was an outcast because he had been the one who had found and freed the U-boat; he could feel the tension in those who looked at him, and somehow he felt ashamed under those hard gazes. Moore was beginning to understand the fear in their faces after what he imagined he'd seen down in the U-boat. Imagined? Was it imagination after all, or the effect of the gases in that airless tomb? The entire thing had been like the nightmares he experienced over the deaths of his wife and son; didn't he awaken shuddering and sweating from those, ready to curse God yet again for allowing it to happen? But it had been so very real in the U-boat: the sounds, the smells, the apparitions rising toward him with gaping, awful faces. *Stop it!* he told himself, pretending to inspect a bunch of green bananas.

He had sat up half the night in the hotel's front room, drinking one dark rum after the next, holding the scorpion paperweight in his left hand and turning it before the bulb of a desk lamp. The colors of the spectrum had gleamed through the newly polished glass, and the imprisoned scorpion was outlined in a dark, bloodlike red glow. Sitting there, staring at the glass, feeling the warmth of the rum deep in his belly, he wondered what kind of a man had held it before him, in the cavernous darkness of the U-boat. Inescapable fate, Moore thought; it had been inescapable fate that those men had gone down together into the Abyss, inescapable fate that he had discovered the U-boat some forty years later. And now he realized his destiny had become strangely interlocked with theirs, through time and circumstance. He had raised the submarine from the dead, drawn to that ledge beneath the glimmering blue surface as surely as if there had been a path cut for him dropping down into the curling waves. It was after three when he had finished the rum and put the paperweight aside, hoping he would sleep. The terrible images still danced inside his head.

And this morning, as he made his way through the crowd of islanders, he understood their fear of the dark things they associated with the boat's decaying mass. They held him responsible for its being on the island, as if he had brought up some kind of Pandora's box filled with . . . what? The things he'd seen in his hallucinations? Jumbies, duppies, monstrous forms that crawled through brackish water like huge dark spiders? He shook the visions off. *Voodoo superstitions,* Moore thought, *and not worth a damn.*

There was some kind of commotion on one edge of the Square; Moore could see several of the islanders stepping aside as if to make way for someone. Heads turned; conversations stopped. The wild clatter of laughter and talking began to die, slowly at first, from that edge of the Square outward, and was replaced by a low whispering and murmuring. Moore couldn't see what was happening because there were too many people around him, so he walked toward a clear spot over by the hut where the fish were being stored. A group of islanders parted and Moore saw Boniface approaching, walking slowly, guided by his cane and dressed in a black suit. The glass eye around his throat caught the sunlight. The man looked straight ahead, not even acknowledging the others but seemingly walking directly toward Moore. Finally the outer fringes of the crowd grew silent in anticipation, and the drummers stopped their rhythms.

Boniface narrowed his eyes slightly, staring into Moore's face, and did not slow his pace until he was standing a few feet away from the white man. Moore saw that the whites of Boniface's eyes were bloodshot, as if he'd been either drinking or smoking ganja. Beneath the eyeglasses they appeared as inflamed, deep circles in the ebony face. Boniface leaned forward on his cane, both hands clasped at its hilt, and studied Moore in silence. Other eyes were on him, from all across the Square, and in the distance he could hear a woman hushing a group of children.

"You've been inside it," Boniface said quietly.

"That's right," Moore replied, meeting the man's gaze.

"Are you a fool? A madman, to disdain what I say? God help you! Ah, *oui*. You see it as historical, a curiosity perhaps. Would you so peer at the fangs of a snake? And now it sits opened behind those frail wooden walls. And tell me, what did you find inside?"

"Nothing. We found nothing at all."

"Liar!" Boniface hissed, his expression fierce. He looked around at the knot of people behind him, and when he returned his gaze to the white man he had regained his control. He said in a voice just above a whisper, "I know what you found there, Moore. Do you hear me? I know! And you thought yourself dreaming, or mad, or cursed with the sight of something you could never begin to understand. Do not return to that place. Leave the boat alone, I warn you!"

"What did I see, Boniface? You tell me."

The man paused for a few seconds, and when he spoke the voice came from the corridors of his soul. "You glimpsed Hades, Moore. You saw the place of eternal torture and damnation. And yet you are a fool to think it was a nightmare, to think you are safe because the things you fail to understand cannot reach you. *But I tell you they can!*" Boniface abruptly turned from Moore, sweeping his gaze across the faces around him. He stepped into the crowd and it parted for him, backing away.

"Listen!" he said, his voice ringing through the silence that had fallen in the Square. "Hear me well, all of you! Some of you heed my word, some of you despise my teachings, but now I beg all of you to listen!" He looked from face to face, his own hard gaze unyielding. "There is a great and terrible danger on Coquina, and I urge all who can to pack belongings and get away from this place now, quickly!" There was a startled murmur across the Square.

Boniface held up a hand. "Wait! Hear me out! If you cannot do as I ask, then do these things! Board your windows, keep your shutters and doors locked! If you have guns, keep them close at hand!" The crowd's uneasiness increased and several people moved about nervously, but none dared turn his back or drop his eyes. "Stay off the streets at night," Boniface continued. "Watch your wives and children, and do not allow them to stray off the paths into the jungle. . . ."

There was a chorus of angered, fearful responses from some of the men. Several of them stepped forward, as if to challenge Boniface. A woman fell to her knees and began to mutter wildly, her hands clasped before her.

"LISTEN TO ME, YOU FOOLS!" Boniface shouted, the veins standing out in his neck. Immediately all noise ceased; the men stood where they were, glowering. The reverend continued softly, "If you value your lives, you will not go down into the boatyard. . . ."

This last warning held them breathless. The breeze swept over them and on inland; at the rear of the crowd a metal pot was knocked over. An elderly man came past Moore and picked up a bucket; he glanced at the white man, his eyes pools of fear, and then vanished. In another moment the rest of the islanders had begun to gather up their goods in silence. The musicians carried their steel drums off; women grasped for their children's hands and pulled them along, ignoring their crying. The Square began to empty rapidly.

"Are you crazy?" Moore asked Boniface, stepping beside him. "This is exactly what the constable didn't want! You've started a goddamned panic!"

"I've told them the truth," Boniface said. "Kip lies to himself. I'll have no blood on *my* hands!"

Moore held back the urge to grab the frail old man

153

and shake him until he cracked open, spilling out his bilious secrets into the sand. "Tell me what it means," he said after a while.

"It may save their lives. It may save yours as well."

"But why won't you just explain?" Moore was infuriated. The islanders had been overpowered by Boniface's voodoo. There was nothing Kip could do.

Moore, knowing that now the islanders had been overpowered by Boniface's voodoo, watched the few people still left carrying away their goods. One of the farmers began to drag his unwilling hogs along, his wife and children switching at their flanks with sticks. Another bent to gather up armloads of sugarcane and throw them into a wheelbarrow.

"Remember," Boniface said, holding Moore's eyes. "Stay away from that boat."

"What in God's name is this all about?" Moore asked again, but the reverend had turned away without a word, retracing the path by which he'd come, moving through the rapidly emptying Square toward Front Street's sand ribbon. "WHAT IS IT?" Moore shouted, but the man didn't stop. He watched Boniface disappear among the clapboard houses.

Moore saw now who held the power; he had seen Mayor Reynard's face among the crowd, and a dozen others he knew. None of them had moved, none had spoken; they'd been frozen under Boniface's gaze. And the man's words had swept the Square, begging, commanding, pleading. None of his believers could dare to disobey.

In another few moments Moore was alone in the Square except for a couple of thin dogs searching for scraps. And above their low, growling challenges Moore thought he heard something, very distant and difficult to define. It was a distant buzzing sound, like a fly circling his head; slowly the noise became the whirring of a cricket, then the close droning of a bee. Moore lifted his face into the sun, shielding his eyes with a hand, and searched the sky. He found it, and the large winged shadow passed close over the village roofs, sending whorls of sand dancing past him.

Steven Kip drove a narrow, rutted goat-track of a road through the greenish-black jungles; the studded tires bounced and crashed over stones and the remnants of uprooted trees. Kip braked the jeep when he came to a crossroads to get his bearings as to which way to drive. He had been at this point on Coquina only twice before, and one of those times he had become hopelessly lost for hours on a road that wound around and around before dropping off into the sea. He lifted his arm and wiped sweat from his forehead. The air was thick and wet here, and the dampness had worked its way beneath his clothes, clinging to his skin in beads. Light streamed through the thick overhang of trees and vines like golden, liquid columns, but in places the darkness was like the bottom of the ocean. Birds screeched and fluttered in the maze of limbs, their forms giving a brief glimpse of red or blue or yellow as they sought safety at higher altitudes.

Kip chose the right-hand pathway and turned onto it, driving through a large circular puddle of standing rainwater that sucked at the tires. Strands of mist clung close to the earth, wrapping themselves around the dark trunks of trees and slithering into the high grasses. Kip had driven for perhaps ten more minutes, wondering if he'd made a mistake again, when he saw a tree lying directly across the road. He stopped the jeep just in front of it; the tree had been living when felled. He could see the marks on the shattered trunk where the axes had been used. This was the right road after all.

Kip climbed out of the jeep, stepped over the tree, and began to walk. In the absence of engine noise the cries of the birds seemed louder, some piercing and arrogant, others sadly sweet. A little farther on Kip saw a face drawn in ashes on a tree trunk; the eyes were wide and staring, the mouth open, showing rows of teeth. A warning, Kip thought. It was a sign to keep the curious out, and perhaps more than an obvious reference to the Carib's heritage of cannibalism. As he passed the symbol he heard someone running in the jungle, bare feet crushing leaves. The sound quickly faded away, and Kip knew he'd been seen.

The jungle had been cleared less than a hundred yards ahead; he could see the Carib village, which consisted of a score of shantylike, unpainted clapboard dwellings, battered from years of hard weather and sun. A rundown store with tin placards advertising COCA-COLA and PRINCE ALBERT TOBACCO stood at the center of the village, its shingled roof half-collapsed and in some spots bared down to the wood. Just beyond the village, on Carib Point overlooking the blue sheen of the Caribbean, was a useless squat tower, now decayed; green vines covered its base and all the glass on its lamp deck had been long broken. Strung between the houses were lines of drying, tattered clothes, and here and there were small square plots of scraggly corn and beans.

A naked child sat on the ground sailing a piece of wood whittled into a boat in a brackish-looking puddle, and he looked up with surprised eyes as Kip entered Caribville. A group of other children had already seen him and had run away, followed by their short-haired yellow dog, who stopped to snarl and bark at the constable. Some men had gathered in front of the store, their eyes sharp and bright, their features appearing more chiseled and harder than those of the Coquina villagers, their complexions a tawny gold. An attractive woman with long black hair who had been carrying a basket balanced on her head stopped in her tracks when she saw Kip; when she had regained her composure she continued on, moving away toward one of the houses. People peered at him from screened doors and windows as he walked deeper into Caribville. He sensed their hostility. They had never accepted him as the authority, as law on the island, and they disliked anyone whose ancestry was tied with the British.

The men at the front of the store began to separate as Kip reached them, and they were gone before he could speak to them. Kip stood at the doorway, his gaze sweeping across the village. A single road headed downhill to a semicircle of beach below. At the Carib harbor, there was a wharf where a few rusty old trawlers lay moored. Kip could see some of the men working on their boats. Farther along the beach stood a huge concrete hulk, just the steel framework and walls of a building. At one time, a British firm had tried to build a hotel and marina there but the project had fallen through. Now it stood as a silent sentinel of progress thwarted: the jungle had grown back around it, and spiders and lizards had claimed the building as a shelter from the heat.

"What do you want?" someone asked, in a heavily accented voice that mixed English and Spanish.

Kip looked around. A heavyset man in a T-shirt stood behind the screen door, his hands on his hips. His hair was cropped very short, but his glossy, black sideburns had been allowed to grow wild and full. His eyes were small burning embers under thick black brows, and they regarded the constable with a mixture of curiosity and disdain.

"I want to see the Chief Father," Kip told him.

The Carib was silent for a few seconds, sizing the other man up. "And why?" he asked.

"Official police business."

"Is that so? Well, then, you can talk to me; I'm Cheyne's brother-in-law."

Kip shook his head. "That won't do. Is Cheyne here or not?"

"He ain't," the man said. "He's took his boat out this morning."

Kip didn't believe the man. When he looked to one side he saw two other Carib men, both burly and tough-looking, leaning against the remnants of a brick wall, watching him. One pretended to pare his nails with a knife blade. "It's Cheyne I want to see," Kip said, gazing at the men. "There's been trouble over in Coquina village. A man's dead, and I want to know . . ."

"We heard about that," the man said. "All about it. So you come up here to ask questions about us, thinking mebbe we had something to do with it? Go away, constable. You ain't welcome here."

"Thanks for your help," Kip told him acidly, watching the other two out of the corner of his eye. "I know where Cheyne lives; I'll find him myself." As he walked away, he heard the man call out, "Better watch your step around here, constable! This ain't no fuckin' pastel pink Coquina village you in now!" There was laughter, and someone cursed and spat, but Kip paid them no attention. He reached a house farther down the row of decrepit shacks, and knocked on the door frame. Waited, knocked again. The door opened a few inches and a smooth-skinned, pretty woman peered out at him cautiously.

"I'm looking for him," Kip said.

She shook her head, spoke a few words in the brisk native dialect. "Gone," she said. "He gone." She pointed toward the ocean.

"When is he coming back?"

The woman shrugged, not understanding. In the dim confines of the house a baby began crying, and Kip heard an aged voice call out. The woman looked over her shoulder, nodding, and then closed the door in the constable's face.

Damn! he thought angrily. Cheyne was the only one who'd talk to him, and he was a hard man to track down; the other Caribs would just as soon spit as look at him. Kip left the house, walking back past the store to his jeep, ignoring the stares of the men and their curses flung at his back. Deep within him he knew the Caribs had had nothing to do with Turk's murder. He was desperately trying to convince himself that the answer was logical, something he could put his finger on, but the more he brooded over it the more the answer seemed to elude him. It led him into a place of darkness, a cramped passage moving him inexorably toward a closed iron hatch.

THAT WAS NOT REAL! he told himself for the thousandth time, trying to make the thought convincing. That was not, could never be, real! Of course, it was his job to be concerned. He was responsible for the Coquina villagers and the Caribs as well, even though those people looked to their Chief Father as the ultimate authority.

As he reached the jeep Kip realized the birds were silent; the myriad noises now were strangely and disturbingly absent. The breeze swept in, rattling foliage and sending the mist through the trees with questioning fingers. Silence swelled in the sun-ribbed shadows, louder than the screeching of the birds. It was an oppressive quiet, and Kip wondered what had caused it.

He started the engine and began to thread his way along the road, away from the red points of eyes that had been watching.

And hungering.

Thirteen

THE SINGLE-ENGINE PLANE circled a few times above the island's interior and then dropped smoothly down into the trees. Moore had seen it and, out of curiosity, he drove his pickup truck along a road into jungle, across open flats and through areas black with thicket, trees, and vines shutting off the sunlight. The road came into a wide clearing; there was a narrow, packed-dirt airstrip and a tin-roofed shed. Beyond the strip, at the fringe of the deeper jungle, was a farmhouse. A black man in dungarees stood there watching the thing that had come from the sky. That didn't happen often on Coquina.

Moore turned onto the airstrip and pulled up alongside the plane. Some sort of symbol was painted on the craft's side, a white circle with the letters JHF in white at its center. He could see movement in the cockpit; a figure in a tan jumpsuit pulled at a duffel bag wedged between two seats. Moore climbed out of the truck and approached the open cockpit door. "Can I give you a hand?"

"Yes," the pilot said, working the bag free and hefting it over the side to Moore. "Take this bloody thing. But be careful; there's expensive camera gear inside."

Moore caught the heavy bag, but stood braced at the cockpit doorway staring.

The pilot was a young woman, her hair pinned up in a cap but a single curl of gold showing at the neck. He had just caught a glimpse of her profile as she turned to give him the bag. She lifted a suitcase and very carefully laid it outside the cockpit as Moore stepped back to give her room. She glanced up, appraising him with her clear gray eyes, and offered her hand. "Jana Thornton," she said; Moore shook her hand and started to speak, but she turned away again for a smaller suitcase on the co-pilot's seat. She put it down on the ground and went on, "I wasn't expecting a welcoming party. I couldn't raise a wireless signal, but if I've plotted correctly this has to be Coquina."

"It is."

"Then I'm where I want to be." She turned to look down the rutted, pot-holed airstrip. "I don't expect you have many commercial flights here, do you?"

"No," Moore agreed. "We're not exactly a tourist mecca."

She nodded thoughtfully, returning to the cockpit and emerging again with a few bricks, which she placed as stops against the plane's tires. Moore carried the bags to his truck and then turned back to her. "What's the JHF stand for?"

"Jamaica Historic Foundation," she said, straightening up. She closed the cockpit door and locked it. "Will my plane be safe out here?"

"We haven't lost any so far."

"I really didn't expect anyone to be meeting me," she laughed as they climbed into the truck's cab. "But I appreciate the ride, Mr.—?"

"David Moore." He started the engine and they began to move along the strip. "You would have had a long hike into the village."

He glanced across at her as they reached the jungle road. It had been a long time since he'd seen a white woman as attractive as she was. She wore very little makeup and didn't really need any; she was a natural beauty with high cheekbones and forehead and a striking facial structure; she was perhaps in her late twenties. Her hair was tucked underneath the cap, of course, but he envisioned it as falling to just about shoulder length. Her skin was deeply tanned, as if she spent a lot of time outdoors; the sun had deepened laugh-lines around her eyes and mouth. She had the hands of a man, toughened and callused. There was a simple gold chain around her neck, and she wore no rings. Moore had seen a look of energy and intelligence, perhaps also of caution in her eyes. They were calm now, and steady, but Moore thought they could probably cut like a heated scalpel when she was angry.

"Where have you come from?" he asked her. "Kingston?"

"That's right."

"Isn't it dangerous flying alone like that?"

She smiled slightly, as if the question was one she heard often. "Not if you know what you're doing. And I do. There's an interesting reef out beyond your harbor. Do you know anything about those two steamer wrecks to the south?"

"I've dived them," he said. "They're in about sixty feet, but only the stern's left of one and the keel of the other." Moore paused for a few seconds. "You're pretty good to recognize them as steamers from the air."

"I know that type of wreck," she said. "And there are objects lying near them that could only be broken steamship funnels."

"What are you doing on Coquina?" Moore asked, fascinated with his passenger. "And what's your Foundation do, anyway?"

"I'm here to find the island's constable. As to the Foundation, we're a research group in alliance with the British Museum."

"I see. Then you're here because of the U-boat."

She glanced over at him and nodded. "Let's say I'm here to investigate something the Foundation doesn't understand. There was a story in the *Jamaica Daily Gleaner* about a submarine hulk surfacing. We contacted the man who reported it—a mail-boat captain—who turned out to be sixty-eight years old and somewhat less than an expert. I'm reserving judgment as to whether what's surfaced off your island actually *is* an authentic World War II relic."

Moore looked at her and noticed her eyes were suspicious and questing, like a cat's. "You can see for yourself."

"I plan to."

They came off the jungle road, turned on Back Street, and drove toward the center of the village. The Square was now completely deserted, and Moore saw that Kip's jeep was still gone from its usual place in front of his office.

"I don't think the constable's in right now," he said. He motioned toward the grocery store. "There's a cafe over there if you'd like something to eat while you wait."

"I can do with some lunch," she acknowledged, and Moore pulled the truck to the curb.

Everybody's Grocers and Cafe was a small stucco building painted a bright mustard yellow; the store was at the front; the cafe was a scattering of tables near a kitchen at the rear. When they sat down, the rotund cook protested that she was leaving soon to go home, but Moore talked her into making lunch for them. He asked for two orders of seafood bouillabaisse and coffee.

"Is it Miss or Mrs. Thornton?" he asked her casually after they'd seated themselves.

She extracted a cigarette from a pack of Players and lit it without waiting for him to find a match. "It's *Dr.* Thornton," she said coolly.

"Oh? A doctor of what?"

"A professor," she corrected. "I'm a marine archaeologist, specializing in the study of sunken wrecks."

"Sounds interesting."

"It is." She tapped ash off her cigarette. She looked up, examining his eyes for a few seconds. She could see intensity in this man's tanned, weather-lined face. The eyes were strange, very blue, warm and yet distant at the same time. There was curiosity and strength; but something dark and disturbing as well, lying deep inside. Then she saw it vanish like the briefest of passing shadows.

"What about you?" she asked, at last. "What are you doing here?"

"I own the Indigo Inn. The hotel at the top of the hill."

"Ah, yes. I saw it from the air." She tilted her chin and exhaled smoke. "I wouldn't think you would attract many guests."

"Not during hurricane season, no. But when the good breezes are blowing we get a few yachtsmen passing through. And I enjoy the life. It's not a bad way to pass the time."

"I want to know about this submarine," she said quietly, after their coffee had been served. "Where is it now?"

"Locked away in an old naval shelter down in the island boatyards. All two hundred feet of the damned thing."

"Two hundred twenty feet," Jana corrected him. "Width twenty feet, displacing approximately 749 tons of water. And, if it is a German boat, most probably a vessel from the VII-C series, if that means anything to you."

"No, it doesn't," Moore admitted.

"The workhorse of the Nazi submarine fleet. They operated by the dozens both in the North Atlantic and in the Caribbean during the war. I've dived on the wrecks of several just off Jamaica, but of course there's not much left to comb through. That's what the Foundation fails to understand, Mr. Moore: The word we received is that this U-boat surfaced unaided . . . and in almost perfect condition. Now, since you're a diver yourself, you tell me how that's possible."

"Okay," he said. "First of all, I guess I should let you know that I'm the one who found the thing. It was buried in sand at a hundred and fifty feet, and an unexploded depth charge blew it free. Both the constable and myself have been inside it. Yes, that's right. It's authentic. The hull's holding tight, all the equipment's still in place, and . . ." He paused. Bodies? Tell her about his vision in that dank tomb? No. "It's still seaworthy," he said. "And I have a theory."

"Fine. I'm listening."

"The U-boat was buried in one hell of a lot of sand. I believe a ledge just above it had given way and covered it over, and it remained there until the last big blow whipped the sea around and slid some of the sand back. If the submarine were completely buried there'd be no way the usual marine organisms could attach themselves to the iron. The sand was a natural buffer against corrosion."

"That would be a great deal of weight crushing the superstructure, wouldn't it?" she reminded him.

"I didn't say the superstructure was unscratched. How much pressure could those boats withstand?"

"Their shipyard guarantee was a little over three hundred feet," Jana said, sipping at her coffee. "Some of them made it to six hundred and back with only minor structural damages. Others may have gone even deeper before they imploded."

"So it depended on the boat?"

"There may have been a difference of degree in the elasticity of the iron from shipyard to shipyard, or even from year to year. But tell me this: Even if your theory is correct, it doesn't explain why the boat surfaced."

"No," Moore agreed, "you're right. But couldn't the explosion have jarred a mechanism or something?"

She gave him a patient smile. "That's rather remote. There is, however, the possibility of a gas buildup within the boat. You see, a submarine rises and falls by means of compressed air; filling the buoyancy cells with air to force the water out lifts it up, and letting the sea flood the cells again will make it descend. It's rather like the action of the human lungs, if you can envision a U-boat breathing. The captain can control the speed of an ascent or descent by regulating the amount of air or water in the cells. Leonardo da Vinci came up with the idea of an underwater boat used for warfare centuries ago, but the concept so frightened him that he never executed a model. Anyway, I can't see that the machinery to pump compressed air into the tanks would still be operable. Of course . . ." She paused for a moment, tapping her finger on the table. "There might already have been compressed air in the tanks, though not enough to displace the weight that lay over it. When the weight shifted the hulk began to rise. One of the crewmen may have bled air into the tanks at the same time your suspected ledge collapsed. But then it was too late."

The cook, still muttering about the lateness of the hour, brought a pot of bouillabaisse filled with chunks of snapper, crabmeat, and scallops simmered with tomatoes and peppers. Moore began eating at once, but Jana tested it cautiously with a spoon before trusting her stomach to the exotic fare.

"Of course," Jana said after she'd taken a bite, "all of the systems were duplicated in each boat. One mechanized, one manual. But I doubt very seriously if there would have been any hands left aboard to operate the levers. I presume the crew got out by means of an escape hatch, or perhaps through the torpedo tubes."

Moore sat motionless. He held a spoonful of food near his mouth, then slowly put it back down onto his plate. The tension in his stomach was palpable. "No," he said huskily.

"What?" Jana asked, looking up, seeing his face cloud over; the look of it put her on edge.

"No," Moore repeated. "That's not what happened at all."

Jana didn't know what he was talking about at first, and then it dawned on her. Of course. Skeletons. "How many are left?" she asked.

"I . . . I'm not sure. I don't think . . . I saw all of them."

"You went from bow to stern?"

He shook his head. "Just from the bow to the control room."

"I'll want to go all the way aft," Jana said. "I've seen skeletons in a sunken ship before."

"Not skeletons," Moore said quietly. "Not skeletons." He blinked and gazed deep into her face. "What do you want to see the thing for?"

"If it's towable and in reasonably good condition the British Museum might be interested in the hulk as a war relic," she said, puzzled by his behavior. "Which would mean a large grant to the Foundation, incidentally."

"I see." Moore pushed his food away. "Then you'll want to go down inside the U-boat?"

"That's right. I'll be checking for damage, taking photographs and tape-recording notes. I've been sent here to determine whether or not a salvage team is merited."

Moore saw the woman's eyes narrow a fraction, and he knew she was seeing beyond the mask of his face, getting a glimpse of the fear he felt. He could virtually sense the iron crypt lying a little more than a mile from where they sat. She looked away from him abruptly, preoccupied with her food. *Tell her,* he told himself. *Tell her what you've seen. YES! SEEN! It wasn't a hallucination, wasn't the product of an oxygen-starved brain! You saw them there! YOU SAW THEM THERE!*

At that instant he realized he was clinging frantically to the edge of reason. What would he say? That he had seen long-dead things moving, reaching, swinging wrenches and hammers? That somehow Death itself had stood still, or had claimed those crewmen but had released an evil rage that made their bodies move in strange mockery of life? *No. God in Heaven, no.*

"How many . . ." Moore began. "How many men did a boat of that size crew?"

"Between forty-four and fifty," Jana said, and thought he seemed to pale slightly. The man knew something important, something she should know as well. She must find out what it was.

My God, Moore almost said aloud. He picked up his coffee, realized he'd finished it, and placed the cup back in its saucer. *Fifty. Fifty. Fifty.* The number thudded in his brain. *Stay away from the boat,* Boniface had said. The Night Boat. A thing of darkness, hiding darkness. A periscope shaft, beckoning him into the depths where he was to carry out the task they had wanted done. *Lock your shutters, your windows, your doors.* Fifty of them, hidden in shadows away from the alien sun. Waiting. Waiting.

Waiting.

Jana said, "I'd like to see the boat now."

Fourteen

ONCE FEAR TAKES HOLD there is no escape. It surfaces to haunt the brain, to lead the eyes down corridors of terror, to taunt the senses with the presence of something unknown, just beyond reach. As Moore drove the girl toward the boatyard he saw that the fear had spread rapidly in the village, a fire fueled by Boniface's eyes and cryptic words. There were bolted doors and shuttered windows everywhere; on some of the walls were hastily drawn voodoo symbols, painted there as talismans of protection. A few people were still moving about the streets, as dusk still was several hours off, and in the harbor men worked on their nets for Monday's fishing, but the air was different. The bar district was almost deserted, and there were no children running along the beaches or playing ball among the fishermen's shanties.

The boatyard gates were unrepaired and Moore drove through. In another few moments he steered the truck around the piles of debris and oil barrels and passed the supply shed. He put on the brakes and slowed. The shed doors were open; one of the large wooden doors had been ripped off its hinges and lay in the sand, and there was a jumble of barrels, splintered crates, and cans around the entrance. Moore knew it should have been securely locked. He continued on across the yard for the naval shelter.

When they reached it he immediately saw that the doorway was wide open, a dark entry leading toward the twisted iron hulk. He stopped the truck and pointed at the shelter. "It's in there," he told her.

Jana went around to the truck bed and began unzipping the duffel bag. "Any electricity in there? Arc lights?"

"No," he said, his gaze fixed on that square of blackness, knowing what lay beyond. "All the juice is cut off."

She opened the bag and took out a camera case and a flash attachment. Zipping the bag up again, she took the Nikon from its case and fit the flash to it, then let it fall around her neck. "Now," she said, "we'll see your precious relic."

They stood together for a long time in the foul-smelling darkness as their eyes slowly made out the sharp lines of the huge craft. A prehistoric monster, Moore thought. Jana coughed into her hand. "Chlorine gas," she said quietly, her voice echoing against metal. "Battery seepage." When she was finally able to see it, from bow to stern, she caught her breath and took a step forward.

Jana blinked, put out a hand as if to touch it. "My God," she said, awed. *"My God."* She moved forward again and Moore moved with her, stepping over an empty crate marked LUBRICANT, TWENTY CANS.

Jana had dived in murky green water twelve miles to the north of Jamaica about six months ago, finding at a depth of ninety-four feet a submarine that had been in its days of glory similar to this one; she had first seen it as a long dark cigar shape, then as she hovered above it, as a mass of coral with twisted iron ribs protruding. The hatches had been open, circular holes all clogged with growth, nothing left of the conning tower but a dark flower of iron where a bomb or shell had struck. And in the center of the veins of tubing were crisscrossed pipes that now served as home to starfish and spotted eels. That boat had been dead, devoid of power and menace. But this one, here only a few feet away . . . was very different. *It's a hoax,* she thought suddenly. *A joke. No boat could be underwater that length of time and not be a rusted, broken hulk.* But no; it was real, the iron hull secure. She had seen boats down only a few months in worse shape than this one, and she couldn't believe what she was seeing. She picked up her camera and switched on the flash to let it charge up, then began to take her pictures carefully and unhurriedly, moving along the port side and then back again. When she called out to Moore he could hear the excitement in her voice. "It's a VII-C, all right. Minor damage to the superstructure, snapped sky periscope . . . Jesus! The eighty-eight millimeter cannon's still intact, so is the twenty-millimeter gun! Deck looks to be broken through in places, but my God, the corrosion hasn't even begun on most of the hull!" As she talked she took picture after picture, the flash outlining a jagged shadow on the opposite wall. "There's water inside?" she asked.

"Not very much."

"Condensation or overflow through a hatch, probably. If that's so, the boat must have gone down in a hurry. Possibly under attack, if you say there was a depth charge near it." She came along the port side and then toward the bow. "Torpedo tubes are clear," she told him. "Bow torpedo-loading hatch is open. Is that how you went in?"

"Yes." Moore nodded.

She took another photograph, the flash a silent white explosion. In its light Moore saw something; he took a step forward, but already she was on her way across the gangplank. She stepped onto the deck, avoiding debris and rats.

"Just a minute . . ." Moore said, trying to figure out what it was he'd seen.

Jana was peering through broken deck timbers. "Pressure hull looks unscathed." She pushed a box away and empty oil cans rolled out. "I can see the explosion you mentioned loosening it from the sand, but what made this boat surface? Compressed-air expansion? Possibly there was already air in the buoyancy tanks?" She was talking to herself, not noticing as Moore moved to the edge of the concrete walkway and stared over at the bow. "For the time being we'll have to accept your theory," she was saying, "until the Foundation comes up with something better. My God, what a weapon!"

"The hatch," Moore said quietly, and the sound of his voice made her look up.

"Through there, that's where the bow torpedoes were loaded," she explained. "There's another at the stern for the aft tube. What are all these crates and cans doing here? This gun mount looks as if someone's greased it. . . ."

"Kip closed this hatch," Moore said in a hollow

tone, staring into the hole. "And now it's opened again."

Jana moved over by the hatch and snapped another picture of the conning tower. "I'll have to look at the mechanisms inside," she told him. "But I'll need the high-intensity lamp from my bag."

"Don't . . . stand near that hole," Moore rasped, his mouth dry. She stood over the hatch now, peering down into it. She hadn't heard, and he raised his voice. "Don't stand near the hatch!" He started across the gangplank toward her.

"What?" she asked, glancing over at him, one foot resting on the hatch rim. "What did you . . ." And then she abruptly sucked in her breath, a half-cry escaping her lips; she stepped away from the hole and Moore saw that her eyes were fixed on something behind him.

He whirled around; a shadow blocked the doorway, moving toward him. He took a step backward, lifting an arm to ward it off, his teeth bared and eyes widened.

The shadow stood motionless, looking at the two of them. "What the hell are you doing here, David?" Kip asked. "And who's she?" He didn't wait for a reply, but raised his voice. "Come off that thing, miss, before you break your neck!"

"Who are you giving orders to?" she asked indignantly.

"I'm the constable of Coquina, and I'm ordering you off that boat!" He glanced at Moore. "Who is *she?*"

"Dr. Thornton. She came from Kingston to examine the submarine."

"Is that so?" Kip watched as she made her way

across the gangplank and approached him. "What were you trying to do," he asked her, "go down in that bastard by yourself?"

"That's exactly right," Jana said, her guard up.

"Wrong. This shelter and that boat are off-limits to everyone without my express permission, and so far I haven't given it to you." He pressed the back of his hand against his face. "It smells of rot in here; let's get out into the sun."

When they had left the shelter Kip closed the door and looked for some way to lock it; he found a thin metal rod in the debris of the yard and jammed it through the door's hasp as a temporary solution.

"I have a letter from the Jamaica Historic Foundation in my bag," Jana said curtly. "If you like I'll get it for you and then we can . . ."

"No," Kip said. "Never mind any letters." He was aware of the woman's growing anger. "How did you get to Coquina?"

"My airplane."

"I see." He glanced over at Moore, then back to the woman. "Well . . . Dr. Thornton, is it? I'm afraid you made a long trip for nothing. First thing Monday morning two trawlers are going to tow the submarine out to deep water. A couple of welders are going to cut holes into it, and it's going back down where it came from."

"Wait a minute," Jana said, her face flushing. "I don't know why you think you can make this decision, but I'm not going to let you do it!"

"I'm sorry. The plans have been made."

"Then unmake them, damn it!" she said, stepping defiantly toward him. Kip stood where he was, but he could feel the heat of her anger. "You don't seem to realize what that boat is! It's a Nazi U-boat in almost perfect condition after forty years or so at the bottom of the Caribbean. We have to know how it stayed that way, what made it cork, and what boat it was. I can have a salvage team down here within three days! You can't sink it!"

"It's a rotting old hulk," Kip said.

"No! It's in remarkable condition, not much deteriorated from the day it went down! And I'll wager the interior is in excellent condition as well, including the engine room! My God, the boat's a naval historian's dream. It's almost certain I can guarantee interest from the British Museum if I can just examine the inside!"

"You ever heard the story of Pandora's Box?" Kip asked her; the question startled her. "Let's just say there's plenty you don't know about the submarine. All manner of hell's been raised here because of it. No, I'm not going to wait any three days. I wouldn't wait three damned hours if I didn't have to!" He reached over and pulled at the metal rod to make certain the door was shut securely. Moore realized he had locked the door as if to keep something in instead of out. Kip turned to him and said, "I was driving past on my way back from Caribville and I saw your truck parked here. I didn't think you would've come back here alone. . . ."

"You're a madman!" Jana said suddenly. "That's a scientific find you want to destroy!"

"I've had enough arguing, miss," Kip told her, looking her straight in the eye. "I've had my say, and that's how things stand. If you want to file a protest with your Foundation when you get back to Kingston, that's fine with me too. Let them get in touch with me, and I'll tell them the same thing. The U-boat's going back into the ocean. David, I'll see you later. Dr. Thornton, have a good trip." He nodded toward her and walked back to his jeep. He started the engine and roared off, leaving them standing together at the side of the shelter.

"What's wrong with that man?" Jana asked. "Is he out of his mind?"

"No," Moore said. "No, he's not." It was getting late; the shadows were thicker, a blue-black mist stretching across the yard. Soon night would cover the island, and Moore realized there was no place on earth he would rather avoid than this boatyard, with the U-boat lying only behind the thickness of a wooden wall after darkness fell. "It's too late for you to make Kingston before dark," he told Jana. "If you'd like I'll give you a room up at the hotel."

"I appreciate that," she said, "but I've no intention of leaving until I've talked some sense into that idiot."

"Suit yourself," Moore said, motioning toward the truck.

Driving into the village, Kip knew there was something terribly wrong; he saw the empty streets, the shuttered windows, the voodoo talismans scrawled on stucco and clapboard. Anger surged within him, and he felt a confusion he couldn't begin to define. One of the symbols, chalked against a sea-green door, held his attention, started the slow stirring of memories— sluggish, nebulous—at the back of his brain. It was the crude drawing of a huge hand, from top to bottom of the door, the fingers spread as if to ward off the invisible. Kip pulled the jeep to the side of the road and stared at it, unable to tear his gaze away.

He was a child again, a boy of thirteen, sitting at a low table eating from a bowl of corn mush and ham bits. He ate slowly, though it was his first meal in over a day. Across the plank-walled room, a few half-charred logs burned erratically in a stone fireplace. On the floor was woven sea-grass, well-worn; the window shutters were closed tight and the only light came from several oil lamps placed around the room. The dim half-glow illuminated the straw tribal masks on the walls, their features cunning and wolfish: heavy-browed seashell eyes gleaming. He thought they were staring directly at him, and that sometimes their features changed to look almost human, but grotesque and freakish.

A man sat in a rocking chair before the fire. He stared into the flames, rattling a jar of dog's teeth distractedly. After a while he took one of the teeth out and tossed it in, then bent forward as if he saw something there. He leaned back, the runners making a soft, catlike murmur on the grass mat. From one corner there was a low rustle; the man turned his head and the boy caught a firelight profile of slitted eyes in an aged, weather-lined face. On a bed of sea-grass across the room there was a large green iguana almost two feet long; a metal collar clamped about its neck secured the reptile to a line tied around an overhead beam with enough slack so that the lizard could move about in the room. Its pale red eyes stared at Kip, the white flesh under the jaw and belly undulating as it breathed. It came forward a few feet, crunching on the grass, stopped, flesh quivering along its spine, slender tail sweeping across the floor. Its head moved jerkily, eyes fixed on Kip.

"Feed it," the man said.

There was a piece of doughy brown bread beside him. He tore off a small chunk and tossed it over. The lizard jerked, scurried back, waited. Then it advanced on the bread and licked at it.

Kip was still dazed from hunger and weak from sleeping. In the past three days he had slept a great deal, intoxicated by the strange fumes eminating from pots the man kept in a circle around the boy's bare mattress. Sometimes his sleep was dreamless and black, the sleep of the dead, but more often it was peopled by phantoms, grinning things like the masks that watched him, always in an anticipatory silence. The faces spun about him in his dreams, calling his name over and over.

Out of necessity, Kip had begun to build a brick wall in his mind to keep the horrors back, the mortar going down smooth and thick, each row of bricks solid and even. But sometimes the things seemed to have more strength, and they reached out with their gray tendrils to pull down the bricks he had erected the night before. No matter how hard he shrieked at the nightmare forms there was no escape; there were too many, and he had to work harder and harder to put the bricks back into place. He worked at the wall like a madman, as if sleep were just another of the many labors set for him by his uncle, who had made him heat and knead balls of wax, to be fashioned into images by the man and sold to furtive customers. Kip had also been made to drain seven white chickens of their blood, and, one night, to accompany his uncle to the pauper's graveyard to sever a recently dead man's head for that fearful death spell, the *Garabanda*. The wall never seemed to be complete, for the things still found holes and weak spots through which to grasp at him. But someday it would be strong enough to hold them back and away forever, and never again would they make him scream that terrible scream from the deep pit of sleep. He vowed it to himself, made the vow as much a part of him as was his fear and dislike of the man who called himself "uncle."

In one of his cold-sweat nightmares he was wandering the wide corridors and empty rooms of a huge, abandoned mansion. Moss draped the windows and doors; no light could penetrate, and he moved through spidery shadows. When he ran into boarded-over doors, sealed windows, bricked passageways, he would turn and retrace his steps. In one room there were older people dressed in bright colors, each of them standing alone and not speaking to the others; in another was a child playing on the floor with a bright green ball that suddenly uncurled and became a lizard that slithered away. Upstairs was a passage with gaping holes in the floor, the black timbers threatening to give way beneath his feet. He guided himself onward, searching, feeling his way along.

As he came through a doorway, the tides suddenly surged around his feet. He resisted the pull of the current and saw the blue water slowly turn a dark-red color. In another room, farther along, were a woman and a little girl who waved to him and smiled. He heard the tolling of a ship's bell from far away, a world away, then silence. He moved on, finding rooms crowded with iron, ship's parts, and rusted equipment; a white man moved across the corridor ahead of him and Kip followed. A skeleton stood before him, arms out, face imploring him for something he couldn't understand; the skeleton crumpled, fell to dust.

And in the next room, almost at the crown of the house, a congregation of shadows. A chair. Open windows, black sky, sheer tattered curtains trailing in an unfelt wind. And in the chair a dark form, unrecognizable, a roiling thing without true substance, but emanating a vast and terrible hate. The door slammed behind him. Alerted by the noise, the hideous form turned what would be its head, slowly, seeking out the intruder. Two blinding crimson orbs fixed Kip to the floor; they burned through to his brain. And then the thing rose from the chair and started for him, dark arms coming up to embrace him. He felt his back against the door, felt the hardness of the wood pressing into his spine. The thing's hot breath touched his cheek and he began to shout for help, over and over; it neared him, smelling of age and rot, uncoiling like a black mamba.

And then the door behind him came open. He fell backward, still screaming.

Opened his eyes.

A hand coming for him, brown and withered. A craggy, staring face behind it. He recoiled; the hand grasped his shoulder and shook him fully awake.

In the corner the lizard had shifted, tiny pinpoints of gleaming red still unblinking.

His uncle stood over him, wiping sweat from his cheeks. "Your future is not with me," he said.

And suddenly the figure of the hand on the green door trembled. The door came open and a man in dungarees peered out at the constable.

Kip stared at him for a few seconds, then composed himself and drove on to the Square, the memories whirling inside his head: bits of remembered faces and colors, sights and smells. He had labored long and hard to wall off that part of his life. He'd thought the bricks were firmly mortared into place. Until the U-boat had come.

I know what you could have been, Boniface had told him.

Bullshit, Kip muttered between clenched teeth. Bullshit.

The evening shadows fell across Coquina. The moon rose, glittering silver on the waves that surged over Kiss Bottom. The breeze began to pick up, gently at first, then strengthening and finally sweeping up sand in the streets, swirling it in gritty puffs that stung the shuttered windows. A dog bayed at the moon until someone cursed and threw a shoe to quiet him.

And no one heard the sound of hammers ringing against iron down in the boatyard.

Fifteen

JOHNNY MAJORS STRETCHED, feeling the ripple of muscles up and down his back. He got out of bed and moved in the dark toward a chair in one corner of the bedroom where his clothes had been thrown down in hasty disarray. As he buttoned his shirt he looked across at the woman's nude form sprawled on the bed, her black body still glistening from their heated lovemaking. She said softly, "It early yet. You don't have to go."

"Ten to eight," he said, struggling into his jeans. "Old lady'll be wonderin' where I am. Someday she gonna go over to the Landfall and see I ain't there and then what gonna happen?"

"You scared?" she asked; a mocking question she knew would get to him.

"No. Hell, no. But I smart too. I ain't gonna play her to the limit." He zipped his fly and buckled his belt.

"Cale and Langstree won't be back 'til tomorrow sometime. You could spend the night."

He grinned, his teeth gleaming in the darkness. "The hell you say. If your man found us here in the mornin' . . . uh uh, no. And my old lady wouldn't be so damn happy about it neither. No, baby, we got to play it smart. There enough of you for both me and Cale."

"Mebbe not," she said petulantly, drawing herself up on the pillows, her heavy breasts hanging over the sheet.

He came and sat on the bed beside her. "Hey. Your old man and Langstree'll have more trips to make. Hell, he's gone most all the time as it is now. So . . ." He stroked the smooth flesh between her breasts. "Damn me, you're a fine woman, Nora," he said in a husky voice.

"I need you to stay with me, Johnny. I don't like to be alone at night."

Leaning over, licking beneath a nipple, he realized he was hard again, but he couldn't spend the time. He had been with Cale's wife for over an hour tonight, and two hours the night before; there was no use in pressing his luck. But damn, what a woman she was. She twisted those soft, beautiful hips a thousand different ways when he was inside her, wringing him out and exhausting him and driving him wild with excitement. But Christ Almighty, if that sonofabitch Cale ever found out his woman was making time there'd be hell to pay. . . .

She reached out to cling to him, her hands grasping his belt buckle, but he stood up and moved away. "No, baby, no. I got to go now." He slipped his shoes on. "There'll be more times."

She smiled at him seductively and he looked at her appreciatively—she was still warm and glowing from the merging of their heated flesh. He stood over by the room's single window, the moonlight streaming in through a broken red shutter. When he bent down to lace his shoes she saw something, a brief glimpse of a dark form moving past the window. She sat up in bed, catching her breath in a sudden gulp of air.

"What's wrong?" he asked, thinking she was playing with him again. "Hey, what's the matter with you?"

Nora sat motionless, not knowing if she had really seen something there or not. Had someone been spying on them through the shutter? Someone her husband sent to keep a watch on her? She reached down for the sodden sheet and drew it around her like a shroud. Maybe it was even Cale himself, the bastard come back early?

Johnny hurriedly finished lacing his shoes, eager to be going. The house was a mile or so from the village, and he had a long ride in the dark on his bicycle. The look in the woman's eyes was giving him the creeps and, only half-joking, he demanded, "Hey. What you lookin' at, damn jumbies?"

The shadow fell across the shutter slats. She raised a hand, palm out as if to ward it off. Her mouth opened, and her voice came out as an eerie whine.

Even as Johnny Majors whirled around, sensing the presence of something beyond the window, there was a sharp crack of splintering wood as a blow struck the front door. He cried out in fear, his mind racing. It was Cale come back, either that or some of Cale's friends come to make him pay for screwing the woman.

Glass and wood shattered, exploding into the bedroom. The shadow was battering its way through the

186

window, and Johnny caught the brief flash of a wrench in the moonlight. There were more shadows out there, two, three, four, five, all merging into one pulsating darkness that ripped at the shutter and tore the glass away. Nora screamed, and backed into a far corner; Johnny looked around desperately for a weapon, hearing the front door being broken open. He picked up the chair beside the window and struck at the shadows, again and again, and for a moment they backed away.

"Jesus," he cried out, his chest heaving, holding the chair before him like a shield. "Jesus God who is that out there WHO IS THAT OUT THERE?"

And in the sudden silence he heard them.

Their breathing was ragged, painful, as if they were unused to the air, as if each lungful was raging fire. He could hear no voices, no movement, only the breathing of men suffering from a hideous, torturous disease, and that alone was enough to make him think he was going mad.

One of the shadows moved forward, reaching slowly through the remnants of the window. The hand grasped a broken slat and began to pull it away.

Johnny stood transfixed; the woman whined like a child from her corner. The hand, illuminated by the moonlight, looked gnarled and brown, the skeletal fingers like the claws of an animal. The nails were long and filthy; they scratched at the glass, a tiny noise which seemed tremendous to the trapped couple. And swirling about the room, borne in by the moist Caribbean winds, was the stench of rot; it caught them in smoky folds like some ancient fungus, or slime vomited up from the guts of the sea.

In the next instant the shadow hurtled itself through

the rest of the glass, its arms outstretched, black talons groping for the man. The woman screamed, a pitched, terrified noise—oh God, why wasn't this Cale *not Cale NOT CALE*. . . .

The man raised the chair and brought it down upon the reeking thing that had crawled over the window-sill; he struck something as solid as bone but could not stop the phantom. He realized too late that the others had broken through the door and were now behind him. Something caught him around the throat: a hand, cold and bony, and another hand gripped his hair. Nora's scream broke through the ceiling of her throat, then fell away to become a childish, insane babble. Johnny tried to fight free of the things, flailing with his arms and legs, but now they were all around him, the shadows pressing close, those terrible hands sharp icicles on his face, his throat, his arms.

He threw out an elbow, striking one of them, and he heard the hissing of foul breath close to his ear; a tremendous strength picked him up and flung him into a wall, where he crashed headlong. He felt the searing pain of a broken shoulder as he slid helplessly to the floor. He twisted around, his heart hammering and the panic chewing at his insides, to face the shadows as they approached. The woman, crazed with fear, was crawling on the floor on her stomach toward a closet. He lay with his back against the wall, blood dripping from a broken nose, and saw the things as they reached out for him.

The darkness covered them, but he could see their eyes. Red pinpoints of hate, they burned deep within withered skulls, unblinking and penetrating. The shadows breathed like the rising and falling of the elbows that fanned Hell's blaze. Johnny Majors held up his hands in horror and supplication, for he knew the hour of his death had arrived.

"Please," he pleaded. He could not hear his voice over the din of his bursting heart. "Please don't kill meeeeeeeee. . . ."

One of the things grinned; moonlight glittered off rotted, broken teeth, and a black tongue licked along what remained of lips.

"Please don't kill . . ." Johnny Majors whispered.

Two claws descended; they grasped the man's face, nails biting deep and drawing blood. And slowly, very slowly, they began to pull the man's face apart, even as he screamed in pure cold pain. Fingers ripped away the nose in tatters of dripping flesh; a hand clamped around the throat, the strong hard nails plunging deep, choking off the screams, puncturing the jugular vein and releasing a dark red river. Johnny Majors lay paralyzed against the splattered wall, his eyes glazed in shock, unseeing, his nerves feeling the agony but his brain gone and unable to respond. The hand at his throat began to peel the flesh away, exposing veins and cords. The shadows moved closer as the odor and warmth of the blood wafted up to them. Another moved in, bent forward, the eyes whirlpools of red; its claw flashed out, ripping away a cheek that dangled on slivers of skin. A three-fingered hand, bare bone showing on the knuckles, probed at an eye, in the next instant digging in and tearing it away like a quivering grape from a vine.

The man opened his mouth and moaned, then shuddered involuntarily. His head fell back, exposing the torn throat to the silver light. The punctured artery in his neck continued to pump blood in widening puddles.

And then the crimson-eyed shadows fell upon him, lips and tongues voraciously consuming the face and throat. Teeth bit at flesh, tearing through and gnawing hungrily on bone; the weight of the things covered him over. He lifted one hand, but it hung useless, in the air, the fingers slowly curling, and then fell back. The room was filled with the noises of their feeding; the grinding of teeth on bone, the sucking at gaping wounds and the tearing away of chunks of flesh. Blood covered the floor, and some of the things bent down to lap at the puddles, maddened and starved for its sweet, strong taste. They began to tear the body to pieces, biting through bone for the marrow and the fluids. They worked faster and faster, more frantically, the sounds of their breathing echoing in the room. The woman whimpered where she lay. They pushed at each other to reach the wounds and when one wound was dry they groped for others, hissing in fury as another pushed them aside. They broke open new rivulets of fluids, like dark wine from fleshy casks. They were impatient and greedy as they feasted, ripping strips of flesh and hoarding them, squeezing out the final drops. And when they were finished with the man, when they had scattered him in grisly pieces and sucked him dry and found they had still not had enough to fill their collapsed veins and arteries, not enough to stop the terrible pain, not to quench the raging fire, they turned with a vengeance upon the woman.

She watched them come, some of them walking, some of them dragging themselves across the floor toward her, and she was powerless to move. They were enraged because they were still not filled, not relieved of their inhuman pain, and their teeth were merciless.

As they fed on her motionless body, one of the things disentangled itself and rose to its feet. Blood smeared its lips and hands, and as it backed away from the mass of bodies it lifted a palm and licked at the human liquids. It stood in a corner, watching as the others tried to satisfy their hungers. The agony still remained, deep within dried and twisted tissues, within muscles drawn hard as stone, within flesh shrunken and wrinkled around the bones. With each breath the agony welled up, fanning the blaze ever higher. The thing in the corner put a hand to its throat in a vain attempt to still the searing pain. No pulse beat there; the heart had become a lump of decayed matter, and the veins had collapsed like the walls of empty houses. The thing shivered suddenly, in agony and rage and madness and hate.

On the wall beside it there was an oval mirror. It turned its head very slowly and peered into the moonlit reflection.

The only thing living in that face were the eyes, and those were sunken and terrible, slits of evil in the shriveled head. At one time, an age ago, those eyes might have been cunning and wolflike, full of glory and the blaze of battle. The once aquiline nose was flattened and almost rotted away, now just a pit into which the face was slowly collapsing. Patches of yellow hair clung to the misshapen scalp, and when the thing opened its mouth to scream against its own image, the broken, ragged-edged teeth glittered in the light.

The thing lifted up its arms and struck the glass. A

crack zigzagged across the mirror, slicing the vision of the corpse's face into two disjointed parts. It struck again and again, the breath coming harshly through twisted lips; and the mirror began to fall to pieces. When all the glass had broken and the frame was empty, the thing let out a hoarse roar of torment and rage, the scream rising up and up and ending in an empty, choked sob.

The others, feeding on the woman's naked body, heard but did not pause in their feast. Currents of blood shifted around them like ebbing tides, staining the tattered remnants of their brown uniforms.

On the front porch of the Indigo Inn, David Moore sat sipping a drink and watched a light far out at sea. A cigarette burned in an ashtray beside his chair; there was a half-empty bottle of rum at his feet. The light came off a freighter, traveling toward the port of a larger island. The sight of it stirred his wanderlust, made him think of distant shores, of people he had known and left behind.

His time in Baltimore seemed like someone else's life now. He had been a different David Moore then, a man naïve and unaware in so many, many ways. If there was such a thing as fate, it had moved swiftly in his case, sweeping him along on a path from which he could never hope to find his way back. Nothing could ever alter his own personal tragedy; the scar would always remain, deep and ragged, on his soul. Since the deaths of his wife and son he had determined not to fall in love again, and though he had fallen in love with places and experiences he could never really get close to people again. It was too dangerous. He had been attracted to other women, yes; he had sought sexual encounters just as the women he spent nights with did, but he found it difficult to express his emotions anymore. He knew he drank too much because he was afraid of both life and death; rather, he was suspended between them, his senses still indulging in the multitudinous experiences his travels had offered him, while his deep-seated emotions were numbed and frozen. He was now just the shell of a man who had once run his hands through Beth's hair and felt the power spark between them like currents of electricity. And yet, in all this time he had only felt himself grow closer to her. Sometimes, locked in a dream, he knew he only had to reach out a few inches and touch her supple naked body, draw her closer to him and hold her so tightly she would never be taken from him again.

And thinking of Brian, his son, was just as difficult: What sort of man would he have become? What would it have been like to watch the boy grow up, go to college? God forbid that he would have taken a position at his grandfather's bank and been stifled just as David had been. No, that was too easy. Perhaps the boy would have been intrigued by the ocean, and would have chosen a life that would have fulfilled him—in ocean engineering, or oceanography, say. Those were fields David might have picked, had not the family decided on his direction in life. He would have made certain that Brian knew there was an entire world of choices; he would have made certain the boy knew his life was his own.

Now, when the rum had him and the sea was crashing across the reef, when he sat alone with the night, he couldn't keep the images at bay very long: he and the boy playing touch-football in a wide, grassy park under fleecy clouds, Beth's hand reaching for his under a long waxed table during a Thanksgiving dinner at the elder Moore's estate, the flashing blare of a carnival merry-go-round, and their lips meeting as Brian, on a red-mouthed palamino, clapped his hands and grinned.

And after it had happened, after the day of storm and terror, after the doctors had diagnosed his listlessness, insomnia, and, later, fits of rage as "survivor's syndrome," his father had confronted him in the sitting room of the family home; the old man's icy eyes had stared at him through a flat haze of blue Cuban cigar smoke. He had not looked at his father, instead remaining intent on the flames that burned within a huge marble hearth.

"If you're in trouble with the police again, David," the old man said finally, his voice a harsh rasp, "I'm not going to help you. I want you to understand that here and now. Your barroom brawls and destruction of public property have gone far enough."

The younger man sat in silence; a log shifted, then burst into flame.

"Well? Have you nothing to say to me?"

Moore slowly turned his head; their eyes met, ice against ice, and locked. "I didn't ask you to help me last time," he said quietly.

"By God, someone had to!" The old man waved his cigar, knocking off ashes onto the Oriental carpet. "What was I to do, leave you in jail for the rest of the night, let some goddamned reporter find you in there drunk and do a story about how Horton Moore's son went wild and shot out every damned traffic light for eight city blocks? Jesus! That would be exactly what my investors would like to see!"

"Fuck your investors," Moore said, in a whisper, too low for his father to hear.

"And you'd be in jail right this minute if I didn't have a lot of friends at City Hall!" the old man continued, his eyes blazing. "My God, boy, what's to become of you? There are no black sheep in the Moore family; I want you to know that! And I won't sit here and watch you become one, not while I have breath left in me, I won't!"

Moore nodded but said nothing; he heard the fire burning and to him it sounded like the noise of the sea over rocks.

"I don't know, I don't know," his father muttered, spewing out a stream of smoke that curled toward the painting above the mantel. The man in the portrait had another pair of accusing, solemn eyes: those of Moore's grandfather. "Maybe because you were my only child, maybe that's why I've been so lenient with you. Maybe I've loved you too much, I don't know. . . . I thank God your mother isn't alive to see what you've become!"

Moore faced his father at last, and the look he gave him was so fierce the old man was silent. "And what *have* I become? You've tried to make something of me that I never wanted to be; nothing bores me more than the thought of that office, those confining walls, the dead rustle of papers. I was a born executive, isn't that what you told your associates? An executive in the Moore mold? No. I'm not going back there again."

"Then what will you do, you idiot? Goddamn it, that's what you've been educated to do! There's nothing else for you! My God, I know you've been through a bad time, but you're behaving like a lunatic! They've been gone six months, David! They're not coming back, and there's nothing else now except putting your nose back to the grindstone and doing what you're supposed to do!"

"No," he said. "I can't."

"I see," the old man said, nodding; he took the cigar from his mouth and his smile was cool, sarcastic. "You can't or you won't?"

"Both."

"Then if you won't pull yourself together like a man," he said, leaning forward slightly, "you're no son of mine. I've been wrong about you. I can see that now."

"Maybe." David Moore stood up; their conversation was coming to an end, as it usually did, like the weakened last blows of weary gladiators. "I'll tell you what I am going to do, and it's something I've been thinking over for a long time. I'm going to travel; I don't care where to. I'm going to keep on moving until I've seen what I want to see, and maybe until I find a place I can belong to again. There's nothing for me here anymore."

"Of course. You're going to run. From me, from yourself. Well, go on and run! I don't care! Where do you think you'll run to? What are you looking for, another girl like her . . . ?" He stopped suddenly; the last word had come out as a half-snarl. His son turned on him, and the heat of his rage made the old man lean back. He closed his mouth, not too obviously because he didn't want David to think he was frightened.

Moore controlled himself and then said, "When I was a child and knew no better," he said, "you told me how much alike we were. I'm a man now, and I see all the differences."

"Then go on," the old man told him. *"Run."*

Moore looked once into his father's face to find the man that was truly there; his father quickly averted his eyes. "I'd better go now," he said finally.

"I'm not holding you here."

"No. Not any longer. I'm sorry; I didn't want to tell you my decision in anger."

"What does it matter? You've told me."

There was an awkward silence; Moore stepped forward, lifted his hand toward his father and extended it. "Good-bye," he said.

"You'll be back," the old man said, ignoring his hand.

And it was then that David Moore had walked away from that life. He worked his way from country to country, living close to the earth or on a boat at sea, not knowing what drew him on but knowing he had to take that next step, and the next, and the next. He began to have the old nightmares again, the whirling scene of wind and wild ocean and *Destiny's Child* breaking into bits beneath him. He began to hear Beth's voice calling to him over a great distance, fading in and out; sometimes even close to his ear, the whisper of his name and then silence. It disturbed him, but he began to listen for it. At times he doubted his sanity, but sometimes he was certain she stood beside him, trying to reach him, separated only by the barrier between life and death.

In a dark clapboard house in Singapore a woman with blackened teeth and the smile of a cat stared at him over a plate of yellowed bones. She reached down and picked them up in her hands, rolled them around and then dropped them back. They were ordinary chicken's bones, but the woman seemed to see something strange and important in them.

A group of sailors from Moore's freighter had gone with him to see the fortune-teller, and they stood in the shadows that fringed the room. "He's going to inherit a fortune, is that it?" one of them asked jokingly, and the others laughed. "Fortune, hell," said another. "He's just going to be lucky enough to get out of this port without a colossal case of the drips."

"Someone waits for you," the woman said in a high-pitched whine. The men laughed again; crude remarks were flung back and forth. Moore watched the woman's eyes and believed her. "No. Two people," she said; she lifted the bones again, rolled them, let them fall.

"What the hell are we doing here?" one of the sailors asked.

The woman looked into Moore's face. "There is a great distance to be traveled yet," she said, wet lips glistening. "I can't see where they are. But they will not leave until you find them."

"Who are they?" Moore asked, and as soon as he spoke the men were quiet.

"A woman. Tall. Very beautiful. A man. No. A boy child. They are very confused, and they don't understand why you can't hear."

"I . . ." Moore began, but then stopped himself. "Is there anything else?"

She rolled the bones, dropped them, and probed as if looking for a particular one. Then she shook her head. "No. Fate reserves the rest." She held out her hand for her money. "Anyone else?" she asked.

The freighter's lights had vanished; the horizon was

black again and above it hung the separate, fiery dots of stars. Moore crushed out his cigarette. It was hard not to believe, but it was equally hard *to* believe. He wanted to believe, though; he desperately needed to, perhaps because of his persistent, unnerving feeling about Coquina. That it was the end of his journey. And the questions still to be answered, the ones that had plagued him day and night and sometimes made him cry out because he couldn't understand. Why had he not died with Beth and Brian? Why had he been saved? Why had he been sent on a path that led . . . here? To Coquina? To find what? *Fate reserves the rest,* the old woman had told him.

"Do you mind if I join you?"

Moore turned his head, his reflexes slowed by the effects of the rum. Jana was standing behind him on the porch, wearing a tight white blouse and jeans. He had no idea how long she'd been there. "Sure," he said, and motioned toward another chair beside him.

She sat down and put her legs up on the porch railing. Her hair was exactly as he'd imagined it: she wore it loose and it touched her shoulders, softly blond and very attractive. "It's quiet," she said after a moment of silence.

"Yes, the bars closed early tonight. Usually there's a lot of noise on a Saturday." He glanced over at her, his eyes tracing the fine line of her profile. "Is your room all right?"

"It's fine, thanks." She sensed that he wanted to be alone, but she wasn't about to leave him. "It's a shame you don't have more visitors. I think your island has a lot of potential."

He grunted. "For what? Another tourist haven, where they destroy the jungle for a Hilton and a shopping center? It would mean more money coming into Coquina, but there are only a few natural places like this left in the Caribbean. That's why I bought the hotel and decided to stay on for a while. I wouldn't have it any other way."

"Are you against progress?"

"Progress, no. Spoilage, yes. A few years ago some businessmen had a plan to build a hotel and marina over on the island's north point. They dredged out a harbor and started blasting the jungle away with dynamite. They never finished it, and they ruined a perfectly good natural cove."

"What made them stop?"

Moore shrugged. "Money, I suppose. And problems with the Carib Indians, who kicked their night watchmen around and stole their supplies; those people claim that part of Coquina, and they guard it jealously. But I'm glad they didn't finish. You can keep your Jamaicas and Haitis; Coquina's better off being left alone."

There was a pause, and then Jana said, "I didn't know I'd touched a nerve."

Moore glanced over at her; he hadn't meant to come across that strongly, and he knew it was partly the rum talking. "I'm sorry," he apologized. "I suppose it's only a matter of time before the tourists move in, but I'm attached to this place. I don't want it to change."

"I can understand your feelings."

"Well," he said, dismissing the subject with a wave of his hand, "enough about Coquina. I'm forgetting my manners. Would you like a drink?"

Jana shook her head. "I don't drink, but thank you all the same."

Moore sipped from his glass, listening for a moment

to the sound of the ocean rolling across Kiss Bottom. The waves were harsher than usual, and that could mean a storm was building somewhere, chopping up the sea. "How long have you been with the Foundation?" he asked her finally.

"A little over a year," she said. "I worked in research for the British Museum after I finished school, and I had the opportunity to dive with Cousteau on the *Britannic*. That was mostly luck, but it helped me win a position in Kingston."

"What exactly does the Foundation do?"

She smiled faintly and nodded toward the open sea. "That's my laboratory. Out there are perhaps thousands of sunken wrecks. Some are charted, some aren't; more are being discovered all the time. We document and study the ones that haven't been identified. There are perhaps more wrecks in the Caribbean than any one place on earth, so that's why I tried my damnedest to get the position. Pirate's galleons, men-o'-war, sailing merchants, steamers, warships; the bottom's a marine archaeologist's paradise. What we're doing is just as much for shipping safety as for the sake of history."

"You're very young to have come so far in your field."

Jana smiled openly; it was a warm smile, filled with a charm Moore had not seen until now. "I've heard that one before. Believe me, I worked my ass off to get where I am. It's never been easy—it still isn't—but I think the work is worth it."

"So what are you planning about the submarine?"

Jana's smile faded at once. She stood up and leaned against the railing, staring out into the night; when she turned back to him he could see the fierce determination in her eyes. "I'm not going to let that man sink it, if that's what you mean. He doesn't seem to realize how valuable it could be. To be perfectly honest, grants to the Foundation from Great Britain haven't been pouring in for some time; the British Museum seems to be losing interest in our work. Something like this could spark a fire throughout the entire scientific community! No. I'm not going to return to Kingston and tell them I had a risen U-boat in my grasp, in remarkable condition, and let it be sunk right under my nose!"

"Wait here a second," Moore said suddenly, standing up. "I want to show you something." He went to his study, found the scorpion paperweight, and brought it out to her. "Look at this," he said.

She stared at the glass object, holding it up to the dim porch light. Her expression was troubled and she seemed agitated. "Where did you find this?" she asked quietly, glancing at him and then back to the paperweight.

"Inside the boat; there was a cabin just forward of the control room."

Jana nodded. "The commander's quarters." She turned it, examining the letters. Moore saw the color suddenly drain from her face. "Korrin," she said.

"What?"

"It's the name here. Korrin. Wilhelm Korrin. Do you see?" Her eyes were bright with excitement.

"I suppose it could say that, yes."

"I know that name," she said with finality.

Moore took it from her, held it into the light.

"And now I know what boat that is," Jana said.

Sixteen

"WE WERE OVER two hundred miles off the mark!" Jana was saying. "It's incredible! If it weren't for this . . ." She held the paperweight up as she sat on the sofa in the hotel's front room. She was constantly turning it, studying the letters as if fearful they would somehow evaporate before her eyes.

"You've been talking for fifteen minutes," Moore called from the kitchen where he was making a pot of coffee, "and I haven't understood a thing you've said. Wait until I get in there."

"When's the earliest I can get a message off to Kingston?"

"Hard to say," Moore called back. "The relay operator sometimes works for an hour or so on Sundays, sometimes not at all."

"I've got to get a message off!"

"Settle down," he said, bringing in a tray with a coffeepot and two cups. He set it down on the table and poured some for her and then for himself. "If it's all that important we'll wake her at daylight." He sat beside her. "All right, I'm listening. Who's Wilhelm Korrin?"

"He was one of the few U-boat aces of World War II," Jana said. "There weren't many others: Prien, Schepke, Kretschmer—and Korrin's tonnage record equaled anything they sunk. Well, at the end of the war the others were all accounted for, either dead or in prison camps, but Korrin had vanished without a trace, and since the war he's been a puzzle to military historians.

"A few months ago a group of sport divers found a U-boat wreckage near Jamaica; there wasn't much left of the boat, but on checking our records we found it was unidentified. Korrin's last known command was in the Caribbean, so of course we assumed we'd found his U-boat. Now finding this paperweight makes all the difference. And it's even more vital to preserve the U-boat now; there'll be war diaries aboard, Korrin's personal log—who knows what else. It's a treasure trove for both the Foundation and military historians."

Moore grunted. "He was that important, was he?"

"Very," Jana said. "Korrin almost single-handedly blocked off the northeastern coast of the United States; on one particular tour of duty his U-boat crept inside a convoy to strike at three tankers. All of them went down, Korrin escaped, and that attack earned a Knight's Cross for him in Berlin, but he never returned to accept it. In the early part of 1942 his area of operations was the Caribbean; he was one of the first U-boat commanders patrolling the area, and he was given a free choice of targets. The unverified reports say his boat shelled the Trinidad oil refineries, slipped into Castries harbor to torpedo an anchored freighter, and sank the British cruiser *Hawklin* with a single concussion torpedo that snapped it amidships. The *Hawklin* survivors testified that the U-boat returned several hours later to fire on their lifeboats; if that incident had ever been proved, Korrin would have gone on trial for his life—if he'd ever returned to take his punishment, that is. Communications between the U-boats were kept at a minimum for the sake of security, and there was no way Korrin's movements could be tracked.

"Then he vanished. His boat's number—U-198—never reappeared on any of the German position logs. He was really quite something—a ruthless, highly intelligent man, a patriotic Nazi who asked for the most demanding missions. But for the last forty years he's been a mystery."

Moore was impressed. "You've been doing your homework."

"I did as much research as I could when I was diving that U-boat off Jamaica. That's primarily the reason I drew this assignment." She put the paperweight down and looked at him. "Now I'd like to know something. This afternoon you didn't even want me near the boat. Why was that?"

He put his cup on the table and paused for a moment, then said very quietly, "Something happened when Kip and I went in; something I can't understand or explain. It's dangerous . . . very dangerous."

"Tell me."

He took a deep breath, realizing Jana was going to

probe until she found it. "The bodies inside aren't skeletons; they've been mummified. It's not a pretty sight. . . ."

"I can handle it."

"No. It's more than that." He paused, feeling her gaze on him; he sipped at his coffee, wondering how to say it. "Something moved inside there," he said finally.

Jana started to laugh, but then she saw he was deadly serious and she stopped herself. "You mean it, don't you?"

"Yes." He let out a deep sigh and clenched his hands together. "I've gone over it in my head a hundred times. Kip says it was a hallucination, the effect of the fumes we breathed; but damn it, I know I saw something real there, in the boat's central passageway. And it looked like a man."

"A man? Perhaps someone else was hiding on board."

Moore shook his head quickly. "I mean it looked like one of the . . . things we found lying together in the control room. I know I sound like I'm losing my mind and maybe I am, but there's something terrible inside, and I'm not going into the boat again."

"Sometimes the imagination . . ." Jana began.

"NO!" Moore looked up at her, and his expression frightened her because she could see his own fear, working deep within him. "It was *not* something I imagined; it was real."

They sat in uneasy silence for a few moments. Jana put the paperweight aside, finished her coffee, and then stood up. "It's time for me to be turning in," she said. "I'm an early riser. I'm afraid I'll have to be depending on you for transportation around Coquina;

if it's too much trouble I suppose I could rent a bicycle down in the village."

"It's no trouble," he said quietly.

"Well, if you're sure. I'd like to make a quick check of my plane in the morning, and of course I'm going to have to talk to the constable."

"I don't think Kip's going to change his mind."

"We'll see. If I have to, I'll fly back to Kingston to get legal intervention." She stood over him for a moment and then she said, "Good night," and moved toward the stairway. When she had gone up a few steps she turned back to reassure him but then thought better of it and continued on to her room.

Moore sat on the sofa for a long time. And then he felt it—the sensation that very near to him was evil, an intense, burning hatred that at any moment could rise up and destroy the village. It was the same sensation he'd had while in the boat, and he was unable to shake it. Then he thought of the forty-five-caliber automatic he kept in a drawer in his room. He stood up and locked both the screen door and the wooden door, walked through the corridor into the kitchen, and bolted the rear door as well. Only when he was satisfied the hotel was secure did he snap off the lights and mount the stairway in the dark.

Thick, bilious clouds swept through the night, covering over the moon and the stars. A brief shower sent droplets spattering against windows and roofs, and rivulets of water crept along gutters. The sea flattened, pocked by the rain, and when the dawn came both sea and sky were plains of slate that merged at the horizon. Only a lighter patch of gray above the turbulent ocean indicated where the sun was hanging.

The wind that had forced the clouds in from the northeast had died away just before morning, and now a grim stillness and silence lay across Coquina.

Kip hadn't slept well. He had been awakened continually by imagined noises: something moving in the brush outside his window, a far-off crying of birds, the scratching of rats at the walls. He had gotten out of bed and read until dawn, trying to keep his attention on the printed pages, but his mind was too full to allow him to concentrate. He turned the pages automatically without really seeing what was there. And now, as gray light filled the small house and Myra cooked breakfast in the kitchen, Kip sat with his hands folded before him, motionless and lost in thought.

"We'll be ready to eat in a few minutes," Myra said, looking in on him. "Shall I wake Mindy?"

"No," Kip said. "Let her sleep a while longer."

The woman understood that her husband wanted to be alone, so she went back into the kitchen and began to get out the silverware.

For the past few days, he knew, he hadn't been as warm to her as he usually was. The enemy has reached us, he thought suddenly; they have found us through the barriers of both time and death, and they will not sleep until they destroy us. The U-boat was eating into him, obsessing his sleep, contaminating the very air he breathed. What kind of men, Kip wondered, had made such a death machine as that? Who drove the rivets, who hammered the iron plates, who strung the miles of wiring beneath the decks? Who packed explosives into the torpedoes, set the equipment into place in that hellish control room, torched the water-tight bulkheads into their frames? Every inch of the thing had been conceived and built for one purpose: destruction. In life it had prowled the currents seeking to carry out its purpose, and in death the thing's image seemed burned into his brain. *The enemy has reached us,* Kip thought, *and there is no escape.*

He ate his breakfast quickly, barely hearing what Myra was saying to him; she knew his way of working out problems was often to draw inside himself until he had found a solution. He helped her with the dishes, kissed her and the still-sleeping child, and then left the house for his morning rounds.

He wondered how he was going to handle the Thornton woman. She would never understand his reasoning; she couldn't see what he had seen or feel what he felt, and there was no use trying to talk to her. He would have to do what he felt was right, because he was the law and he was responsible for all of them.

And he was still pondering the problem when he saw a man running wildly toward him, almost tripping over himself. He waved his arms, calling out frantically; it was Andrew Cale, co-manager of the boatyard. The man was almost hysterical; his eyes were sunken, glassy hollows, and tears streamed down his face. There were marks on his bare arms where thorns had scratched him.

"KIP!" he cried out, his chest heaving. "Oh, mon, thank God I find you!" He grasped the constable's arm and pulled at him.

"What's wrong with you?" Kip asked. "What's happened?"

"My house . . ." he said, unable to catch his breath. "Oh God . . . my house . . ."

Kip's spine went rigid. "Get in," he said, and reached over to help the man.

"Me . . . and Mr. Langstree just got back . . . from Steele Cay . . . and my house . . . I can't go in there . . . I doan know . . . I doan know . . ." Cale whimpered.

Kip turned on the road that would take them to the man's home. He stopped the jeep next to the cinder-block steps leading to the door and Cale struggled out. "Come on, Kip!" he said breathlessly. "Please, mon!"

Kip stared at the house. The front door had been torn off its hinges and lay against the porch railing. Windows had been shattered, the pieces of glass speckling the yard. Floral-printed curtains still hung in the remnants of the frames. They had been shred-ded into strips. Cale grasped at him. "Please . . ."

As soon as Kip stepped across the threshold into the house he smelled it: the reek of blood and above that another smell. Rotting flesh.

Cale pushed ahead of him and started down the hallway. The man stopped and stood framed in a doorway staring at something. "NORA!" he called out suddenly, his voice trembling. But he did not move, even as Kip reached him and put a hand on his shoulder.

"There," Cale said, pointing a finger.

Kip's eyes followed his finger, and he froze in horror at what he saw.

On the floor, amid shattered wood and glass, was something that at one time had been a man.

Now bare, savaged bone glistened. The eyes were gone, as was the nose, and the teeth seemed oddly white and perfect in the remains of the head. On the torso, arms, and legs there were innumerable sickle-shaped wounds, where hunks of flesh had been ripped away right down to the bone. *Bites,* Kip thought suddenly. *Rat bites.* There was nothing left of the throat; it had been peeled and stripped away down to the spinal cord, all the veins brutally torn. The body lay in a clotted, wine-red ooze. Cale choked and turned away, staggering for the door but unable to keep from vomiting. Kip used all his strength to control the wave of nausea that surged inside him, but he felt dizzy and off-balance.

When the sickness had passed he forced himself to go into the bedroom. The window had been broken open; in one corner of the room there was a blood-matted sheet, and droplets spattered the mattress. Kip steeled himself, bent down, groped in the corpse's rear pocket and found a wallet. He opened it and looked for identification.

Johnny Majors. Jesus Christ in Heaven!

"WHERE'S MY WIFE?" Cale asked, wiping his mouth, his eyes swollen and heavy-lidded. "Where is she?"

"I . . . don't know," Kip said, surprised at the hollowness of his own voice. One of the man's hands lay beside the head; it had been gnawed or broken from the wrist, exposed bones licked clean.

"WHAT DID THIS?" Cale screamed suddenly. He backed away from Kip, his hands clawing at the corridor wall.

Kip bent to the floor, swatting at flies that whirled around the body. There were boot marks in the liquid pools. He caught the tremble of panic that welled within him. Covering the corpse with the sheet and struggling to control himself, he quickly made his way out of the house and supported himself against the hood of the jeep. Cale came out on the porch, his eyes glazed and lost. "Where's Nora?" Cale said hoarsely, in a voice barely audible. "What happened to her?"

But Kip hadn't heard. He was staring off into the jungle, not really knowing what he was seeing; at last his mind cleared and he was aware that vegetation had been crushed in a path that led away from the house. Approaching the jungle fringe, he saw the impression of a boot in the still-damp earth. Then three others. Cale called out again, "Where's my wife?" but then the constable was out of earshot, following the path of crushed thorns and snapped vines.

Every few feet there were drops of blood, and ahead the pathway turned through a grove of dead, rotting trees. He followed it for perhaps twenty minutes, knowing he was insane for going alone and without a weapon, but still, he was compelled to follow. And then, breaking through a high growth of thorns, he saw he had come to one of the old, decaying plantation great houses, a square slab of a structure over which dead trees hung in a tangle of shriveled branches. The roof had collapsed into the second floor, and black timbers protruded from the open sockets of windows. A second-floor balcony sagged, its supports fallen away, and vines crept along the gray, weather-battered wood.

And here the boot marks ended.

In the distance a bird shrieked sharply, then was silent. Kip looked around, found a branch he could use as a club if necessary, and walked toward the concrete stairs leading up to the massive doorway.

There were more droplets of dried blood; Kip stopped just in front of the door, listening, but he heard nothing. He tightened his grip around the club and kicked the door open; it swung out, ripping off its hinges and falling to the bare floor with a loud, echoing crash. Kip stepped into the cold dampness of the room, his skin crawling as he saw the puddles of blood and a bloody smear where something—the woman's body?—had been dragged. He stood in a huge, high-ceilinged room with corridors branching off on all sides; a wide stairway with a broken banister reached the second floor before plummeting into darkness. Kip could see the tree limbs through the holes above.

He moved slowly along one of the halls, the club held up before him, his free hand feeling the way. A few feet farther and something streaked across his hand: a lizard scrambling for the safety of a hole. He pulled his arm back, stifling a cry, and waited until his pulse had calmed down before going on. He heard the lizard racing along the corridor. At his feet there were more droplets and smears of blood, leading him into another room. *Get out of this place,* he told himself. *Get a gun, bring back more men to help, but get out of here before it's too late!* But then the next step brought him into the room, and the terrible stench of rot choked him. Timbers had fallen in from the ceiling, littering the floor; there were square windows, devoid of glass, from ceiling to floor, and through them streamed thick columns of gray light.

A body lay on its back in a corner.

Kip moved forward, slowly, his eyes widening and his teeth gritted against the stench.

It was not the corpse of Nora Cale. It was a skeleton from which almost all trace of flesh had fallen away; it wore the tatters of a uniform—brown, matted with grime and fungus like the cloth Turk had clutched in his death-grip—and its arms were outstretched as if seeking either death or mercy . . . or perhaps both. Kip stared down into the empty eye sockets, feeling his practical, trained resolve seep away.

It was madness, he thought; the real world was a place of boundaries, of blue sea and sky, green jungle, clapboard and stucco buildings, flesh-and-blood people. There was no Damballah, nor Baron Samedi, nor jumbies that haunted the village. But what was this, then, this skeleton in the remnants of a Nazi uniform? His soul cringed away from the things that lurked beyond the edge of the fire; all his life he had tried to reach a balance, to make reality his base and core. But that central part of him, hidden from all others and often even from himself, *did* believe. It had faith in the same superstitions, the power of voodoo, the evil things that sucked life from night sleepers, that moved through graveyards carrying cold steel scythes, that stood in shadows and regarded the world of light through hooded eyes.

And now here this dead thing lay, miles from the risen U-boat; time had finally caught up with it, collapsing its bones and flesh with a touch of sea air. Kip backed away from it; he had seen more blood on a windowsill and he knew the things had taken whatever was left of the woman with them. NO! NO IT CANNOT BE! *Yes,* the voice whispered, the voice of his "uncle," his teacher, *yes, it is true remember the forces of a man live on after death after death after death after death. . . .*

These things that he had feared all his life, that he had buried at the back of his mind, were real.

And suddenly the brick wall he had built inside him so long ago broke open, a cracking of mortar grown weak and useless, and the howling dark forms swept over him.

Seventeen

THEY DID NOT LIKE the foreigner. If he had approached any of them, if he had sat in on any of their card games, or taken a shot of rum or even talked to them, perhaps their feelings might have been different. But he had locked himself away in his below-decks cabin, not speaking to anyone, even paying extra to have a steward bring his meals to him. The black, hard-eyed seamen didn't like that; he would only be on board for a three-day trip, but they didn't trust whites anyway, and this foreigner was very strange.

The man seemed to dislike the sun; his flesh was a pasty white, his hair dull, tinged with yellow and combed straight back in an old style. He had never come up on the freighter's deck during the day, but there were stories circulating that he'd been seen walking the forward deck in the dead of night, standing at the bow as if trying to sight something off in the distance. And he had spoken to the galley steward in a strange accent: not British or American, but something else. When the freighter tied up at the commercial wharf in Coquina harbor, the seamen were glad to be rid of him. The captain had told the first mate and talk had trickled down through the men that he would not be returning to Kingston with them.

As the seamen worked their lines, the foreigner emerged through a hatchway onto the deck; he squinted, though the sun was dim in the gray sky, and walked past the men toward the port side where the gangplank would be lowered. He carried a battered brown suitcase and wore a suit, once-white, that had yellowed with age. The men moved out of his way so he could pass. He walked slowly, stepping over lines and cables, and he winced occasionally because today his leg was bothering him; he thought it must be the humidity and the heat, perhaps even rain coming. One could often judge the weather from the pain of shattered bone.

He waited until the gangplank was secured and squinted again, the light almost painful to him. When he crossed over onto the wharf, one of the seamen behind him muttered, "Damn good riddance . . ."

The man walked along the wharf for a moment, limping slightly, then stopped to gaze across the village ahead. A small boy lugging a basket of bananas was passing, and the man asked him, "Please. Is there a hotel here?"

The boy looked up at the stranger, turned, and pointed at the blue house on the hill. "Indigo Inn," he said, then quickly moved on.

"Danke," the foreigner replied. He gripped his suitcase and began to walk toward the street beyond.

The jukebox began to throb in the Landfall Tavern as coins tinkled down through metal cylinders. Its treble range had deteriorated, so all that came through the speakers was the bass guitar and the low thud-thudding of drums. The bartender, annoyed because he'd expected this to be an easy day, drew mugs of beer and poured rum for the group of seamen who'd come in off the freighter to quench their thirsts.

At a back table, sitting alone, the foreigner sipped from a mug of beer; the corner was dark, and he was glad because he was not eager to have the men notice him there. Before him on the table was a tattered piece of the *Daily Gleaner* dated four days earlier, which he had bought in Jamaica. When he saw the item on the third page he'd had to sit down in his room at the boarding house and read it again very carefully. Then again. He'd made a telephone call to the paper and was referred to an officer at the police station by the name of Cyril McKay. "Yes," the officer had told him, "it's under investigation now, yes, a small island called Coquina to the southwest of Jamaica. Do you have any particular interest?"

"No," he'd said. "Only curiosity. I was a naval man, you see."

And now he'd reached the island. He'd wanted to get out of the sun before starting that long walk up the hill. He looked down again at the two-paragraph item, staring at the headline: WRECKAGE DISCOVERED.

So strange, so strange, he mused, how one's past never really releases its hold; it always remains—in a phrase, a remembered sight, sound, or smell—a sharp, aching feeling one might have watching the freighters cast off their lines and head for the open sea. He felt swallowed up by those two words. *Wreckage Discovered.* After all those years? Thirty-five, thirty-six? He had just turned sixty. More like forty years. Enough time for him to grow older and grayer, for the muscles that had been firm and tight to turn to flab, for his long-unused sea instincts to become dull.

And though he was barely sixty he looked older. That was because of his time spent in the prison, suffering humiliations and beatings from a patriot of a jailer who had spent his fury through his fists, then had calmly sat down outside his cell to discuss the hopelessness of the Nazi cause. The man knew how to beat his prisoners where the bruises didn't show, and they were told that if they cried out they might be smothered in their sleep. The medical records would record them as having died of heart attacks.

He had never said a word. When they took him to the black room and opened up a hole in the roof for the hot tropical sun to burn down on him he had kept his lips a tight, grim line. *Who was your commander?* the one who spoke German had asked, while the other, a younger man, had watched. *You're the only one who survived; there's no use in being loyal to them anymore. They're dead, food for the fishes. They wouldn't have been so cruel to you! There are women and children back in the Fatherland who want to know what's become of their loved ones! Whose names are they going to have chiseled on the gravestones? Your boat destroyed the* Hawklin, *isn't that right? And then it got into Castries harbor and torpedoed a freighter moored there, isn't that right?*

Sweat had streamed down his face; the sun had cooked him, searing his flesh through that ceiling hole, but he had not spoken because he was still one of them, still under orders, and he would never betray them as long as he lived.

"Refill?" someone asked.

He looked up; the bartender stood over him. "Excuse me?"

"Another beer?"

"No." The bartender nodded, moved away. The German glanced around the room at the freighter's crew. They hadn't liked him, he knew; they had scorned him, as if his pale flesh carried a disease they were afraid of catching. But the freighter was the quickest way to get here and though the cabin he'd shared with a dozen cockroaches had been cramped he hadn't paid very much for it. He had been on a lower deck, and at night he could hear the racket of the huge diesels coming through the bulkheads. It was a good sound, a sound that reminded him of good men and other times and places.

Someone nudged him roughly on the shoulder and he turned his head. Who was it, grinning from the dark with teeth as large as tombstones? Yes, yes. VonStagel, with his bushy red beard that made him look like a wild Viking. And beside him in the smoky bar the morose, brooding Kreps. Everyone at their cluster of tables was drinking, laughing and shouting; the sounds came from everywhere at once, glasses clinking, someone cursing drunkenly, others singing a bawdy mariner's song about the ladies left behind.

"Hear, hear!" shouted Bruno, the big-shouldered diesel mechanic. "Bring on the dancing girls!"

A roar of laughter, plates clattering, chairs scraping the floor. The waiter placed a pink mound of pork on a bed of potatoes and sauerkraut before him. He dug into it hungrily, for tomorrow it would be rations—moist eggs, lukewarm coffee, stale bread, and sausages that would rapidly collect fungus from the dank air.

". . . and so what was I to think?" Hanlin, the

senior radioman, was asking VonStagel. "There was the petty officer—you remember Stindler, the pompous asshole—standing in the whorehouse balcony holding his prick out and parading so the good people of Berlin could see! My God! Well, anyway, the patrol wasn't long in coming, I can tell you, and they hauled him off in a wagon with his dick still hanging out of his pants! And to think we all thought of him as a saint! St. Stindler we called him on U-172. My God, how wrong could we have been?"

"And what happened to him?" VonStagel asked. "Did he get his piece or not?"

"Who knows about that? I only know he's not signed on the new boat. . . ."

Farther down the table, Lujax, the E-motor mate, and Bittner, the diesel stoker, were talking quietly, absorbed in their conversation. ". . . dangerous waters," Lujax was saying. ". . . Atlantic boiling . . ."

". . . it's all dangerous now," Bittner replied. "It's a question of strategies. Who's the smartest, not who's the strongest. . . ."

A large Nazi flag had been tacked tightly across one wall so there wasn't a single wrinkle. The chair just beneath it was vacant; the Commander was noticeably, perhaps pointedly, absent. The executive officers were talking, eating, drinking, but watching the door that led out into the street.

"Sonofabitching Tommies almost got Ernst's boat last week," Hanlin was saying between mouthfuls.

"I heard something about that," added Drexil, a fresh-faced, raw recruit sitting beside Hanlin. "It happened just off Iceland. . . ."

"Sonsofbitches came out of the sun," Hanlin continued. "Slammed bombs all around the boat, doused their tower pretty well, but they managed an emergency dive. . . ."

"Damned lucky," Kreps muttered.

Bruno was admiring the tavern girls; there were three of them carrying big trays laden with mugs of beer back and forth from bar to men, from bar to men. Two of them looked fine—blond girls, firm-fleshed and youthful—and he'd heard stories about the taller one from Rudy. The third was a snaggle-toothed monstrosity and not worth crossing the street for. Yet she was the most gregarious of the three, throwing herself down in the laps of the men and joining in their bawdy choruses. "The Paradise," Bruno said. "They've got women over there who dance on your tables!"

"Ahhhhhhh! You're horny as hell!" VonStagel chided.

"I admit it, then! The Paradise! We've got to go! You friggers think it's a joy breaking your back in an engine room for a tour of duty, you're mad! I want to fill my lungs with perfume before I have to smell the stench of oil and piss! The Paradise and then the Seamen's Club! We'll make the rounds tonight."

"I'm for it!" Drexil shouted.

"What the hell?" VonStagel looked around. "Schiller, what about you?"

And then there was a silence in the room as the door came open. A chill seemed to spread from the door into the Celestial Bar. The noises of eating and drinking died away; in the quiet the sailors could hear a tug chugging off in the harbor, and the distant wail of a foghorn. Boots clattered sharply on the hardwood floor.

Korrin had come in from the street; two other men

had accompanied him, but now they stood back as he swung his gaze around the bar, meeting the eyes of the crew one after one. "Heil Hitler!" he said sharply, clicking his heels together and raising his arm in the Nazi salute.

The men stood to attention. "Heil Hitler," they replied as one.

Beneath Korrin's U-boat officer's cap the reddish-blond hair was just taking on flecks of gray, and his face was hard, the eyes fierce and compelling, intensely dark and powerful. He was a tall man, well over six feet, and he was lean and athletic-looking. A slight scar slashed across his upper lip gave it the trace of a scornful curl, and his cheeks bore the jagged scars of fencing wounds. He wore black gloves; a dark brown, rain-dappled coat was draped over his shoulders. Schiller squirmed under his gaze; he felt like an insect being probed by a microscope lens.

"My name is Wilhelm Korrin," the commander said quietly, his voice softer than Schiller would have expected. "So!" He looked around the room again, the dark eyes narrowing, as cold as the touch of ice on each man's spine. "This is to be my crew." He turned his head toward one of the men who had come in with him. "Gert, they become younger with every new command . . . but they age quickly." The aide gave a brief, thin-lipped smile and the commander returned his attention to the seamen.

"You'll age," he said. "Some of you may be old men when we return. Some of you may die. Some of you may be heroes. But rest assured there will be no cowards." He held his gaze steady for a few seconds, and the man under his scrutiny nervously shifted his position.

"Some of you I know from other boats; some of you will be under my command for the first time. What I require is very simple: You will carry out your duties as seamen under the German flag, and you will obey my orders without question."

VonStagel lifted his beer, and the commander immediately sensed the movement; Korrin stared at him in silence, and VonStagel lowered the mug from his lips. "We are sailing in the finest weapon the German navy has ever built," Korrin continued. "And as long as you sail under my command each one of you will be a vital part of that weapon. You will breathe with the boat; you'll roll with her, you'll feel her vibrations down in the pit of your guts, and you'll know her like a lover."

Korrin rested his hands on the back of a chair, the fingers in those black gloves as long and delicate as a surgeon's. "I regret I won't be joining you for the evening, but I'm needed at Command. Enjoy yourselves tonight; do what you like with whom you like, but be warned. We leave harbor at first light, and any man unable to report must answer to me. Is that understood?" He reached down for a bottle of red wine, poured half a glass, and then held the goblet up. For an instant Schiller saw the commander's face through the glass: distorted, something barely human floating in a sea of blood. "A toast, gentlemen," Korrin said.

Glasses were hurriedly filled, lifted in silence. "To our good hunting," the commander proposed. He drank a bit of the wine and returned the goblet to the table; without looking at his crew again he rejoined the other two officers and they left the bar together, their boots clattering in the street.

224

There was a long silence in the room; someone muttered, and very slowly the activity resumed.

Bruno shook his head. "It's the Paradise for me," he said. "Now or never."

Wreckage Discovered. Those two words had been seared across Schiller's brain. Was it the wreckage of U-198? And if so, why wasn't it where it was supposed to be, down in the murky vault of the sea? He had been the only one to escape, that terrible night so long ago, and now the past had resurfaced, summoning him here to this forgotten place.

They were all dead, of course. All his friends and crewmates. He had been there at the end, watching the slow fall of the depth charges, seeing the ocean erupt again and again in geysers of white, roiling foam. But something still bound him to them, even after all these years; he was still part of them, still part of that weapon, U-198. Though he was older now, weaker, with failing eyesight and migraine headaches, living a life very different from the one he had once envisioned for himself, he was still a sailor in the German navy, and still a crewman of U-198.

And perhaps, he thought, if it was his boat he should be there to say a final good-bye to his companions.

He held up a hand for the bartender to see, and when the man approached he said, "Please. I'd like another beer. . . ."

Eighteen

KIP RAISED THE HAMMER, brought it sharply down on a nail; another blow and the nailhead was flush with the plank. He reached for a third piece of wood from a pile lying next to the shelter wall and carefully hammered it into place across the closed door. Kip pulled at the timber reinforcement, decided another was needed, and hammered until the door was sealed tight. He stepped back a few paces, wiping the moisture from his forehead.

He was soaked with sweat from his efforts and exhausted from carrying the planks across the boatyard. He stood where he was for a moment, staring at the blocked doorway. He needed a chain, a thick chain to pull across the door. And a padlock, something heavy and tough. *There must be a length of chain here somewhere,* he thought, *or else I could get one off a boat moored in the harbor. But the shelter must be sealed. It must be sealed so nothing . . . so none of them . . . can get out. Another timber,* he thought. *Nail another timber in place there at the bottom of the door.*

"Hey! What in God's name are you doin' there!"

Kip tensed, turned toward the voice. A heavyset black in denims and a bright-blue shirt was walking quickly and purposefully across the yard. The man was almost bald except for tufts of white hair on both sides of his head, and his eyes were wary, untrusting. He clenched a pipe between his teeth, and trailed gray whorls of smoke behind him. Kip stood where he was, the hammer still in his hand, and watched Kevin Langstree approach.

The boatyard owner stopped abruptly, his eyes moving from the hammer to the timbers and back again. "What do you think you're doin'?" he asked, not taking the pipe from his mouth.

Kip moved past him, laying the hammer down on the jeep's rear floorboard, beside the loaded rifle he'd brought along as a measure of safety. Langstree snorted in anger, stepped forward, and wrenched at the timbers.

"STOP THAT!" Kip yelled angrily.

Langstree whirled on him, teeth bared. "You lost your mind? Goddamn it, what goin' on here, mon?"

"I've sealed the shelter," Kip said evenly, "so no one can get in."

"And I know what you *got* in there, too! Oh, yeah, Cochran told me all about it this mornin'! I know you got that bastard boat in there! Now you listen to me! I own this yard . . . ain't nobody else own it but Kevin Langstree! What damn right you got to use my yard while I'm away?"

"I had to get the boat out of the harbor. . . ."

"I DON'T WANT TO HEAR THAT FUCKIN' STUFF!" Langstree yanked the pipe out of his mouth; he was trembling with rage, and Kip fully expected the man to strike him. "You got no right, no right at all!

227

Any other boat maybe okay . . . but NOT THAT ONE!" He motioned with a hand toward the shelter. "YOU KNOW WHAT THAT THING DONE TO ME? Do you? Blew my yard to bits forty years back, set it afire, and killed a score of my best men! Those men died bad—crushed by metal, burned to crisps, torn apart—and me standin' there in the middle of it, watchin' the hell come down on us! No, mon, I can't forget that! AND NOW THE GODDAMN THING BACK AGAIN! I don't know where from, or how, but by God I want it out of my yard!" He turned again toward the doorway and began to pull at the timbers. There was a crack as one of the nails came loose.

Kip grasped Langstree's shoulder; he said in a grim, forceful voice, "I told you not to do that."

There was heat burning behind Kip's eyes. The boatyard owner started to tell Kip to get away from him, but he thought better of it and took his hands from the timbers. "This is still my yard, by God . . ." he began.

"Your yard, yes," Kip said. "My island."

"I won't have you tellin' me what I can and can't do, mon, no matter if you the law here or not! I'm away a week and the whole place gone to hell . . . this god-damn boat in here, my supply shed broke open and God knows what all stolen, everybody scared and not wantin' to even come to their doors. . . ."

"What was stolen from your supply shed?" Kip asked him, a note of urgency in his voice.

Langstree paused, searching the other man's eyes. "Take a walk over there and you see, by God! The whole thing broke into, crates of oil, rope, timbers, barrels of fuckin' diesel fuel gone. I don't know what else—marine batteries, heavy-duty cable . . . "

"Maybe it was requisitioned while you were gone?"

"Hell, no! Ain't no way that much stuff be used in a week's time. We just got paintin' and patchin' jobs in the yard now. . . . That's heavy stuff been stolen, right out from under your damn eyes!"

Kip caught the man's collar. "Now you listen to me, Langstree," he said very quietly. "You do as I say and leave the shelter alone. We're towing the U-boat out in the morning and sinking it, but for now *just leave it alone!* DO YOU HEAR WHAT I'M SAYING?"

The other man nodded, frightened by Kip's intensity. He pulled free of the constable's grasp and stepped back a few paces. "You crazy, mon, you crazy as all hell!"

But Kip had already turned away. He climbed into his jeep and started the engine. Leaving Langstree standing there alone, he wheeled past the shelter and raced back for the village, anxious to get home and make sure his wife and daughter were safe. Kip felt infected by a strange madness, a fear that threatened to rise up and crush him. He had caught a glimpse of the truth today, and he realized how powerless he was to prevent what would happen. Oil, Langstree had said. Barrels of diesel fuel, ropes, cable. And batteries. *God, no.* He had seen the truth in Cale's mad stare, in the half-consumed corpse of Johnny Majors, in the remains of the Nazi U-boat sailor lying on a bare plank floor. And now, worst of all, in the theft of marine supplies from the unguarded shed.

In all the world there was one man who might be able to help.

Boniface.

* * *

Driving along the jungle road to the airstrip with the woman on the seat beside him, Moore could smell a storm in the air—a damp smell, full of heat, and the breezes had died completely. The entire sky was a gray, featureless canopy, the sun hidden, the clouds hanging motionless over Coquina. Jana had awakened more angry at Kip than she had been the day before, and he could still see her anger working in her face. She had hardly spoken to him this morning, just insisting she had to check her plane before sending her message to Kingston. Now, as Moore drove into the clearing, he saw the airplane ahead; it was still as they'd left it. But as he pulled up beside it he realized he was wrong.

"JESUS!" she cried out, leaping from the cab even before Moore had braked. She ran alongside the plane, and Moore followed.

"Goddamn it!" Jana raged, tears of anger springing up quickly and streaking her cheeks. She ran a hand along the jagged dents in the plane's fuselage. The canopy glass had been broken out; in the front were the smashed remains of the instrument panel; wires hung loose, and the seats were ripped. She shook her head in disbelief and rushed past Moore to the open engine cowling. Moore saw the confusion of torn wires, cables and plugs missing. Someone had completely wrecked the plane. Jana slammed the cowling shut and stepped back, trembling. "Vandalism!" she said. "Pure goddamned vandalism and in the meantime Mr. Kip is sitting his ass in the village! He thinks he's such a hotshot, telling people what they can and can't do, and meanwhile he can't even maintain law and order!"

"I don't understand it," Moore said. "There's no reason anyone would . . ."

"It'll take days to fix this engine," the young woman raged, "if I can even get parts out here! Somebody's going to pay for this mess!"

Moore motioned toward the farmhouse beyond the strip. "Maybe they heard or saw something during the night. Come on." He reached out to take her arm and she jerked away, then stalked along after him to the truck.

Silence hung like a storm cloud over the clapboard house. There was an empty pen, a shed, a square of tobacco plants. On the porch was a bicycle frame without tires, and to one side of the house the hulk of an old car. The trees clustered above like a painted green ceiling, and only a few yards away the jungle grew wild.

Moore and Jana climbed a couple of cinder-block steps to the porch. There was a screen door and beyond that the front door, which was wide open.

"Hello!" he called into the house. "Anyone home?" He waited, expecting a reply. He thought he heard an odd drone, like the buzzing of insects, but he wasn't sure.

Jana reached past him and knocked on the door. "Is anyone there, for God's sake?"

But Moore had located the insect noise; he moved to the far side of the porch and looked down. Then he stiffened and stepped back a pace.

Jana reached him. "What is it?"

A dog lay on the ground, where it had probably been trying to squeeze its way under the porch. The head was almost severed from the body, and circles of flies groped around the gaping wound. In the animal's midsection there was a second wound, exposing intestine. The hind legs had been torn away and the bones gnawed clean. "God . . ." Jana said quietly.

Moore shuddered and returned to the door. He opened it and stepped into the front room.

Chairs were overturned, tables shattered; glass had been broken from windows and lay glittering on the floor. "Watch your feet," Moore told Jana as she came in behind him. And then his heartbeat quickened. He felt a crawling sensation at the base of his spine, and he knew they were not alone.

Jana fought the urge to cry out, because suddenly the odor of blood had come to her, as strong as the taste of rusted metal in her mouth. She wanted to avert her eyes but couldn't, and she stared at the body huddled in the corner.

It was the corpse of a middle-aged black man; the face registered a look of shock and horror unlike any Moore had ever before imagined. The top of the head had been peeled back, a hideous mass of ravaged tissue remaining, and the throat was ripped open just as the dog's had been. His right arm had been snapped off at the elbow and the ulna and radius both shattered as if something had tried to get at the marrow. A trail of smeared blood led from the room, along a hallway and through another open door.

Moore moved forward cautiously, his heart hammering in his chest; Jana stood where she was for a few seconds, staring at the strange pattern the blood had made on a plastered wall, waiting for the surge of nausea to either flood over or pass. At last she took a breath of air with her teeth clenched, trying futilely to strain out the death smell.

The second room, the kitchen, had been wrecked as

well; it had no door, and only a few shattered windows. Utensils lay scattered about on the floor and there was a lot of blood but no more bodies. Looking at the scene of violence and murder, Moore felt a nameless, vaporish dread settle on him, as if something were whispering a message to him that he couldn't quite understand. He shuddered. What had happened here? His mind dismissed the question abruptly, for the sake of his own sanity.

Jana's eyes searched his face. "What in the name of God . . . ?" she whispered.

"I don't know," Moore said quickly. He grasped her arm, tightly. "Let's get out of here." He stepped away from the window.

And it was then that the shadow fell across them, a thing framed in the doorway, reeking of rot and blood, claws lunging for Moore's throat.

Moore flung Jana backward and she screamed in utter terror; the thing grasped him, nails sinking into his neck, its weight bearing down on him. It hissed and drew back decayed lips from its yellow fangs. Moore struck at the thing wildly, trying to force it back, but it had him in its grip now, and in the nightmarish eye sockets he saw the red, volcanic fury of hatred.

He crashed to the floor with an impact that almost knocked the breath from him; the thing, its once-human face a rotted horror streaked with fungus, struck Moore's head against the floor and then, mouth gaping, straddled his torso to rip his throat away. Moore pushed against the sunken chest, feeling bones and hardened intestine, but he was weakened by the blow to his head. The darkness spun past his face like black trails of mist. He saw the mouth opening,

opening, the points of teeth descending for the jugular vein.

Jana was on her knees immediately, crawling forward. She threw aside the kitchen utensils, desperate for the object she knew must be there, and then her hand closed around it: a large, sharp-bladed butcher knife. She saw the thing's teeth about to close on Moore's throat, and she had no time to think; she tensed herself and leaped forward, grasping at the horror's face with one hand and with the other driving the knife into its back, using all the power she could summon.

The body shuddered beneath her; pieces of flesh came away in her hand, and the stench of rot choked her. She screamed in fear and anger, pulling the knife out and driving it in again, out, in, out, in, feeling the body begin to tense. Somewhere, she knew, this walking corpse must feel pain. Her forearm ached with the force of her blows, and as she wrenched at the face she felt something—the remnants of a nose, a cheek, or a lip—tear away.

And with the next solid plunge of the knife the thing shrieked—a high, hoarse sound driving through its throat—and reared up, knocking the woman backward. She lost her grip on the knife and it remained planted in the thing's back, just below the left shoulder blade. Moore shook his head dazedly, crawled away, and watched as the nightmare collapsed to its knees, vainly trying to reach the knife; it shook its head from side to side, like a dying animal, its mouth opening but uttering no sound. It flopped on its belly and began to squirm and shudder as it crawled for the doorway, its breath quickening, the fetid smell filling the room. The thing lay full-length, one hand inching very slowly toward the door frame, trying to pull itself into the corridor. Then it expelled a long, terrible hiss and lay motionless, its arm still thrust out, fingers grasping at the frame, its body sprawled in a broken S-shape.

Jana heard herself screaming; she couldn't stop, even though the noise was frightening her, as if someone else were screaming at a distance, louder, louder, louder, more uncontrollably. *Is that me?* she heard herself say. *Is that me is that me is that me screaminggggggggggg* · · ·

"JANA!" Moore said harshly, shaking her. "JANA!" He wrenched her around and she abruptly stopped screaming; she looked at Moore as if she didn't know who he was or where they were or what had just happened. He put a hand to his throat, feeling the marks of the nails welling up on his flesh, and looked again at the corpse. Standing up, bracing himself against a wall, he moved toward it and then pulled the knife from its grip. There was no blood on the blade, no blood around the dead thing on the floor. It was totally dry, a thing without life fluids. He put the toe of a shoe under it, grasped the remnants of a shirt, and turned it over onto the back. That red fire he'd seen burning in the sockets was gone; all that remained was empty darkness. The skull grinned at him, its lips still pulled away from the teeth, a mockery of both life and death.

Staring into those hollow sockets, Moore realized the U-boat's legacy. They were condemned to a life-in-death, a torment of souls suspended in decaying flesh. Some unholy power had kept them alive, as living corpses in an iron coffin . . . and he had helped free them from the crypt.

Jana had to search to find her voice. "What . . . is it . . . ?" she whispered, unable to stop trembling. "My God . . . my God . . ."

Moore turned toward her and pulled her up from the floor. He led her out of the farmhouse, keeping his grip tight on the butcher knife because he knew there could be more of them lurking very near. They quickly crossed the porch to his truck, and he told her to get in and lock the door behind her.

As he climbed behind the wheel, Moore heard a crashing noise coming through the foliage perhaps twenty yards behind him; he twisted around, hearing Jana cry out, and saw the shadows approaching from the deeper jungle, the dark things plowing through the tangle of brush and vines. Moore turned the key in the ignition; the engine started, and he pressed his foot to the floor. The truck roared in response, its tires throwing up clumps of wet earth as Moore raced away up the road. In the side mirror, he saw them break through the jungle fringe, and then he was across the airstrip and heading back for Coquina village, his hands holding the wheel so tightly his knuckles were white as bone.

"WHAT WERE THEY?" Jana clutched at his sleeve, her eyes wild and confused; the fear had her now, and she was unable to think.

"They're alive," he said, his eyes darting left and right to pierce the green shadows on each side of the twisted road; the reality of what he was saying numbed him, and his temples were bathed in a cold sweat. "I saw them in the U-boat, and Kip saw them. I didn't believe . . . I didn't want to believe . . ." He touched the red marks at his throat. "I don't know why or how, but I know they're alive. . . ."

He reached the village, speeding along the deserted streets; he saw the jeep was gone from its space in front of Kip's office, but he hammered on the door repeatedly in the vain hope that Kip might be there. As he turned away from the door he looked up and saw the thick roil of clouds in the sky, dull gray, blinding white, traces of black far in the distance. He crossed the Square, finding the grocery locked and the blinds down over the windows; he reached the hardware store and knocked on the front door there, but the place was deserted. He looked down High Street from store to store; everything was locked up and quiet, the streets empty, a ghost town. A white circle of gulls swirled above Kiss Bottom, their screams coming to him on currents of wind; they swept down across the surface and then back again toward the sky. Moore watched them flying in formation out to sea, as if abandoning Coquina.

When he returned to the truck he couldn't look in Jana's eyes because of what he would see in them, and because he was afraid of what she might see in his. He started the engine, put the truck into gear, and drove on through the Square, climbing High Street.

And at the hotel he saw the front door was open.

He tensed involuntarily. Though he'd left the door unlocked, he remembered closing it that morning. Moore slid the butcher knife into his waistband, his nerves raw.

"Wait here," he said to Jana. "I'm going in first." He left her sitting in the truck and walked cautiously up onto the porch; with one hand he drew out the knife, and with the other pulled open the screen door.

He stepped across the threshold, his senses as aware as those of an animal; abruptly, he froze in place, trying to see into the dim room.

There was a man sitting in a chair; a suitcase sat on the floor beside him. He held the glass paperweight in his hands, his eyes focused on it as if he had found something that had been lost for a very long time. Moore let the screen door bang shut behind him, and the man hastily—and awkwardly—rose to his feet.

Nineteen

"FORGIVE ME," the stranger said in a thickly accented voice. "The door was open, and I came in to wait." He held up the paperweight. "Please . . . where did you get this?" The man dropped his gaze, saw the knife in Moore's hand. "I . . . meant no harm," he said very quietly.

"Who are you?" Moore asked.

"My name is Frederick Schiller. I was told I could find a room here, and when I walked up from the village I couldn't find anyone . . ."

Moore stood where he was for a moment trying to place the accent. Of course; it was German. He put the knife down on a table, still cautious.

"Where did you get this?" Schiller asked again, holding the paperweight as if it were a precious jewel.

Moore ignored his interest. "How did you get here?"

"By freighter from Jamaica." He paused for a few seconds, then reached inside his coat and brought out a cheap brown wallet. "I can pay," he said.

Moore waved the wallet aside. "I don't know what your business is on Coquina, Mr. Schiller, but it's a bad time for you to be here."

"Oh? Why is that?"

"There's a storm building. I can see it gathering in the sky, and the last hurricane we had almost tore this place apart."

"My business won't take very long," Schiller replied. "Now . . . please. This object . . . where did you find it?"

"Aboard a boat . . ."

Schiller closed his eyes.

". . . or to be more exact, what's left of one." The screen door opened behind Moore and Jana came through. She looked from Moore to Schiller and then back again. "Are you all right?" he asked her anxiously.

She nodded, running a hand across her forehead. "Yes . . . I'm just very tired. I can't . . . I can't think very coherently yet."

"Is the young lady ill?" Schiller asked.

"I think I'd better lie down for a while," she said to Moore.

He glanced over at the German. "The kitchen's at the back if you want a cup of coffee. I am going to take her upstairs." He was intrigued by the man now and wondered what his story was. He helped Jana up the stairway to her room at the end of the hall and threw back the covers of the bed for her. When he started to move away she reached up and grasped his forearm, her hair fanning out across the pillows. "I don't understand," she said, searching his face. "I don't understand what's happening here, and I'm afraid, and I don't know what to do. . . ."

He stood looking down at her for a moment and then smoothed the hair away from her forehead, gently, as he had done for another woman a long time ago. "Rest," he said. "Do you want a light on in here?"

"No," she said. She lay very still for a few seconds and then she put her hands to her face. "I saw it . . . I touched it . . . Dear God, I can still smell the rot of it on me. . . ."

Moore crossed the room, shutting the terrace doors. When he looked at her again her head was turned away from him, the blond hair almost silver in the pale light. He wondered if she would drift off to sleep; if she did, what would she dream of? The corpse with the mangled brains? The grinning face of a thing that should have been dead forty years ago? She shifted her position, her hands still at her face, and Moore heard her take a long, painful breath. He stood beside her a while longer, then left the door open as he went out.

He walked to his own room and checked the forty-five in the drawer. It was loaded with one clip, and there were two spare clips. He returned the gun to the drawer and went back downstairs.

The German sat holding the scorpion paperweight, a whorl of blue cigarette smoke around his head. When Moore came back into the room he put the object on a table beside his chair. Moore paid no attention to him, but poured himself a shot of rum and took a long swallow. With the afternoon sun hidden behind clouds, the light was a pale gray; though the room was dim and cobwebbed with shadows, he made no move to turn on a lamp.

"So," Moore began, finally turning to him. "What's your business?"

Schiller exhaled a stream of smoke. "The U-boat."

"I thought as much."

The German reached inside a shirt pocket and offered the newspaper clipping. Moore looked at it briefly. "That woman . . . Dr. Thornton . . . is a marine archaeologist here to take a look at the boat too. I don't know what interest you might have in the thing, but aside from the historic value it's a worthless hulk. I wish to God I'd never found the damned thing. . . ." His voice trailed off, and he took another drink from his glass.

"And you've been inside?"

"Yes."

Schiller sat back, sighed, pulled from his cigarette. "How much remains?" he asked in a strange, distant voice.

Moore examined him: white hair, sharp nose and chin, high cheekbones, weary, tormented eyes, deep lines across the forehead. Representative of a salvage firm, perhaps, sent from Jamaica to appraise the hulk as scrap iron? No. He was German, and that was too much of a coincidence. "Not enough for salvage," Moore said, testing him.

A thin smile crept across the man's face, then quickly faded. "Salvage? No. I don't care about salvage; I would think she's beyond that by now. It's incredible, you know. I thought by now the sea would have broken her into pieces, that there would be nothing left at all." He raised his eyes to meet Moore's. "It's true, then, just as the paper said." It was a statement, not a question.

Moore sat where he could see the man's face. "It's true."

The German raised the paperweight again; Moore

saw that his hand was trembling slightly. Schiller turned it in his grasp, running a finger along its smooth surface. "In 1942," he said, "I was a seaman in the German navy. I was aboard U-198 when she was attacked and sunk by British subchasers out beyond your island."

Moore leaned forward, his expression frozen.

"Yes," Schiller said. His gaze was hard; the eyes, like bits of glass, focused on a spot at Moore's forehead. "I was the only survivor. All the others . . . except one . . . went down with the boat, and that man who didn't was burned to death in a spillage of flaming oil. I called for him . . . I tried to find him but the sea was littered with bodies. The air stunk of smoke and crisped flesh. My boat was gone; it had dropped out from underneath me. Oh yes, I would have done the same had I been the commander. There wasn't time you see. And then I was left alone with the noise of shelling and alarms and screaming . . . " He caught himself; his eyes softened a fraction and he stabbed the cigarette out in an ashtray. "Forgive me," he said. "I didn't mean to go into that."

"No," Moore said, still stunned. "I understand. But how is it you came to be on Jamaica?"

Schiller absentmindedly wiped his lips with the back of his hand; it was a habit he had kept over the years. All the men who held bridge watch on U-boats had done it to varying degrees, wiping away salt crust as the sea spray thundered against the iron bulwark, again and again, a hundred thousand times a day. Another link with the dead, he realized, touching his mouth. "I live on Jamaica now," Schiller said. "I came back in the late fifties to teach history and the German language at the University of the West Indies at Mona. At least that's what I first told myself. I think perhaps I really returned to the Caribbean because of the boat."

Moore waited for him to continue, but when Schiller was silent he asked, "The boat? Why?"

"Because," Schiller said, with an effort, "as long as I shall live I will be a crewman . . . the last crewman of that boat." He felt along the sides of the paperweight again and then put it down. "I was never a loyal patriot to the Nazi cause, and perhaps I realized all along that Hitler was driving our country to utter ruin. But for a brief instant of history . . . a very brief instant . . . we were glorious, like a flame burning itself into oblivion. That I will never forget."

The room was still; there was a steady drone of insects outside, and the breeze sang through the screen door mesh in a soft whisper. "I don't believe you've told me your name," Schiller said.

"David Moore," the other man told him, putting the glass of rum down and getting to his feet. He switched on a lamp; in the sudden light the German looked more aged than he was. His eyes were filled with memories.

"I would very much like a drink," Schiller said. "Sometimes I need it, you know."

"Yes. Me too." Moore poured rum into another glass and gave it to the man.

Schiller took it gratefully, sipped at it, and then listened to the song of the insects. He stood up, went to the door, and stared out across the darkening harbor. "A beautiful island," he said after another moment. He did not turn back toward Moore. "You do know that my U-boat almost destroyed it?"

"Yes, I do."

"Do you . . . feel any bitterness?"

"Some would."

Schiller nodded. "An honest answer. This island lay within our patrol grid, you see, and we were ordered to shell the naval yards. We knew the British were repairing some of their ships there . . . and, well, it was war. . . ."

Moore sat down again, watching the man.

"I remember . . ." Schiller said quietly, "I stood on the bridge during the first shelling, and I counted the explosions on shore. I felt so distant and detached from what was happening. I knew we were destroying human beings, yes, but still . . . they were the enemy. On that particular night the subchasers didn't come, and the shelling seemed to go on for hours. Oh, there were shore batteries firing back, but we lay beyond their range, and we watched the flames grow against the night like wild red flowers on a field of black velvet. The commander observed through his binoculars, and after he ordered cease fire, when the echoes of the deck gun had finally all died away, we could hear the screaming. . . ." Schiller was quiet for a long time; Moore stared at him. "When the commander was satisfied, we continued our patrol."

"And you never felt remorse over something like that?" Moore asked.

Schiller turned toward him, his brow furrowed, as if pondering a question he couldn't fully understand. "It was my duty," he said. "But be assured I paid for it, yes, and many times again. We returned to the area some days later; the commander suspected work had been done to repair the yards, and he wished to shell them again, before the work could be completed. Some distance from your island the watch sighted a ship, moving slowly just ahead; we submerged and tracked it for some time. It was a freighter. We attacked with torpedoes, but the warships lying in your harbor were alerted by the flares and caught us from behind. I was on deck at the time, along with the man I've already mentioned. We were swept off in the crash dive. . . ." He paused, staring out toward the sea.

"What happened to the boat?"

"I don't know," the German whispered. "Or rather I should say, I'm not certain." He drank from his glass. "The subchasers circled the area in which the boat had gone down, and they began to release their charges. Their Asdic and sensor devices had targeted my boat and they hammered at it, hour after hour. All this I was forced to observe from the deck of one of the British ships after I'd been hauled into a dinghy. The sea boiled like a volcanic crater, vomiting up sand and coral and fish blown to pieces. I thought about the men inside the U-boat, hoping to find safety beneath tons of water.

"A depth-charge attack is a savage thing, Mr. Moore. You hear the iron bend under the detonations, and you pray to God it will not bend too much and that the rivets will stay sealed. A thread of water bursting through a pin-hole break can cut a man's head off at the greater depths, and a rivet can ricochet like a bullet, pass through flesh and bone and metal bulkheads. And the noise . . . the thundering shriek of underwater explosions, the squeal of an iron plate, the sound of the Asdic beams like handfuls of gravel tossed against the sides of the boat." He shuddered and looked away. "But *you* must not make a sound. You must hold back your fear and the screams that threaten to burst from your throat. Because if you scream the men with earphones at their stations perhaps three hundred feet above will hear you, and they will send more charges tumbling down to seek you out. It is a vicious game, a war of taut nerves, when water becomes the enemy instead of the protector and a single cry can seal your death warrant.

"For two days the British subchasers kept up their attack; they knew they had the boat trapped, and though there were long periods of silence the explosions always resumed. They dropped what seemed like a thousand depth charges, then waited for the sound of a cough, or a rattling bucket, or the hissing of breath through clenched teeth, or the shrill scream of imploding iron." His eyes were wild, and they unnerved Moore. "But the U-boat never surfaced. There was some oil, but nothing to indicate a direct hit. From what I could understand the British Asdic had lost the boat, as if it had suddenly vanished, but they were still certain it remained down there. Somewhere."

Moore remembered his dive vividly in that moment—the mountain of sand and coral, and the jagged remnants of what had once been an underwater ledge overhead. Perhaps the U-boat commander had tried to escape the enemy by *rising* along the Abyss wall, instead of sinking lower, and then had lodged the submarine beneath that ledge to hide from the sensors. And perhaps at the same instant a crewman had operated a lever that had delivered compressed air to the buoyancy tanks. The concussions had caused the ledge to collapse, burying the submarine under tons of sand. That would account for its disappearance. Then the men would have been imprisoned, waiting hour after hour for the air to give out, as the gases and the stench collected and suffocated them. When enough sand had shifted away from the hulk, aided by the hurricane and that final charge blast, the remaining compressed air had lifted the U-boat.

"In time," Schiller was saying quietly, "the subchasers gave up their hunt. I was questioned and put into prison where I remained until the war's end. I returned to Germany, to Berlin. I remember walking the streets to my parents' house. There was hardly anything left. A lone chimney, the front wall and door still standing like a facade. And across the door, in bright-red paint, someone had scrawled 'The Schiller Family Is Dead.'" He blinked, looking away from the other man. "They'd been killed in an air raid."

"I'm sorry."

"No, no. It was war, you see." He finished the rum and put the glass down. "Where is the boat now?"

"In the yard."

Schiller smiled grimly and nodded. "Strange, isn't it, how the fates work? Perhaps, after all this time, my boat has a destiny still."

"Destiny?" Moore was taken aback by his use of the word. "What do you mean?"

Schiller shrugged. "Where will the hulk go? Some maritime museum? Or even the British Museum itself? It's a possibility, I would think. So my boat is not yet dead after all, is it? Perhaps it will sit in a huge hall of warfare on a linoleum floor surrounded by great artillery pieces and even an old, battle-torn Panzer tank. Further down the exhibit there will be a shining Spitfire, or perhaps a reconditioned Junkers. It will be a place for old men to come and relive their days of glory as they slip toward senility; young people will come too, but they'll fail to understand any of it, and they'll laugh and point and wonder how any of this ancient junk could ever have been useful at all."

"Useful!" Moore snorted.

Schiller stared at him for a long time, then finally dropped his gaze. Yes, the man was probably right. Now it could only be a battered, rusted shade of what it once had been, filled with seawater and ghosts.

"In March of 1942," he said, in a voice so low Moore could barely hear him, "it was the most awesome weapon I had ever beheld. I saw it at night, after I'd been transferred from another boat, and the lights in Kiel harbor where it was moored burned a dim yellow to save power. The mist had come in from the sea, and it hung over the boat in thick gray strands; the diesels were in operation, their noise echoing across the water, making the pilings tremble under my feet. I watched the mist being drawn in through the diesel intakes along the superstructure. From where I stood the periscope towers seemed to vanish into the sky; there were men already at work on the decks, and through the open forward hatch a column of smoky white light filtered out. It was a magnificent sight, preparing for sea duty. I can never forget it, nor do I wish to. Yet . . . I suppose now the boat is nothing."

Moore sat there a moment longer, then walked across the room to refill his glass. Outside, the clouds were heavy in the early evening sky and lights were coming on in some of the village houses. The breeze had quieted, and through the screened door Moore saw a sudden flash on the distant horizon, perhaps heat lightning or a storm crawling across the earth's curve. He didn't want darkness to fall tonight. If only he could keep the light from fading, so he would be reassured of a measure of safety. His eyes scanned the jungle's dark folds. They were out there; he didn't know how many, but they were out there. Waiting.

"I didn't mean to go on about the boat," Schiller said. "It's ancient history. But, you see, that's all I have left."

"The crew," Moore said suddenly, turning to face the German. "Something's happened . . ." He stopped, and Schiller leaned forward slightly.

"What about them?"

Moore paused, wondering what to say. It was madness to think the man would believe him.

"You found their remains?" Schiller asked. "I'm prepared to help with the identification, as much as I can."

The silence stretched between them, Moore lost in thought and wishing the man sitting opposite had never seen that newspaper item, never come to Coquina. Finally, he motioned toward the kitchen. "If you're hungry I can throw some snapper in a skillet."

"Yes . . . *Danke*. That would be very good."

"Why don't you go on back there," Moore said, "and I'll check on Dr. Thornton." When the German had walked through the hallway Moore went upstairs and found that Jana was still sleeping. Before going to the kitchen he went outside, closing and latching all the shutters. He locked the screen door as the darkness rolled slowly across Coquina. Then he latched the front door, as if he could hold the night back with a single slab of wood.

Twenty

A THIN BEAM of light moved along a pile of empty battery crates; there was a sudden, frantic rustling and squeaking, and Lenny Cochran kicked at one of the crates. Instantly a small dark shape, then another, burst from the debris and scrambled toward the wharf pilings. He followed them with the light until they disappeared behind a skiff that had been overturned for keel patching. *Big damn rats everywhere,* he thought. He could hear others moving around the center of the crates. *Probably a nest of the buggers in there,* he told himself. *One good fire would sear their asses and clean 'em out.*

He turned away from the crates and continued on, moving his flashlight from side to side. The barnacle-scarred hull of a trawler tied up at the wharfs caught the reflections of the light in the water; he shone the flashlight the length of the boat, then turned away and walked up through the hard-packed sand, stopping every so often to examine other heaps of junk, clusters of barrels, pieces of engines laid out on the ground.

251

The tin-roofed supply shed was directly ahead; its doors had been hastily repaired and boarded over. He paused only a moment around the shed before moving toward the far side of the yard, where the sea lapped quietly against the sliding bulkhead of the abandoned naval shelter.

He'd tried to get some of the other men to act as night watchman for Mr. Langstree, but none of them would have any part of it. Mason and Percy had whined when he'd asked them; J.R. had flatly refused to do it, and so had the others. He couldn't force any of the men to do it, so the job had fallen to him. He felt guilty about having that boat put into Mr. Langstree's yard without proper permission anyway, and this was a way to ease his own conscience and get back into Mr. Langstree's good graces.

He knew exactly what bothered the others; it was the stories they heard, and Boniface's warning about staying away from the yard. He'd heard the whispers around the bars: Something bad was going on, something nobody wanted to talk about, and it had to do with the damned boat. The Night Boat, that's what they called it. It gave him the willies to think about what the two trawler captains had said. Jumbies, dead souls flying on the wind and coming down at you to go for your eyeballs and tear out your heart. . . .

He shivered. *Stop that kind of thinkin', mon!* he told himself severely. *That only gets a body in trouble!* He felt again for the old skeleton-gripped revolver he'd brought as protection. He'd only been able to find three shells at home but he figured one would be enough anyway, to scare off anybody who might come to steal more supplies. *Damn, but it's dark out here!* he thought. *No moon, no stars, the smell of a storm building up, mebbe one, two days away at most.*

And in another few moments he was at the door of the dark naval shelter.

He moved the light along it; whoever had nailed it up had done a hell of a job. Nobody was going to be breaking in there tonight. He looked along the wall, probed with the point of the light down toward the rotten pilings at the seaside and then, satisfied no one was lurking there, started to move quickly toward the other side of the yard.

And then stopped.

Flesh writhed along his spine and at the back of his neck. His heart was hammering in his chest and he swallowed, trying to shake off the fear. *What the hell was . . . ?* He turned, thrusting the flashlight forward as if it were a weapon.

He waited, not daring to breathe, listening for the noise that had sounded like . . . something . . . scratching. . . .

Something scratching behind that door.

Rats. Rats caught in there, seeking a way out.

And as he watched he saw the door slowly bulge outward, pushed by a tremendous force. Wood creaked and whined, then settled back on its frame. He couldn't move, his mouth opened in a silent scream, the door bulging outward, outward, the noise of nails giving way around timbers, the splitting of wood . . . *Jesus!* The light was shaking in his hand; he couldn't hold it still, and when he drew the gun he couldn't keep that steady either.

The door cried out eerily with the force of whatever was on the other side; with a noise like a pistol shot a split appeared in its center. A jagged gap grew down the weathered wood.

From the inside a gnarled, misshapen hand emerged, reaching down and snapping away one of the reinforcing timbers.

Cochran stepped back, unable to summon the strength to flee. He raised the gun and squeezed the trigger, hearing the sound of his own labored breathing loudly in his ears.

But the hammer fell dully upon one of the empty cylinders.

The door shattered in a ripping of wood and nails; a half-dozen claws probed through, tearing a way out. Cochran tried to lift the gun again, but it seemed too heavy and he knew he couldn't aim it and he had to get away from this place, get to the village, tell them yes the jumbies were real, the evil things had descended upon Coquina.

And it was then that one of the things that had come up through the darkness behind him leaped upon him, its teeth sinking through the back of his neck and crunching on the spinal cord. Another grasped his left arm and savagely twisted it, ripping it from its socket. A third clawed at the man's chest in frenzy, broke open the ribs, and tore the heart out like a dripping treasure.

The commander stood apart from the others. Wilhelm Korrin let them feast, then motioned with a shriveled arm for them to help free their comrades.

There was a faint glow in the sky, and Steven Kip was driving toward it.

He had left home in the early evening, leaving Myra with a loaded rifle and telling her to keep the doors and shutters locked. He'd gone down to his office to get the second rifle and a can of gasoline before patrolling the village. Now, driving along the harbor, he saw the light over the treetops in the distance, and he knew it was coming from near Boniface's church. *More voodoo?* he asked himself, as he raced through the empty streets. *Damn it to hell!* A large fire blazed in a circle that had been dug out and ringed with red and black painted stones in front of the church. Kip could see shards of timber, clothing, and what looked like shattered sections of the church pews piled in it. At the fire's base a heap of ashes glowed a bright red-orange, and the heat of it seared his face as he left his vehicle. He walked around the circle and hammered on the door. No answer. Kip knocked again with the strength of anger, the heat touching him like a hand with bright-red nails. The church windows, like watchful eyes, reflected the flames, and no lights showed through the shutter slats.

"BONIFACE!" Kip called out.

And then, very slowly, the door opened.

Boniface stood before him in a stained white shirt, bright beads of sweat, each one reflecting fire, glistening on his face. In his eyes the blaze seemed white-hot. "Get away from here!" he said sharply. He started to shut the door again, but Kip slammed his arm against it and forced his way in.

The church was filled with the red glow, alive with the frenzied slithering of shadows. Many of the seats had indeed been torn out as fuel for the flames, and there was an axe propped in a corner. On the altar were the pots and strange bottles Kip had seen at the jungle ceremony; three or four cheap metal crucifixes hung on the walls, and the floor around the altar was sprinkled with sawdust and ashes. Kip shook his head and stared at the old man; around Boniface's neck was the glass eye, its pupil a gleaming red circle.

Boniface reached forward and bolted the door, then turned to the constable. A drop of sweat ran down across his cheek and spattered onto the floor.

"What are you doing, old man?" Kip asked. "What's this fire for?"

"Get away!" Boniface repeated. "As quickly as you can!"

Kip ignored him and walked to the altar, examining the materials spread out there, liquids in bottles and dark things in black pots. All voodoo things, he remembered, used to communicate with the spirit world. One of the pots had been overturned, an oily-looking liquid spilled from it; a bottle had been thrown against a wall, leaving its remains in red smears on the paint.

"Get back to your home!" Boniface said. "Get back to your woman and child!"

"What's all this for?" he asked, motioning toward the objects. He was beginning to feel a coldness working its way into him, slowly and insidiously.

Boniface opened his mouth, paused, his eyes fearful and half-crazed. "To . . . keep them away . . ." he said, very quietly.

"Talk sense!" Kip said, fighting to hold back his anger.

"They . . . fear the fire. I've been trying to break it . . . it's too difficult now, and I'm old, and I'm weak . . . and I'm very tired. . . ."

"Break it? Break *what*, damn it?"

Boniface started to say something but the words never came. He seemed to shrivel up, even as Kip watched him, all the life leaving him at once until only a shell of flesh with weary, frightened eyes remained. He held out a hand to steady himself, leaning on a shattered pew; he sat down, put his face in his hands, and stayed that way for almost a minute. When he looked up his face was drawn and anxious, as if he'd heard something approaching. His eyes glittered wildly in the red light and came to rest on Kip's face. "Help me," he said in a whisper. "Can't you . . . help me?"

"Help you do what?"

"It's too late . . ." Boniface said, as if he were speaking to himself. "I never thought they would . . ."

"Listen to me." Kip walked over and stood next to the *houngan*. "Two more people are dead . . . probably others as well. I want to know what those things are, and I think you can tell me."

"The boat," Boniface whispered. "That beast from Hell. The Night Boat. No one can help now. They're free; I can feel it. They're free, all of them, and no man can turn them back until they've done what they must do."

Kip leaned over the pew, his gaze boring deep. "Tell me." The chill inside him made his bones ache.

Drawing a long breath, Boniface put a hand to his face. The gesture cast a huge shadow on the opposite wall. He nodded, as if giving himself up to something. "The Sect Rouge. Do you know it?"

"Only from hearsay," Kip said.

"The most powerful and secret society in all the islands. They use the dark things as their weapons; for power or a price they cause famine and pestilence, they commit murders cold-bloodedly and efficiently. I know. Because I was a member of the Haitian Sect

Rouge for five years, and in that time I created much that was evil. I learned the art of fashioning the waxen images of my enemies or those I was paid to assassinate, to slowly force nails one by one through the opening of the mouth, or draw a garotte tight around the throat. I learned the art of the *wanga*—poisons— and how to leave a trace of it on a marked man's pillow, or smeared along the rim of a glass, so that death came painfully and stretched into weeks. I conjured the evil *loa,* and conspired with them for the souls of my enemies. I have made a corpse scream for revenge; I have worked the sorcery that transfigures time and breaks the barriers between the living and the dead, and I have unleashed evil things onto this world.

"I left Haiti in 1937, after the murder of a rival *houngan* who was threatening to expose my Sect Rouge activities to the local police. To escape those who would avenge that man's death, I came here. Those were my days of youth . . . and strength. Now I cannot control it . . . I cannot, and I am very tired. . . ."

"What are those things from the U-boat?" Kip demanded.

The fear had pooled up in Boniface's eyes; now it brimmed over. "Think of it. What would be the most horrible means of execution? A death by inches, the body and brain starving for air, flesh writhing in total agony. The minutes stretching into hours, days, years; an eternity of torture. Flesh drying over bones, intestines hardening, brains and skulls shriveling, nerves screaming in unendurable pain. No air, no sun, no chance for escape; only the agony and the darkness, each a hideous partner to the other. But still Death delays its merciful touch; he will not free them until they have paid with their flesh. Their souls will be trapped within a rotting house, and even after their bodies have begun to fall to pieces there will be no peace. Not until the decay is complete, or until their black, evil hearts are pierced, or until they are burned into ashes." He lifted his gaze. "Half-human, living corpses, driven mad with pain and rage, hungering for the fluids of life in the vain hope their burning will be cooled. I know. Because I made them as they are . . ."

Kip stood motionless, feeling that chill creeping around him. Shadows flickered huge and monstrous across the walls, diminished, and leaped again.

"When I came to Coquina in 1937," Boniface said, "there was no constable, no officials of the law. This church was a dilapidated ruin; the Catholic priest had caught the fever and died some months before. So I set myself up as a minister; it was a logical way to gain some measure of power over the people, and to hide from my Haitian enemies. The priest hadn't understood their voodoo beliefs, and I found it easy to gain a following. The people looked to me for guidance, to act as both their *houngan* and their legal guardian; the law I enforced was stern, harsh perhaps, and I punished evil by the only means I knew: an eye for an eye.

"And then came that war. The British brought their men and their ships; they assigned a constable to look after the island. And though he was a good and fair man, like you, I was still Coquina's real law. I had the power, and with it the responsibility. When that damned iron monster came up from the depths, when it rained fire on the island and killed those I loved, I knew I must take a hand against it.

"I saw the bodies after they had been blown to

bloody bits; the sight haunted my nightmares. The dead reached from their graves, calling me, whispering in the still darkness, until I could take no more; I had the power, the spells taught me by the *zobop*, the master magicians, and that power was greater than any weapon on earth."

Boniface was silent for a moment, staring at his wrinkled hands. "I knew the monster would return; in a drug-induced vision, through the sweat and pain, I saw the Night Boat nearing Coquina, saw a burning freighter and death floating on the sea. That terrible thing was returning, and I knew I must await it.

"And on that night when the sky was filled with red streaks and flame, when the battle raged over the Abyss and we could see the ships circling their prey, I built a fire on the beach and began my work. I asked help from Damballah, to entrap the thing in the sea, and from Baron Samedi, to withhold his mercy. It was difficult . . . it took many hours, and I prayed that the thing would not escape before I was finished.

"In a trance I could see the boat hidden there in the Abyss, in the midst of black, churning currents; I saw the sand fall over it, crushing it under. They were trapped, they would never return to hurt my people again. They would starve for air, they would decay . . . but their deaths would be withheld. I could see through the sand and the iron, as if my eyes were everywhere, and I saw them there . . . huddled together, their air slowly giving out, their lungs heaving. In my mind I saw a black, gnarled hand reach out to touch them; they trembled, as if they had been touched by the Devil. A voice reached me—soft, of velvet and steel, whether male or female I did not know—whispering: *It has begun.* I don't know when I awoke from the trance, but I was sitting before a cold fire and all the British ships had gone. It had taken two days.

"Now those things exist on the border between life and death. But I can't hurry the process, Kip, and now they possess a power that I hadn't foreseen. *Hate*— because of their agony, because *we* are human and they . . . no longer are. To them we are still the enemy, and the year is still 1942. And so you understand now why I wanted you to sink it. . . ."

"No . . ." Kip whispered. He shook his head. "No!"

"I created them, and there is nothing any man can do."

"THERE HAS TO BE!" Kip said, his voice echoing throughout the church. "YOU MUST KNOW WHAT TO DO!"

"I've been trying, again and again, to quicken the process toward their death, but the spell is too strong, and I don't know what . . ."

Kip grasped the man's shirt and pulled him around. "YOU'VE GOT TO DO SOMETHING!" he said hoarsely. "For God's sake, you're the only one who can help us now!"

"I . . . can't," Boniface said wearily. "But you . . . you might do something. *Oui, oui,* you. Your uncle was one of the greatest *houngans* in all the islands!" Boniface gripped the constable's sleeve. "He taught you the art . . . you were his young apprentice . . . now you can help me . . . !"

"NO!" Kip shook his head. "I shut it out of my mind; I've forgotten everything that man tried to teach me!"

"But you must possess a power of your own," Boniface insisted, "or he would not have chosen you as his successor! It's inside you, if you allow it to come out, if you allow yourself to take control of it!"

Kip pulled away and stepped back. His mind was filled with conflicting emotions. He turned toward the altar, staring at the voodoo implements there, and in a sudden burst of rage he lunged at them, kicking away the bottles and pots.

"It's junk, all of it!" he said tersely. "It's goddamned junk!" He reached down for a bottle and smashed it against the far wall, splattering clear liquid; he kicked a pot that clattered away across the floor. Then he stood panting, furious, and listened to the sound of his own ragged breath. "It's madness," he said finally. "What do they . . . want with us?"

"We have their boat," the other man said. "And they want it back."

Kip looked over at him; the supplies missing from the yard—the oil, diesel fuel, cables, and rope. *My God, is it possible?* The timbers piled on the U-boat's deck, as if they were being used to shore up bulkheads below. He shuddered; he could imagine the things working within the U-boat, hour after hour, never resting nor stopping. No, no; their batteries would be long dead and corroded with salt. But then he remembered the marine batteries Langstree said had been stolen. If enough power could be coaxed from them, if the diesels could be brought up even to a fraction of power . . . The images ate at him. If the U-boat ever reached the sea lanes between Coquina and Jamaica . . .

"First they've tried to quench their thirsts for the fluids of life," Boniface said. "But they have failed, and now their fury will be uncontrollable. They will try to kill as many as they can."

"I saw one today—dead—in a house a mile or so from the village."

Boniface nodded. "The air is taking its toll on them, but very slowly. Too slowly to save us." He stared at the constable, his expression clouded and distant.

"I will not last this night," he whispered. "I close my eyes—like this—and I see the moment of my death fast approaching. It is taking shape now, grasping for me . . ." He turned his head and peered through the shutter slats. Then he garnered his strength again. "The fire is dying. They fear the flames; I've got to build it back." He took a few pieces of shattered wood, opened the door, and went outside. The fire had burned down dangerously low.

Kip was transfixed, unable to think clearly. There were Myra and Mindy . . . He had to get them off the island somehow, get them to safety. But what about all the others, the people who looked to him for protection? How to save their lives? How to shield them from the onrushing evil?

Outside, Boniface bent down and threw the wood into the smoldering red and orange ashes. *Build it back,* he told himself. *Build it huge and roaring, hot and vivid in the night!* The flames began to grow back, licking at the new timbers.

Boniface stepped away from the circle; the eye hanging on his neck flared blood scarlet, cooled to a violet, darker, darker, to a deep gray, and finally to ebony.

And he felt the coarse, ancient hand of Death on him; it touched his neck very lightly, but it was enough to send an electric chill of warning through him. He twisted around, looking toward the jungle, and as the shadows fell upon him he knew the moment had finally come. And though he saw his fate clearly he would not give himself up to them.

"KIP!" he shouted, his voice breaking. He turned toward the open church door.

Before he had taken more than a step he tripped over an exposed root and fell to the ground, the glass eye shattering to bits beneath him. "KIP!" he screamed, feeling the shadows reach him.

Boniface's glasses had fallen off; almost blind, he crawled away from the things, his mouth trying, but unable now, to make a sound, his fingers gripping into sand and earth. And then one of them placed a booted foot on the old man's throat and crunched down. Boniface tried to fight back, but his strength was rapidly fading; he was choking on his own blood. The living corpses hissed all around him, illuminated by the building fire, and their claws flashed down to rend him apart.

When Kip reached the door, he stood paralyzed with shock at what he saw. The things turned their heads toward him, the fiery caverns of their eyes seeking fresh blood.

Kip saw the faces of Hell's warriors, things that had crewed a boat through the dark currents of the underworld. There were five, and more coming through the jungle. The one that had crushed the reverend's throat had a face half covered with a yellowish fungus; white tufts of hair clung to the head, and the sunken remains of its eyes burned into Kip with a searing hatred. When the thing's tight gray lips parted in a death's-head grin, Kip heard it hiss. A ring emblazoned with a swastika on its right hand caught the firelight.

And then they came for Kip, their talons groping for his throat, teeth bared.

Kip steeled himself. When they were almost upon him he raised the ax he'd taken from the corner of the church and brought it smashing down onto a grisly skull of a head.

The thing shrieked, a high rattle of reed-dry cords, and fell backward. The others were coming for him, moving so fast he had no time to think, no time to step back, slam and bolt the door to gain a few extra minutes. He clenched his teeth, smelling their dead reek, and swung back and forth with the ax, wading into their midst as they grasped at his chest and arms and legs, tearing at his clothing and then his skin. The ones he struck down dragged themselves back to grasp at his legs; he kicked at them, staggering and almost falling. A hideous face streaked with fungus hissed at him; he chopped at it with the ax and it smashed into fragments. Something caught at his knees and he almost fell forward into their midst. He knew that if he fell he was dead.

He fought for balance, swinging wildly, listening to their evil rattles and high, eerie moans. A claw emerged from the mass of bodies, probing for his eyes; he ducked his head, began to fight with fists, feet, elbows, and knees, kicking them back, hammering at them, crushing their skulls with the gleaming blade. One of them leaped forward, seizing him around the throat; another grasped his back and began to chew at his exposed shoulder, making hungry grunting noises. Powerful fingers caught at the ax, trying to wrench it away from him. They closed in on all sides, flinging themselves at him, trying to tear through his throat with teeth and nails. A wrench glittered in the light, coming straight at him, but he caught the shock of the blow with the ax handle and then slammed the blade into an arm socket.

Panic choked him; there were too many. *TOO MANY!* he shrieked. The ones with crushed faces and broken bones would not give up, they still struggled to devour him. He fought away from the thing on his back, and another took its place, sucking at the blood that trickled from his shoulder gash. *THE JEEP!* he heard himself cry out. *The jeep! Get to the jeep!* He caught on to the side of his vehicle for support, holding his arms over his face to ward off the claws, then battering with the blade left and right. He fought away, dragging himself into the back of the jeep, feeling the things grasping at his legs to pull him into their ravenous midst. Kicking at them, wrenching his legs free, Kip watched them ring the jeep to prevent his escape, saw the terrible fury in their mad eyes.

A thing with a remnant of a red beard started to climb up after him, but Kip brought the ax down with all his strength. The head was almost torn from the body; the mummy fell backward, yellow bone glinting in the gaping wound. More claws reached for him; the dead eyes were cunning and desperate.

Kip backed away, his muscles throbbing, sweat streaming from his body and the blood dripping from his fingertips.

And then his foot bumped the gas can he'd brought along.

He slammed the ax into it, ripping it open; he lifted it, splattering gasoline over the things and throwing the rest of it into the fire just behind them.

The explosion threw him over the front seat against the windshield. The flames roared into the sky, embers swirling in a whirlwind. Several of the things burst into flame; the fire caused a panic among the others. They fought away from each other and began to run toward the green wall of the jungle, flaking into ashes with each step. They crawled across the ground like maddened animals, screaming and moaning under the fire's blazing touch. A few of them reached the jungle and crashed through into the foliage; the others lay where they had fallen, melting like waxwork figures.

Kip threw himself behind the wheel and roared away from the church, feeling that in another moment he might go totally mad; his entire body shook, his heart pounded, and cold sweat dripped from every pore.

The village lay ahead, dark and quiet, peaceful and unaware in the night.

And a long time yet before morning.

Twenty-one

DAVID MOORE THREW the sodden sheet off and leaped from his bed; he was awake as soon as his feet hit the floor. He stood in the hot darkness, his mind a nightmare landscape, trying to pinpoint what it was that had filled him with terrible alarm.

Moore opened the terrace doors and stepped out, gripping the railing. On the horizon there was a brief flash of lightning, followed by the hollow, still-distant rumbling of thunder. The ocean was churned high and white, and somewhere the storm was building. Moore stood where he was a moment longer, listening, wondering if it was the thunder that had awakened him; he went back into the room, switched on a lamp, and hurriedly dressed in a cotton shirt and jeans.

There was an insistent knock at his door. "Who is it?" he said.

"Jana. Let me in, please."

He opened the door. She came in, wearing the same clothes she'd fallen asleep in; her eyes were red-rimmed, and beneath them there were dark hollows.

"I heard something," she said. "I know I heard something." She had rested for only moments at a time, and in her nightmares were things that watched her from thick shadows, licking their lips with bloated tongues.

"Thunder," he said quickly. "It woke me too . . ."

"No!" She shook her head and moved past him to the terrace, where she peered down into the darkness. "I thought I heard a woman's scream."

Lightning flashed, making Jana wince. Moore came up beside her. "Are you all right?" he asked.

"I think so. I don't know. I tell you, I heard a woman's scream!" She rubbed her arms, as if to get the circulation going.

"The man who was here . . . when we came in," Jana went on. "Who is he?"

"His name is Schiller; he was on the U-boat when it went down."

"Then . . . he knows? About what's happened?"

Moore shook his head. "No, I didn't tell him."

In the darkness there was a sharp, distant sound of breaking glass. Moore grasped the railing, straining to see. The next streak of lightning cast strange, long shadows across the streets of the village; there were no lights on, and nothing moved.

"What is it?" Jana was tense beside him, her voice a taut whisper.

"I don't know . . ." Thunder boomed across the sea, but behind it Moore thought he heard the sudden splitting of timber. A light switched on, almost at the farthest fringe of the village, and he could hear someone—a man's voice—shouting in a high, frantic pitch. A noise like a pistol shot echoed across the roofs, and there was the sound of more glass cracking;

another square of yellow light appeared, nearer to them, and Moore saw a shadow dart by the window. In a blue lightning flash he thought he could make out figures in the streets, but then the darkness claimed the earth again. A coil was winding within him, tightening his muscles. He turned from the railing, went inside to the dresser drawer, and withdrew the automatic.

"What are you going to do?" Jana asked him, framed on the terrace, the fear creeping across her face.

"I'm going downstairs to check the doors and windows." He put the automatic on safety and stuck it into his waistband. "I want you to stay in your room and be sure the terrace doors are bolted."

"They're coming, aren't they?" It was more of a statement than a question, the voice cold behind it.

"Go on."

"No. I'm staying with you."

"You'll be safer up here."

"No," she repeated, holding his eyes with her own.

He shrugged; there was no time for argument. Moore and Jana went into the hallway and were about to descend the stairs when Moore saw a sliver of light beneath the German's door.

He knocked, waited, heard movement inside, knocked again. Schiller opened the door and stood bleary-eyed, his tie loosened and the top buttons of his shirt undone. A chair had been positioned before the open terrace doors, and the bed was still made. Schiller rubbed his eyes and yawned. "I fell asleep," he said. "I was listening to the thunder." Then he noticed the pistol at Moore's waistband, and he was instantly alert. "What . . . is going on?" he asked, looking quizzically into their faces.

Moore stalked past the man, grasping the terrace doors; he was shutting them when another streak of lightning cut the sky in half, and the thunder echoed. He saw that a few more lights had come on, a scattering of fireflies across Coquina village.

"The gun," the German was saying behind him. "What is it for?" He took a step toward the other man. "I don't understand."

And before Moore could reply there was a *crack!* near Front Street, from the fishermen's shanties. Whether it was a gunshot or the noise of glass being broken he couldn't tell, but then there came an eerie, ragged wail, one of terrified desperation. Moore's mouth was dry, his mind racing. The lightning flashed again and in that brief light he saw figures . . . the things . . . moving through the streets below. The scream ceased abruptly, then came a man's voice, shouting, and a woman's shrill and hysterical. Moore threw the bolt on the doors and, turning away, saw Schiller's face a drawn, pale mask.

"What was that scream?" the German asked; his face was ashen, a blue vein throbbing rapidly at his temple.

Moore pushed past Schiller and Jana into the hallway, descended the stairs three at a time in the dark. In the distance he heard another voice, shouting incoherently, then drowned in a wave of thunder. A nameless dread had gripped him, and he couldn't move fast enough. *Check the windows, the doors. The shutters—some of the shutters are weak, the storm damage not yet replaced—get them bolted.* He felt the way he had inside the submarine, his legs out of control, functioning crazily in slow motion, as if he were inside a stranger's body.

He reached the front door and shook the knob to test the lock. It was secure. One of the windows facing the porch hadn't been pushed down flush to the frame; Moore cursed himself, reached it in two strides, and grasped the window's top to push it into place and lock it.

Lightning streaked, a thin white thread. And in its light Moore saw the forms that stood on the porch, groping from the darkness at the doorway.

Moore caught his breath, slammed the window down, locked it.

From the rear of the Indigo Inn there was the sudden, electrifying sound of shattering glass.

He heard the screen door open, heard the wood splinter as it was ripped from its hinges by a dozen hands. Someone in the village screamed again, and someone else called out for God. The rear windows were being broken out; he could hear something hammering at the back door, trying to get through. Moore whirled around, slammed and locked the door that connected the kitchen with the rest of the hotel. He dragged a table across it, at the same time bringing out the automatic and switching off the safety.

And then silence, broken only by his own rapid breathing and the noise of chaos in the village: screams and shouts, a gun firing, a cry of pain.

Someone was coming down the stairs: Schiller and Jana, feeling their way in the dark.

"SCHILLER!" Moore shouted. "WATCH THAT REAR DOOR . . . !"

Something suddenly pounded against the front door . . . *wham! wham! wham!* . . . with a tremendous force. *A hammer,* Moore thought, ice flowing in his veins. *The things have a hammer.*

He heard the door at the back of the hotel come off its frame; there was a wild crash of glass and crockery from the kitchen.

A front window shattered, the glass exploding into the room along with pieces of the aged shutter. Jana cried out, and Moore saw the black outline of a figure throw back a powerful arm to break out the rest of the wood. The door was struck, again and again; there was a sharp splintering sound.

Moore raised the gun, aimed directly at the thing that tore at the shutter, and fired.

A gout of flame spewed from the automatic's muzzle; the gun's roar momentarily deafened him. The dark figure was thrown backward, and glass tinkled from the broken frame.

"You killed it . . ." Schiller said, sweat glistening on his face.

"Wait," Moore told him, not moving. "Keep your eye on that back door, for God's sake!"

A heavy blow struck the door that sealed off the kitchen; glass broke on the other side of it. Moore jerked around and fired through the wood, filling the air with splinters and the acrid odor of gunpowder. At the same time, that hammer blow struck the front door again, and Jana could see it slowly bending inward; she grabbed a chair and wedged it under the knob. The shutter at another window was being attacked, the claws scratching their way in. Moore brought his arm up and fired; the things ducked away on either side of the frame.

Schiller saw a split growing in the center of the rear door; he backed away from it, watching the wood being broken with a horrified fascination.

A window on the room's far side buckled inward in a shower of slats and glass. One of them had thrown itself partway through and now grasped the window's ledges to pull itself the rest of the way in. Jana reached to her side for the decanter of rum and threw it, but the bottle broke just above the thing's head; Moore stepped forward, firing point-blank.

The muzzle flame exposed a face cancerous with rot and fungus; a lipless mouth gaped, the eyes holes of hate. Moore fired again, and again, seeing the face explode into bits of bone and dried flesh; it hissed and fell back through the window.

Now the rear door was buckling. Schiller forced his legs to move, putting his hands against the wood to hold the things back. He could feel the incredible force of whatever was behind the door.

A window breaking, another, two more. A skeleton's shoulders pushed forward, the grisly brown scalp glistening with glass. Jana hefted a wicker chair and struck at it, but then the arms were in and it was too late.

Three more bullets remained in the automatic. They were fighting their way in now through all the windows, and it was only moments before the doors would give way. Moore felt the wild touch of panic grip him, shook it off, felt it return with a vengeance. There was no time to get those shells from upstairs, but was there a chance they could make it to a terrace and leap from the porch before the zombies reached them?

He turned and fired at the one Jana was trying to fight back. It shrieked and collapsed, sliding through the window.

The rear door split; Schiller stepped away from a gnarled claw that had burst through. But others reached through as well, and they would be inside within seconds.

With a tremendous noise of cracking wood the front door caved in, and hideous shapes came through the jagged aperture, the one in the lead wielding a hammer, others carrying crowbars and wrenches. Moore fired into their midst and knew he'd hit one of them, but even as he prepared to fire his final bullet, he heard Schiller shout that the rear door was down as well. A stench of rot wafted over him, and a shadow loomed up, striking a blunt object down on Moore's right shoulder. He cried out in pain; the gun slipped from his numbed fingers.

Then they engulfed him, clawing and biting, the teeth grinning and terrible; a hand flashed out, clubbing him across the forehead, and he fought back, his teeth clenched, not willing to let them take him without a battle. He was thrown backward over a chair and lay sprawled on his back. They huddled over Jana in a corner, their claws and fangs flashing; Moore crawled toward her as one of them grasped his throat and began to twist his head to one side, about to rip it from the neck.

"GOD HAVE MERCY!" Schiller shrieked in German, backing against a wall at their approach. "GOD HAVE MERCY!"

And a voice hissed, "Stopppppppp . . ." The sound was as cold as the touch of the grave.

The thing strangling Moore released its grip and stood up. Moore coughed violently, shaking his head from side to side, a black curtain still obscuring the field of his vision. They released Jana; she crumpled to the floor in a heap.

Schiller stood where he was, pinned to the wall, his mouth making whimpering sounds.

The things stood motionless, waiting, eager for blood.

A shadow moved, the clatter of boots across the floor; lightning flashed, illuminating a face destroyed by the ruin of rot, a face that had seen its own horror in a mirror. One arm, wrapped in a tattered brown sleeve, slowly rose, the finger pointing. The hand came out, almost touching Schiller's chin, but when Schiller recoiled in stark terror the thing paused. Its head cocked to one side, it examined Schiller with burning eyes.

Moore crawled toward Jana; she was semiconscious, her face gashed and her clothing in shreds. He huddled beside her and watched.

"Nein . . ." Schiller whispered. *"Nein . . ."*

The figure before him breathed heavily, the stare penetrating. Then, with a tremendous effort, the gray lips moved. "Schillerrrr . . . ?"

The German shrank back, his shoulders pressed into the wall.

"Mein Gott . . ." the thing whispered, its voice a dry rasp that made Moore's skin crawl.

Schiller blinked, screams of madness echoing within his head. He couldn't believe it, wouldn't believe it, but he seemed to recognize the man—or what had once been a man—from a long time ago. Another life. *"Nein . . ."* he rasped, shaking his head. "Not you!

276

You should be . . . dead . . . all of you should BE DEAD!"

Korrin held Schiller's eyes for a moment more, then slowly moved his gaze to Moore and Jana. He raised the arm again, flesh hanging in strings from the exposed bone, and pointed toward them. *"Feindlich Teufel . . ."* he whispered.

"Nein," Schiller breathed. *"Nein, nein . . ."*

Korrin turned from Schiller; as he approached, Moore pulled Jana back against him, trying to shield her body with his own. The living corpse towered over them, and Moore could feel the touch of its fetid breath.

"ALL OF YOU ARE DEAD!" Schiller shrieked, his voice breaking, slithering into a moan.

Korrin's eyes were flaming slithering whorls of destruction. They seared through Moore's flesh and muscles, into the bone and the brain. The arm extended, and the hand, with its long, filthy nails, came down for Moore's throat. He held his own arms up weakly to ward it off, but he was powerless to move.

And then suddenly, in a blur of motion, Schiller had picked up the gun lying on the floor. He fired without aiming; a tongue of orange pierced the shadows.

Moore saw Korrin's head jerk to one side, saw the lower jaw hang on threads for an instant before being ripped away, leaving a ragged edge of flesh. Korrin staggered backward, almost falling, but then regaining his balance. He put his hands to his face, and the scream roaring through that broken mouth cast Schiller over the brink of insanity. Still screaming, Korrin moved forward, his claws rising; Schiller squeezed the trigger again, aiming between the eyes, but the hammer fell on an empty clip.

At once the other crewmen had turned on Schiller; one of them struck out with a crowbar that smashed across the German's chest, and then they were on him, going for his eyes. Korrin reached him, bending down toward the offered throat.

"RUN!" Schiller screamed, his eyes glinting as the things covered him over. "RUN!"

Moore hesitated; Schiller had saved them, but now the man was beyond hope, and the instant they finished with him they'd crave more blood and fluids. He pulled Jana up, shaking her to make her move, and dragged her through the shattered rear door toward the kitchen. Beyond the broken opening where the back door had been was the jungle's blackness.

Moore turned back. They were shredding the flesh from Schiller's body.

Then he pulled Jana after him into the thick, clinging underbrush. She was still dazed and tripped across vines. He picked her up, ignoring the sharp protest of his injured shoulder, and struggled into the walls of foliage, feeling thorns grasp at his trousers and scrape across his arm.

There was no time to think, no time to let his nerves feel the pain; he had to get them as far away from the hotel as he could. The terror still throbbed within him like the beating of a second heart. He moved deeper into darkness, heedless of their direction, only knowing they had to find a place of safety. His feet sank into the soft earth, slipping in standing puddles of water. On the next step he lost his footing and crashed to the ground with Jana still in his arms; the shock on his injured shoulder made him cry out in pain. Jana shook her head dazedly, the scratches livid on her face. She tried to crawl away but Moore reached out and caught her.

And he heard the terrifying noises he had expected all along. They were following; he could hear brush being crushed down beneath boots. *Closer. Closer.*

He pulled her up and went on, as though he were running headlong into a deep pit from which there was no escape. He tore frantically at the vines which blocked their way. A wild bird cried out and burst from the brush just in front of them. The things were still coming, assisted by the path that Moore was breaking. When he looked back over his shoulder he thought he could see a dozen or more of them approaching, shadows moving among other shadows. The entire jungle was a morass of shadows, which burst through the foliage, reaching out for him with shapeless, spidery fingers. Panic exploded within him and he fought on, dragging the girl with him, the muscles of his injured arm numb and useless. There was nowhere to go, nowhere to hide, nowhere to find safety.

The things were almost on them, only a few yards behind and closing quickly. *Don't stop! Don't weaken! DON'T STOP!* He lost his footing, staggered to his knees, pulled himself up, grasping Jana's wrist in a fierce grip. Thorns whipped into his face, his chest heaving with the exertion; around him birds screeched in a wild, loud cacophony, and through their piercing clamor Moore could hear a horribly familiar harsh, rasping breath. His skin crawled, already sensing the claws that would reach for the back of his neck.

And then the shadows rose up in front of him.

He opened his mouth to scream, but the scream was drowned out by the ear-splitting roar of a shotgun blast.

The muzzle flare exploded past Moore and Jana into the shapes that reached toward them. Shrieking in pain, they split their closed ranks and fought back the way they'd come. The man with the shotgun raised his weapon again, bracing it against his bare shoulder; the gun bucked again, but the forms had already vanished into the all-consuming night.

Moore collapsed to his knees, his body racked with pain, and retched into the brush. When he looked up he saw perhaps six or seven men, a few of them holding torches. A firm hand reached down and caught Moore's wrist, drawing him to his feet.

The man who stood over him cradled the smoking shotgun in the crook of his muscular arm. He was completely bald but had a full white beard and mustache. A small gold ring in the lobe of an ear glittered in the light of a torch, and a golden amulet hung about his thick neck. But it was the face that both commanded Moore's attention and repelled him; it was actually repellent to him—black, deep-set eyes glowered from beneath a high forehead, and the nose was as hooked as an eagle's beak. One side of the face was terribly scarred and thickened, the scars streaking pink across the tawny skin, crisscrossing that side of the neck, as well as a large gouge across a shoulder. He wore a T-shirt and dark trousers which had been ripped in numerous places by thorns. The man motioned silently to several of the others, who began to move off in pursuit of the fleeing shapes. They all carried guns or wicked-looking knives.

The man turned his attention to Moore and Jana. "Follow," he ordered, and without waiting for them he began tracking back into the jungle from the direction he'd come.

Twenty-two

SMOKE WHIRLED ACROSS the Coquina roofs in the grip of a rising storm wind. A lamp had been thrown over in a tinderbox shack near the wharfs, and red tendrils of flame greedily consumed the roof. The dancing sparks spread, rapidly devouring other dwellings, leaping from roof to roof, caving in fiery timbers on the bodies that lay beneath.

The fires took hold, strengthened by the wind, and began to gnaw away at the semicircle of shanties clustered around the harbor. The reddish light in the sky grew in intensity, the sea mirroring the flames. A silence had fallen across the village, broken only by the noise of wood giving way beneath the fires and the thrashing of the ocean against Kiss Bottom. Still, there remained the echoes of chaos, the screams that had filled the streets, the moaning and crying that had spilled through windows and doorways.

Kip roared through the smoke in his jeep, his eyes

red and wild, his shirt hanging in tatters around his chest, ashes all over him, ragged scratches on his throat and cheeks. His eyebrows had been singed, the flesh around them puffed from the heat. He gripped the wheel, swerving to avoid the bodies littering High Street as he headed down for the harbor. A corpse lay in a doorway frame—a woman, her face mangled beyond recognition—and another—a man in a pool of blood—alongside. A body sprawled directly in his path, a mass of torn flesh he had known as James Davis; he wrenched the wheel to one side and whipped past. More bodies, more pools of blood. A child, arms and legs spread-eagled, eyes lifted to the sky; the man called Youngblood, the head almost torn from the body. Windows above the Landfall Tavern had been shattered, and he saw the heavyset woman who had worked there sprawled out with sightless eyes. There was a rotting corpse crumpled in a heap —one of the things from the U-boat—grinning even in death; a young girl—yes, the high yellow on her way to Trinidad—now beaten and torn, her beauty ravaged. He shuddered, looked away, was forced to look back to keep from running over a corpse.

He had reached the village just before they attacked in full force; he had fired his rifle at them, struck some of them down with his jeep, shouted until he was hoarse to alert the sleeping islanders. But he had known he was too late. He heard the screaming begin, saw them crashing through glass and doors. There were too many . . . *too many* . . . *too many* . . . the streets crawling with death. He'd fought them away even as they rushed him, trying to pull him

283

from his jeep, and then he had raced to protect his own family.

And there he had found his house a shambles, windows broken, the doors caved in. Tears stinging his eyes, he had rushed inside. His wife and daughter were gone. There was a smear of blood across a wall, a bullet hole in a door, another in a window frame; the sight made him freeze in shock. He had fought his way out of there, sobbing, not knowing if they were alive or slaughtered.

Kip saw figures struggling through the pall of smoke as he neared the harbor. He tensed, slammed on his brakes, and reached for the rifle on the seat beside him. The forms emerging from the darkness were islanders, terrified people running wildly past him toward the jungle beyond. He saw their glazed, mad eyes and knew there was nothing he could do.

Except one thing.

He jammed his foot to the floor, blared the horn to avoid a man who staggered through a doorway into the street. The jeep roared along the harbor through the blazing heat. A bucket brigade had been started, the men moving in slow motion, their clothes smoking. Wet wood whined and shrilled; to Kip it sounded like what he imagined a shell from a U-boat's deck gun, screaming from the sea, might sound like.

"WHERE ARE YOU!" he shouted, his throat raw. "WHERE ARE YOU!" Smoke whirled before him, stinging his eyes, filling his mouth. But he knew where they were.

It was war. War, just as it had been in 1942. Time had stood still for the U-boat's crew, and now it was frozen for the villagers as well. But this was not war. It was a massacre, a hideous and inhuman massacre of the innocents. But, that was the way it was done, wasn't it? War always took the innocents first, and then the things that had done the killing slipped back into the shadows to wait and plan for another day. By all that was holy, he swore he would kill as many as he could with his bare hands if need be. He left the burning village behind, sweat and tears mingling on his face, his pulse pounding with the knowledge of what was to come.

And then he was at the boatyard, crashing through the remnants of the gates, swerving past the junk piles, one hand guiding the wheel and the other gripping his rifle. The naval shelter lay before him, a streak of lightning illuminating it for an instant. The doorway was open. He stopped the jeep, leaped over its side, and ran toward the shelter with the rifle clasped in his arms.

But before he reached it there came a hollow rumbling noise that seemed to make the earth tremble beneath his feet.

He stood where he was, listening, new sweat beading up on his face. The noise came again, harsher, shaking the shelter's walls. The distant sound of thunder, yes, thunder.

"Noooooooo," Kip hissed through clenched teeth, his mind reeling. "NO!" He took a step forward.

The noise died away, came back, growing, growing, growing, making the ground tremble. With a shriek of metal the huge sliding bulkhead crumpled.

Kip forced himself to move, one sluggish step at a time. "I won't let you get away . . . !" he shouted against the brittle wind, the words flying out to al' directions. "GODDAMN YOU, I WON'T LET YOU GET . . ."

The bulkhead bent outward, a blister of metal. It collapsed into the water with a metallic ripping noise.

And from the shelter, inch by inch, the U-boat's stern emerged.

The battered propellors churned oily water; the boat's aft deck slid out, then the conning tower. Kip could see formless shapes on the dark bridge. He raised the rifle and fired, hearing the bullet ricochet off iron. The U-boat emerged like a reptile slithering from its den, and the entire length of it shuddered from the straining power of the engines. It moved free of the shelter and began to turn, gradually, the iron protesting, toward the reef passage with foam streaking along its bow.

The U-boat ground itself over a skiff, rammed broadside into a small trawler at anchor and cast it away. The sea was already filling the trawler's shattered port deck. Lightning jabbed the sky, and Kip saw the iron monster cross the harbor, veering away from the sandbars; the boat gained the passage and began to move, sluggishly against the surge of whitecapped breakers. Kip ran past the water's edge and on into the sea, bringing the rifle up, firing without aiming, again and again. The gun jammed; the U-boat was out of the harbor now, the ocean thundering against its hull, and when the next sheet of lightning came it was gone, swept away into the night, on a final and terrifying voyage.

The waves thrashed around his knees, almost throwing him off balance. Wind sucked at him, howling within the empty shelter. *The Night Boat*, Boniface had said. *The Night Boat*, the most terrible of all creatures of the deep. "Nooooo," he whispered. "I won't let you get away . . ."

Lightning flashed overhead, and the thunder's boom sounded like the laugh of a war god, savage and victorious.

Rain began to fall, first in single heavy drops, then in sheets that rippled across the sea. Kip stood in the downpour, his eyes fixed on the limitless blackness. Very slowly he made his way out of the water and when he reached shore he crumpled to his knees in the sand, driven down by the weight of the storm.

Moore and Jana clung to each other, following the men through the curtains of rain. They were Caribs, Moore realized, although he didn't recognize any of them. They were moving across a high-grassed clearing into a part of Coquina he didn't know. He could see the glimmer of lights in the distance. The crowded shacks took shape out of the rain, and he saw the outline of the muddy street stretching down to the north harbor. Caribville. One of the Indians stepped from the path into thicket and sat on his haunches, facing back the way they'd come, with a rifle across his knees. Another took his position a few yards away.

The streets were empty. The heavy raindrops on tin roofs sounded like gunshots. The man with the shotgun spoke quietly to the others and the group split in different directions; he motioned with his head for Moore and Jana to follow, and he led them to a shack where an oil lamp burned behind a window screen. He opened the door and waved them in with an impatient gesture.

Inside there was a dim glow of low-burning lamps, the faint smell of tar and tobacco and food. An emaciated old woman in a patchwork gown sat rocking in a chair in front of a cast-iron stove. Her hair was knotted behind her head; her leathery flesh was stretched tight over her prominent facial bones. Another woman, perhaps in her late thirties, stepped away from the door as they came through.

They stood in a large room; Moore could see another in the back. There were a few chairs, a sun-faded wooden table with a lamp set at its center, cane blinds across the windows, a mat of intricately woven sea-grass on the floor. Framed pictures that had obviously been scissored from travel magazines hung from nails around the room. On one wall was a gun rack, now empty; near it hung a beautifully carved and smoothed wooden tribal mask, light gleaming on its oiled surface. Its triangular teeth were bared, the eyes set in a fierce, warriorlike glare.

Moore put his arm protectively around Jana, supporting her as the man closed and bolted the door behind them. As she swept her wet hair from her face, Moore saw an angry red welt on one cheek.

The man shook his head like a dog, spraying droplets of water from his beard and shoulders, and placed his shotgun in the rack. At once the younger woman was at his side, speaking to him in the Carib language. He didn't reply, but waved her back to her place. Across the room the old woman rocked back and forth, her hands clenched in her lap, her gaze boring through Moore's skull. She muttered something and laughed abruptly.

The man took up one of the lamps in his large hand and stepped toward Moore. With the light falling directly upon them, Moore could see his horribly ravaged face. The eyes were as hard and cold as chunks of new granite.

"Who are you?" Moore asked him.

The man ignored him and spoke to the young woman, who hurried from the room. She returned a moment later with a brown blanket and offered it to Moore, but he could see no charity in her face; he took it and wrapped it gently around Jana's shoulders.

The Carib held the lamp steady, its light painting his flesh the color of waxed mahogany. He held Moore's gaze and motioned with the lamp toward a window. "Rain before wind," he said in English, his voice like the rumble of a diesel engine. "The storm will follow."

"You saved our lives," Moore said. "If you hadn't . . ."

"There are many who are beyond saving now," the Carib said. His speech pattern had a mixture of British and West Indian rhythms, and he sounded as if he might be fairly well educated. "Your name is David Moore; you're the one who bought the hotel, aren't you?" He stood like a massive tree rooted to the floor.

"That's right."

"What happened to your shoulder?"

"I can't remember. I think one of them hit me with something."

"Broken bone?"

Moore shook his head.

The man grunted, played the light across Jana's face. Behind him the old woman muttered on, her voice rising and falling.

"What place is this?" Jana asked.

"My village. My house." He looked from one to the other. "I am Cheyne, Chief Father of the Caribs."

And now Moore made the connection: The man reminded him of that statue in the Square. Cheyne, a distant ancestor of the chieftain who'd battled pirates?

"Those things . . ." Jana said softly. She picked at the dried blood on her lower lip and then raised her face to Moore's. "What about Schiller?"

"Dead," he replied, his mind sheering away from the image of Schiller pinned to the floor. He weaved back and forth, the pain now flaming under his flesh. Cheyne spoke to the woman, who left the room again. He clamped a firm hand around Moore's arm and eased him into a chair. Cheyne motioned for Jana to sit on the mat beside Moore and she did, drawing her knees up to her chin and pulling the blanket around her. Then Cheyne withdrew a gleaming, jagged-edged blade from his waistband. He picked up a flat black whetting stone from the table and began to draw the blade slowly across it; then he walked over to the window and stood peering out. Moore sat silent with his head in his hands.

"The constable made a mistake bringing that boat into the harbor." Cheyne said suddenly. "A long time past, it brought death and evil here. Now again. It's not a machine; it's a living thing, and it has the soul of *Héhué*, the serpent. . . ."

Moore looked up. "You've got to take your men back there and help them!"

The Carib continued sharpening his blade, turning it under his hand. "Some men have gone back to help those who may reach the jungle," he said after a pause.

"We went over there when we heard the shooting, and many of the young bucks wanted to go down and fight. But I wouldn't let them. None of my people are going into Coquina village."

"Christ!" Moore blurted out, shaking his head. "Do you hate those villagers so much you could stand by and let them be slaughtered?"

"They're not *my* people," Cheyne said. "But this is not the point—a good fighter wouldn't last a minute against those creatures. No. If and when they reach Caribville the men will have to protect their own women and children."

"This isn't the time for counting heads, damn it! For God's sake, help them!"

"*Oua!*" Cheyne said, turning from the window, his stare bitter and forceful. "What had God to do with this? Everyone dies, Moore, whether in pain or at peace."

The young woman came back in, carrying a pot of a strong-smelling, vinegary liquid. She knelt before Jana, dipped a cloth into the pot, and began to dab rather roughly at the cuts. Jana winced and jerked her head back; the woman grasped the nape of her neck and finished the job.

The noise of the rainfall had quieted somewhat; now Moore could hear the water rushing through gutters. He got to his feet, feeling the heaviness of his shoulder. "Then I'm going back. Give me a gun."

Cheyne sharpened his knife in silence. In the distance thunder crashed.

"I said I'm going back, damn you!"

Cheyne put the stone and the knife back on the table, reached over for the shotgun, broke it open, and withdrew two shells from a back pocket. He slipped the shells into the breech, closed it, and slung it over to Moore.

"Go on," he said quietly. He put his hands on the table and leaned forward. "But you won't be coming back. And you won't be able to help any of them, because before you reach the village those things will have smelled you out, and they'll find you. They'll bleed you dry; then they'll feast on your corpse and leave your bones for the lizards. Go on."

"Lalouene," the old woman said, the rocker creaking. "He's a dead man." She stared at Moore, her eyes fathomless depths.

Jana shook off the Carib woman, ignoring her angered chattering. "Don't," she said to Moore. "Please don't go back there!"

Moore said, "I've got to find Kip. I'll come for you when I can." He paused a moment, looking back at the Carib in hope the man might go with him, but Cheyne glowered at him and did not move. Moore knew there was no use asking again; he'd have to take his chances alone in the jungle.

There was a loud knock on the door. Moore tensed, whirled around. Cheyne moved forward like a panther, his hand gripped around the knife. He looked out the window and then threw back the bolt.

Two rain-soaked Carib men, both armed with rifles, stood in the doorway. Cheyne motioned them in and the man in the lead—tall and bony with black, ferretlike eyes—began to talk in an excited voice, gesturing with his large hands toward the sea. He talked on for a full minute before Cheyne spoke, and then the man answered a question Cheyne had posed.

Moore was watching Cheyne's face; he could see a coldness creeping across it from the chin upward, first tensing the jaws, then drawing the lips tight, flaring the thick nostrils, settling in the eyes like circles of frozen steel. But in the eyes also, very deep, there was a flash of something he recognized because he had seen it before, in his own mirrored gaze: a powerful, soul-aching fear. Then it passed, and Cheyne found his stern mask again. He seemed to be giving the men some kind of instructions. They listened intently.

When he'd finished the two men returned into the night. Cheyne stood watching them go, and then he rebolted the door. "OUA!" the old woman shouted wildly. "NO!" She shook her head from side to side and the younger woman left Jana to try to calm her. At the back of the house, a baby began to cry.

"What is it?" Moore asked him.

Cheyne reached out and took the shotgun from Moore's grasp. "You will not need this. They're gone."

"How?"

"They've taken their boat," Cheyne said, "and left Coquina."

At once Jana was on her feet. "That can't be!"

"Those men saw the boat move around the point and disappear into the northwest."

Moore shook his head, his shoulder burning, his mind whirling with the horrifying events of the night.

"It can't be!" Jana said forcefully. She looked over at Moore, her gaze helpless, almost childlike.

Moore slowly let himself sink back into the chair. He felt the Carib watching him. "We helped them," he said wearily. "God save us, we helped them repair their boat. We put them in the boatyard, gave them access to fuel and oil and tools. And all along, while we were sleeping, they were piecing that terrible machine back together—and we never knew. God . . . we never knew. . . ."

"Now listen to me!" Jana said, rallying suddenly. "Even if they have worked on the diesels and replaced enough of the battery cells, they can't be getting but a fraction of their former power out of those old engines! I don't care what sort of equipment they had, they couldn't have repaired all of the systems! Their steering will be sluggish, they'll be slowed to a crawl and forced to keep to the surface!"

"You said the systems were duplicated," Moore reminded her. "One operated by machinery. One by hand."

"No!" She looked from Moore to Cheyne, back to Moore. "They may have gotten the skeleton moving and maybe a portion of the brain working, but the veins and nerves are still dead!"

"Can you be certain of that? What about their torpedoes, their deck gun? And that damned boat itself, with its blade of a bow, could batter a hole through a timber-hulled freighter . . . !"

Jana was silent, trying to piece together what he was saying. "No. What you're thinking is . . . madness. This isn't 1942 . . . this isn't World War II. . . ."

"To them it is," Moore said. "If they're moving northwest they may be going back toward Jamaica. And there are shipping lanes between here and there.

Lanes that they may have prowled forty years ago. They're bound to have known the charts and how to reach the lanes from here. . . ."

"God!" Jana whispered. "What's kept them . . . alive after more than forty years underwater? What sort of *things* have they become?"

The baby's crying was louder; the Carib woman left the room, went back through a doorway, and returned holding a black-haired infant cradled in her arms. The baby groped for a breast, and she unbuttoned her blouse to let it suck from a nipple. She kept her eyes fixed on Cheyne's back, as he stood at the window.

"You can go back to your village now," Cheyne said after a long silence. "It's safe."

"They may still need your help," Moore told him.

"No. I have no time to waste on them." He turned and spoke to the young woman, whose face was taut with apprehension. The woman struggled to rise, her arms trembling with the effort, and Cheyne crossed the room to her. He whispered gently and stroked her hair while she muttered pleadingly, clutching at his arm, holding the child close to her body. He looked into Moore's face. "I say go back to your own kind."

Moore rose and took a single step toward him. There was a fierceness in Cheyne's face that made him the living duplicate of that hand-hewn tribal mask. In the light of a nearby lamp the scars seemed only the exterior wounds of something that had mauled his soul. "What are you going to do?"

"It's no concern of yours. Now leave, both of you!"

Tears had begun to stream along the old woman's face.

Moore's voice was unyielding. "What are you going to do?"

Cheyne continued to stroke the woman's hair. When he looked again at the white man his jaw was set and firm, the eyes shotgun barrels.

"I'm going after the *Héhué*," Cheyne said. "And I'm going to destroy it."

Twenty-three

MOORE WAS SILENT under the Carib's powerful stare. Overhead a crack of thunder shrilled through the sky like a shell, burning it blood-red.

"How?" Jana asked. "With a shotgun, or a knife? You don't know what you're dealing with! If you're planning to sink it you'd better find yourself an armor-piercing projectile and some heavy artillery, or a bomb, or a limpet mine . . . !"

Cheyne turned his attention to her; moving past the old woman, he came to her side and scowled down at her. "If need be, yes, I'll fight it with a blade. I'll rip those plates open with my bare hands. It has a debt to pay me . . . "—his hand came up, the callused fingers touching the terrible plain of scars—". . . here and within." He held his hand over his heart and glanced at Moore. "What's to prevent it from returning here, where they realize they can find fuel . . . and food? What will prevent it from entering those sea lanes and churning blood all the way from here to Kingston?"

"I've got to think," Jana said, pacing the room. "Now they can't have stored enough diesel fuel for a long voyage, and they can't be moving very quickly, not with the sea running high."

"If the boat is headed for the lanes, the nearest route from here is between Big Danny Cay and Jacob's Teeth. And if I reach them in time I can force the boat across the reefs and rip its hull open," Cheyne told her.

"No. We can use the wireless here to reach the Coast Guard," Jana said. "They can stop it before . . ."

"Now *you're* talking nonsense. Do you think they'd listen for one minute to what you'd have to say? And by then the bastard would have made it through the passage, and it would be lost to me. No! It's mine, damn it! I've waited a long time to meet it, on the open seas where I'd have a fighting chance, and by all that's holy in this world I mean to follow it!"

"I saw those trawlers down in the harbor," she said. "If you're going after it in one of those you're mad! That U-boat will make matchsticks out of . . ."

"That's enough." Cheyne's voice was hard. "Go away from here. Both of you go tend to your dead in Coquina village. I don't want you around Caribville; there's an hour until dawn light and I have much work to do."

He held Jana's gaze for a few seconds, then abruptly turned back to the old woman; he knelt before her, looking into her eyes, and kissed her cheek. She ran a withered hand along the unscarred side of his face. When he stood up again she clutched at his legs, but then he went to stand beside his wife and the baby. He took the child in his arms and held it close.

"My son," he said softly, speaking to Moore. "He'll be the next Chief Father, after I'm gone. He'll rule justly and fairly, and he'll be strong, and he'll never know fear because fear eats the insides out of a man and leaves him weak and crying out in the middle of the night. No. Keth will be free and unafraid, and he'll grow straight and unscarred." He returned the baby to his mother, whispered to her, and kissed her on the cheek. When he drew back, Jana saw a solitary tear streaking his wife's face, but her eyes remained strong and cool, full of courage. Without looking at her again, Cheyne took up the shotgun, picked up one of the oil lamps, and strode through the door.

His wife ran out after him. The old woman struggled from her chair and stood balanced precariously, like a frail thing of straw, in the doorway. She turned her head toward Moore, her eyes swimming. "Help him," she whispered.

Moore stood up and made his way out the door. The rain was still falling, but not as heavily as before. The Carib woman stood watching her man disappear toward the harbor. Moore could see dozens of lanterns and flashlights moving down there, each one a spot of yellow in the rain's veil. He wiped the drops from his eyes.

After another moment Jana joined him; the old woman, her clothes soaked, came and put her arm around the wife's waist, pulling at her. *Widows of the sea,* he thought, watching them. *Widows? No, no. Not yet.* They began to walk back through the mud to the chief's house. "Why?" Moore asked the old woman as they passed him.

There was a hard certainty, perhaps even a wisdom on her face, that rooted him to the spot. "His destiny," she answered, and then she and Cheyne's wife were gone.

Destiny. Destiny. Destiny. The word drove into his brain, exploded into a thousand steel fragments there. He remembered the transom of a broken boat thrashed by the sea: *Destiny's Child.* There was nothing he could have done then except be pulled along by the swift and hidden currents of his own destiny, no matter how hard he fought against it, not understanding why. He was unable to win the fight because life is like the sea, and its powers pull a man into the deep and mysterious Abyss of his own future.

Perhaps the Night Boat's returning to the surface had only been a matter of time; perhaps he had only speeded the inevitable. Now as he looked back on the chain of deaths and destruction, he saw them as part of the chain of events that had brought him around the world and left him here, in this place of all places, standing in a harsh tropical rain. Cheyne was right, he realized: There was nothing to prevent the things from returning for more supplies and more lives. Years ago, on another day of storm, when the earth had closed over him, something inside had given way. Part of him had died then, making him like those tortured things that crewed the boat, out of place and time, caught in the clutch of a destiny that had hidden itself until now. Only in the past few days had it given him a sharp, terrifying look at what lay ahead.

He loved this island, these people, for good or for bad. He loved them like the family he had lost. And with God's help or without it, he must not, could not, would not lose another to the dark, sudden upheaval of his fate.

"I'm going to help him," he heard himself say.

Jana clutched at his arm as he started to push past her. She wiped the rain out of her eyes and shook her head. "He's out of his mind, David! If he finds the U-boat they'll cut his trawler in two! He won't come back, and he knows he won't!"

A white-hot flame had begun to burn in his muscles. *We are born alone and we must face death alone.* Who said that? A philosophy instructor, ages ago, in a college classroom of another world. Everyone must die, Cheyne had said, whether in pain or at peace. He knew there was a high chance of losing his life, but he accepted it. He would take that chance, clench it in his fist, dare the dark gods, because he had seen the end of his voyage, a brief vision that had filled his head and then vanished. He had seen the knife-blade bow of the Night Boat waiting.

He pulled free of Jana and began to walk through the mud down the winding road to the harbor, where he could still see the flashlights moving.

Cheyne's weather-beaten fishing trawler rubbed up against a tire-browed wharf. It was the largest of the Carib fleet, perhaps a shade more than fifty feet from stem to stern, with a wide, low-slung hull. Most of the hull paint had been flayed off and there were some patches, but they were all well above the marked discoloration of the waterline. A broad cabin, painted maroon, with several metal-rimmed portholes stood just aft of amidships. Naked masts, their sails tightly furled, pointed at the sky as the rain dripped off the rigging. At the stern there were booms and hoists, a pile of nets, and a few metal drums strewn about. It seemed a stocky, seaworthy boat, with her spoon bow and pulpit giving her a clean, sharp line.

As Moore approached he could see the faded image

of a name that had once been painted in red on the transom board: *Pride*. The sea swelled underneath it, lifting the boat up and nuzzling the tires; timbers creaked and groaned and there was a dull thud as water broke under the bow.

Several bare-chested Caribs moved on the after deck, some of them clearing nets and cables away. Water spilled from a duct at the stern; the pumps had been started up. One of the men carried a bundle of something wrapped in clear plastic but Moore couldn't see what it was. He waited as another man opened the cabin doorway and vanished within.

"Where's Cheyne?" Moore shouted to the man nearest him.

The Carib looked up with a sullen expression, then turned his back on Moore and continued moving a heavy metal drum.

"Hey!" Moore grasped a wharf piling and leaned over, speaking to another man further down the deck. "Hey! Get Cheyne out here!"

But then the cabin doorway opened again; the man who had carried in the bundle came out, followed by Cheyne, who was giving him orders in a clipped, brusque tone. Cheyne saw Moore and came over to the starboard gunwale. "What are you doing here?" he asked, his gaze dangerous. "I told you to get away!"

"I want to go with you," Moore told him.

Cheyne was silent for a few seconds. Then he said, "Go back home, white man. This isn't for you." He turned away.

Moore gestured wildly. "Wait! Please. You won't understand, but it's important to me. I won't be in the way, and I can hold my own with any of your crew; I used to be a sailor. I can handle myself."

302

"Why?" the Carib asked him.

"I . . . want to be there," Moore said. "I want to make sure the boat doesn't come back. Let me go."

"You're crazy," Cheyne said.

"No. *I* found the bastard and caused it to come up. If it wasn't for me there'd be no death on Coquina tonight. Don't you see? I've got to be there, and I have a right to help stop that thing . . . maybe even more than you."

Cheyne grunted. "No, not more than me."

"How about it?" Moore persisted, disregarding the Carib's remark.

Cheyne examined him cautiously. He reached out and grasped Moore's wrist, pulling him over the side before the trawler could heave again. "All right," he said. "But stay out of my way."

The *Pride* lurched again, a wash of wild foam breaking underneath, and settled back. When it did, a figure leaped from the wharf, landing solidly on the deck. Cheyne twisted around and a few of the other men gaped.

Jana pushed her hair back from her face; it lay sodden and stringy across her shoulders. "I'm going with you," she said forcefully to the two men.

Before Cheyne could speak she had stepped forward, and he was forced back. "Hear me out. What you want to do is insane, I want you to know that first of all. I'm a crazy fool for being here, but you'll need me if you're going to try to get the U-boat, even to slow it enough to make a difference. I know the U-boat inside and out; I know where the armor is weakest, I know where you might be able to ram it to knock out its maneuverability. I know also that a trawler matched against a U-boat, even one that old and slow, is suicide. And don't start that bullshit about a woman being bad luck aboard a boat, because I won't stand for it and you'd only be wasting time."

Cheyne stared at her, his mouth half-open. Rain streamed down the scarred side of his face. "If either one of you gets in my way you're going over the side, do you understand? If you're so anxious, help those men with the drums of diesel fuel. Go on!" He threw Jana a withering glance and then made his way back into the wheelhouse.

A hatch into the hold had been thrown open; Moore helped a Carib haul one of the drums across the deck and down into the hold while Jana cast heavy cables out of the way. *It was a nightmare,* he thought as he worked, rolling three more drums across the deck; what if they were wrong, and the U-boat wasn't headed for Jamaica after all, but instead toward Trinidad and South America? No, no; he felt certain that the monstrosity who had once been a military man would, in his rage and blood-lust, take the U-boat prowling for the freighters in the shipping lanes. *But what if they were too late, what if the boat had slipped through the teeth, what if there was no stopping that grisly crew of horrors?*

In about forty minutes the boat was buttoned down tight. A throaty rumble grew from belowdecks; white smoke churned briefly at the exhausts; the hatch was secured. Some of the Caribs leaped over to the wharf and began to throw off lines. There was an empty wooden crate at Moore's feet, with the word CAUTION stenciled across it in faded lettering; he kicked it aside. The other Caribs left the wheelhouse, those at the bow came aft. As he watched, they left the trawler and stood in the rain watching the *Pride* leave the wharf when the stern lines were cast off. One of them raised a hand in a farewell gesture.

"Cheyne's leaving them!" Moore said to Jana. He made his way to the wheelhouse.

Inside was a roomy cabin with dark-varnished plank bulkheads and a chart table; there was a lighted oil lamp set in a gimbaled fixture at the rear of the wheelhouse. Overhead were thick, exposed wooden beams; Cheyne's head almost touched them. The Carib stood over a polished eight-spoked wheel, before a dimly lit instrumentation panel. A radio receiver sat on a shelf at shoulder level. Moore said, loudly over the noise of the twin diesels, "What about the others?"

Cheyne did not take his eyes off the sea, which he watched through a wooden-framed windshield. He moved the wheel a few points to port and foam specked the glass. "They are staying behind with their families. You and the woman asked to come, Moore. If you've changed your minds you can swim back, both of you."

"You'll need those men!"

"I don't ask of any man more than he is willing to give," Cheyne said. "Their places are in Caribville with their families. They helped me prepare and that's all I required of them."

"You can't do this alone," Moore said.

"I'm not alone."

Jana came into the wheelhouse and glanced quizzically at Moore.

A flurry of rain and seawater smashed against glass; the bow rose high, dropped sharply. Jana grasped an exposed roof beam for support.

"If you're having second thoughts . . ." Cheyne said.

"I'm not," Moore replied. He turned to Jana. "You shouldn't be here."

"I can take care of myself."

Cheyne snorted. "Either get off my boat now or get to the bow and watch for bommies."

Moore saw the sea swirling beyond the glass; the sky was turning from black to gray now, as morning fast approached. The cloud ceiling was low and moved before a rapid wind, opening up holes though which a dank yellowish light appeared. Moore went out onto the deck, into the wind's bite, and saw a black column of smoke scrawled in the sky. It hung directly over the Coquina village, and instantly his heart rose to his throat.

"Cheyne," he called, motioning toward it. The Carib peered out, his powerful hands clamped about the wheel. "The village is burning," he said, a lump of rage rising to his throat. Cheyne turned the trawler very slowly to keep the rising sea from smashing over the port side; he pulled back on his twin throttles and the diesel's noise quieted. His gaze was cold and grim, the eyes unmoving.

In a few minutes Moore could see well enough to make out the ruins of the fishermen's shanties. Cheyne's trawler moved through green-slimed bommies into the smoother harbor water. The smell of smoke was thick and acrid, and Moore was consumed with rage. As the trawler neared the commercial wharf Moore saw a group of ragged-looking islanders and shouted to them, throwing a line. Without waiting for Cheyne to cut his engines he had jumped across to the wharf, moving through the knot of men toward the shanties.

Cheyne came out on deck, "Moore!" he roared. "There's no time . . . !"

But he had already gone, the rage burning within him, his feet sinking in wet sand. The scorched smell hung across the harbor and it sickened him. Bodies were being pulled from the ruins, and lay on the street, charred black; it was hard to tell that many of them had ever been walking, living, breathing human beings. Moore clenched his teeth, looking to see if he knew any of them but not being able to recognize the faces. Someone working with another crew of men farther along Front Street cried out, "Here's one!" and a woman wailed.

Moore walked forward, dazed; the faces around him were weary, filthy. Some he recognized, some he did not, but in all he saw a pain, a numbness, a horror. A woman rocked the corpse of a child while a man stood over her, eyes darting madly in all directions. The man knew he must do something but was unable to think. "Go sleep," the woman whispered through her tears. "Sweet baby go sleep . . ." A wailing pierced the dim light; he saw the burned hulks of the bars, the smoke still rising. Other buildings had caught fire again now that the rain had almost stopped, and he could see bucket brigades working feverishly. The Indigo Inn stood unscathed, at the top of the hill, too far away to be touched by the fire but empty and dead nevertheless.

He was stunned by the carnage. "Moore!" he heard Cheyne shout from the harbor. "Goddamn you . . . !"

There were corpses lying in rows on Front Street

covered with sheets; he caught a glimpse of Dr. Maxwell and one of the nurses from the clinic bandaging the injured. With his next step he almost tripped over a body curled before him; he made himself look down, and saw it was the old man who'd spoken reverentially of jumbies. Now his skull was crushed and his eyes were glazed, sunken.

He shook his head, forcing his breath out between his teeth. God, no . . . no . . . no . . . *History repeating itself,* he thought; *the Nazis have come, the seawolves, the conquerors, and they have been cunning and merciless. Horror upon horror, death upon death.* And on the seas now the Night Boat, moving toward the shipping lanes to carry out a timeless mission of destruction.

And then Moore saw Reynard. The man's forehead was gashed, his clothes smeared with ashes. One of his hands was badly burned, the flesh puffing up in yellow blisters. He stepped forward, making a choking noise, and grasped at Moore's collar. "You did this . . ." he rasped hoarsely. "Look what you've brought upon us. LOOK AT IT, DAMN YOU!"

Moore blinked, unable to move or push the man away.

Heads turned toward them. "You brought that Hell's boat up," Reynard hissed. "You brought that thing from the Abyss!"

"No," Moore said. "I didn't know . . ."

"Open your eyes and look at the dead!" Reynard shrieked, tears streaming down his cheeks. "YOU BROUGHT IT TO THE ISLAND!"

"It was the white man did this!" someone else, a thin, wild-eyed black shouted. "He killed my wife and

babies, burned my house! He brung that boat up from
the sea! He brung it up!"

Moore felt the electricity closing in; he shook away
from Reynard and the man sprawled face forward into
the sand. Another came forward, the hatred palpable:
"FILTHY BROTHER TO THEM THINGS!" it
shrieked. "YOU KILLED HER!"

A hand appeared, holding an extra finger of slim
silver. Someone else shouted, a knot of people
surrounding Moore, nowhere to go. Their breath hot
on him, dried blood on the faces, the eyes gone mad
with fury.

"Spill his blood!" a woman cried out. The group of
men moved closer; someone bent down, broke a beer
bottle against a stone, and held out the glittering
weapon. Moore backed away from it, tripped over
charred timbers, and fell onto his injured shoulder.
He cried out in pain, and then they were upon him,
hauling him up, other hands groping for him, Reynard
shouting in a broken voice. He was pulled forward,
through a cloud of ashes, and he tried to fight them
but there were too many.

The black with the knife was moving in; Moore
caught a glimpse of enraged eyes, a flash of metal. The
knife arm went back in a short, brutal arc, poised for
an instant, and started to drive home through Moore's
rib cage.

There was a blur of motion and bodies, an abrupt
cry of pain; a piece of timber came crashing down
across the head of the man with the knife, and he
groaned in agony as he toppled forward, the knife
spinning from his grip.

The timber swung out, caught another man in the

chest, and drove him to his knees. They all stood back from Moore, breathing heavily.

Cheyne held the jagged piece of wood ready to strike again. His gaze flickered across the maddened faces; then he said quietly to Moore, "Step away from them."

Moore, nursing his throbbing shoulder, moved nearer the Carib. Knives glittered around them.

"Come on," Cheyne muttered defiantly. "Let's make short work of it."

One of the men, larger than the others, stepped from the group, a broken bottle gripped in a hamlike hand; another followed close behind. But a sharp *click!* froze them in their tracks.

"I swear before God I'll shoot the first one of you who lays a hand on those two men," Kip said, holding a rifle into their midst. There were sunken hollows beneath his eyes and he blinked sluggishly, fighting exhaustion. Behind him stood Myra, her clothes dirty and a bandage wrapped around one arm; she held their little girl, Mindy, whose eyes were glazed in shock. "Do any of you think this is going to bring back a wife, a child, or a husband? If we start killing each other we'll be finishing the job those things began . . . !"

The men watched Kip, their faces still eager for revenge.

"There's nothing you can do now," he told them. "They're gone . . ."

"AND WHAT ARE YOU GOING TO DO?" It was Reynard, struggling through the knot of men, sweat shining on his face. "You're the law here, there must be something you can do, some way you can . . ."

"When the weather clears we can use the radio to get help," Kip said calmly. "Until then, no."

Reynard shook his head. "That's not enough! Look at these people, mon! Look at those bodies on the ground! What we going to do if they come back? How we going to fight?"

"Here are your friends," Cheyne said to Moore. "See them as they are." He raised his voice. "I'll tell you how we'll fight, old man! I'm going to sea after the boat; I'm going to try to run it across Jacob's Teeth." He glanced at Moore and said with grudging respect, "And this man's going with me."

Kip looked over his shoulder at the Carib, then at Moore. "Jacob's Teeth? Then you think it's moving toward Jamaica?"

"Maybe," Cheyne answered. "It's the fastest route into the heart of the sea lanes. If we've guessed wrong, or if we're too late, we won't have another chance to find it."

"You won't make it, Cheyne," Kip said. "There's no way you can . . ."

"And what else are we to do?" The Carib glowered at him. "Let that goddamned thing slip away, maybe to return here and do this again? They know our weaknesses now, and they know where to find diesel fuel for their boat. They'll get into the sea lanes and if they do . . . no. I won't have that on my conscience. This time they didn't attack Caribville, but once a long time ago I remember the scream of the shells and burning Caribs crawling through ashes. No! I won't let them get away! Not this time! Not ever again!" He glanced at Moore. "I've waited long enough. If you don't come with me now I'm leaving you behind!" He turned and began walking back to the harbor.

Moore paused for a moment, looking into Kip's face. "I've got to help him," he said. "There's no other way."

"Just you two alone?"

"And Jana Thornton."

Kip stared at him, shook his head, looked back at the islanders. The fear and sickness had overtaken them again, driving out the lust for violence. Reynard staggered back through the group of men, muttering wildly. "I . . . can't think anymore," he said in a strained voice. "I don't know what I should do." He stood there for a moment, his shoulders sagged; he drew a hand across his face and stared down as if he might find an answer in the ashes.

Kip's eyes flickered. He looked around until he saw a face he knew. "J.R., you'll be in charge until we return. Here. The keys to my office. There are guns up there if you need them. Clear away as many of these people as you can from the harbor, get them up to the clinic. David, can we use your hotel as shelter?"

Moore nodded.

"Then that's settled." He turned back to J.R. "Get as many as you can up there. The storm's not far away, from the looks of that sky. Just get them in out of the wind." Kip turned to his wife and clutched her hand. "Go on. You'll be all right. Hurry."

She hesitated, clinging to him; he called another woman's name and she came over to lead Myra away from her husband. "Remember," he said to J.R. before handing him the rifle. "Make sure these people get in some shelter."

Kip and Moore made their way silently along Front Street; they could hear the racket of the trawler's engines, and Cheyne shouting at some boys to help him throw off his bow lines. "I've been trying to raise someone on the radio for the past two hours," Kip explained. "I've just been getting fragments from ships at sea. There's a godawful blow working out there somewhere."

"You don't have to come with us. Coquina's your responsibility and that's all."

Kip shook his head. "I know that boat is still out there, David. And I won't be able to live with myself if I don't try—at least try—to stop it before it takes its evil elsewhere. There'll be more killing, and more innocent people will die. If I turn my back on that I turn my back on everything I've ever believed in."

They reached the boat where Cheyne was already hauling in the lines, Jana working right beside him. The Carib stared at Kip for a few seconds but said nothing.

Moore climbed aboard and helped the Carib and Jana with the bow lines; Cheyne then disappeared into the wheelhouse and the trawler began to move toward Kiss Bottom's passage, its diesels rumbling.

The ocean became a shifting plain of blacks and whites around the trawler. The waves lifted them and then dropped them into liquid, glassine pits that shimmered like a thousand eyes. Foam broke over the trawler's prow, streaming along the deck and through the scuppers. Moore, at the bow watching for bommies, looked to the sky. It was a forbidding, featureless mass of grays and yellows. As they swung in a northeasterly course, black, thick clouds loomed in the distance, closing off the horizon, making it a vast, empty doorway.

He turned to look back at Coquina, a mass of green against the gray. Then a cresting wave, streaked with weed, rose up and blocked his view. They were through the passage, moving across the deep Abyss, the sea striking up underneath the hull.

And with a cold shudder he realized what that horizon was.

A doorway, yawning wide.

A doorway into the realm of the dead.

He made his way aft, clinging to the gunwale, past Kip and into the wheelhouse.

Twenty-four

"BAD WEATHER AHEAD," Cheyne said grimly, the muscles standing out on his forearms with the effort of handling the wheel. Timbers creaked the length of the boat; water struck the windshield with a noise like a handclap. Though the wind had quieted, the sea was rising. A bad sign.

The sea was being churned into a frenzy further ahead, nearer Jamaica. They weren't moving fast enough, although Cheyne knew that the waves would be holding the U-boat back as well.

Cheyne let the *Pride* run for openings through the waves, seeking smoother water before the foam crashed back and closed the holes; there was a strong current thrashing that wanted to take the rudder and spin the boat broadside. Cheyne cherished the *Pride* like a strong, responsive woman. He had built this boat with his own hands, with lumber stolen from Langstree's yard and salvaged engine parts. He'd captained the craft for seven years, using it to fish with a Carib crew. She was a fine, fast boat, with a good

315

balance. He kept his attention focused directly ahead, at times checking a compass and a brass barometer mounted on the panel before him. The glass was low and still falling.

"The sea can pound hell out of the U-boat," Jana said, "and it'll keep right on going because of the way it's built, low to the water. There's no capsizing it."

"All those years," Kip said to Moore, "those things were working to put the boat back to sea . . . maybe they'd been maintaining the engines as best they could even when they were on the bottom. All that time with a single purpose. A desire to strike back, a burning hate and need." He'd related everything Boniface had said.

"U-boat crewmen were trained to improve," Jana told him. "They used whatever was at hand—wires, cables, pieces of timber, even the bulkhead iron. There are documented cases of submarines being raised from the bottom after several days—just before their air gave out for good—due to the sheer guts and ingenuity of the crewmen. In some ways I think they must have been the bravest of all warriors."

"The Night Boat," Kip whispered to himself from where he stood at the rear of the wheelhouse, an arm hooked around a beam. He felt weary and battered, and he wondered what he would have done if his fears had been realized, if Myra and Mindy had been killed. When he'd seen that blood on the wall of his house, his world had begun to collapse. Two of the horrors had broken in and one had slashed his daughter with a claw, but Myra had fought them off with the rifle and had run to the village with Mindy in her arms. There she'd found more of the things, and they would have killed her in the street had a group of men not appeared through the smoke and held them back. She'd remembered Langstree, she'd told Kip, beating at the things with an iron pipe before he was dragged into their midst. Myra had found refuge in the grocery's cellar, along with a few other men and women. The things had almost ripped away the overhead trapdoor, but then the grocery had caught fire and they had scurried away, fearful of the flames. Myra and the others had barely gotten out before the burning roof had collapsed.

"God," Kip said aloud, shaking off the terrible memory of her story. "What if it's taken another passage, moved toward Trinidad, or Haiti, or even the States? You said you'd force the boat onto Jacob's Teeth if you could catch it, Cheyne. I want to know how."

Cheyne didn't turn his head. He watched the storm curtain thickening. "When the time comes," he said. "I'll find it, all right. It's not through with me, just as I'm not through with it."

"Why?" Moore asked, moving alongside Cheyne and supporting himself against the instrumentation panel. "I've seen the hate and the fear in you. How did it get there?"

"I think," Cheyne responded, light glinting off his golden amulet, "you see too much, Moore." He paused a moment, as if weighing a decision. Then he nodded and spoke: "I have a nightmare, Moore. It won't let me be. I can't free myself of it. I am in a room, lying on the bare frame of a bed. I'm a child, and I know nothing of terror or the evil in man because my world is enclosed by the huge cathedral of the sea and sky. I lie in a darkened room and I listen to the nightbirds. But then they're silent, and there's another noise. A thin wailing noise that comes closer and closer, but I cannot escape. And then the noise is all around me, hot and screaming. There is no way to get out of that room.

"I see a crack zigzag across the ceiling; I see the ceiling fall to pieces just as the rain of hot metal and fire pours through. Something jagged strikes my head and I try to scream but I have no voice. I cup my own blood in my hands, and the blood is bubbling. And then the pain. White hot. Unendurable. God, the pain . . ." Tiny beads of sweat had risen on his forehead.

"I can smell myself burning, in this nightmare, and no one can help me because they can't reach me beneath the flaming timbers. And then darkness, a long terrible darkness. Finally there are people in white who tell me to rest. I lie in a green-walled room without mirrors. But one day I struggle up from my bed and I catch a glimpse of something reflected in the window glass. A monstrous face wrapped in yellowed bandages, shriveled and distorted, peering back, the swollen eyes widening. I smash my hand through the glass because I am afraid of what I see. I want to destroy that creature because I know someday its vision will destroy me. This is no longer the face of a man, but the face of *anacri,* a demon; and what is inside is no longer bravery but doglike cowardice."

Cheyne glanced at Moore; his face was drawn tight, the sweat standing out in relief. "When the Nazis shelled Caribville from their boat, my house was the first hit. My mother was driven to the edge of madness. You saw her. My father and a few of the others armed themselves with rifles and harpoons and went out in a small fishing boat to seek the monster. And that was the last I saw of him. The creatures in that Hell-spawned boat took away my life, Moore. They took away something good and replaced it with part of themselves; they're still reaching for me, in each hour of my waking, in every moment of my sleep. They keep returning to rip pieces of my soul away, and they won't stop until they have the all of me. I fear them as no man ever feared anything on this earth, Moore. Even now I tremble and sweat, and I despise myself for it. To a Carib, courage is life, and if I die as a coward my soul will never find peace."

He paused a moment, licked his lips, his eyes judging the width of the sea's corridors. "I left Caribville for ten years; I went to South America and worked as a hand on one of the coffee plantations in Brazil, later in the Colombia stone quarries, where I learned how to blast rock with dynamite. I was shunned and cursed by all as a symbol of bad luck, as a man with two faces, one good, the other twisted. A British woman was my only friend—the widow of a freighter captain killed in a wreck, who lived near the quarries and worked as a cook for the men. She was maybe twenty years older than me; she showed an interest, taught me how to read and write.

"When I returned to Coquina to take on my responsibilities as Chief Father I knew I wasn't fit for the position. But someone had to do it, and I have the royal blood. For years, I managed to lead my people as best I could. I tried to exert some influence, tried to change enough of the old ways to allow us to live in peace with the white man. But then one day, as I stood on the point, I saw that huge boat rise from the Abyss. I trembled as I watched. The rage, the fear, the weakness: All of it flooded over me again. I forced myself to go down to the boatyard. I stood outside the shelter for a long time, but I couldn't make myself cross the threshold. In my arms I held a crate of dynamite: I was going to blow it to pieces. Instead I ran from that place, shaking like a cur. If I had destroyed it that night, if I had set the caps and fuses and lit them, none of what's happened on Coquina would have come about. There is much on my soul now. But I have a last chance. One last chance to find them, to destroy them before they slip away. I don't know if I can. But by God . . . by God, I must try."

The men were silent for a long time. Then Kip said, "Where'd you get that crate of dynamite?"

"When they were building their hotel and marina," Cheyne said. "We stole it from them by the crateload and hid it in a shack out in the jungle. Most of it's rotted now, but there's still some fit for use."

Ahead the sky was a mass of rolling clouds, yellow with black, swollen underbellies. The sea thundered against the hull, bursting around the bow and making the entire boat shudder. Cheyne pointed at the radio receiver. "Moore, see what you can pick up on that."

Moore switched it on and turned the dial; there was nothing but the loud crackle and blare of static. A voice faded in, then evaporated. The trawler was being rocked from side to side, the noise of a giant's fist pounding the keel. Moore turned away from the radio and looked toward Jana. "You should be back on Coquina," he told her.

"I can make it," she said. "I've spent most of my life researching sunken wrecks, U-boats, and otherwise. Now, to see a boat like this one come back to life, riding the high seas . . . it may be evil, yes, it may destroy us . . . but I have to see it."

Moore shook his head. "You're either a fool or the gutsiest damn woman I ever met." Something in her eyes kept him from saying anything else, although he couldn't for the life of him figure out what it was. There seemed to be a thin wall of mist between them, as lazy and serpentine as the deep Caribbean tides. He wanted to reach through, to pierce it with his fingers, to lay a hand against her cheek and feel the warmth of her flesh coursing through him. He was glad they were together but was deeply afraid for her as well. She was a beautiful woman, filled with life and hope, and he did not even attempt to raise his hand to reach for her. He knew it couldn't be. What was that about being of two different worlds? One of them was dark, the other light, and she was not part of what lay before him.

"Bommies ahead," Cheyne said quietly.

Moore turned to look; Kip joined them.

The sea just beyond was a boiling maelstrom of black. When the waters parted for an instant Moore caught the glimpse of the green and brown hooks of a surface-grazing reef. Cheyne twisted the wheel to starboard, and as he did a wave struck the side, shaking them roughly. He brought the wheel back quickly, and began to zigzag through the waves that now lifted in all directions, swamping the foredeck and streaming through the scuppers. Something scraped noisily along the port side, just below the waterline. Cheyne hissed the breath out between his teeth. "We're in the midst of it," he said. "I need a watch at the bow." He eased back on the throttles, cutting his speed.

Moore glanced over. "I'll go," he said.

"There's a coil of rope on the flooring back there. Tie it around your waist good and tight. Kip, you take

321

the other end of it and do the same. When Moore goes out that doorway you hold yourself firm to one of those beams and let him have slack real slow. Keep the rope taut between you."

Kip helped Moore secure the rope, then slipped the other end beneath his arms and knotted it around his chest. "Be damned careful out there, David," he said, raising his voice over the noise of the sea.

Moore nodded and then went out the doorway into the weather. A surge of spray slapped against him, almost knocking him back, but he clenched his teeth and began to move, hanging on to the starboard gunwale, creeping inch by inch toward the prow. Kip grasped the overhead beam behind him with one hand, bracing his feet against the door frame and letting out the line. A wave pounded diagonally across the *Pride*, hammering at Moore; he clung against a capstan for balance, the trawler pitching beneath him.

He watched for the telltale coral swirls. A plateau of growth lay to port; Moore motioned in a starboard direction and the *Pride* responded. Other reefheads were exposed beyond, as the sea rose away from them; Moore waved his arm frantically. One of the bommies ground up under the hull with a long grating noise, but then they were through and Moore, straining his eyes, couldn't see any others. He stayed where he was, his arms aching and his lungs heaving to draw in air through the bitter salt spray. The trawler suddenly bucked upward as a green-veined wave crashed beneath, and Moore was driven to his knees, feeling the rope gnaw at his waist. With a shriek that was unlike anything he had ever heard before, the sea parted, sending the *Pride* racing down into a black gully before tossing it high again.

Moore hung on; suddenly he was wearing his yellow slicker. Around him the crashing and grinding of water, the wind screaming in a high wail. He lay at the stern, fighting to control the rudder, hoping beyond all hope he could make harbor before this freak storm consumed his boat. Panic welled up within him: *Don't lose control,* he shouted to himself. *For God's sake, don't lose control!*

"DAVID!" his wife screamed from the cabin companionway. And there they stood, both of them watching, their eyes frozen in white faces.

"GET BACK INSIDE!" he shouted, the words twisted and hurled over his head.

"PLEASE . . . !" she cried hopelessly.

Ice filled his veins; he had seen it over her head: a wave that blocked out the sky, staining it deepest black, a churning wall of water that was going to sweep over them. He opened his mouth to shout because he knew she hadn't seen, but nothing came from his throat. *Don't lose control!* he shouted mentally. *Let the wave break over the bow, let it break and keep control of this boat! It will lift the boat high and send it tumbling across its huge precipice, but KEEP YOUR HAND ON THIS TILLER!*

He watched it coming, could not speak, could not breathe, could not think. He saw their eyes fixed on him.

An instant before the wave hit he took his hand away from the tiller, a self-protective instinct, throwing an arm over his face and screaming even as he knew it was a fatal, senseless mistake.

A single cry tore at his heart before the water twisted the boat, before the black wave crashed broadside and covered *Destiny's Child:* "DAVID . . . !"

When he reached back for the tiller it was gone; he was sealed in a coffin of water, twisted and mauled by the sheer force of the wave. He went down choking, hands gripping emptiness, around him the tangled timbers that had been *Destiny's Child*. He'd lost control for one instant; it had been enough to sweep them away from him forever. He'd failed them, failed them even as they trusted him with their lives.

And now, on the *Pride*'s pitching forward deck, Moore forced himself back from a voyage through rage and bitterness through the dark caverns of his own soul. He clutched at the capstan, his muscles aching; he ignored the sharp pulling at the line around him. He was afraid to move. The storm-swept sky and sea, the wind now building and hitting his face, the waves dancing madly before the bow all combined to haunt him with fragmented, horrible images of the past. Water crashed over him, streaming around his feet and threatening to suck him away from his hold.

Yes, yes. Why not let go? Why not let the sea take you? This is the time you've waited for; this is the moment, the second, the place. When the next white sheet of water covers you over, let go . . . let go. Only an instant of pain, perhaps, as the sea fills your lungs and chokes the brain. An instant. That's all. He shook his head. No. *Yes. No. NO!* It was not suicide he'd followed across the world; no, the thought of that was repugnant to him. He had followed his beckoning destiny and now was not yet the time.

Then from the blackness of the sea, crashing through the next wave that loomed overhead, a huge and terrible shape materialized. Foam swept the decks, shimmered like glass along its hull. A haunted boat, its railings strung with weed, chasms of water opening beneath it. The iron bow raced toward Moore.

"Cheyne!" he shouted, twisting his head around.

He saw the Carib's face through the glass: drawn, mouth open, eyes staring in cold terror. The man's hands clamped around the wheel, frozen in a collision course. Kip peered out behind Cheyne, reaching forward.

"Cheyne!" Moore shouted again, unable to move.

Water splattered the windshield and rolled off. When it had cleared Moore saw that the Carib's eyes were fierce holes, and his teeth were bared. Cheyne threw his shoulder into the wheel, spinning it to starboard; the *Pride* responded, sending another wall of water over Moore.

The Night Boat passed to the port side only feet away; Moore could hear the hoarse rumblings of its engines, the taunting roar of a creature from the depths. The trawler listed to starboard and Moore lost his grip. He fell away from the capstan, slamming hard into the starboard gunwale. He heard the Night Boat's iron flesh rasp against wood. "God . . ." Moore hissed, salt stinging his eyes; he wiped the water away, saw the thing vanish through another high wave, trailing streaks of green luminescence. The rope tightened, almost cutting him in two; he pushed himself away from the gunwale and was dragged back into the wheelhouse.

Cheyne fought to regain control of the rudder. The *Pride* wanted to break free and run, but he wouldn't let her go. "I won't lose it!" he breathed. "By God, I won't lose it!" The trawler shuddered, pitched high, but began to answer the helm. Cheyne worked against the wheel, the muscles of his back aching; Kip leaped to his side and together they righted the boat.

Moore lay back against the wheelhouse bulkhead trying to catch his breath, coughing and trembling. Jana was suddenly at his side, bending over him. "It came out of the dark," he told her between coughs. "I didn't have time to . . ."

"It's all right," she said. "It's gone."

"No, not gone," Cheyne said. "They turned back to ram us under; they know we're here, and they know we're following. Now maybe they're after us, playing with us a little bit, biding their time." He shook his fist at the dark sea. "Damn you, where are you? I'll follow you into Hell, you sonofabitch!"

Moore waited a few minutes longer, until his strength had returned, then he rose shakily to his feet and came alongside Cheyne; he reached up and searched the radio band. There was only more static. Ahead the sky was solid black; a dozen or more jagged white bolts of lightning cut the wide range of the horizon. Now they couldn't be certain where the U-boat was. It could be moving alongside them, turning to ram them from behind, or waiting ahead for a confrontation of flesh and iron.

The black door was wide open; the *Pride* hurtled through.

Twenty-five

MOORE STOOD PEERING out through the windshield, his eyes probing the dark for the thing he knew must be here, somewhere, perhaps dangerously close, perhaps a dozen miles away. Bolts of lightning crackled, striking deep into the sea. Wind whistled around the edges of the wheelhouse, died away, built back up.

Moore had no idea how long they'd been tracking the U-boat—or was the U-boat tracking them now?—because his wristwatch had shattered when he'd fallen to the deck. It was a matter of hours, he was certain, but time here was elusive, something alien. His body was fatigued, his eyes ached from straining out to the horizon. They had not sighted any land nor any other ships, and once when Kip had gone out onto the deck, he let a blast of air into the wheelhouse that felt thick and hot, as if the sun were beating down directly overhead.

"Turn us back to Coquina, Cheyne," Jana called from where she sat at the rear of the wheelhouse.

"Your trawler can't take the force of these waves much longer. The U-boat's gone. It's gotten away and you won't be able to find it again."

Cheyne said nothing; he paid no attention to her.

She rose and made her way forward. "Damn it!" she said, her gray eyes blazing. "Listen to me! You can't cover the whole of the Caribbean! And if you do find the boat again, how can you ever hope to force it to the reef? It will crush this trawler to pieces!"

Cheyne glanced over at her and then at the other two men. "I've returned to original course, directly into the passage between Big Danny Cay and Jacob's Teeth toward the sea lanes. I know where they're headed. Turning back to grind us under cost them time; if they hadn't we would've lost them for sure."

He stared into Jana's face. "I didn't ask you to come. I didn't ask any of you. You all came of your own free will; I didn't have to tell you what you'd be facing out here." He looked away, his gaze sweeping the wild horizon. "The currents come together between the cay and the Teeth; they drive a boat through there like a bullet. And that's where they'll try to go through into the lanes a few miles beyond. No. I'm not turning back now."

"You can't stop them," Jana said. "You're mad if you think you can!"

"Maybe I am," he acknowledged. "But if I can't drive the boat over the Teeth, then . . . As for the artillery, or a bomb . . . Moore, take that lantern from back there and step down into the cabin. I want this woman to see something."

Moore turned up the wick and went down, carefully, through the narrow opening. "Go take a look," Cheyne told Jana.

The light illuminated a small galley, a couple of bare-mattressed bunks, and more coils of rope and crates. Moore edged forward, watching his footing, and Jana followed close behind. Where the frames and plankings came together near the bow the crates were piled on top of each other and secured with heavy ropes. On some of them he could make out faded letters: CAUTION. HIGH EXPLOSIVES. He remembered the crate he'd kicked away on the deck. Dynamite. The fuses led out from cracks in the boxes, winding around each other to make a single, thick fuse, which was attached to a small reel. Bundles wrapped in clear plastic were tied to plankings, the cord fuses bound to the others. He raised the light and saw the long, brown sticks. There were four crates and two bundles of the plastic-wrapped dynamite. Enough for a tremendous explosion.

They made their way silently back into the wheelhouse. "Put that lamp back on the shelf," Cheyne said. He saw an opening beyond, spun the wheel for it; the *Pride* vibrated. Jana stared at him, her face pale. "That's the dynamite we stole from those company men," Cheyne said. "So you see, I did come prepared."

"The entire boat . . . ?" Jana asked softly.

"Dynamite packed in the bow, drums of diesel fuel in the hold. When the primary fuse is wound out there'll be three minutes before the flame sets off the first case. When the explosion comes it'll take off the bow section and turn those hardwood plankings into spears. Then the hold will go, and those fuel drums will blow like . . ."

". . . depth charges," Moore said.

Cheyne glanced quickly at him, sweat shining on his

face, his massive shoulders glistening with the effort of controlling the rudder. Then he returned his gaze to the sea. "Three minutes to get off before the bow blows."

"Off? Where?" Jana thrust out her arm. "Into that sea?"

"If it happens . . . if I have to light that primary fuse," Cheyne told her, "you'll gladly take your chances in the water, storm or no. Now stop your chatter and get out of my way." He saw holes opening ahead, veered for the nearest; the sea streamed over the port beam and then rolled off, as if the *Pride* had shrugged her shoulders of the ocean.

Cheyne kept the wheel under firm control. He saw the barometer was still descending; a pulse throbbed at the base of his throat. He looked across as the floating compass rose, and slowly corrected two points. Sweat dripped from his chin and spattered onto the instrumentation panel. He was listening for a noise over the gobbling racket of the diesels: the faint rattling of the warning buoys on the southeastern point of Jacob's Teeth. The sea would be twisting them around, making their bells hammer. Cheyne was staring off to port at about ninety degrees when the next few flashes of lightning cut the darkness. He had sailed these waters a thousand times with the Carib fishing fleet, and sheer instinct told him the cay should be within sight, though some miles distant; beyond them would be the treacherous, hundred-yard-long stretch of the reefs.

But the lightning revealed only the wind-whipped sea. Something was wrong. Was it possible the compass was off, he wondered, or had his instincts been fooled by the storm? He leaned forward slightly, over the wheel, staring into the sea. *It's not right, damn it!* he told himself, his eyes flint-hard. *Nothing is right!* He should be hearing those warning buoys by now, and even seeing the wash around the first of the blunt, green-slimed bommies that would sharpen into knife blades ahead. "Try the radio," he said to Moore.

Moore twisted the dial; this time there was no sound from the radio. He turned up the volume. No squeak of static or electrical interference.

Only silence.

"That's funny," Moore said. "Something's wrong with it . . ."

"No," Cheyne said. "The radio's not out. I don't know what it is. I'm not sure where we are."

The wind hissed around the wheelhouse, whispering through cracks in the ceiling.

"What's the matter?" Kip asked, his voice tight.

Cheyne looked from side to side, searching for the bommies. There was nothing. He turned to port a few degrees. The wind filtering through the ceiling stank of rot, of something decayed, yet refusing to die.

The sea stretched out before them, huge and empty, a universe of water. No Big Danny Cay, no landmark bommies. Cheyne eased back on both throttles, his skin beginning to crawl. *The boat . . . where was the boat . . . ?*

"I haven't lost it!" he said through clenched teeth. "I haven't lost it! No! It's out there. And it's waiting for me."

"Where are we?" Jana asked, looking first at Moore and than at the Carib.

A wave slammed hard into the hull, rocking the *Pride* to both sides. The wind pulled at the windshield frame.

Then there was an abrupt, deafening silence.

Sea crashed across the bow; Cheyne drove straight through the rising wave, and on the other side of it he clenched his hand tight around the wheel and stared.

The ocean had flattened into a black, limitless plain. No wind, no slap of sea across the trawler. There was a strange, unnerving stillness.

"Where are you, bastard?" Cheyne whispered. "Come on, let's be done with it!"

Cheyne cut back the engines until the *Pride* was almost sitting still. Lightning flashed across his field of vision. Moore, standing beside him, gripped the instrumentation panel for support.

"Listen . . . !" Kip said.

The wind. Rising in the distance. Shrieking, turning, thrashing against itself like a maddened beast.

Veins of yellow broke open in the sky, cutting the sea into a jigsaw pattern of black and ocher. Lightning made the water shimmer. In the half-light Moore caught his breath; he'd seen the entire horizon roiling. The hurricane was advancing rapidly, a storm of gargantuan magnitude.

At the same instant the entire plain of the ocean seemed to rise up, throwing the *Pride* forward so fast Jana and Kip were slammed against the bulkheads. Cheyne fought with all his strength to hold the rudder, shouting for Moore to help. The wind howled the length of the boat, and as the next roaring water flooded across the *Pride* there was a snapping noise— wood giving way. One of the masts toppling.

Moore's head was thrown back, his teeth almost biting through his tongue. Cheyne gasped, pushing against the vibrating wheel, fearful that the rudder would break. The *Pride* was thrown high, almost free of the water; in the next moment it was toppling down a black wall, the sea smashing against them so hard Moore thought the windshield would shatter. Something hit the boat; there was a grinding noise beneath. Cheyne cursed, fought the rudder.

The sea was littered with broken planks, pieces of boats, here a huge tree with naked branches—they could see it all by the intermittent lightning's illumination. The battered tin roof of a house whirled past the starboard beam. Floating crates, the bow of a skiff, jagged bits of a storm-broken wharf swept by on each side of the trawler. Sheets of spray drove over the boat, the scream of the wind like a man's outcry. As Moore watched, his shoulder pressing against the wheel, a dark object hurtled across the prow directly toward the wheelhouse: the trunk of a tree, trailing clumps of seaweed. It struck the windshield; glass cracked, stinging Moore's face. Water exploded into the wheelhouse, breaking out more of the glass. The tree trunk twisted, broke off, plunged away into the sea again. Cheyne wrenched at the wheel, his back about to give way, the sweat of pain running down his face. The rudder wouldn't respond!

And then suddenly, from the darkness straight ahead, as if borne toward them by the hurricane, came the looming, monstrous war machine.

The Night Boat.

Cheyne glared at the iron behemoth. "PUSH!" he shouted, his voice ragged. Kip moved forward to help, his feet slipping in water.

The rudder was still sluggish; the sea had it locked in a powerful grip. The *Pride* began to turn broadside, helpless before the rush of the oncoming monster. It would strike them on the port side, crushing across the wheelhouse; Moore opened his mouth but could not manage to cry out.

The iron prow lifted up, up, towering over them. Foam roared beneath it, the noise of certain destruction.

But then something else rose out of the storm: an apparition, flaming green and ghostly, a vision from a nightmare.

A freighter. It appeared to be aflame—its length twisted, glowing metal. Burning figures on the decks. A hideous noise of screaming and moaning that made Moore cry out and clap his hands to his ears.

The freighter, moving with incredible speed, roared between the trawler and the Night Boat; Moore could still see the submarine through a mist of fiery timbers. The U-boat veered away, water thundering against its superstructure; it swept past the trawler, and the grim freighter disappeared within the folds of the sea.

Cheyne strained at the wheel, his teeth clenched. There was a loud crack that both Moore and Kip first mistook for breaking wood. Cheyne cried out in pain; bone protruded from his left elbow. The rudder came free, the wheel spinning. The Carib fell to his knees. "TAKE THE WHEEL!" he shouted.

And Moore, his senses reeling, found himself reaching for it, gripping it, his wrists almost breaking. He let the wheel play out and then fought back, feeling the ocean's tremendous strength wrenching at the rudder.

"KEEP YOUR HANDS ON IT!" Cheyne roared, pulling himself up, his arm dragging uselessly. "DON'T LET IT SLIP!"

Moore held on, his arms about to rip from their sockets. Spray whipped into his eyes through the broken glass.

"HOLD HER STEADY!" the Carib shouted.

The wheelhouse door was suddenly torn from its hinges; in the next white-hot sear of lightning Jana saw the huge form take shape, saw it hurtling toward the *Pride*'s starboard, saw the waves churning at its prow. "It's coming back!" she cried out, holding herself in the doorway. "There! It's coming back!"

Kip twisted his head around, struggling toward her. He saw it approaching, could imagine the things aboard grinning as they sighted their easy prey.

It raced onward, parting the sea, the rumble of its diesels and oil-stink filling the wheelhouse. Jana saw the dripping holes of the torpedo tubes as the submarine was lifted high; in that instant she fought for her sanity.

In the far distance came a sound of metal against metal, a clattering racket borne in by the wind, swiftly carried away. The buoys marking Jacob's Teeth!

When the submarine was almost upon them Moore felt the rudder respond; he spun the wheel to port. The Night Boat roared alongside, only feet away.

Kip and Jana were shoved aside by the boat's turning. Cheyne, his broken arm hanging, stood between them, his eyes blazing. Then he staggered along the bucking deck, moving for the bow. He stumbled, fell, regained his footing. The noise of the buoys was more strident now, closer. The Night Boat shuddered, struck the *Pride,* and then was thrown back by a wave. It came in again, iron grinding along the trawler's hull. Timbers shattered.

And finally Cheyne had reached the bow; he grasped a thick line and pulled at it. There was a crude twin-grappled anchor attached to the other end used for mooring on reefs. The thick, coarse line was coiled on the deck and made fast to a winch. He heard the buoys rattling dead ahead. If he could lift the anchor, throw it, get it hooked into the submarine's deck railing there was a chance of dragging it across the reefs and splitting that hull open. With one arm he hefted the anchor, the muscles cramping; he couldn't find strength enough to throw it. The Night Boat again crashed against the starboard gunwale. There was no time. In another moment it would be veering off from the Teeth.

Cheyne pulled the anchor with him and leaped over the gunwale.

He slammed against the superstructure, pain taking his breath away. He began to slide down the iron, his feet scrabbling at vents. With his good hand he sought to spike the anchor in, like a harpoon, but there was no place to hook it. The sea pounded him. He drove out with the anchor, feeling it catch into something: A collapsed, hanging section of railing.

The rope snapped tight before his face and he clung to it, dragging in the water. Beside him, the monster vibrated. *Hold!* he commanded the bolts around the winch on deck. *Hold!* "I'VE GOT YOU!" he shouted, his mouth filling with water.

And then the Night Boat swerved toward the *Pride*. Cheyne was caught between, but still he held the anchor firm into the railing, gasping for breath.

The two vessels crashed together; the entire starboard gunwale split open. When the submarine pulled away, tightening the rope again, Moore looked for Cheyne but saw he was gone.

The rattling of the warning buoys rang through the wheelhouse and Moore saw one of the red cans pass to port. They were in the danger zone. He threw the throttles forward, the *Pride*'s diesels screaming. Ahead were the twisted outgrowths of coral; he turned directly for them. The only hope was the trawler's powerful engines against the submarine's ancient ones. The *Pride*, shuddering with the weight, pulled the Night Boat onward.

There was a splitting noise, a snapping of coral; Moore heard iron being scraped and gouged as the Night Boat was dragged alongside. Kip saw figures on the conning tower, the terrible things watching with greedy, flaming eyes. A flash of lightning revealed a grim, jawless face.

Moore continued on into the field of reefs, feeling the *Pride* being bitten and knifed by the coral. Water streamed into the wheelhouse, almost pulling him away from the wheel, but he fought it off, steering straight for the treacherous growths. Kip and Jana, holding on at the doorway, saw the submarine slam onto a sharp coral slab; iron shrieked, began to fold back.

And then, the diesels still racketing, the *Pride* was held firm by the Teeth's bite; mere feet away the Night Boat came to a stop, its guts pierced by a reef spear, oil leaking from its tank. The two boats hung side by side, each doomed. Waves swirled around them, seeking to break them free.

Moore turned from the wheel, his eyes searching the shadows. The oil lamp had gone over; it lay on its side and where the glass had cracked a single, weak finger of flame burned. "Take Jana and get off," he told Kip. "Use that broken door as a raft. Hurry!"

Kip stared, shook his head. "No, David. NO!"

Moore ducked down through the hatch into the cabin. He reappeared a moment later with the reel of fuse, unwinding it as he backed up the steps. "Get off, I said!" he shouted.

"There's time for all of us," Kip told him. "Please . . . !" He turned his head; a movement had attracted his attention. The zombies were climbing down from the conning tower, moving across the deck toward the *Pride*.

"Take Jana!" Moore shouted. "Go on!"

Kip grasped his arm. "You're going with us!"

"If you don't try to fight the sea you can make it. I did . . . a long time ago. Two can make it on that door. Three can't." He came to the end of the fuse, threw the reel aside; the things were scurrying down the conning tower ladder. One of them tried to pull the anchor free.

Moore bent down and touched the fuse to the dying flame. It hissed, sparked; a red cinder burned past him, along the plank flooring and toward the bow-section cabin.

"DAVID!" Jana pulled at his arm. "Please!"

"I can't leave you," Kip said.

"They need you on Coquina," Moore told him, his voice hurried. "The things are coming to board the trawler. If they find the fuse and put it out, they may be able to work their boat free of the shoals. They'll find someplace—maybe another Coquina—to repair it. Go on! Get out of here!"

Kip paused. There was something cold and resolute in Moore's eyes; he had seen a vision beyond Kip's sight. There was nothing else to be said. Kip grasped his good shoulder tightly, then took Jana's hand and dragged her out over her shouted protests. He hauled the battered slab of the door over to the port side. The water was black and wild underneath, dotted with coral. "Listen to me!" Kip shook her hard. "I SAID LISTEN TO ME! Hang on to my back. There'll be a shock when we hit, but don't let go!"

And then, gripping the door before him like a shield, he leaped over with Jana clinging to him. It was like hitting a solid wall when they struck; water crashed over them, tossed them high and then back down. Kip pushed off from coral, shredding one hand. He kicked with all his strength, trying to catch his breath, hearing Jana cry out in pain as her leg brushed one of the Teeth's needles. The bulk of the door kept them afloat and away from most of the coral. Kip clung to it with all the power he could manage.

Moore whirled around in the *Pride*'s wheelhouse as two of the zombies appeared in the doorway. They crept forward, claws outstretched. He backed away from them, counting off the seconds. One of them rushed him and he swung at it; the other grasped his arm, throwing him off balance. He staggered and fell through the companionway into the lower cabin. Fingers jabbed at his eyes; he kicked them back, struggling to his feet. Behind him glowed the eye of the fuse. Others came down after him, yellow fangs slavering, talons seeking his throat. He kept backing away, making them follow him toward the bow compartment. *How long?* his brain shrieked. His flesh was crawling. *HOW LONG?*

With another few steps he twisted around to look. The primary fuse sparked higher, separated into four fuses that snaked toward the crates. There was a hiss of fetid breath in his ear; a spidery thing with gaping eye sockets leaped for him, forcing him to the plankings, a claw reaching to rip at his throat. He threw it off, kicked at it, crawled away. He found an odd piece of wood and stood up, brandishing it like a club. The cabin was filled with the stench of smoke and rot; whorls of smoke from the burning fuses undulated around them. One of the things reached out—a face eaten by gray fungus, red eyes staring—and Moore slammed the wood into its chin. It fell back, colliding into the others.

"COME ON!" he dared them, beckoning with his club. "COME ON AFTER ME!"

They stopped suddenly, watching him, the eyes moving past to probe the bow shadows. They saw; in the next instant they surged forward, flailing at him, trying to reach the dynamite and tear out the racing fuses. Moore swung wildly, felt the wood break beneath his grip, felt himself flung back by a tremendous, inhuman strength. *Only seconds now, the seconds breaking into fragments. Seconds. Hurry. Hurry. Hurry.*

Moore stood his ground, blood streaming from a hairline slash; he fought madly with his bare hands against the hideous things that advanced upon him, throwing them to each side, slamming fists against brittle bone.

And through the knot of living corpses came the one that Moore recognized: the tall, livid-eyed form of Wilhelm Korrin. Moore saw the jawless face illuminated in the faint red glow of the fuses. Korrin stepped forward slowly, a man in the grip of horrible pain; his arm came up, the finger pointing toward Moore. The hand became a claw, grasping, reaching. The others were motionless, watching their commander.

And then the hand stopped, inches from Moore's throat. Korrin stood looking at the burning fuse. His head fell back slightly, the eyes closing, the lids blocking off that hellish gaze, as if in expectation of death's final and merciful deliverance.

An instant before the heat seared him Moore had a split-second sensation: the touch of someone's hand, cool, kind, reaching for his through a wall of mist. He held it tightly. And his last thought was that he was staring toward the sea, that he had seen a beautiful boat in the distance and he must swim to it, must swim to it because he had recognized the name on the transom and they were waiting for him.

The blast parted the sea. Kip and Jana, struggling through the churning waves, twisted around to look. There was a yellow glare so fierce it hurt their eyes; jagged shards of wood flew through the sky, leaving fiery trails. The bow section of the *Pride* had disappeared; beside the trawler the fist of a giant pounded the Night Boat, slamming a tremendous rent in the iron just at the waterline. The forward deck collapsed—crumpling, metal shrieking—the conning tower was almost ripped from the superstructure. Iron plates spun into the air, up into blackness. Bits of railing were thrown to all sides. In another roar of flame the *Pride*'s wheelhouse vanished; the second blast deafened them. Drums of fuel were tossed high, and as they dropped back into the sea they exploded just over the surface, covering the submarine with sheets of flame. As Kip watched, he saw the Night Boat thrown free of the reef. Its twisted, smoking bulk veered toward him and Jana, faster and faster, driven by the rolling currents.

And then came the collapse of the entire deck, the conning tower falling away, the periscopes snapping off. Kip felt the pull of the water at him; he fought it, his legs kicking wildly. A whirlpool had opened and the Night Boat began to whirl around the rim of a huge, black pit; as the submarine was sucked down, the bow peeled back, the noise of a dying beast screaming in agony. The ocean's thunder drowned out the death cries.

The boat was folding in on itself, its iron caving in, being hammered into a misshapen mass. It was happening, Kip realized, just as Boniface had tried to make it happen when he twisted that bit of wax cast in the submarine's image and tossed it to the flames.

The Night Boat's stern pitched high, dripping red flame; the bow vanished into the whirlpool. There was a loud hissing as the sea swept over hot iron. On the rising stern the screws glistened in the firelight.

Water crashed over them, forcing them down; Kip clenched the door and pulled them back to the surface.

And when his head broke free he saw the thing was gone.

Though the plain of the sea was studded with fire, the whirlpool's action was lessening. A rush of bubbles exploded on the surface; then the whirlpool stopped, covering over the boat, its own deep grave.

Kip and Jana clung to the platform of wood, exhausted, breathing raggedly. Kip shook his head to clear it, shrugging off water. Jana was limp, one hand still clamped to his shoulder. He could feel the strong beating of her heart.

On the horizon, silhouetted in a gash of orange sky, was a flat mass of land. Kip blinked, unsure of what he was seeing. It lay about two miles distant, but he could already feel the currents dragging them in. "Big

Danny Cay," he said hoarsely. Beside him Jana stirred, lifted her head.

They began to kick for it, slowly because the water was still rough. Kip looked over his shoulder, trying to pinpoint the spot where the submarine had gone down, but now the fires were dying and there was no way to tell. The creature was gone, and there was no cause to look back again. Now he could only think of all he would have to do, because he was the law on Coquina and there were people he was responsible for, people who looked to him for the kind of strength he knew he would find deep within himself.

And swinging his vision back across the sea he thought he saw something, there against the warmth of the horizon, something like a small boat heading into the sun with her sails filled and all the great expanse of the sky beyond it.

His eyes filled with tears and, looking away, he knew it would soon be out of sight.

Afterword

Robert McCammon Tells How He Wrote *The Night Boat*

The Night Boat was the second novel I wrote, but the third one published. If you'd like to know why that was, write me a letter and I'll be glad to tell you a tale of dark and twisted passages.

The Night Boat actually had its beginnings in a drawing of a dinosaur that scared the jelly out of me as a kid. It showed an aquatic beast with a mouthful of gleaming teeth emerging from dark water to snap at a pterodactyl's leg, the full moon shining down and gleaming off the white-capped waves. Long after everyone else in the house had gone to sleep, I lay in bed and heard the sound of waves on prehistoric shores, and the thrashing of a huge and hideous body emerging from the depths. The hero in *The Night Boat*, David Moore, remembers the same drawing.

I also am fascinated by machines. Particularly ships

and submarines. I can imagine nothing more grim than to be two hundred feet underwater in a leaking, moldering submarine. They didn't call them Iron Coffins for nothing, and it took iron-willed men to survive in them. Most of the German submarine crews didn't.

The Night Boat is a mixture of dream and nightmare. A dream in that the location, the colors, the language are idyllic; nightmarish because the Night Boat invades the dream and destroys it. I took scuba-diving lessons in researching *The Night Boat,* but I wasn't able to afford a trip to the Caribbean. It amazes me still that a review I got for the book went to lengths to say how accurate the reviewer thought I'd gotten the cadences of island language. I listened to many hours of calypso music and spoken Caribbean dialect records.

Events and impressions in an author's everyday life are always mirrored in the work he or she is doing at the time. While I was writing *The Night Boat,* I lived in a cramped little roachhole of an apartment on Birmingham's Southside. Honestly, I could hear the roaches running wild in the ceiling over my bed as I tried to sleep. And my upstairs neighbors played their stereo at an ungodly volume all hours of the night, so round about two or three in the morning you could hear the other neighbors banging on their walls to get the music shut down. That weird, rhythmic hammering in the early hours remained with me and found its way into *The Night Boat.* When the crew hammers at the rotting hulk of the submarine, it's actually irate neighbors at two o'clock in the morning trying to get Led Zeppelin silenced. The roaches in the ceiling I saved for another book.

Now, eight or nine years after *The Night Boat* was first published, I think often of Coquina Island. It is a beautiful place, surrounded by emerald water, with fresh trade winds and golden sand, green palms swaying in the breeze, the scent of cinnamon and coconut in the air. It was created by a young man whose apartment looked out over a junk car lot, the smell of burned onions wafting from somebody's kitchen, and burglar bars on the windows. Ah, the luxury of the imagination . . .

The Night Boat is about the merging of dream and nightmare, confinement and escape, and what I think of as the whirlpool of Fate. David Moore thought he'd escaped that whirlpool, but it was waiting for him, there below the surface of emerald waters, where the monsters doze but never sleep.

Robert McCammon
June 1988